"Side effects?" I sa

"Well, yeah," said Norton, ignoring Ralph. "All medicines got side effects."

"*What* side effects?" I demanded.

"Heh, heh, well, you see, we don't exactly know, Princess. I mean, it's different for everybody, and you bein' a mort and all . . ." He finished with a shrug.

I was beginning to see that help from these guys might not be the gift on a silver platter that I thought. "What's going to happen to me?"

"We don't know what. Just keep your eyes out for them, and if they give you trouble, let us know, okay?"

"Yeah," I said dubiously. "Okay." I began to wish I had listened more when my mom or Grandma Kaminski had talked about folklore and fairy tales. One thing I did remember now, though, was that whenever a magical beastie did you a favor, there was usually a price.

STEEL ROSE

Kara Dalkey

A ROC BOOK

ROC
Published by the Penguin Group
Penguin Putnam Inc., 375 Hudson Street,
New York, New York 10014, U.S.A.
Penguin Books Ltd, 27 Wrights Lane,
London W8 5TZ, England
Penguin Books Australia Ltd, Ringwood,
Victoria, Australia
Penguin Books Canada Ltd, 10 Alcorn Avenue,
Toronto, Ontario, Canada M4V 3B2
Penguin Books (N.Z.) Ltd, 182–190 Wairau Road,
Auckland 10, New Zealand

Penguin Books Ltd, Registered Offices:
Harmondsworth, Middlesex, England

First published by Roc, an imprint of Dutton Signet,
a member of Penguin Putnam Inc.

First Printing, December, 1997
10 9 8 7 6 5 4 3 2 1

 REGISTERED TRADEMARK—MARCA REGISTRADA

Printed in the United States of America

To John,
without whom this book
would never have been conceived,
let alone written

Chapter 1

"For whom do the trees bleed?" I cried as I poured maple syrup down my right arm.

Some jerk in the back of the club pretended to snore.

"For whom does the earth bleed?" I picked up a cup of ink mixed with Karo syrup and poured it down my left arm.

"Take it off!" yelled a girl from a table to the right.

"For whom does Nature bleed?" I staggered to center stage. Picking up the plastic ketchup bottle I'd set there, I held it out, top pointed toward my face.

"Oooh, squeeze it, baby!" yelled a heckler off to my left.

I waited, prolonging the dramatic moment. I couldn't help but hear the murmured conversation at the table just in front of me:

"So, what are you doing after finals?"

"Dunno. Maybe some rafting on the Ohiopyle. You?"

"Gotta do Kennywood, for sure."

The jerks weren't even paying attention. I concentrated on my next line. "Is it for *me*?" I squeezed the ketchup bottle hard, squirting a gout of thick red goop onto my face.

Snickering laughter and scattered applause.

I raised the bottle high over my head. "Is it for us?" Squirt. Then I pointed the bottle toward the audience. "Is it for YOU?" I crushed the plastic between my hands, sending a fountain of ketchup out into the unsuspecting faces.

More laughter.

"Hey!"

"Ya missed me!"

Ignoring them, I collapsed to the stage in feigned tragic death.

For a moment there was only embarrassed silence. Then some girl giggled. "Is it over?"

You aren't supposed to know, I thought at her. I lay still.

"Hope so," said the heckler. "Puts us out of our misery at least."

The Per Forma Club has no stage curtain. When the spotlights went off, I stood and matter-of-factly picked up my props. Two of the seven or eight people in the audience clapped politely. The rest were already talking with each other, but not about my act. The heckler and another guy got up and headed toward the door.

"Pigs!" I yelled after them.

"Get a life!" the heckler yelled back.

"Fuck you, too," I muttered as I made my way toward the dressing room. Welcome to the theater, to the magic, to the fun. Well, at least he'd been paying attention to the act, unlike some others. Any reaction to performance art is worthwhile, even a negative one. Mine wasn't even the main act for the evening. I had been just a warm-up. The things we tell ourselves to keep despair at bay.

The "dressing room" was just some storage space left over from when the building served as a warehouse. It was painted seasick green and fitted with a cheap shower and a full-length mirror. As I stumbled in with an armful of props, I met with a cloud of smoke that didn't add to the homey ambience.

"Hey, California girl. Good job." It was Barb, the Per Forma's waitress-du-jour, puffing away on her cigarette break. The smoke twined among the curls of her hair.

I coughed as I set my props down, more parts of me irritated than my throat. I'd really been looking forward to some relaxing time alone, to get rid of the stage jitters. "Thanks. Do you have to smoke in here?" It came out as a whine.

"Yep," she said with a good-natured nod. "Warren's made the main room nonsmoking. Man, I hate this health 'n fitness kick the whole world is on."

"I know what you mean," I said, as I fished a towel out of my knapsack. "It's a bad sign when even Pittsburgh starts taking on Yuppie habits." Ah, Pittsburgh, land of pretzels, pierogies, Philly cheese steaks. Heart Attack City and proud of it.

"You got that right. Hey, I been meaning to ask—how do you like the 'Burgh so far?"

I really began to wish she would leave before I changed clothes. "It's not like I'm a stranger to the place," I said. "I was born here and only left when I was eight. I been back a little over a year. The way I see it, if you gotta live somewhere, you could do worse."

Barb laughed. "Guess you miss the beach, huh?"

I paused. My mind filled with memories of huddling under a towel as blond bimbettes and sun-bronzed guys strolled by and being too ashamed of my skinny, pale, boobless bod to go much farther than the car. Remembering the acrid smell of salt water, the sickening scent of suntan oil, and the shrieking of seagulls, I said, "Not really."

Since Barb seemed not to be going anywhere for a while, I turned my back and carefully stripped off my leotard and tights. I've heard some people say you're not ready for performance art if you can't perform naked. Screw it—it's not my body I want people thinking about.

"Born here, huh?" said Barb. "What hospital?"

"Sheesh, I don't remember. I was awfully young at the time."

"Oh. What neighborhood does your family live in, then?"

"We lived in Bloomfield, mostly. But my grandma's now down in South Side."

"Aha. And what was your last name again?"

"Kaminski."

Pittsburghers. I swear, half of them are walking genealogy charts. As Barb stared at me over her cigarette, I knew she was thinking of everybody she ever knew who lived in Bloomfield or South Side, or if any of them had been a Kaminski, or if she knew of anyone who had ever mentioned a Kaminski. Playing connect-the-dots, only the dots were people and the game the size of a city.

Before she could start in on "Do you know . . ." I said, "But it sure feels different coming back here after L.A."

"Yeah? How so?"

She was fishing for civic compliments, but I didn't give her any. "I dunno, kinda . . . claustrophobic. Out west, the streets are wider, buildings aren't packed so close together. When it isn't smoggy, you can see the mountains or the ocean or both, depending on where you stand. Here it's all narrow little houses crowded on narrow little streets on steep little hills. Kinda like San Francisco without the charm."

"Heh. The 'Burgh's got its own charm. You'll see. Anyways, at least out here we don't get earthquakes."

"Out there they've got sunny days more than half the year." I bundled up the leotard, trying not to drip anything on the floor, and stuffed it into a garbage bag. Then I stepped into the tiny shower and pulled the grimy plastic curtain shut. "So you're a real yunser, aren't you?"

"Hey, watch it! But, yeah. I've lived here all my life. North Side. Wouldn't live anywhere else."

"Why not?"

"Why leave? Everything I need is here. My family is here, my friends . . . there's so much to do. Crime's low. People are friendly, an'at. I don't have any reason to go."

"Guess not," I said, and I turned on the hot water. Pittsburghers. Half of them never leave, half of them can't wait to. I was only here because when my dad died I needed someplace to go. I hadn't made many friends in California. Mom had let me move into her Bloomfield apartment rent-free while she was off teaching in Georgia. She was even paying my tuition at the University of Pittsburgh. I wasn't in a position to turn down such a deal.

God, the shower felt good. The warm water eased my frustration, my jitters, my loneliness. I felt like I could wash away the stupid indifference of the crowd, along with the syrup and the ink. For the thousandth time, I wished Mom had lived in Seattle, where they appreciate performance artists.

All too soon and too suddenly the water turned cold. "Shit," I grumbled, turning it off. The Per Forma always did have a lousy water heater. I shoved aside the plastic curtain and stepped out dripping wet.

Barb was still there. "Do you like sports? Pittsburgh is a great sports town. The Pirates, the Penguins, an'at."

"Nope," I muttered into my towel as I rubbed it over my short hair. 'Not into sports at all."

"Do you like beer?"

"Yeah, I like beer."

"Good. I was beginning to wonder if you were human." Barb stood and stubbed out her cigarette. "Welcome back to town, anyways. Give the 'Burgh a chance. It'll grow on you."

Yeah, I thought as she left. *Like slime mold*. As the door closed behind her, I felt my back unwind, my whole body relax. *Alone at last.* For a moment, I had the mad desire to curl up and sleep on the cool, bare concrete floor. Then I remembered the cockroaches and decided to get dressed instead.

I could hear Marissa, the main act of the night, doing her thing onstage. She was getting all sorts of cheers and applause. Sure, I could have gotten an enthusiastic crowd too, if I pranced around onstage naked, moaning like a cow having orgasms. Where's the art in that? What kind of message does that send?

I jumped as the door opened again. It was Angela, the club manager, walking in with mop in hand. "Thanks for using a drop cloth this time," she said. "I only had to clean up the stuff that fell between the tables."

My hands shook as I struggled to put on the other leg of my sweats. "Hey, no problem. We clean because we care." I hate the way I get nervous around people who impress me. I envied Angela her long, wavy red hair. Mine is so thin and dark. Angela managed to have earth-mother hips without looking fat. If I'd been gay, I would have fallen for her. I hurried over to my knapsack and threw on my usual black T-shirt and jeans jacket.

"Want a ride home?" Angela asked. There was something odd in her tone, but I couldn't read it. It's always been a problem with me—reading people. Sometimes I feel like I'm the only blockhead in a world full of psychics.

"Uh, yeah. Sure. Thanks," I said, wondering what I was in for.

It's not like she never offered me rides home before. The Per Forma is in a neighborhood called the Strip District, a warehouse area down near the banks of the Allegheny River. It's pretty run-down, but it's slowly becoming sort of an artists' quarter, with a few trendy clubs for music, dancing, and so on. The Per Forma could be there because the rent is low. During the day, Penn Avenue is a busy open market with fruit stalls, ethnic food booths, and all sorts of stuff cheap. After dark, with most places closed and the booths gone and the huge, empty old warehouses nearby, well, a small woman probably shouldn't walk alone.

As I packed all my stuff into my knapsack, I heard Marissa finish up her act to great applause. She breezed into the dressing room, and my nervousness ratcheted up another notch.

"Hi, Marissa," I said, being the good sport, as she threw on a big sweater and chinos.

"Hi. T.J. Hey, what's with the crowd? I thought we were supposed to have more people this evening."

"Beats me," said Angela with a halfhearted shrug. "Thanks for a good show, anyway."

"Sure. Always." Marissa turned and looked at me funny for a second. Like I said, I can't read people. But I usually assume the worst, and I thought she was blaming me for driving people away. "Listen, Ange, I got some ideas I wanna run by you. You gonna be at Warren's on Saturday?"

Some people might claim I'm paranoid, but I'd have sworn she said "Warren's" just to needle me. Warren is the owner of the Per Forma, and he threw a party once a month for friends and staff. Lots of performers and regulars at the club got invited too, but not me. Never me, even though I'd been showing up for six months and had been onstage three times. But I figured it wouldn't be cool to look like I was horning my way in, so I never asked about it. I kept my mouth shut and pretended I didn't hear her.

"Sure I'll be there," Angela said. Was that an odd glance she was giving me over her shoulder? "But not until evening."

"Okay," said Marissa with a too sweet smile. "See ya then. 'Bye, T.J." Throwing her purse strap over her arm, she strode out the door.

And that was it. No "Good job" to a fellow artist, or hanging around to gossip. While Angela scooted the last customers out and shut down the place, I

checked to make sure I hadn't left any junk on the
floor. She didn't say anything as she locked the front
door and we walked to her car. She seemed preoccu-
pied and I didn't want to butt in on her thoughts.

Angela used to be a favorite student when my
mom taught at Carnegie Mellon. When I told Mom
I wanted to do performance art, naturally she put me
in touch with Angela, who got me my first chance
on a real stage. I didn't want to look this particular
gift horse in the mouth.

We got into her '88 Olds Cutlass—hey, nobody
gets rich in the performance art biz except maybe
Laurie Anderson or Spaulding Gray—just as a light
rain began to fall. Angela still hadn't said much as
we pulled onto Penn Avenue, and I began to get a
sinking feeling where my stomach should be. Like I
said, I can't read people, so I usually assume the
worst. Sometimes I'm right.

"So," I began. Despite my attempt at seeming casual, my voice came out as anxious as I felt. "Warren's having another beerfest on Saturday, huh?"

Angela tilted her shoulder in half a shrug. "Yeah,
well, you know." A long, heavy silence followed.

So. No invite for me this time either. "Well, um,
what'd you think about tonight? My act getting better? I tried to project more, like you suggested."

Angela stared straight ahead, her hands gripping
the steering wheel as though she'd fall over without
it. Guess I'd asked the wrong question.

The rain fell harder, turning the neon lights of
passing bars and pizza parlors into garish smears on
the windshield. Angela turned on the wipers and
they chanted at me, "Dumb chick, dumb chick,
dumb chick."

"T.J.," Angela began, "we've got to talk."

Oh, shit. I swallowed hard. My hands curled into
fists in my lap. "Talk? About what?" I squeaked.

"You know. Your act."

"Wh-what about it?" We had to be somewhere

near Bloomfield, but the world outside the car seemed to fade away, unrecognizable.

Slowly Angela said, "I think you need to do more work. On your technique. You know, put more thought into what you're doing. Into what you want to do."

"What do you mean? I always put a lot of thought into my acts. I stay up nights—"

"That's not what I mean," Angela said sharply. "I mean . . . maybe you need to take some time out."

"Time out?" I said. "Like, take the next gig in three weeks instead of two? I'd guess I'd be willing to do that, if that's what you're thinking."

The stoplight ahead of us turned red, and as Angela slowed she closed her eyes. "T.J., Warren told me not to give you another gig."

I opened my mouth and shut it. Tears formed in my eyes, and I curled my fists so tight my nails hurt my palms. *No! I can't cry now. Mustn't act like a baby. Gotta be cool and try to talk her out of it somehow.*

We pulled up to the curb in front of Mom's apartment building, a two-story yellow-brick place on Cypress Street. I didn't get out. "What's Warren's problem?" I blurted out through gritted teeth. "Is he pissed because I don't take my clothes off onstage?"

Angela pounded the steering wheel once with the heel of her hand. "No! That's not it." She still wouldn't look at me.

"So what is *it*?"

Her hands flailed the air in front of her. "It's just that . . . people aren't responding to what you do."

"How can you say that? I was engaging them tonight—"

"T.J., they were laughing at you. At *you*. They weren't paying attention to your message. Is that what you wanted? Are you trying to do a parody of performance art?" She glared at me, and I had to turn away.

"No," I said softly.

"I didn't think so," Angela said, more gently. "I'm sorry, but it seems like once you get onstage, you forget the basic things about performance. It's like casting a spell over an audience—you have to hold them, captivate them. Then the images, words and stuff that you present to them will sink in."

"I know all that."

"Yeah, well, right now you've got a big gap between knowing and doing."

"I've only been onstage three times! How can I close that gap without practice?"

"Look, you really oughta just take some time and think about your approach. How you can present a theme without trivializing it."

"What's trivial about ecology?"

Angela sighed and rubbed her forehead. "That's not what I said. I meant not making it seem trivial to you. Maybe . . . maybe you need to work on a more personal topic, something close to you. Like your dad's death."

"No."

"Okay, okay. I'm sorry. That's none of my business. But do you see what I'm saying? Do you ever watch the other acts—you know, Marissa, Ankoya, or Daniel?"

Sure I had. Marissa took her clothes off while chanting poetry in grunts. Ankoya dressed in little girl clothes to talk about being abused as a child. Daniel did stuff you'd see in geek shows. "What about them? I'm not going to nail myself to a Volkswagen or do sex with a cucumber onstage, if that's what Warren's looking for."

"T.J.!" Angela grabbed her bangs as if ready to tear her hair out. "You're not getting it! It's not the content, it's the delivery. You're boring people and they are walking out. We're losing customers because of you!"

"Oh."

"Look, I didn't want to go into this, but see it our way. The Per Forma is a tiny club. We need to keep every person we drag in. With luck, we want to drag them back. We rely on good word of mouth, with the reputation that we provide interesting, thought-provoking performance. We need good acts. Right now, you are not a good act."

"Oh." The tears came back, and I hated myself for what I was about to do. "Please," I begged. "Please, Ange, let me have another chance. This is so important to me."

"I can see that," Angela whispered.

My hands did a strange mating dance in my lap. "See, onstage, it doesn't matter that I'm shy, because people will sit there and watch whatever I do, and I can't see their faces because of the lights so I know they're there and watching but I don't have to . . . you know . . ."

"I know."

"And they *listen* to me. And I can tell them about the stupidity and the greed and the hate that I see. And I can say it any way I want and they will listen. And I've got so much to say that people really ought to hear, truths that people won't talk about. That they'd rather ignore. Oh, Ange, this is so important!" I gasped to keep from sobbing.

I felt her hand on my shoulder. "I'm not saying you're finished as an artist, T.J. It's good to see that you're so . . . motivated. That's what I mean. You should take some time to think about how you can draw upon that inner passion and show it to your audience. That'll grab them more than pious lectures about Mother Nature."

I sucked in more air to try to gain control over my breathing. Every muscle felt tense and I was shaking. "So, okay. I'll work on a new act. Would Warren go for that? One more chance?" A few sobs finally betrayed me as I said, "I'm not asking just because you know my mom."

Angela rested her forehead on the steering wheel. She took several deep breaths also as I waited. I blinked and let the tears run shamefully down my face.

At last, with a sigh heavier than all the ones before, she sat back. "One of our bookings skipped town the other day. I'd given him the seven o'clock slot a week from Tuesday. We don't have anyone yet to replace him."

"Yeah?" I said softly.

"I don't know how I'll sell it to Warren. But if you want that Tuesday slot, I'll give it to you."

My shaking got worse, if anything, with the relief. "Thanks, Ange. Thanks a lot. I'll do good, I swear it. I'll come up with something better."

She sort of smiled at me. "Yeah, okay. But if we're going to get this past Warren, you gotta promise me something. You've got to bring in people, lots of people, or my name will be worse than mud. So tell every friend you've got to come see you. Make a bunch of new friends. Or enemies. Drag in strangers off the street. Whatever. Just bring 'em in."

"I will, Ange, I will. I promise." I wanted to hug her but didn't dare. With my luck, I'd have gotten snot all over her sweater. I unbuckled my seat belt and clambered out of the car. As the rain pelted down on my head, I turned toward her one last time. "Thanks again, Ange. I'll see that you won't regret it. Thanks a lot."

Angela nodded. "Yeah. Take care. See you a week from Tuesday."

"See you." I waved and dashed up the stairs and fumbled my way into Mom's apartment. Funny how it's always been. "Mom's"— It's never felt like mine. I went to the living room window and turned on the lamp. I thought I saw Angela wave as she pulled away from the curb.

When her car went around the corner, I turned off the light. I flicked the TV on and curled up in front of it, letting the pictures bounce off my eyeballs as I surfed from channel to channel. I felt sick and humiliated and victorious and hopeful all at the same time. One more chance. One more chance.

As my nerves calmed down to normal, I went to sleep in the middle of an infomercial for the Psychic Hotline. I dreamed that I called them and got a busy signal.

Chapter 2

I woke up still wearing my clothes. Sometime in the night I had sleepwalked to my bed. I staggered into the living room, yawning and scratching my head. The TV was still on. A purple dinosaur was dancing on the screen. I punched it off on the third "I love you" and wobbled into the kitchenette. Good thing Mom was off teaching anthropology in Geórgia for the year. She'd be pissed as hell if she saw the way I was living.

I opened the fridge to see what was for breakfast. Beer and cold pizza. Yum. I didn't bother to nuke the pizza slice. Just sat on the barstool next to the island counter and ate, trying to jump-start my brain. *Lessee. It's Friday. No classes today. Good. Finals coming up soon. Bad.* I had a paper I had to finish for English Comp, studying to do for Spanish and Art Appreciation, and a monologue to memorize for Acting. But none of it seemed important compared to working on a new act for the Per Forma. I mean, I confess I wasn't really a serious student—I only went to Pitt because Mom was paying for it, and if I suddenly dropped out I'd have to get a real, soul-sucking job out in the world somewhere. *But what good will all this book learning do me if I can't make it in the one thing that means the most to me? Ugh. Too heavy a thought for so early in the morning. Morning?* I looked at the kitchen clock. Yeah, it was still morning. Barely. I noticed the answering machine by my elbow. The little red light was blinking.

"Geez, did I sleep through the phone ringing?" I pushed the message-retrieve button.

"Hello? Hello? Tiffany, dear, this is your grandmother. Listen, I'd like you to call me. We're having dinner Sunday and I'd like you to come. I've been a little worried about you since I haven't heard from you for so long. So call me, will you? Thank you." Long pause. "Love you, dear. Give me a call, now." Another long pause. "Bye-bye. I'll talk to you later. Take care now." And yet another long pause before the final *beeeep.* I love Grandma Kaminski, but she'd never gotten used to some kinds of technology.

I picked up the phone and pressed her automatic dial number.

She answered on the first ring. "Hello?"

"Hi, Mamu. It's T.J." I've called her Mamu since I was three. She still calls me Tiffany, though I've told her a thousand times not to.

"Tiffany, dear. How good to hear from you. What's new?"

"Um, you called me, Mamu. I'm returning your call."

"Oh, that's right. Listen, honey, we're having dinner on Sunday. Some of the ladies from church are coming over, and I'd like you to meet them. I've told them all about you. I know you've been lonely being back in Pittsburgh and all, so I thought it would be nice for you to socialize a little."

Yeah. Socialize with blue-haired biddies three times my age. My favorite kind of party. Not. "I'll come if I can, Mamu."

"I'm so glad, dear. It's so good to hear from you. How are you doing?"

"Oh, I'm okay. I'm thinking of getting my nose pierced."

"Nose pierced! Nose pierced! Last month it was tattoos, now it's nose pierced!"

"Oh, but the tattoo turned out great!" I kidded her. "It's a big, flaming skull with this humongous tongue hanging out of its jaws." I love Mamu, but I just can't help yanking her chain sometimes.

"A skull! Oh, my . . . You're gonna wear that the rest of your life? Oh, you're not . . . Tiffany, dear, I never know when you're joking."

"Please don't call me Tiffany, Mamu."

"Never know when you're kidding. Well you'll just have to show us your tattoo on Sunday. How have you been feeling, dear?"

It sounded like she was fishing for something. "I'm fine, Mamu. Why?"

"Well, you know, I was down at St. Aldabert's the other day."

Uh-oh. "You been talking to angels again, Mamu?"

"It's not nice to mock, dear. I know you don't believe, but it's not nice to mock. Anyway, I just thought I should see that you were all right."

"Am I not supposed to be all right?"

"Well, I just got a message that maybe something not so good was gonna happen to you. So I'm glad you're all right, dear."

I paused. I've never been sure if Grandma Kaminski had the sight or whatever, but she could say some pretty spooky things sometimes. "Um, actually, Mamu, something not so good did happen to me last night."

She gasped. "Oh, no! What happened, dear?"

"I lost my gig at the Per Forma. They told me I couldn't do my act there anymore. I had to talk the manager into giving me one more chance."

"Oh." Long pause. "That's a relief. I thought it was going to be something awful."

I had to clench my jaw to keep from screaming. "It was awful, Mamu," I growled. "That gig is really important to me."

"Oh. Well, I hope that was it, then. But will you do your poor grandmother a favor, dear?"

Oh, no, she's going to ask something really stupid.
"Sure, Mamu. Anything."

"Did your mother give you my lucky scarf before she left, like I asked her to?"

"Lucky scarf? Uh, no."

She sighed and muttered in Polish. "I guess I should have given it to you myself. I know your mother doesn't always appreciate my gifts."

Actually, Mom had tried to have little to do with Grandma Kaminski since the divorce. But I think Mamu believes that marriage is forever, and she stubbornly pretends the divorce never happened. And I get stuck in the middle.

Mom also takes a pretty dim view of Grandma's superstitions. Especially ever since the day Grandma Kaminski told me about cats. When I was five or so, she told me that when you see a cat staring off into space, if you get behind the cat and look right between its ears, you can see the ghost that the cat is watching. I was kinda freaked around cats for a while after that.

Now that I was older, I didn't think much of the ghosts and angels and demons stuff either. But like I said, Grandma could be kinda spooky sometimes.

"I'll look around for it, Mamu. I think she left some stuff in a drawer in the bedroom."

"Oh, good. I'd appreciate it, dear. If you find it, would you wear it for me today?"

"Wear it?"

"Well, you know, carry it or something. Just keep it near you. And treat it nicely. It's an heirloom. It was old when my mother gave it to me, so it must be over . . . oh, I don't remember. Anyway, will you do that for me, dear?"

"Sure, Mamu. Just for you."

"Thank you. I feel much better now. You're a good girl, Tiffany, dear, even if you are a little wild sometimes. I remember Harry, your father, always said to me you were solid as steel."

I felt a funny constriction in my throat. "Yeah. Well, thanks, Mamu. Gotta go. I haven't eaten breakfast yet."

"You haven't—it's nearly time for lunch, dear! Go and eat. And be sure to look for that scarf. It's blue and has silver threads in it. And remember dinner on Sunday, dear. Four o'clock."

"I will, Mamu. Thanks. Loveya, 'bye." I hung up. She's sweet, but it bugs me when she treats me like a baby. I drummed my fingers on the countertop, feeling antsy. Finally I jumped up and grabbed a mug out of the cupboard. I dumped in a teaspoon of ground coffee, filled the mug with water, and nuked it in the microwave. *Beep.* Instant caffeine fix. Tasted awful. Fuck it, I don't drink it for the taste.

Lucky scarf. Heh. Reminded me of those candles you can buy in New Age shops that you can burn for luck or money or love or whatever. I once even saw an aerosol spray can for Devil-Be-Gone. Raid for those pesky household demons. *But isn't luck exactly what I need right now?* I thought *And it will make Mamu happy, and I won't have to lie when she asks. And she will ask.*

I decided to go look for the scarf before I forgot. It was in the bottom dresser drawer in the bedroom, all right, along with the other stuff Mom hadn't wanted to take to Georgia. I found it way in the back, under a box. It was a deep, deep blue, maybe made of silk, and had a border of silver threads, some of which were missing. It was kinda pretty, the way it caught the light. There were no mystic symbols on it or anything—it was just a nice old scarf. I draped it over my shoulders and shut the drawer.

I went back to the kitchen and mulled matters over while I ate the slice of cold pizza. So. The new act. What to do. What was it Angela said I wasn't doing right? Oh yeah, delivery. I guess I knew what she meant. Sometimes when you say the words just right, you get a thrumming feeling in your stomach and head. You just know the message is coming across. Maybe that's why it's called "delivery"—the Meaning of Humanity in thirty minutes or your ticket free. Well, maybe not.

Anyway, my problem was that it's hard to get that feeling onstage. I get so nervous and excited, it's like I want to shout out everything all at once, so that sometimes it comes out all garbled. Pacing, that's what I need. And what else was supposed to help with delivery?

I thought about getting some more coffee. Grounds. Grounding . . . that was it. Planting yourself on the stage in balance with the Earth beneath you, making your body a solid platform from which to project yourself, or some such garbage. Almost as woo-woo as Grandma's lucky scarf. Again, a problem—nervous energy doesn't let me stay planted in one place too long.

Maybe I'd better wait to work on that once I've got my theme and props. So . . . what theme? Angela said I should pick a personal issue. Heh. My best performance of that would be one long scream. But that's been done. All the cool things have been done. It's hard being original, anymore.

So what are the usual ways of working up a piece? *Hmmm . . . write a diary. Naw, I always forget to write the entries. Put myself in a confrontational situation— naw, I hate those. Draw a map—can't draw for shit. Find an interesting location and explore sound and movement in that space—that could be cool . . . get me out of the apartment at least. Take randomly found objects and tie them together with a narrative . . . hmmm.* That, at least, I could do in my state of semiconsciousness.

On a whim, I draped Grandma's scarf over my head and intoned, "Ooooh, lucky scarf, lead me to something to use in my act!" I spun around three times and walked forward. Naturally, I bumped into a bookshelf.

Mom's got books on shelves all over the apartment, kind of like thick wallpaper. I guess she just collects books the way some people collect spoons or troll dolls. I pulled the scarf off my head and ran my finger along the book spines in front of me, making a *rat-a-tat* sound. The names on the old, frayed bindings brought back memories. I remembered them from my childhood, back before my folks' divorce. As a kid, I used to pick a book off the shelf and read its title and imagine what the stories inside were about. 'Course, it was pretty challenging, with titles like *An Analysis of Harvest Festivals of Mid-Alpine Europe,* but you'd be surprised what a kid can think up.

In a theater class I once had, we learned about the overlap between performance and ritual. Mom's got lots of books on ritual, since she's an ethnologist. And these books were part of my personal life . . . so maybe there was something here that could go into my new act. But which book?

I sat cross-legged on the floor. I could almost hear my acting teacher from last semester, Professor White, saying, "Don't think! Your problem is you're thinking too much. Do the first thing that comes to mind."

I closed my eyes, reached forward, and grabbed the first book my hand came to rest on. I didn't even look at what the book was. I just took it and put it in my backpack. One down. A few more things to go.

I tied the blue scarf around my eyes like a blindfold and stumbled through the apartment again, until I banged my knee against something. It was the knob of the lower kitchen cabinet—where the hardware drawer was. I opened it and discovered an old hammer of Dad's. *Why'd Mom have that?* I wondered. My parents never ceased to baffle me. I never was told the full story behind their divorce. I guess they figured a child wouldn't have understood. When I got old enough to ask, I didn't—I guess because it would just hurt too much.

It's funny how grown-ups always try to keep the

Dark Stuff hidden from kids. It's not like we don't
know it's there. Anger, hate, evil . . . the ugly side
of being human that people, Boomers and Yuppies
especially, don't want to admit is there. All you need
is love, yeah, yeah, yeah. Love wasn't enough for my
folks. No love for me, 'cept for Mom and Mamu, and
they only smother me with it. Trouble is, you keep
the Dark Stuff hidden and it starts to look good, se-
ductive, something only grown-ups get to do. Guess
that's part of why I like performance art. The Dark
Stuff is part of it, all the unpleasant, not-nice emotions and attitudes and Things Polite People Don't
Talk About. There's no keeping secrets. It's all gotta
be out there, bleeding where everyone can see it.

Things like death. Well, maybe now that Dad was
gone, Mom had just wanted a keepsake. The hammer's handle had been scrunched and splintered, but
I put it in my pack anyway. There was a ball of
twine on the shelf behind it, so I put that in my
backpack too.

Naturally, I threw in the Creative Whack-Pack(tm).
Some people swear by their tarot deck, but if you
have to use cards I think the Whack-Pack is better.
It's not just a bunch of pictures and symbols—the
Whack-Pack cards actually suggest things to do.

Figuring I had enough props to start with, I stuffed
the lucky scarf in last, tied up the backpack, and
caught a bus to Schenley Park.

When I was a kid, Schenley Park was a spooky
place, a forest of dark shadows. I was especially
afraid of Panther Hollow. Dad used to kid me, saying
that real panthers still lurked there. Now that I'm
back, and older, I think Schenley Park is kinda cool.
It has a social ecology all its own. On the higher
trails, near the rim of the hollow where there's more
light, you'll see joggers and sometimes a horseback
rider. On the middle trails, where the shadows are
deeper, there'll be students reading or couples making out. But on the lowest, darkest trails, beside the

creek, that's where the solitary hikers go, that's where you'll find me.

I thought it was kind of a shame that they cleaned up the little lake and the creek bed a few years back. I liked the idea of it being wild and overgrown, a real urban jungle. But the creek still flows over broken old concrete steps and waterways as if an ancient civilization had fallen there. In the shade of the trees, hearing the birds and skittering of small animals in the underbrush, you can feel like you're in another world.

I went down the steps next to the Schenley Park Historical Center and headed up the trail to a place I knew: a stone bridge, eroded, pitted, and blackened by the pollution of the Bad Old Days. If ever a bridge might have trolls living under it, this was it. Pittsburgh is sometimes called the City of Bridges—bridges to everywhere, bridges to nowhere. A bridge for everyone. For the afternoon, this ugly bridge would be mine.

I scrambled down the creek bank and noticed that somebody had accented the pitting in one rock to make it look like a skull. Wow, cool. Perfect. I ducked and walked under the bridge arch. At its highest point there was just enough room for me to stand up. Good thing the creek was just a thin trickle—there'd be dry ground to work on. The air smelled musty and moldy. Suited my mood just fine.

There were even a few rocks sticking out of the hard mud banks that I could use as platforms for my props. I yelled "Hey!" a couple of times to sound out the acoustics. The sound didn't carry—it was reflected back on me. Whatever I did here, it would be hidden and private. I could work with that.

The first thing I pulled out of my backpack was Dad's broken hammer. I put it on the rock in front of me and stared at it a while. I took out the twine and tied the hammer to the rock. Didn't know what it meant, but I liked the effect.

So now I needed an action or words to go with

the prop. I was mentally drawing blanks, so I pulled out the Whack-Pack and shuffled it. Then I picked a card. It was card number 17, from the Artist suit— "Think Like a Kid." I put myself in the mental place of a child and looked at the bound, broken hammer. I felt a slow, welling pain rising from my chest, into my throat. I swallowed hard, fearing that if I let that tide of sorrow reach my eyes, they would overflow with tears. I had to look away.

"Lean into the blade," an acting instructor told me once. *"If it hurts, you are on the right path. Seek the danger."* I decided I'd seek it some other time. This was supposed to be just practice.

I turned and put my hand into the backpack. It closed on something soft and kinda squishy. *I don't remember putting anything like that in there.* I carefully pinched it between my fingers and drew it out into the light of day. It was an old peanut-butter-and-jelly sandwich in a plastic bag. I vaguely remembered packing it three days before. Must have forgotten about it. Well, it counted as a found object. Might as well add it to the act.

I set the sandwich down and pulled another card from the pack. Number 20, from the Warrior suit— "Get Support." Huh? That one stumped me. How could I get support, and from whom, with an old peanut-butter-and-jelly sandwich? I could feed it to the squirrels—but what support could tree rats offer me? Offer. Offering. Has mythic resonance. Okay it was a dumb idea, but it was somewhere to start. Maybe it would fit in later.

I took out Grandma's scarf and draped it across a flat rock behind me. I carefully unwrapped the sandwich and placed it on its plastic bag on top of the scarf. "For whoever can help me," I intoned, "gods, demons, or small furry critters, this is yours."

I reached into the backpack again and came up with the book from Mom's shelf. It was bound in black and in silver on the spine was the title: *Rem-*

nants of Pagan Belief in Eastern Europe. Great. I'd get to speak academese for my script. Well, they say anything can work in performance art. I set the book down on a rock and pulled another card from the Whack-Pack.

It was number 20 from the Artist suit—"Be Whacky." Okay. I decided I would open the book at random and do whatever was suggested by the page I picked. I held the book open in one hand and riffled the pages with the other. When I felt like it, I stopped and put my finger on a page—page 129. I scanned the text; it was about work songs and dances in a Polish village named Tyczyn. There was a verse of one of the songs, in Polish, of course. My dad had taught me some Polish pronunciation, but I had forgotten a lot of it.

Still, I chose to stick with my whacky plan, and I began to dance around, singing the Polish verse, making up a tune. It was kind of awkward because I had to dance on uneven ground, but I managed a hopping, swaying sort of movement. The stones of the bridge echoed my voice in strange ways.

After going through the verse once, I put the book down and continued the dance, singing the words as well as I could remember them. Which wasn't very well, so it deteriorated rapidly, until I was doing something more like a Native American chant. I kept hopping from one leg to the other and moving as far side to side as the space would let me. I allowed my voice to get louder and louder, until I could feel the echoes from the rocks as subtle vibrations on my skin. It felt . . . powerful, like I could move mighty boulders with my voice alone. The vibration sank into my bones and I felt that thrumming that comes in the stomach and head when one finds the right voice. I was grounded, balanced, moving in time to the quantum hum of the universe.

I danced harder, until my singing became rough, meaningless syllables—Pla Ayala Yough Mough Glawala!—The sounds just came out of me any way they wanted. I swung my arms and shook my head, spittle flying from my lips. I felt like an ape. A force of nature. It was great!

At last, exhausted, I fell forward on my hands and knees. My gaze fell on the hammer tied to the rock. A spear of pale green sunlight had somehow made it down into the Hollow and lay across the broken, bound tool.

Wow! I didn't know exactly what I had done, but I knew it was Art. Here I had done some sort of primal ritual. The hammer on the rock was the sacred icon, my mom's book had been the sacred text, and I had done the sacred dance. I had even made a votive "offering." I turned around to look at the sandwich.

It was gone. And two pairs of iron-gray eyes were staring back at me.

Chapter 3

They weren't squirrels.

In fact, it was hard to tell just what they were. "Hello?" I said, reaching for my backpack. I wondered if I'd remembered to pack the Mace.

"Hiya, kid!" one of them said in a hearty, gruff voice. I blinked and the two figures became more visible, but it didn't help. I seemed to be seeing two fleshy gray fire hydrants, about four feet tall, with pointy gray, Hershey kiss–shaped heads and no neck. Their arms and legs were really thin, like tree twigs. Each had a little fringe of gray beard beneath the wide slash that passed for a mouth, and each wore a brown leather apron. If they had noses, they were hiding them somewhere.

I remembered Mom once nattering about some mystic types doing dance rituals in order to have hallucinations. But she said they danced for *days* to get that effect. I knew I was in lousy shape, but this was ridiculous. I shook my head and squinted at them. No difference. Still hydrants. But I was too tired and out of breath to run away screaming.

"Hey, thanks for the sandwich," said the other, thinner one in a dopey voice. "I ain't had one of them in a while. Forgot how good they tasted."

"Yeah," said the fatter, gruff one. "And thanks for the piece of cloth, too. Nice workmanship."

Oh, shit They've got Grandma's scarf.

"Yeah, most people ain't so generous nowadays,"

said dopey guy. "Some people call on us and give us junk, or nuthin'. But you, you got taste. Good to see that."

Great. Guess I'd better not be rude. "Um . . . you're welcome. I guess. How long have you guys been standing there?" I glanced around to see if the rest of the world still looked normal. Seemed to be.

"How d'you mean?" said gruff guy. "We live here, 'mongst other places." He shrugged. How can something with no neck shrug?

Okay. Either I've completely flipped out, or these are a couple of homeless midgets in costume. "I, uh, meant that I hope I wasn't disturbing you. You guys shooting a movie around here or something?"

They laughed. At least I think it was laughter. Sounded more like rocks being pounded together. "Hey, thanks," said gruff guy, "but despite our good looks, we ain't in motion pictures. We was just sittin' near here when you showed up. You sang your song, and here we are."

"Yeah," said the dopey one. "But, uh, if I might ask, just what was that other stuff you was doin' here? We got the song, an'at, but what was the rest of it?"

"Um, it's kind of hard to explain. I was working on a performance piece. That's what I do. Performance art."

The two gray hydrants looked at one another. The thinner one said, "You mean like something onstage, like Shakyspear?"

Oh, brother, I thought. *It's hard enough to explain to normal people. What do I tell these . . . things?* "No, it's not like plays and stuff. You see, there's usually just one person doing it, although sometimes a bunch of people do it. And sometimes there's a script, but a lot of times there isn't. And the props and the actions might be telling a story, but a lot of times they don't—they just symbolize something, though sometimes they don't even do that. The idea is that the

audience should figure out the meaning for themselves, in their own heads, and like that. You know?"

They stared at me.

"I guess I'm not being too clear," I went on. "See,
the idea is you set up a bunch of symbols in front
of an audience, and they make their own meanings
and stories from what they see. That way, they get
involved, and you can get them thinking about stuff,
maybe stuff they don't want to think about but which
is really important, you know?"

They scratched their scraggly beards. "Sounds, uh,
interestin'," said dopey guy. Both of the gray critters
waddled over to me. They weren't any prettier
close up.

"So," said the gruff, fatter one. "How can we
help ya?"

I shrank back against the cold stones of the bridge.
"Excuse me, but I don't know you and—"

"Oh. Where are our manners? Allow us to introduce ourselves. We're—" They made noises like
rocks grinding together again. I think they were saying their names. "We fix things," gruff guy added.
"We do all sorts of work. You got a job needs done,
we do it!" He stood taller and stuck a thumb proudly
through the strap of his apron.

"I see," I said, not seeing at all. "Um, I'm T.J." I
slowly held out my hand.

Gruff guy grasped my hand and shook it. It was
like shaking with a tree branch. "Pleased to meet-
cha, T.J."

"You guys aren't from, like, Mars, are you?"

"Mars? Naw, we don't get north of here much."

"I didn't mean Mars, Pennsylvania . . ." I
muttered.

"So, anyways, what's the job?"

"Job?"

"Yeah," said thin and dopey. "You called. We're
here. Watcha want us to do?"

"I called . . . oh." A light switched on in my head

and I didn't like what it showed me. "Um, I think there may have been some mistake—"

"Oh, I get it," said fatso. "You wanna see our credentials. Just a minute, here." He swiveled his gray head around until his gaze fixed on Dad's hammer tied to the rock. "How about that hammer there? That's a lousy way to fix a hammer, by the way."

"I wasn't trying to fix it."

"Just a sec." In a blur of movement, he untied the hammer and picked it up. He spit on the handle and rubbed it very fast between his twiggy hands. Then he handed it to me. "There ya go. Good as new."

And it was. The handle was whole and shiny as if it had been made yesterday. The steel head gleamed. "Um," I said. *Holy shit. He really fixed it. With . . . magic of some sort. Right before my eyes.* "How'd you do that?"

The gray fireplug grinned. His teeth were triangular and pointed, like a shark's. "Secret of the profession. So, do we qualify?"

"Well, yeah. I guess." I kept turning the hammer over and over in my hands. It looked and felt just like a new tool bought at Sears. I kept glancing at the rock, where the twine now hung loose and frayed. It was weird. It was crazy. But what if they were real and could do real magic? Didn't I, in fact, need help, and a lot of it? Any help I could get? "See, what I need is a good new performance act. Because the club I perform in has told me I have just one more chance to do it good. And I have to bring in lots of people to watch, or I won't get any more stage time. I don't suppose you guys can help with that?"

"Sure we can." They nodded as if I were asking the most reasonable thing in the world. "You'd be surprised what we can do."

"I already am."

"So there ya go. Tell us more about this, uh act you was doin' here."

"Well, I'm hoping to make a really powerful statement."

They blinked. "Statement?" said the gruff guy. "What is it you wanna say?"

I clenched my fists. "What I really wanna do . . . is shake up the Boomers."

"Boomers? What's a Boomer?"

"You know, those people who act like their kind are the most important that were ever born. They want to hold all the jobs and control the world and never let go. They think they'll be young and beautiful forever. They think they're morally and philosophically superior to everybody else, but really they're messing up the world for everybody else. And they think the world, and anybody who isn't them, only exists to entertain them."

The gray guys' eyes got wide. "Oh! Yeah!" They looked at each other and nodded enthusiastically. "We know folk like that."

"Anyway, I want to slap them out of their smug complacency. I want to offend them. I want to shake 'em up and say, 'Wake up and smell the garbage, assholes!' Y'know?"

"Yeah! Yeah!" the fireplugs said. "You do that. Go get 'em!"

"Any help you want on that," said dopey guy, "we'll give it to ya."

Wow, I thought. *I've never had a cheering section before. I could get to like these guys, whatever hospital for mutants they've escaped from.* "Well, look, um, I'm still working it out right now, but if you guys could figure out how to get lots of people to come see my act at the Per Forma Club—that's in the Strip District— a week from this Tuesday night, that'd be a really big help."

Gruff guy nodded once. "We're on the job. Listen, kid, you're our kind of mort. We like what you stand for. Anytime you want something done, just call on us. We'll be there in a jiff."

"Yeah. Right. You got a phone number?"

Dopey nudged gruff guy. "Heh, heh, she thinks we got a phone."

"Naw, naw, naw, you just hold the token and say our names. Ooops, almost forgot to give you the token. Lesseee, what have we got here . . ." He felt around the folds of his flesh as if they were pockets. "Aha! Here ya go. Use this." He handed me a rectangle of slightly bent manila card.

I took it cautiously. It was an old-fashioned time card, like my dad used to use when he worked at the mill. At the top it was "LTV Steel Corporation." Its slots were filled with stamped hours and dates. The last one was May 1, 1953.

"So you just hold that and say our names and we show up."

"Uh, what were your names again?"

They made the same horrible grinding noises they did before.

"Sorry, but I can't say that."

"Oh. Uh . . . that's okay. How's about you pick names for us and we'll answer to those."

"Pick names for you? All right. Let me think." I remembered a TV show I'd seen the other night on the Nostalgia Channel. Pointing at the fat, gruff one, I said, "Ralph." Pointing at the thinner one, I said, "Norton."

They nodded and grinned. "Hokay. Ralph an' Norton it is. Call us anytime. We oughta be going now. We'll get working on that crowd thing for ya. See ya later."

"Thanks. I appreciate it. 'Bye."

They didn't walk away. They just slowly faded from view. The last part of them I could see was their eyes. Then they blinked and were gone.

Just . . . gone. I sat for some moments, staring. I waved my arm back and forth through the air where they had been. Nothing. *Did I imagine*—I looked down at my hand. I was still holding the manila time

card. *That was so . . . fucking . . . weird.* The hammer
beside me was still bright, shiny, and new. Shredded
string still hung on the rock. I could have found the
card, but I couldn't have fixed the hammer. *What
were those guys? Moonmen who talk like mill jocks?*

I rested my head in my hands and took several
deep breaths. *I gotta get out of here. I gotta get someplace
normal. Fast.* I began to pack up my stuff. The scarf
was gone, and there wasn't a crumb left from the
sandwich. They seemed to have eaten the plastic bag
too. In went the hammer, the book, the Whack-Pack,
fast as I could stuff them. I left the string.

I put the time card in my jeans pocket and stepped
out from under the bridge. It was midafternoon already. *Where did the time go? Have I been here that
long?* I felt suddenly ravenous and realized I hadn't
had any food all day except coffee and cold pizza. I
stretched and my back cracked. The air smelled moist
and metallic, like rusty iron. The light coming down
through the trees seemed an unnatural shade of
green.

*Shit. God, don't let me be going crazy. I've got enough
problems already.*

I ran up the winding trails of Panther Hollow,
passing the few joggers still out. When I got up to
the Panther Hollow Bridge, I half expected the life-
size bronze statues of panthers on each of its corners
to raise their heads and snarl at me. They didn't.

I have never been so aware of how many statues
line the route from Schenley Park to Oakland: Bobby
Burns, Columbus, Mr. Schenley himself, Stephen Foster, not to mention the occasional soldier or goddess.
I expected them all to shout something at me as I
passed. I didn't even look up at the Pan Fountain—
the big pointy-eared guy might wink and blow a kiss
at me.

But up ahead, to my relief, was the Cathedral of
Learning. It's a huge gothic tower, like something out
of a Batman movie. I'm kinda fond of it and seeing

the place was reassuring, even if it is mostly filled with ordinary classrooms for the University of Pittsburgh. Somebody in a lit class I once had called it "Minas Pitt"—said it was a reference to a tower in a fantasy book by a guy named Tolkien. I've never read that dragon-and-elf shit. Maybe I should have.

Anyway, I thought about going into the C-of-L because I could eat at the Roy Rogers down in the basement—that would feel real normal. But if I did that, I might run into classmates and I might blurt out something crazy or stupid to them about what I'd just been through. So I changed my mind. There was someplace better to go.

I headed on down Forbes Avenue. The traffic, the jabbering students, the panhandlers, the concrete buildings, all helped bring me back to reality. But was concrete ever so colorful before, or was it just the light?

Maybe I'm not exactly going crazy. Maybe I just really did some powerful art and so I'm seeing the world different. I'd heard somewhere that learning a new language creates new neural pathways in the brain. Why wouldn't doing a new work of art do the same? My shoulders relaxed and I breathed a little easier.

What was I afraid of, anyway? I wasn't too familiar with fairy tales and stuff—I tended to tune out whenever Mom would go on her long explanations of what goblins and dragons and witches were supposed to really stand for. And Grandma Kaminski's odd mixture of faith and folktales just confused me. I knew that deals with the devil don't go well for the dealer. *But those whatever-they-weres didn't make me sign anything in my own blood. They didn't hurt or threaten me. Didn't try to kidnap me. They were friendly—they even fixed Dad's hammer. And they said they'd get people to the Per Forma for me. That's all. If I just imagined them, or if somebody was playing tricks on me, I'll feel real stupid, but it's no harm done. But if*

*they're real . . . well, hey, I just might have some powerful
new friends on my side.*

Half a block ahead of me, two bow-head fluff-
chicks came out of C. J. Barney's. I realized I sort of
knew them from my Intro to Performance class at
Pitt. The girls walked toward me and I froze in my
tracks. Damn, I hadn't wanted to run into anyone I
knew so soon. *What if they talk to me? What do I say?
Well, I could mention my next gig, since I have to bring
in lots of people. Time to get the word of mouth going.
As they came closer, I rehearsed in my head what to say.*

Some things I guess even art and magic can't
change. See, in some ways, being born shy is the
worst handicap you can have, because no one can
see you have it. Blind people got their canes, pleeges
got their wheelchairs. Shy people just have faces no
one can see behind, and everyone assumes you're
stuck up, hostile, or weird just because you're quiet
and awkward.

Normal people just don't get it. "Give others a
chance," they tell me when I try to explain. "Nobody's out to hurt you. Open up a little and you'll
see how friendly people are." Right. That's like telling someone with a snake phobia, "Oh, but it's a *pet*
python. It won't hurt you." It doesn't matter, see?
People are snakes and they make me nervous, and
anyone who doesn't understand that is luckier than
I'll ever be.

So here I was, facing two girls I didn't even *like*,
and my tongue felt frozen because I had to ask something of them.

"So, I'm like, totally freaked, you know?" said one.
I remembered her name was Crystal.

"Oh, my gawwd, I don't believe it! He didn't!"
Her name was Cindi.

"And he goes, 'What's your prob, babe?' real
macho, you know?"

"Oh, my gawwd! What did you do? Oh, hi, T.J."

I thought they were going to walk right over me.

"Hi, Cindi, hi, Crystal. Hey, I'm doing another gig at the Per Forma a week from Tuesday, and I'd like some people from the Theater Department to come see it."

"You're in a play?"

"No, I'm at the Per Forma. It's a performance art club."

"Oh" Their blue-eye-shadowed faces fell. "You mean, like, barfing on stage and stuff?"

"That's not what I do. I'm into meaningful messages about the environment and how the world is really messed up and stuff like that. You guys think you can make it?"

"Well, gee, thanks for letting us know, T.J. We'll keep that in mind. Tuesday, huh?"

"A week from Tuesday. At seven."

"Okay. Maybe we'll see you there."

"Right. See ya." I passed around them and heard them giggling behind me. *Sure. What do you two care about art? You get wet dreams about guest-starring on* Baywatch.

Don't know why I bothered. Up ahead was my haven of refuge—the Beehive Coffeehouse. It's more home than home. It's also one of the coolest places in the 'Burgh, I think. It's in this building that looks like a small castle, with a tower and everything. Part of the place is a movie theater, the King's Court, which shows art films and stuff the staff thinks is neat. The rest of the building is the Beehive.

I bought a cup of Yrgachef coffee and a fudgie brownie called a mud bar at the counter and went up the iron spiral staircase to the larger of the two upstairs rooms.

The big room has walls painted orange and a sculpture hanging at the far end that looks like a huge fish skeleton. The floor, tables, and plastic chairs are black. It's the room for people who want to study or have quiet conversations.

It was kind of empty at the moment, so I sat in

one of the two booths, next to the Space Traveler
Dude mural. The mural is kind of a comic strip in
which Space Traveler Dude finds the Earth, only to
discover that it's a lifeless, toxic wasteball. Space
Traveler Dude is my hero.

I munched down the mud bar and swigged some
coffee, trying not to think much for a while. I felt
really tired. I hadn't had that much sleep the night
before, and I guess that dancing under the bridge
took it out of me. I leaned my head against the wall
and closed my eyes—

—And fell into a dream. I was following Space
Traveler Dude as he zipped ahead in his saucer. He
disappeared down a huge, round well, and I stopped
just at the rim. One more step and I'd have fallen in.
The ripples on the water faded until the surface became a smooth flat black disk. The disk tilted and
rose up until it was vertical, now a round portal in
front of me. Beyond the portal was a nightscape, stars
twinkling over shadowy hills in the distance. A cool
breeze blew out of the portal, smelling of wet dirt
and rust. Iron-gray eyes glimmered in that Land of
Night. I could walk right in, anytime I wanted to.
And I wanted to. I leaned forward and—

A massive earthquake shook the ground and I lost
my balance. I wobbled about, falling backward away
from the portal. Someone yanked on my shoulder
and I was awake.

Sam was standing beside me, his hand on my arm.
"You been partyin' too much, T.J.? Weekend's only
just begun, girl."

Sam's black and tall and has got gorgeous muscles.
They say he's a gentleman to all his girlfriends. If I
had the guts, I'd ask him out myself—heck, it would
freak the shit out of Mom. Why he bothered to be
my friend I'll never know.

"Hey, gotta keep the fires burning," I said,
stretching.

"Looks more like you're burning out. Studying for

finals getting to you?" He shook the sleeve of my oversize black T-shirt. "You gotta get some more flesh on you, girl, or you're gonna blow away."

"Oh, shut *up.*" I slapped his hand away, but I was blushing and grinning. "Besides, I thought men liked skinny women."

"Not me. Going to bed with skinny women is like sleeping on coat hangers, if you ask me."

"You are *rude.*"

"Just telling the truth." Sam sat down on the bench across from me. "So, what you been up to?"

"Working on a new act."

"Really? How's it coming?"

"Good. I got a good start on it today."

"What's it about? Or is that a stupid question?"

I shrugged. "It's not together enough to really tell yet. But it feels powerful, you know? Like I'm moving in the right direction."

"Good. That's real good."

Seeing him nod and smile made me a little braver. "I'll be doing the new act a week from Tuesday, at the Per Forma. Think you could come see it?"

Sam leaned back and looked at the ceiling. "Tuesday . . . Tuesday . . . shit."

"What?"

"I have a rehearsal that night. Show's going up that Friday."

"Damn." At this rate, I'd need magic to get any audience at all. "Couldn't you skip rehearsal for one night?"

Sam stared at me, wide-eyed. "Skip out of rehearsal? I'm gonna pretend I didn't hear you say that."

"Okay, okay, I'm sorry. What's the play?"

"*Midsummer.* I'm Oberon, King of the Fairies." He dangled a hand from a limp wrist.

"Very funny. Well, at least it's not *Othello.*"

"What? Don't you think I'd make a fine Desdemona?" He batted his eyelashes at me.

I had to laugh. I was beginning to feel like part of
the real world again. I hadn't wanted to tell anyone
about Ralph and Norton, but I was pretty sure Sam
would go easy on me if anybody would. "Um, Sam,
can I ask you something?"

He tilted his head. "Depends on the question."

"Listen, what would you think if you were, say,
rehearsing by yourself, and a couple of really weird-
looking guys showed up and started talking to you."

"I'd say it's a typical night in the Pitt Theatre
Green Room. Why?"

"No, no, I'm not saying this right. I mean really
weird. Like, not human. Short and all gray and
pointy."

"You mean, like him?" Sam jerked a thumb at the
mural of Space Traveler Dude.

I craned my head to check out the Dude again.
"Yeah, now that you mention it. But with longer bod-
ies. And their heads were pointy, not flat on top.
And they didn't wear shades."

Sam fixed his gaze on me. "I'd say I'd been doing
some bad shit lately and I should stop that stuff."

I sighed and put my chin down on my arms on
the table. "I'm not doing drugs, Sam. Wish I was. It
would give me an excuse."

Sam frowned. "These guys mess with you?"

"No. They were helpful, in fact. They fixed my
dad's broken hammer just by rubbing their hands
over it. They were even interested in my act and
wanted to help bring people in to see it. Apparently
something I did while working up the performance
piece actually summoned them. And when they left,
they didn't just *leave*, you know, they faded away
right in front of me."

Sam blinked. "Uh-huh. They didn't even offer to
take you up in their saucer?"

"Sam, I'm serious!"

"Well, people who say they been carried off by
aliens are serious, too. You really saw this, huh?"

I sighed heavily. "Yeah. I did."

"Hey, Sam," called a guy from the doorway behind me. "Time to go, man. Game's startin'."

"Yeah. Be right there." Sam leaned toward me. "You talk to anyone at the health service about this?"

"Well, no. It just happened an hour ago. I haven't sorted it all out yet."

"Well, maybe you should think about that as a next step. Them or the cops. Or the FBI, maybe. Up to you." Sam stood and put his huge hand on my shoulder. He looked down at me, concern all over his face. "I gotta go now, T.J. But you take care of yourself, you hear?"

"Yeah. I will."

"Okay." He patted my shoulder and left.

I put my head down on the table. *Idiot, idiot, idiot. Why did I blurt all that stuff out? Now he thinks I'm crazy. I'll be lucky if he ever speaks to me again!* I decided right then not to mention Ralph and Norton to anyone else. Ever.

Chapter 4

When at last I dared to sit up again, the room was empty. I took a sip of my coffee but it was cold. There was something scratchy in my jeans pocket. I reached into it and pulled out the manila card. Hm. Maybe I should have shown the card to Sam. It probably wouldn't have proved anything, though. *But maybe I could prove something to myself if I try it now.* For the hell of it, I said softly, "Ralph. Norton."

Nothing happened. Well, what did I expect? I put my head down on my arms again and sighed.

"Hiya, T.J.!"

I jumped so hard my knees banged against the table. There they were, sitting on the bench across from me, wide grins on their faces.

"Uh . . . hi. You . . . you're here!" I looked around to see if there was anyone to notice, but we were alone.

"Sorry, didn't mean to scare ya," said Ralph.

"We woulda come sooner," said Norton, "but your voice was so soft it was hard to find ya. You gotta speak up a little next time."

"Okay," I said.

"So, what's up?" said Ralph.

"Um. I was just, uh, testing the card. I wanted to make sure it worked."

"Good idea," said Ralph. "Always smart to check your equipment, I always say."

"You do not," said Norton.

"Shaddup," said Ralph.

Approaching footsteps and voices drifted up the stairwell behind me. I watched Ralph and Norton, but they didn't seem concerned. "People are coming. Aren't you guys gonna hide?"

"Naw," said Ralph. "They won't see us."

"They won't? Why not?"

" 'Cause we don't want 'em to."

The clump of talkative students came shuffling into the room. They never even looked our way. They took over one of the big tables in the middle of the room and became rapidly embroiled in a discussion of philosophers and *Star Trek.*

So much for the craziness theory. No proof either way.

Ralph and Norton were staring hungrily at my plate. "Um, you guys want the rest of my mud bar?"

"Thanks!" said Norton. He plucked it up and broke the chunk in half. He handed one half to Ralph, and they both tossed the brownie down their gullets without bothering to chew.

"So's about this performance act thing," said Ralph, "we haven't gotten too far yet, but we've been thinking'. What you need is something grabby. Something to really bring 'em in."

"Well, I'm hoping to do something shocking, you know?"

"Shocking's good. We can work with that. "We're thinkin' posters or something."

"You guys studied marketing?"

Norton shrugged. "We learn whatever a job needs."

"That's all we got for you right now," said Ralph. "Need anything else?"

"Um. No. Just wanted to test the card. And posters sounds like a good idea. Thanks."

"No problem. Call us anytime. Be seeing ya." And again, as before, they faded from view, leaving the eyes for last.

My hands were shaking so hard the card was rattling on the tabletop. I still hadn't proved anything. Except that I could imagine them again. I put the time card into my backpack. *Maybe I need a visit to the health circus after all. Or just a nap.* I went home, and even though it was only late afternoon, I took a long, hot shower and staggered off to bed. I'm not sure why I was so tired—being frazzled abut the new act, or meeting Ralph and Norton, or just that I'd been keeping weird hours and not eating much lately. Or maybe doing magic really takes it out of you. Anyway, I fell asleep right away. Slept through the night, too. I don't think I dreamed anything. At least I hope not.

Next morning's breakfast was a bowl of Cocoa Puffs without milk. I sat on the couch and dumped out the book bag. I hoped that examining all the stuff, like reading goat's entrails, would explain the past and foretell the future. I hoped it would tell me yesterday was a bad dream.

No luck. There was the manila card. There was the hammer, still bright, shiny, and new. I picked the hammer up and ran my hands over it again. It sure looked good. But some quality was missing . . it just wasn't Dad's old hammer anymore. Maybe that was part of making it new. All those years of his hands building things with it had just gone away.

But what if my brain was playing tricks on me? Out of curiosity, I went to the kitchen and opened the hardware drawer. No other hammer there. I briefly thought about calling Mom and asking her if she remembered a broken hammer in the drawer, but I didn't. Didn't need her thinking I was taking bad drugs either.

Could go to the health service . . . But it was Saturday. Their hours are short on Saturday and it was already noon and I hadn't made an appointment. I was relieved to realize I had an excuse not to go. I didn't really want confirmation that I was nuts. Besides, aren't artists supposed to be a little flaky?

So. What to do with the day. I could work on the act some more. But my muscles felt sore, and my shoulders felt tense, and my stomach began to not feel so good. I didn't want to move. *Okay. I'm not ready to get back to that right now. God knows, I don't want to conjure anything else up.*

There's always studying. Got plenty to study and write for finals week. I fetched my notebook from the bedroom and flipped it open. On the inside cover was a Post-it Note with a message to myself in red ink: "Owe two more hours to scene shop."

Shit. I'd forgotten. Probably deliberately. I never looked forward to doing shop hours. It's not that I don't like to build things—I liked putting stuff together as a kid. I'm just not anal about it, that's all. Like, my lines aren't always straight. I mean, what's the big deal about a fucking eighth of an inch?

Anyway, I don't get along real well with the grad students who kind of run the place. But every theater student has to do time in the scene shop. And I owed two hours. *Better get it over with.* I put everything but the hammer back in the backpack, slung it over my shoulder, and headed out to campus.

The University of Pittsburgh is spread out all over the Oakland neighborhood, some say like an octopus or a blob because it keeps sucking up more and more property. Eventually it'll own everything Carnegie Mellon doesn't. Pitt is so big, it's split into an upper and a lower campus; Pitt Stadium, for example, is up on the Hill, the law building and Hillman Library are down by Schenley Plaza. Most of Pitt's buildings are the dull, square, glass and concrete type, except for the Litchfield Towers, which are round glass and concrete. But there is Heinz Chapel, which is a scaled-down copy of some French gothic church— funny to think it's named after a brand of ketchup. And there is William Pitt Student Union, which used to be an old hotel. Its claim to fame is that an old-time actress, Eleonora Duse, died there. And there is Forbes Quadrangle, one box sitting atop another, that was built where Forbes Field used to be—there's even a plaque noting the former site of home plate. And there is the mighty gothic tower of the Cathedral of Learning, where most of my classes were.

The Cathedral of Learning seems to change moods, depending on what time of day you see it, and the weather, and so on. That Saturday afternoon, it was confident. Just sitting there in the bright sunlight, saying, "Here I am." I ran up the steps, through the revolving door, into the cool interior.

The first floor of the C-of-L is called the Commons. It looks just like the inside of a huge medieval cathedral, but without the pews and altar and stuff. It has a tall, ornate iron gate by the elevators, big fireplaces at the four corners, and lots of thick wood tables and carved high-backed chairs for studying. It's always kind of hushed and echoey in there. If a real church is called God's house, the Commons must be where God hangs out to chill for a while.

I bopped down the stairs to Roy's for a burger. You wouldn't expect to find a fast-food joint in the basement of a building like this, but that's Pittsburgh for you. Expect the unexpected. I wolfed down a cheeseburger and put the large fries in my pack for later. Then I finally had to face the inevitable and head down another set of stairs to the scene shop.

The shop door was closed. Odd—someone's always in there this time of day. I push-pulled on the door a couple of times and it opened. So I walked in. "Hello?"

No one was there. Some tools and paper sketches were out, so somebody must have been working in there earlier. I knew I shouldn't be in the shop unsupervised, but I wasn't sure what to do. I could go hang out in the hall until someone came back, but that seemed stupid. It wasn't like I was going to mess up anything, anyway.

I pulled the sack of fries out of my backpack and munched a few while I waited. Still no one showed. I wandered around the work area and looked at the sketches laying on the table. They were plans for wooden cutouts for an elaborate stage set. Some designer for the Shakespeare Festival was clearly having too much fun. From the due date at the top of the sketch, I could see these guys were under the gun to get the set finished. Not surprising. The director had probably changed his or her mind for the third or fourth time. Pretty typical in the Theater Department.

I reached into my backpack to get my notebook, but my hand closed on the manila time card instead. I pulled it out. And a bizarre idea entered my idle brain. *I need proof that they are real. Something someone else can see. And Ralph and Norton like to work. Bingo.*

I held the card up in front of me, my hand shaking again. I swallowed hard and whispered, "Ralph? Norton?" Nothing happened. Then I remembered I had to speak up. I looked around, hoping nobody was about to come in, then said louder, "Ralph! Norton! I got a job for you guys." *C'mon, don't fail me now.*

There was a rustling behind me and I turned around. The gray fireplugs were sitting up on one of the tables, chowing down on the rest of my french fries. "Hiya, T.J. Good thing you spoke up. It was hard to find you here in the Upsy-Down Mineshaft."

"The what?"

"You know, this building. Thanks for the fries. I love these things."

"Um. Hi. You're welcome. Can't you get them where you, uh, live?"

"Not like these, we can't," said Ralph. "So whatcha got for us?" He licked his lips with an enormous tongue and wiped his twiggy hands on his leather apron.

"Come take a look at this." I led them over to the sketched plans. "We need these shapes of wood cut out and put together."

"Boy," said Norton, "these are the strangest shapes I ever seen. This ain't no birdhouse, I can tell ya that."

"Is this for your performance thing?" said Ralph.

"No, this is for a stage set for a play somebody else is putting up. But I'm supposed to be helping out. It's part of my grade."

"I gotcha," said Ralph. "What's the layout?"

"Well, I think these pieces here are supposed to be layered on top of each other, and these should be stood up at an angle."

Norton stared off into space a moment. "Dat's gonna look pretty strange."

"It's a set for *Midsummer Night's Dream*. It's supposed to look strange. It's part of the forest where the fairies live."

"O-ho," said Ralph. "That makes sense, then. Gimme those plans." He snatched the sketches out of Norton's twiggy paws and held the paper close to his face. He scratched his fringe of a beard. "Hmm. Tricky. But we can do it." He swiveled his bulbous head to look around the room. "Pretty good tools here. Let's get to work, Norton."

What happened next was a blur. Really. Like a pair of gray dust devils was whirling around the shop. Now and then I'd get a glimpse of them if they hovered still for a moment. Once Ralph stopped and asked me, "Do they really want these hinges here?"

"Yep. I think they want to be able to get the bigger pieces out of this room, through that door."

"Ohhhhh." The gray tornadoes went back to work. I wondered if they were related to the Tasmanian Devil cartoon character. In another couple of minutes, all the lumber was cut and the finished pieces were neatly assembled and stacked.

"Want us to paint 'em for ya?"

"No, we'd better leave something for the grad students to do."

"Hokay, whatever you say. Hey, we're still workin' on that promotion thing for your performance. But we gotta talk about what you're gonna be doing, an'at."

"Uh, sure. I'm still working on it. I'll let you know when I've got enough for us to talk about."

"Well, we got some ideas for you, in case you need inspiration or something. Just let us know."

"I will." I heard voices coming toward the door. "You guys better scoot now."

"We was just leavin' anyways," said Ralph. "Thanks for calling on us."

"Yeah, this was fun," said Norton. "See ya 'round." They waved and faded away again, as usual.

" 'Bye." I waved back at the empty air. I looked at the cut pieces. They were done beautifully. I could never take credit for this. Nobody would believe it.

The shop door opened just as I slung my backpack over my shoulder and posed in a nonchalant slouch.

There's this one older grad student who's a bear of a guy, balding, bearded, and heavy. He's tried to be patient with me, but I knew I really pissed him off sometimes. Wouldn't you know, the guy coming through the door was him.

"Damn, I thought I locked this door," he said to the doorknob. Then he looked up. "T.J.! How long have you been in here?"

"Just got in," I said coolly. "I was supposed to put in a couple of hours, but it looks like there's not much to do."

He frowned at me. "You didn't touch anything, did you?"

"Me?" I smiled. "Not a thing. Nice job you guys are doing on that set, by the way."

"What do you mean? We haven't started building it yet."

"I meant the cutouts." I jerked my thumb toward Ralph and Norton's work. *Now comes the moment of truth.*

It was worth it to see the expression on his face as he turned and saw the assembled pieces. Surprised doesn't begin to describe it. His mouth fell open. His eyes went wide. He scratched his head. "When . . . who . . . I could swear this was all lumber half an hour ago. T.J., did you see who did this?"

I shrugged. "Like I said, I just got here."

"Jeez, who could've . . ." he ran his fingers over the wood. "This is really nice work." He muttered possible suspects among the grad students or MFA's under his breath.

"Well, I'm gonna go," I said. I feared if I stayed any longer I was going to bust a gut laughing. "I'll come back sometime next week when there's something I can do."

"Sure. Yeah. Next week . . ." He continued muttering and walking around the set pieces.

I walked as fast as I could to the stairwell and collapsed against the wall. *I'm not crazy! They're real! And they can do anything!* I covered my mouth to keep my shrieks of relief inside and just sat huddled there. My heart thudded inside my chest. Every part of me shook. My world had just turned inside out.

They're real. And they'll show up any time I call them. They're gonna help me with my act. They like my philosophy. They even seem to like me! With magic like theirs on my side, I can do anything! The Whack-Pack was right. I got help. And Mamu, that was one hell of a lucky scarf.

Chapter 5

When I couldn't hold it in any longer, I ran up the stairs and out of the C-of-L. I nearly skipped down the sloping lawn, past Stephen Foster's cabin to Forbes Avenue. I didn't care where I was going, I just needed to be moving. I went past the Carnegie museum, saluting the statue of Shakespeare and thumbing my nose at Galileo. *There are more things in heaven and earth than are dreamt of in your philosophy.* Anyone else walking by probably thought I was nuts. Didn't matter—for once I knew I wasn't.

I holed up in the Arabica coffeehouse on Craig with a glass of lime Italian soda and a chocolate biscotti, savoring my newfound luck. *Magic. Power. A pair of little gray men are going to help me do a performance act like the world has never seen. No more dweebs ignoring me or laughing at me. No, sir. They're gonna have to watch. They're gonna have to listen. I'm going to hold up a magic mirror and they're gonna see themselves as the blind, insignificant airheads they really are.* I sat in a besotted, power-mad daze the rest of the afternoon.

It was frustrating to not be able to tell anyone about it. Not that I had many friends to tell. But Sam clearly wouldn't believe me. Angela? No, I didn't want her getting any doubts about me and changing her mind about the gig. Maybe Grandma Kaminski . . . then I'd have to tell her I'd lost the scarf. She'd be mad. No, worse—she'd be hurt. I couldn't do that. I'd have to keep the good news all to myself for a while.

Afternoon was starting to become evening, but I still didn't want to go home. Home was where ordinary things happened, and the world wasn't ordinary anymore. I went back to the Cathedral of Learning, now glowing golden in the late sunlight. They were starting to close up the Nationality Rooms when I walked in. I found a partly hidden table in a corner of the Commons and pulled out my notebook.

And found myself staring uselessly at the page. My class notes read like the scrawlings of an idiot. I tried to jot down ideas for the new act, based on what I'd done in Schenley Park, but I felt stuck. When possibilities are endless, it makes it pretty hard to choose where to start. I tried imagining myself standing onstage, roaring fury like a lion at the crowded room, the audience cowering in their seats, aware and ashamed.

But what had seemed natural and right while daydreaming in the Arabica now felt hateful, mean, and shrill. I began to get the scary feeling that there was something major I didn't understand, that I was missing an important point. Like there was always this bulletproof glass wall between me and the audience, me and other people. What good was it to use a magical bullhorn to shout at people when they couldn't hear me through the wall? And the wall wasn't their fault.

I couldn't write. The atmosphere in the Commons was beginning to feel . . . oppressive. It's a good place to be when you're feeling lonely because you can be around other people without having to talk to them. But sometimes it's a place that can remind you just how lonely you are.

I got an itchy feeling between my shoulder blades and turned around. Nothing there but a stone column, topped with a carving of an angel with two gargoyle heads on either side of it. I had the feeling they were staring at me.

"Oh, what would *you* know about it?" I snarked at them. I packed up my stuff and left.

I went down to the Roy's in the C-of-L basement for dinner. A fish sandwich, just for variety. Then I had no choice but to finally head for home.

It was dark out as I left the Cathedral. The air was a little chilly for mid-April, and I wished I'd brought a jacket. I walked quickly past Heinz Chapel, not wanting to look at the light shining through the stained-glass windows—it hurt my eyes for some reason. I took my usual shortcut to Craig Street, where I could catch the bus home, through the alley at Dittridge.

I was usually cautious in that alley—there's dumpsters and construction stuff cluttering it up and the sidewalk narrows as you walk in. My strange mood must have distracted me. I didn't notice the car idling in the alley to my left.

Someone jumped out from behind one of the dumpsters to my right, knocking me against the concrete wall. Something cold and hard and sharp was pressed against my neck.

"Get in the car!" he growled. His breath reeked of cigarettes and beer.

Shit. Not this. Why now? I knew if I got in the car, I would be dead meat or wish I were. "Like hell," I said.

I had taken a self-defense course once. They teach you not to fight back against an armed attacker, but I figured I had to try. I got my left arm and shoulder, on which my backpack rode, against his knife hand and pushed it away. I tried to drive my sharp little elbow into his chest. For good measure, I kicked him in the shin.

But then my backpack slid down onto my left arm, making it useless. Now off balance, I stumbled forward. I felt a line of pain in my right cheek. Then his fist drove into my gut, knocking the wind out of me.

Surprise, rage, pain, and sudden weakness all fought for my attention. Then it was all I could do to focus on getting the next breath. My attacker was able to pick me up like a rag doll.

The dark interior of the car was just a few steps ahead. He shifted his hold in order to shove me in. My backpack slid onto my forearm suddenly, forcing his grip to slip until I was hanging upside down, my nose inches from the pavement. I could smell the stone and sand of the concrete, see glittering chips of rock.

Something fluttered by. It was Ralph and Norton's time card, fallen out of the backpack. From somewhere I found the strength to reach out and grab it.

"Ralph, Norton," I whispered.

"Shut up, bitch." He grabbed my legs and tried to shove me in the car backwards, but a limp body is pretty awkward to handle.

"Hey, put her down!" came Ralph's gruff voice from somewhere in front of me. "That's no way to treat a lady."

"Yeah, she's a friend of ours," said Norton. "You be nice to her."

I smiled, but it hurt, so I stopped.

My attacker turned, with my legs half in the car. Again I felt the knife against my neck. "Stay back or I'll—what the fuck?"

I heard twanging sounds, like someone playing musical rubber bands. The knife fell away from my skin. My chest and cheek hit the cold concrete. The guy fell down onto the sidewalk, and for the first time I saw him clearly; jeans, T-shirt with a flannel shirt over it. He probably wasn't much older than me. Maybe even a Pitt student. The anger on his face was rapidly turning into terror. Three tiny silvery arrows were sticking out of his chest.

Ralph and Norton ran up beside him, each holding a small bow. They wrapped cords around the guy's wrists. He didn't fight them off—just seemed to stare

at them, his eyes wide with fear. Ralph waved at me
and said, "Hang on, T.J. We'll be right back." He
and Norton began to sink into the sidewalk as if
walking down stairs. They tugged on the cords and
my attacker sank with them, as though the concrete
were quicksand.

He worked his mouth but no sound came out. His
gaze fixed on me, pleading, begging me for help. As
if I could do something. As if I would.

I lay alone, in that awkward position, for long moments. I heard cars and people go by on Dittridge
and Craig, but no one came down the alley. A relief,
I guess; I would have been so embarrassed if someone had seen me that way. What would I tell them?
Hi, don't mind me, I was attacked but my friends,
just dragged the jerk underground so I'll be fine,
thanks. My cheek and neck began to sting, and I
realized that I was bleeding.

Ralph and Norton popped up out of the pavement
again and bobbed toward me. They picked me up in
their branchlike arms, Ralph at my shoulders and
Norton at my legs. With little effort, they moved me
to one side of the alley, setting me down on my back.

"That bastard," growled Ralph. "He sliced her
real good."

"Lemme see," said Norton. They bent over me,
their iron-gray eyes inspecting my face. Their breath
smelled like moist earth. Like fresh mushrooms.

"Yeah?" I wheezed. "How bad is it?"

"Shhh. Hold still, Princess. We'll fix you right up."

Princess. That was what my dad had called me
when I was a little girl. It was soothing to hear. I
closed my eyes. Ralph's and Norton's thin, cool fingers patted over my face and neck. I let my thoughts
drift elsewhere, enjoying being able to suck in more
air with each breath.

"That should do it," said Norton. "But we better
get her home."

"Yeah, but we gotta do it the hard way," Ralph

muttered. "To make sure the fixings hold. Time to go walkies, Princess."

I opened my eyes as Ralph reached under my shoulders and hoisted me up. I tried to stand and doubled over. "Sheesh, it's worse than I thought," said Ralph. "Take it easy, T.J. We'll be beside you every step."

So, one of them on each side, I staggered toward my bus stop on Craig. "Are you sure people won't see you?" I moaned.

"Trust us. They won't."

I decided to concentrate more on walking and shut up. I felt nauseous and weak, but calm. *Where did the adrenaline go? I should be as jumpy as if I'd had three pots of coffee.*

The few people walking past me looked at me a little funny, but they didn't seem to see the gray fireplugs holding me up. Fortunately, the bus came quickly. Somehow we squeezed the three of us up the bus steps, and somehow the right change appeared in my hand.

The black lady bus driver stared at me as I sank onto the front bench—the place where the old and the handicapped usually sit. "Are you all right?" she asked.

I nodded.

"You don't want me to call anyone for you? Ambulance or something?"

"No, really. Thanks," I rasped.

"Okay," she said dubiously and pulled away from the curb. I wondered what I must look like. I could have glanced up at the window across from me to check out my reflection, but I didn't.

The face of my attacker as he sank into the concrete was stuck in my mind. "What did you do to him?" I whispered to Ralph.

"To whom?"

"The guy who jumped me."

"Oh. Him. You don't wanna know." Ralph

grinned, displaying pointed triangular teeth. Nope. I didn't wanna know.

My thoughts were so scattered, I almost missed my stop. As the familiar landmarks went past, I jumped up and puled on the cord. My gut reminded me I shouldn't have done that, and I had to grit my teeth not to groan aloud. Ralph and Norton practically carried me down the bus steps. I wonder how *that* looked to the driver.

I pointed at Mom's apartment, and they hustled me to it and up the stairs. I unlocked the door and they guided me inside, all the way to the bedroom. I stretched out on the bed, not wanting to move anymore.

"Just stay right there Princess," said Ralph.

Yeah, right. Like I could go anywhere.

Ralph returned in a few moments with a steaming mug. Norton propped me up against the pillows, and Ralph put the mug to my lips. "Here, drink this. It'll fix you right up. Help you sleep."

I took the warm mug in my hands and sipped from it. It tasted like some kind of ginseng tea, made with really hard water. I could only take a few swallows, but it felt good going down. "Not bad," I said. "You guys oughta open a health food store."

Norton snorted. "Not our line. But, like I said, we learn whatever we need to get the job done."

"You sleep now," Ralph said to me, tucking the blanket under my chin.

And I did.

When I awoke, I didn't know who I was. Or what day it was. Or where I was. Not that I was anyplace new. The ceiling was still the one in Mom's apartment. But it took several seconds to remember that. A few seconds more to get the feeling that "I" was present and accounted for. A whole minute at least to figure out that it ought to be Sunday. And that I'd met two funny-looking creatures named Ralph and Norton on Friday. And that I'd been attacked Saturday night.

I sat up slowly. My stomach felt fine. There was a lot of sunlight coming through the windows. It sounded like the TV in the living room was on.

I stood up and padded to the bathroom. No muscles were sore. I took a piss and then looked at myself in the mirror. My short hair was really scraggly and spiky. I peered at the reflection of my face and saw on my right cheek a long, faint, shiny scar. It was noticeable only when the light hit it just right. It made my look kinda . . . dangerous. *Huh. Cool,* I thought.

I pulled off my clothes and got into the shower. The hot water felt good, and slowly I woke up. Enough to know things still weren't quite right. But the strange thing I was feeling was . . . nothing.

Other girls I knew about who had been assaulted had said they felt awful for weeks, sometimes years afterward. I should have been pissed as hell, or scared out of my mind, or crying a lot or *something.* Instead, I felt blank. As though it had happened to someone else, a long time ago.

Maybe it's shock, I thought. *Maybe the feelings will all come crashing down on me later.* More rage to add to the pile. But something within me said, *No, you'll never feel it.*

A creepy feeling stole over me. *What if they took it all?* I wondered. Ralph and Norton wanted to "fix" me. What if that meant removing all my strong emotions? Like Dad's hammer . . . bright, shiny, and new . . . and all character gone. A performance artist needs strong emotions. Heck, every kind of artist needs passions. *What if mine are all gone?*

I finished the shower and threw on a baggy black T-shirt and jeans, then finally set foot into the living room. Ralph and Norton were sitting on the floor in front of the TV, surrounded by a nest of Twinkies and Ho-hos wrappers. Looked like they'd found my secret junk-food stash. They were watching the Home Shopping Network.

"Hi, guys."

"Hey, she's up!" said Ralph, jumping to his feet and grinning.

"Hey, have you seen this, T.J.?" said Norton, pointing at the tube. "This is really funny. We never had this when we last watched TV. An' you got so many channels!"

"Yeah. Cable," I said, toweling my hair. "Fifty-seven channels and nothing on. Listen, guys, I want to thank you for rescuing me last night—"

"Think nothin' of it. Part of the service. Free of charge."

"Yeah, thanks, but, not meaning to be rude or anything, but I gotta ask you something. Um. What have you done to me?"

"Whaddya mean?" said Ralph.

"Okay, I mean, I was jumped last night, right?"

"Yeah. And you called for us and we rescued you."

"Yeah, I know, and I'm grateful, I really am. But . . . something isn't right this morning. I'm feeling really strange. That is, I mean, I'm not feeling much of anything, and that's really strange."

Ralph frowned. "You don't hurt or nothin', do ya? I thought we took care of that."

"Yeah. You did. You took care of it real good. That's kind of the problem. I don't feel anything about last night. Not even scared or sad or angry. It's like it didn't really happen, you know?"

"That's 'cause we fixed ya. You don't hafta go through all that weepy stuff an'at. That way you won't get distracted from working up your act."

"I know, but . . . you don't quite understand." I sighed and flopped down on the sofa. "See, I might need those feelings. For the act."

"Why?" said Norton. "That guy wasn't a Boomer or a Yuppie."

"I know, but that doesn't matter. I mean . . . are *all* my strong emotions gone, or just the ones I should have had last night?"

Ralph and Norton scratched their beards, looking so confused I would have laughed if I hadn't felt so worried. "Look, T.J.," said Ralph, "I don't know what it is you're goin' on about here, but all we did was fix ya so's you wouldn't be damaged by what happened last night. So's your body would be healed and you wouldn't be feeling no pain. That's all. We can't undo that. And like we said, that stuff woulda only distracted you from the work you gotta do."

I was about to tell him about artists and passions, but I realized these guys just wouldn't understand. Most normal people don't, so why should they?

"Sorry about the scar, by the way," Ralph went on. "It was the best we could do. The guy's knife musta been dirty or something."

"That's okay," I said. "I kinda like the scar. So, I won't notice any changes other than not feeling stuff that would have hurt me from last night?"

Norton shrugged. "Well, except for the side effects."

Ralph tried to shush him with gestures.

"Side effects?" I said coldly.

"Well, yeah," said Norton, ignoring Ralph. "All medicines got side effects."

"*What* side effects?" I demanded.

Ralph put on an embarrassed grin. "Heh, heh, well, you see, we don't exactly know, Princess. I mean, it's different for everybody, and you bein' a mort and all—" he finished with a shrug.

"And we ain't exactly doctors," said Norton.

I was beginning to see that help from these guys might not be the gift on the silver platter that I had thought. "And all what? What's going to happen to me?"

"Look, it's not gonna be any big deal," said Ralph. "We didn't work any major mojo on you or nothin'.

If you get any side effects, they'll be little things. We just don't know what. Just keep your eye out for them, and if they give you trouble, let us know, okay?"

"Yeah," I said dubiously. "Okay." I began to wish I had listened more when my mom or Grandma Kaminski had talked about folklore and fairy tales. One thing I did remember now, though, was that whenever a magical beastie did you a favor, there was usually a price.

Chapter 6

After some moments of awkward silence, Ralph asked, "Anything more we can do for you, T.J.?"

The Home Shopping Network was displaying a fake diamond necklace that cost more than my yearly tuition at Pitt. My mind kept wrapping around the concept of price . . . and whether some things are worth it. "Coffee," I said. "I could use some coffee."

"One cuppa joe, coming right up."

I heard what sounded like a muted chain saw buzzing around in the kitchen. Moments later Ralph put a warm mug in my hands. I took a sip. Jeez, it was strong. But it helped to clear my head.

"Listen, guys," I began, "don't get me wrong. I'm still grateful for your help and all. But can I ask you a few questions?"

"Sure, T.J.," said Norton. "You're our pal. Ask whatever you want."

"Okay. To start with, what are you? I mean, is there a name for your . . . species, or something?"

Norton looked wary. "If I tell you, you're gonna laugh."

"I won't laugh."

"Yeah, you will."

"I promise I won't."

"Okay, then. Your kinda people call us . . . knockers."

I nearly snorted coffee out my nose.

"Hey, Ralph, she's laughing."

"I am *not*," I said.

"It's not like it's any worse than Boomers or Yuppies."

"Sorry," I said. "I was just surprised. You mean like knockers like tommyknockers? I think I once saw a Stephen King book called that."

"Yeah, tommyknocker's another name. So's knackers, coblyanu, hammerlings, mountain monks, shaft dwarfs, buccas, gathorns, spriggans, nuggies, and a buncha others."

"Nuggies?"

"She's laughing again."

"I'm sorry! It's just, well, the names don't tell me anything about you. They just sound silly."

"Look," said Ralph, beginning to pace the room. "It's kinda hard to explain to you young people 'cause you don't know about us. But we been here a long time. We came over with the folks from the Old Country, ya know? They knew about us, even if most of 'em never seen us. But they'd tell stories about us."

"My grandmother's Polish, but she never mentioned . . . nuggies."

"That's the problem," said Ralph. "Stories about us are being forgotten. We're the working guys. We're the kinda folks who help out in the house and on the farms and in the mines and the factories."

"Oh," I said, "you mean like those little people who'd sew up people's clothes or make their shoes and the people would leave milk and cookies out for them?"

"Yeah, like that," said Ralph.

"But we don't do no clothes and shoes," said Norton.

"Right, we like the mines and factories ourselves," said Ralph.

"I get it," I said. "So you came to me because I kinda called for help and you guys wanted a job. Is that it?"

"Yeah, mostly," said Ralph. "See, me an' Norton, we been talkin' a long time about the changes that are happening in this town. When we first got here, long time ago, this was the greatest place on earth. Lotsa hard work. Lotsa people making things by the sweat of their brow. Lotsa opportunity for us to do what we was meant for."

"And lotsa pollution," I muttered.

"Now, see, it's that kind of thinking that's started ruining this place. There are elements out there, folk who didn't like the way we were digging into the earth and becoming powerful. Or that you people were becoming powerful. Folk who want it all to go back to forests 'n flowers and stuff. Folk who want all people to go away. Well, they've started making inroads in this town, and we don't like it. Not one bit."

"That's where you come in," said Norton.

"Right," said Ralph. "Here you come along, wanting help against these hoity-toity, whatchamacall-em. Yuppers."

"Yuppies. Boomers."

"Whatever. Back home, we call them the Sidhe, or the Seelie folk. So, anyway, with you being such a fellow traveler and all, it was natural that we team up. By us helping you, you're helping us."

I hadn't heard the terms "Shee" or "Seelie" before. They might have been a reference to mattresses, for all I knew. *But I'm against pollution*, I thought. *Am I misunderstanding these guys or are they misunderstanding me?* "The thing about Yuppies and Boomers and such," I said, "is that they think they're all for nature, but in reality their greedy, ignorant lifestyle is ruining the world for humanity *and* nature."

"Exactly!" said Ralph. "You got that right on the nose, Princess. So with that kind of keen perception, and your enormous talent, and our know-how, we figured we could make a real difference in this town."

"Enormous talent? You guys are flattering me, right? Angela and Warren don't think I have talent."

" 'Course you got talent. Norton and me, we wouldn't have showed up when you called if you didn't have the talent. We don't offer our services to just anybody, you know."

"I have special powers? I thought you answered because I used my grandmother's lucky scarf."

Ralph said, "But you had to have the power to use it. Wouldn't have worked otherwise."

"You mean I'm kind of a witch?"

"We prefer the word 'thaumaturge'," said Norton. "It flows more trippingly off the tongue."

"Shaddup," said Ralph. "Anyways, that's probably why you got into this performance stuff, T.J. I bet you always wanted to cast spells on people, you was just searching for a way how."

"Yeah," I said, thinking it over. "I bet you're right. But if I'm so powerful, how come my life is so shitty? I mean, I don't get along well with people at all."

"Every thaumaturge I ever known was an odd-ball," said Norton. He quickly added, "No offense, beggin' your pardon."

I looked at my hands as if they were strangers. "Could you guys teach me how to use my . . . powers?"

"Well, thaumaturgy ain't exactly our line," said Ralph. "But we'll show you enough to make your performance stuff work really swell."

"Wow," I said. *This is getting even weirder than I thought.* "Um, there's still one thing I gotta know, guys. There's gonna be a price for your helping me out, isn't there? Something you want from me, and rules I gotta follow, right? I want to know what those are."

"She wants to know The Rules, Ralph," said Norton.

"I heard her. That's a perfectly legit question.

Hokay. You already know Rule Number 1. That is, whenever we show up, you gotta feed us."

"Oh." So that explained why they always seemed hungry whenever I saw them. "The milk and cookies thing?"

"Please," Ralph begged, "no milk and cookies, okay? We had enough of that decades ago. We like variety. Hokay, Rule Number 2: Don't ask us our real names."

"From what you told me under the bridge, I probably couldn't pronounce your real names," I said. "It's okay. I don't like my real name either. I mean, of all the stupid things, my dad went and named me Tiffany Jeannine."

Ralph's eyes shot wide open, and he seemed about to say something. Then he seemed to think better of it and closed his mouth. He and Norton looked at each other and shrugged.

"Yeah," I went on, "disgusting, huh? Like I was going to grow up to be a beautician or a cheerleader or something. That's why I use my initials, T.J. So you guys got named something silly too? Like that guy in the fairy tale . . . Rumpelwhatsit?"

"Uh, yeah, that's it, like Rumpelstiltskin. But, really, what idiot would go shouting his real name out in the middle of the forest to make it easy for some bimbo to go breaking the contract? I ask ya. But it's okay, T.J. Your name is safe with us. We won't tell a soul."

"Thanks. Um. You aren't going to ask for my firstborn child, are you?"

Ralph scowled. "Do I look like father material? What would I do with a kid? Don't worry, T.J. Just feed us and let us help you."

"Okay. Any other rules?"

"Yeah, Rule Number 3: No whistling."

"No whistling?"

"It drives us nuts."

"Just as well I don't know how to whistle, then."

"Good," said Ralph.

"And another thing," said Norton. "No swearing."

"What?"

"It ain't nice," said Ralph.

"Uh, I might find that one pretty tough to follow."

"Well, okay, we'll go easy on that rule, then. And last but not least: Don't break the contract. Don't try to cheat us or double-cross us. That sorta thing."

"Yeah," said Norton. "It makes us grouchy and mean." He grinned his sharp-toothed grin.

"I see," I said, getting a bad case of the pricklies up my spine.

"But we know you're a good kid, T.J. You wouldn't do that to us."

"No." I said. "Of course not."

"Great. Then we are all agreed. Shake on it?" Solemnly he walked up to me, his twiggy hand extended.

So. This was the point of no return. "Uh, don't I get it in writing? Like something I have to sign my name in blood on?"

Ralph drew himself up, offended. "Who the hell do you think we work for? We're independent contractors. We don't do that sort of thing. A handshake is good enough for us."

"Sorry!" I said. "I've never done this before. I just wanted to be clear on, uh, procedures. So, all you want from me is to let you help out with my performance act, right?"

"And sock it to the Yuppies!" said Norton.

"And sock it to the Yuppies," I agreed. I could probably have sent them away then, maybe with no penalty. But, I wondered, where would that leave me? I'd still be nothing. Just a theater student, my career going nowhere. I probably couldn't learn this thaumaturgy stuff on my own. Without something special on my side, I'd be a flop at the Per Forma again, Angela and Warren would never speak to me again, and probably nobody else would hire me. This was my chance at something big. And I figured I'd probably never get another. "Okay. It's a deal." I grasped his twiggy hand and pumped it up and down a few times.

Ralph's face split in an enormous grin. "All righhhht!" He turned and high-fived Norton. Then they danced a little jig together. It was all I could do not to laugh.

"Hey!" Ralph snapped his fingers. "I almost forgot. We got a poster to show ya."

"Yeah, show her the poster, Ralph."

"Here, looky this." Ralph handed me an eight-by-eleven sheet of paper.

"But it's too soon!" I said. "I haven't even decided what's going to be in the act yet." I turned the paper over and looked at it. It was 3-D and in color, better than I'd ever seen holograms done before. It showed a beautiful pale blond woman caught in a huge industrial vice. When I tilted the paper slightly, her head turned and her mouth opened in a scream; the vice tightened and blood dribbled from where the vice squeezed her. The title, in iron-gray letters across the top, read DEATH TO THE QUEEN, a performance act by T.J.

"Um. Wow. That's really gross."

"See, the way we figure it," said Ralph, "is you said that what you do is put out symbols and stuff to shock people. It doesn't matter whether what you do is really like this, so long as they wake up to your message, right?"

"Yeah, I guess you've got a point there. I guess it doesn't really matter. But will this poster bring the kind of people we want into the club?"

"Oh-ho-ho. Just leave it to us. It'll bring 'em in."

"If you say so. This hologram must have been expensive to make."

"Hollow what?"

"You know, a 3-D photograph. I couldn't afford a lot of these."

"Hey, no problem. No charge," said Ralph. "We make as many as you want. We'll even stick 'em up in the best places in town for you."

"Wow, that's . . . really nice, guys."

"For you, only the best," said Norton.

"Hey, you want your last name on here, or just T.J.?"

"Well, my last name is Kaminski."

"Good name." Ralph ran the tip of his twiglike finger over the "T.J." on the poster. "Kaminski" appeared beside it as if it had been there from the start. "There. How's that?"

"Cool," I said.

"Great. We'll start making these up, then. You just go do whatever it was you was gonna do today. We'll let you know when we're done."

"By the way," said Norton, "mind if we call out for pizzas? I ain't had a good pizza in the longest time."

"Um, okay. But try to keep the order under twenty dollars, okay?" My mom usually sent me more money per month than I used, but I didn't want these guys to start any bad habits.

"No problem," said Norton.

Ralph and Norton huddled together, talking about where to put up the poster. I took my coffee into the bedroom, where I had a little desk, with an old Apple IIC on it. Suddenly I realized what I most wanted to do with the day was . . . homework. Finals were coming up, after all. *That's strange*, I thought. *I never want to study, usually. I wonder if this is one of those "side effects" they warned me about. A useful one, if it is.* I felt ready, even eager to get down to work.

I turned on the Apple IIC and the image on the monitor snowed and danced, not settling down. *It hasn't done that before. Gotta upgrade one of these days.* I slapped the side of the monitor, and it immediately behaved itself. *That's better.*

I brought up the file on my Comp paper. The class

had been given the theme "Pittsburgh History." The paper I had been working on was titled "Pollution in the History of Pittsburgh." I stared at it. The file was mostly dry statistics.

I deleted the file and began a new one. "My Dad, a Steelworker," I typed at the top. Ideas, words, sentences, paragraphs began pouring into my mind so fast, I couldn't type fast enough to keep up with them. *Wow. Side effects that make me smarter I can live with.* After a few minutes I had to sit back and rub my hands to keep them from cramping up.

Amazing. Yesterday I couldn't have written this paper. It would have hurt too much. Now, no problem. Whatever was I worried about, making the deal with Ralph and Norton? They didn't ask for my soul or my firstborn son. Didn't even ask me to sign anything. All they want is a job. Best deal I've ever made.

Anyway, even if it isn't, it's too late to back out now.

Chapter 7

Fast-forward through the next week. No, really—the days that followed went by in a blur. Even though it was finals week and I was working hard on the performance act. Looking back on it, here's what I remember.

Monday—I remember the smell of rain on stone, the smell of metal and rust, the smell of mud. Usually I hate rain, especially in the spring, but not now. I drifted into my Art Appreciation final, feeling alert but detached. I think I aced it. I remember that while studying I discovered I actually liked the paintings of Thomas Hart Benton and Diego Rivera. And that social realism wasn't as stupid as I'd first thought.

Monday evening, Grandma Kaminski called to ask why I hadn't shown up at dinner. I put her off with the explanation that I had to study. It was true, anyway. I didn't tell her about the attack because she would have insisted I call the cops. She still sounded worried about me. I told her to light some candles for me and let it go.

Tuesday—More lovely rain. I handed in my paper on my dad to English Comp. I hadn't written about his—passing away. I'd just stuck to my memories of his stories about working in the mill in Pittsburgh. But I had a warm feeling about the paper. I hoped I did him justice.

Wednesday—I began picking out props for the new act, based somewhat on the stuff I had done under the bridge. If it had been powerful once, it ought to be powerful again, right? A hammer had to be in it, of course. And a book. And a rock. Ralph and Norton suggested a doll. Sounded good—dolls are often used in performance art. I suggested using the blue scarf as maybe a dress for the doll, hoping that way I might get it back. But no, Ralph said the scarf wouldn't be right and that they'd bring the material for the doll's clothing themselves. Oh, well.

By this time, I was noticing the posters starting to go up for my performance. They seemed to be popping up everywhere; on the bulletin boards at the Beehive and Arabica, on every lamppost near Pitt, on display boards in the C-of-L. Ralph and Norton had been busy boys. And, in the evenings especially, I saw people looking at the posters. Tall blond people wearing loose-fitting, blousy shirts and long skirts or trousers. People with figures-too-perfect in suits-too-well-tailored. Just the ones we wanted to reach. They pointed at the posters, talked excitedly to one another, and wrote things down.

Wow, I thought, both happy and scared. *It's really going to happen. People are going to come to my show—the ones I've been wanting to reach all along. And they'll listen to me. And Angela and Warren will see I was right. I'll get more gigs, maybe even move on to bigger theaters!* Visions of my name on off-Broadway marquees danced in my head.

Thursday—slow down to real time. On this day, I had the final in Acting. Everyone in the class had to perform a short monologue out of a Shakespeare play. Usually I had a bitch of a time memorizing lines that I hadn't written myself. But this time the lines stuck in my head as if they were superglued to my brain cells.

I had hoped, at the beginning of the term, that we would be allowed to choose our own monologue. I had wanted to do Caliban, the monster from *The*

Tempest. Or maybe Lady Macbeth. No luck—the instructor chose them, and rumor had it that Professor Caldwell liked to match the part to the personality of the student. I don't know what she thought of me. I got Paulina's speech in *The Winter's Tale.* A real nobody of a character.

But I was curious to see what parts the professor had matched with which students. I wondered if Ralph and Norton's special tea had maybe "fixed" my lousy talent at reading people. That would be a fix worth having—we shy people like to *think* that we're keen observers of the world around us. It'd be nice to be right, for once.

I sat down in the back of the room and tried to force myself to relax and pay attention to the other students, so I wouldn't get too nervous about my own upcoming monologue.

Julie was the first one up. She's a really mousy, shy kid, worse than me. She did Portia from *The Merchant of Venice,* stumbling through her lines as though they were snares entangling her tongue:

"You see me, Lord Bassanio, where I stand,
   Such as I am. Though for myself alone
   I would not be ambitious in my wish
   To wish myself much better, yet for you
   I would be trebled twenty times myself . . ."

Sheesh, I thought. *Pathetic. Get a spine, girl.* She painfully plodded her way through the monologue and sat down, hanging her head. The class, of course, gave her supportive applause. They have more heart than taste.

Curt, a tall, gangly blond guy who's kinda gonzo, was next. He got to do Mercutio from *Romeo and Juliet:*

"O, then I see Queen Mab hath been with you.
She is the fairies midwife and she comes
In shape no bigger than an agate stone."

Hah, I thought. *Shakespeare must never have put out
milk and cookies for help with his plays, or his fairies
would have been short gray fireplugs.*

". . . This is that very Mab
That plaits the manes of horses in the night
And bakes the elflocks in foul, sluttish hairs.
Which once entangled much misfortune bodes."

Only if you break the contract, I thought. Curt did his
part so broadly that he got laughs where he probably
shouldn't have. But we all enjoyed his mugging and
bouncing around, and he got wild applause when
he finished.

What an act to follow. Just my luck, I was up next.
Paulina is in a throne room, yelling at some king:

"What studied torments, tyrant, hast for me?
What wheels, racks, fires? What flaying, boiling
In lead or oils . . ."

Paulina's really pissed because the king has ordered someone she cares for killed, so I tried to play
it on the edge of rage. But it was hard to make the
words make sense. Especially the lines about the
devil shedding water out of fire and casting a baby
daughter to the crows. At last, I reached the final
lines;

". . . but the last—O lords,
When I have said, cry 'woe'; the Queen, the Queen,
The sweet'st, dear'st, creature's *dead*; and vengeance
    for't
Not dropped down yet."

I heard applause but didn't move. So strange that I hadn't noticed it before . . . my performance act was going to be titled "Death to the Queen," and here I was mouthing words of fury at just such a thing. The coincidence sent the *Twilight Zone* theme doo-doo-dooing through my head.

Professor Caldwell squawked at me to sit down, so I did. I guess I must have done the monologue all right. The words "vengeance for't not dropped down yet" rang over and over, ominously, in my mind.

I was so wrapped up in my own thoughts that I hadn't noticed Sam was the next person up—I wanted to cheer for him, but he had already begun. He was doing the role of the sprite, Ariel, from *The Tempest*:

"You fools! I and my fellows
  Are ministers of Fate. The elements
  Of whom your swords are tempered, may as well
  Wound the loud winds or with be-mocked-at
    stabs
  Kill the still-closing waters, as diminish
  One dowle that's in my plume."

He's so good. Now that's more like the supernatural critters I know. All-powerful and sure of themselves. Sam got a big round of applause when he was done. I tried to catch his eye, but he didn't happen to look my way, and his seat was on the other side of the room.

There were others not nearly as entertaining. Of the girl who played Lady Macbeth, I thought, *The lady doth chew the scenery too much.* Of the guy who did Julius Caesar, *Indeed, better off buried than praised.* And so on. I had fun.

There was a brief discussion afterward of who did what well and why. My name never came up. Typical. As the class broke up, Sam breezed by me, say-

ing, "Hey, T.J., lookin' good!" but he was out the
door before I could even say "Hi."

As I was getting up from my chair, I bumped into
Julie, the wimp. "Sorry," she said, avoiding my gaze.

A thousand snarky, clever put-downs went
through my head. I normally wouldn't have said any
of them, would have just grunted and walked on.
But I felt a condensing of warmth and energy in my
chest, and my mouth opened without my thinking
about it. "Hey, Squirt," I said, "about your scene
up there . . ."

"What?" She looked up at me, wary.

What came out next was, "That was the best thing
I've seen you do. That was a tough part she gave
you, but I liked the way you handled it. You should
try out for some plays next term."

Her eyes opened wide. "You think so? Really?"

"Yeah. Really."

"Oh. Um. Thanks." Julie wrapped her arms
around her books and walked off, staring at the
ground as usual. But she was smiling, and there was
a little bit of bounce in her step.

Why did I say that? I wondered, I mean, I was kinda
glad I did, now that I could see the result. *It's not
like I lied or anything. And the kind words seemed to
change her. My words have power now. Is this part of the
thaumaturgy stuff Ralph and Norton were talking about?
Or is this another side effect of whatever they did to fix
me?*

I still had some of that bound-energy feeling inside. *A test. I need another test.* Professor Caldwell was
standing by the classroom door, talking to some
other students. I walked up behind them and started
thinking at her, *Give me an A. I want an A for this class.*

The students in front of me suddenly left and I
found myself staring into Professor Caldwell's tired
and perhaps . . . disappointed eyes.

"Going to stand there all day?" she said in her

usual sardonic tone, "or is there something I can do for you?"

My mouth opened and I heard myself say, "I'm sorry. I'm sorry I wasn't a better student."

She blinked. "Beg your pardon?"

"I've been slacking this term, and it wasn't fair of me to waste your time. You had a lot of important things to teach us, and I hope I remember some of them after this."

Professor Caldwell smiled but her eyes narrowed. "Well, thank you, but if you think buttering me up is going to affect your grade—"

"I don't deserve a better grade," I said. "Thanks. 'Bye." I zipped out of the classroom, my feet having more smarts than my mouth at that moment. As I ran down the hall, I wanted to beat myself over the head with my notebook. *What was I thinking? What's wrong with me?* I mean, some part of me knew what I had said was true, but that wasn't the kind of truth I wanted to go around blurting out. I was a performance artist—I had to speak in-your-face-wake-up-and-smell-the-garbage-type truths. I had to be able to tell people what they needed to hear. The uglier the truth, the better. If I couldn't do that anymore, my career was in trouble. *I've gotta ask Ralph and Norton abut this,* I thought, *when I get a good chance.*

The rest of the weekend was taken up with preparing the new act. Other Pitt students were throwing end-of-term going-away parties, but I didn't go to any. Not that I was invited to many. The great thing was, I didn't care. I was so caught up in working out the performance that nothing else mattered. Sometimes that's the wonderful thing about art; it can consume all your attention, take you out of the mundane world, make you forget your problems and feel really alive. I almost forgot to eat. If Ralph and Norton hadn't needed to be fed, I probably would have skipped meals all weekend.

I had decided to do an "inscribed space" piece. It's

not often done in performance art anymore, but it just seemed the right framework to use. In this method, certain props would be placed in specific positions on the stage. The way I moved between the props, and the things I said at each prop "station" would imply certain meanings and connections between meanings.

The rock would be centered at the front edge of the stage. And I would tie my dad's hammer on it just as it had been, under the bridge. There was something so . . . important about that image I just couldn't leave it out. To stage left would be a pedestal with the book on it. For balance, I sketched in two more pedestals, one at stage right and one at the back of the stage in line with the rock.

Ralph and Norton made approving noises when I showed them the sketch. I had fixed us a lunch of pierogies—the good kind; stuffed with mashed potatoes and coated with butter and sour cream. Real heart-attack-on-a-plate stuff. They popped the pastries into their mouths as they nodded over the sketch.

"This is good, T.J., this setup here. Kinda like a cross shape. We can work with that. You got good instincts, kid."

"You're a good cook, too," said Norton, sneaking a pierogie off Ralph's plate.

"Thanks, guys," I said. "But I still don't have all the props lined up."

"Well, there's that doll we suggested."

"Oh, yeah. I'm not sure what kind of doll to use. One artist I've heard of uses little baby dolls—"

"Naw, naw," said Ralph, butter dripping down into his scraggly beard. "Get one of them Barbie-type dolls. Blond, you know, with the big gazongas."

"Uh. Right. Why?"

"Look more like a Yuppie-type person. That's what this act is about, right?"

"Oh. Yeah." The trouble with brainstorming with

Ralph and Norton was that it was too easy to forget whose act it was.

"We got some phrases for you to say, too," said Norton.

"Wait a minute—you're gonna put words in my mouth?"

"T.J., Princess. listen," said Ralph. "You wanted us to help you use your special powers, right? You wanted a powerful act. Well, that's what these phrases are; they're words of power. Magical words, if you wanna call 'em that. Here." He showed me a piece of paper with some kind of foreign writing on it.

"I can't read that."

"We'll teach 'em to ya."

"And another thing," Norton put in, "when you rehearse this, just do it in bits. Don't do the whole thing all together. Not until you're doing it for real, onstage."

That didn't sound like a good way to practice. "Why?"

Ralph slapped his forehead, leaving an buttery smear between his eyes. "Whaddya think you're doing here? You don't wanna set off a spell before its time. S'dugs! No wonder you never learned you was a wizard. You drain your energy before you even use it. You gotta conserve yourself. Got it?"

"Um. Yeah. Speaking of magical words, guys, there's something I've been meaning to ask you. Remember when you said there might be side effects from that fixing you did after I got jumped?"

"Yeah, why? You notice anything?"

"I sure have. Lately I sometimes get this feeling like I've got this light bulb or one of them lightning-plasma spheres in my chest, and when it switches on I say really strange things to people. Stuff I'd never actually say."

Ralph scratched his beard. "What, bad things? Like swearing and stuff?"

"No, not bad things. Truthful things, mostly. Or kind and helpful things. But it's just not me talking and it's scary, you know?"

Ralph and Norton turned to each other. "Gift of Gab, maybe?" Norton suggested.

"Doesn't sound like it," said Ralph. "Doesn't exactly sound like Truthsayer, either. Wouldn't be if it's only intermittent."

"Hmmm. Did you use fresh pennyroyal in that tea, Ralph?"

" 'Course I did. The freshest. Picked it myself."

"Well, there's the problem, you dope!" said Norton. "It's supposed to be *dried* pennyroyal. Forty days dried at least!"

"Well, how was I supposed to know that?" Ralph roared. "I ain't no apocalypsy."

"Apothecary."

"Whatever! Herbs ain't our line. You said so yourself." Ralph turned and suddenly seemed to remember I was still in the room. He smiled like a kid caught snitching from the cookie jar. "Heh-heh."

"Let me get this straight," I growled. "You guys gave me some magical potion, using the wrong ingredients, that give side effects that you don't understand?"

"Don't worry, Princess! Probably it'll wear off soon anyway. If it's not doing any harm, why make a big deal of it?"

"Because," I said through gritted teeth, "it just might get in the way of my performance career."

"Nothin's gonna get in our way, T.J. You can count on that. If it starts givin' you real problems, let us know. We got specialists who can handle that sort of thing."

"Ralph—"

"Anyways, I wouldn't be thikin' of breaking the contract over such a little thing if I was you. If you know what I'm sayin'. We're like family now, and we always take care of our own, you know? So just relax, T.J. We'll take good care of you."

His tone was friendly, but I wasn't sure I liked the words much. It was beginning to sink in just how in over my head I was. And I was beginning to lose confidence in my lifeguards.

More clues came later that night. I was going through my CD collection and Mom's old folk-song books, trying to come up with the music I wanted to use, if any. Ralph and Norton had gone off on a "midnight procurement run."

About 1:00 A.M. they popped back into the living room. Ralph was holding a box. Norton was holding a long pole with a cloth bag tied at one end. He was treating the bag like there was something radioactive in it.

"Hi, guys. What did you bring me?"

Ralph held out his box. "Material for the doll's dress. Treat it with care, willya? It's rare stuff."

"Okay." I took the little wooden box and opened the lid. Inside was a swatch of gossamer cloth, glimmering in the light. "Ooooh!" I said and reached in for it.

"Uh, just leave it in there for now, willya?" said Ralph. "It cost me a lot to get that, and I, uh, wouldn't want anything to happen to it."

"Cost you?"

"Don't ask."

"Right." I reclosed the box and set it on the coffee table. "What have you got, Norton?"

Norton set the bag down cautiously on the rug. "Uh, dirt."

"Dirt? You brought me dirt?"

"Well, special dirt."

It was too late at night, or too early in the morning, to play Twenty Questions. My growing fears were making me impatient. "What kind of special dirt, Norton?"

Norton looked at Ralph. Ralph nodded. Norton said, "Graveyard dirt."

"Grave—eeeeww!" It was my turn to smack my forehead. "What are you guys getting me into!"

"Look, sweetcakes," said Ralph, "you wanna do thaumaturgy or doncha? You wanna do powerful spells, you gotta have powerful ingredients."

"Like fresh pennyroyal?" I was so nervous and fried I began to laugh. "You're not going to make me use eye of newt or tongue of bat next, are you?"

"Eeeeeuuuwww," said Norton with a shudder.

"Not unless it works," said Ralph. "Besides, I remember hearing that performance artists like gross stuff. Anyway, there's one more thing."

"Now what?"

"You gotta make this." Ralph held out a piece of paper to me. I took it and read it. "This is a bread recipe."

"That's right."

"Barley meal, heather, goat's milk, elderberries? I don't have these ingredients!"

"Yeah, you do." Out from behind his apron, Ralph produced another sack. He pulled a set of covered wooden bowls out of the sack and placed them on the kitchen counter.

"Oh. Okay. I'll do it in the morning, I guess."

"No, you gotta make it now. It's the dark of the night, after midnight."

"Now? Oh, c'mon. Couldn't you guys do it?" I whined.

"Hey, who's the thaumaturge here? It's your spell. You gotta bake the bread."

"Doesn't sound very tasty," I grumbled.

"You're not gonna eat it. It's just one of the props."

"But I'm so *tired*."

"Oh. We can fix that." There came the sound of buzzing from the kitchen and Ralph returned with a mug of hot, aromatic tea.

Just smelling it put zing into my synapses and

made my nerves vibrate. *And what side effects might this give me, and do fairy potions have drug interaction problems?* "Uh, no, thanks," I said. "I've had enough fixing for now. I'll just have some coffee and wake myself up."

Ralph looked disappointed. "Okay, Princess. Whatever."

I went to the kitchen and got to work. The dough took a lot of kneading, but I pounded away at it. Then I threw the dough in the oven and set the timer. And collapsed. I draped myself over the island counter, feeling drained. All around me were dirty bowls and spoons. I noticed the living room was a mess too, with pizza boxes, Twinkies wrappers, greasy napkins, paper cups and plates scattered everywhere. I mean, I wasn't the tidiest person in the world, but since Ralph and Norton had shown up, the place was a sty.

"Sheesh, what a mess! Would it be too much to ask, for you guys to clean up the place for me? You don't have to be a thama-whatever to do that, do you?"

Ralph made a face. "Domestic stuff ain't our line either. But you been workin' hard, T.J. You deserve a break. We'll see if we can find somebody on the local grapevine to help out."

I put my head down on my arms. "Thanks. I appreciate it."

"Hey, no problem," said Ralph. He snapped his fingers and muttered something like a chant at high speed.

A gust of wind blew through the room. Paper began to accumulate into a pile in the air, and then, presto! stuffed itself into a garbage bag. Dishes seemed to stack themselves and flew to the kitchen where they landed safely in the sink. Bowls spun under the water tap, frothing with bubbles, then came out sparkly clean and dry on the counter. If I blinked or watched it sideways, I sometimes got a glimpse of a little hand or foot, but only for a fraction of a second. It was like watching *The Invisible Man* on fast-forward video.

In less than two minutes by the microwave's clock, it was done. The apartment was cleaner than I usually kept it. "Bravo!" I said tiredly and applauded. Instantly, a little man appeared, standing on the island counter. He was only two feet high or so and perfectly proportioned. He had pale olive skin, curly dark brown hair, and big brown eyes. He wore a black velvet jacket and knickers and a soft velvet cap with a red feather in it. He swept his cap off his head and bowed to me. "Buona sera, bella signorina," he said.

I don't speak Italian, but somehow I was able to understand him and I blushed. Nobody ever called me beautiful miss unless they were trying to sell me something. "Um. Thank you."

The little man looked at me expectantly.

"Psst!" Ralph hissed. "He wants some wine."

"Oh. Sure. Uh, wine . . ." I remembered Mom had some in the lower cupboard. *Should still be there if Ralph and Norton haven't drunk it up.* I don't drink wine myself. I prefer beer.

I opened the cupboard and saw three bottles in the rack. "Uh, does he want white or red?"

"Vino Bianco, per favore," said the little man.

"White it is." I pulled out a green bottle. It seemed to be a decent California vintage. I poured a glass and set it before the dapper little guy. It seemed so big compared to him that I said, "Would you like a straw?"

He shook his head and grasped the bowl of the glass in both hands. His mouth widened impossibly as he lifted the glass and downed all the wine in one chug. He set the glass down with a sigh and a satisfied smack. Then he drew a lace-edged handkerchief from within his jacket and daintily dabbed at his lips.

"T.J.," said Ralph, "meet Luigi. Luigi, that's T.J. You be nice now, Luigi."

Luigi extended his hand and I reached out mine to let him shake it. Instead, he leaned forward and genteelly kissed my knuckle.

"Gotta watch out for Luigi," said Norton. "He really likes the ladies."

"Aw," I said, "I think he's kinda cute."

Luigi's eyes got very big, and his lips stretched into a dreamy smile. He rose into the air, saying, "Che felicità! Che dolcezza!"

"Now you've gone and done it," said Ralph. "He's gonna be impossible!"

"You're just jealous."

Ralph and Norton looked at each other and shrugged.

Luigi waggled his feet and zipped away through the air, through the bedroom doorway and into my closet. "What's he doing?"

"Mending any clothes that need mending," said Norton. "Polishing shoes, straightening hangers, that sorta thing. Shows he likes ya."

"Huh. Guess you *can* find good help these days. Even if it's from little Italian leprechauns."

"He's not a leprechaun, he's a folletti," said Ralph. "Leprechauns are Irish. They get insulted if you mix 'em up."

"Luigi's okay," said Norton, "if you don't ask too much of him." They hopped onto the couch and turned on the TV. "Go ahead and get some shut-eye, T.J. We'll watch the bread for you."

Sleep sounded good to me, so I showered and went to bed. I fell asleep quickly and dreamed I lay on a sunny, Mediterranean beach. I was naked but felt completely comfortable on the soft sand, the warm sun on my skin. In the distance, I could hear the cries of seabirds and the hiss of waves, like someone's slow breathing. The tide was coming in, and the warm water lapped up against my feet. Slowly it flowed up my calves. Then onto my thighs. The warm water felt wonderful, sending pulses of pleasure up my entire body. I sighed and arched my body and I woke up just as I realized I was having the biggest orgasm I'd ever had. I cried out and grabbed my pillow and hugged it tight, reaching for the lamp switch.

I blinked in the bright light. Something was moving. Under the covers. Between my legs. I flung the sheet back.

Luigi sat up, a huge grin on his face. "Va bene, bella mia, no?"

I smacked him with the pillow.

"Aieeeee!" He flew off the bed and into the wall, then slid down onto the floor.

"Ralph!" I yelled.

I heard Ralph trundle to the door. He opened it a crack. "What's the matter—*ulp!*" His eyes went wide and he shut the door again. "Sorry, Princess, I didn't know you weren't decent!"

I pulled the sheet up to my neck. "It's okay, Ralph. Get in here."

The door opened and Ralph tiptoed in, holding his hands over his eyes. "So, uh, what's up, T.J.?"

Luigi moaned in the corner.

"I got tongue-raped by your little Italian imp!"

"Luigi? Aw, now, we told you not to encourage him."

"Encourage him?!"

"Okay, okay, I'll take care of it. Luigi, get outta here. Scram. Vamoose. Don't bug the lady no more. Got it?"

Luigi stood holding his head. He looked sadly at me and blew me a kiss. Then he spun on one leg and popped out of sight.

"Anything else I can do for you, T.J.?"

"Yeah, don't do me any more favors."

Ralph shook his head and rolled his eyes. "Okay. Sleep tight." He shut the door carefully behind him.

"Yeah. Thanks." Sleep. Right. I sat hugging the pillow and fuming. It wasn't fair. I mean, between shyness and not being too good-looking, well, at nineteen I was still a virgin. Still was. Technically. I guess. The only sex I'd known before was what I could do for myself and a couple of kiss-fests with insecure dweebs who didn't know what they were doing. I didn't know what it was like with a regular boy yet, and here I'd gotten something that felt incredibly wonderful from a weird nonhuman little . . . thing who I didn't even know. It didn't feel right. And the damnable thing was, I'd probably want it again. *What if I get the chance for sex with a real boy someday, and it isn't as good? Is it spoiled for me forever?*

There was a soft pattering outside my window. I turned and peered through the curtain behind my bed. It was just rain. I put my hand up to the cold windowpane and watched the liquid reflections of the streetlights run through my fingers, just out of reach.

Chapter 8

So we come to the Big Night.

I got to the Per Forma extra early to set up any props and to give Ralph and Norton time to check the place out. They told me they were going to set up the special effects, as well as extra protections. But they didn't say what they were protecting me against. "Just a precaution. Nuttin' to worry about," Ralph said. "Trust us. You'll be fine." Well, what are friends without trust? I wasn't going to back out now.

Angela was there early too, looking tense and pale. Turned out the main act had suddenly caught sick. So as far as performers for that night, I was it. From overhearing Angela talking on the club phone to Warren, I knew that more than just her job was on the line. I didn't know what to say to reassure her, so I just concentrated on my setup.

First off, I covered the stage with a drop cloth again. On the cloth I drew the hollow cross, as Ralph and Norton had instructed. Then I poured the grave-yard dirt over the outline. The dirt smelled musty and moldy. Phew!

Norton went bouncing past the stage, humming cheerfully. I looked around but didn't see Angela.

"I hope those posters work," I told him. "Looks like it's up to us to fill this place. Poor Angela. Just her luck the headline performer took sick."

"O-ho!" said Norton. "You think it was luck, do ya? You think it was some kind of coinkidink?"

"You mean, you guys—"

"Shhh. Tonight you're gonna be the star, T.J. It's your night to shine. Hee hee hee."

Jeez, I thought as Norton bounced away, *that was a shitty thing for them to do. Just how costly is this performance going to be? And to how many people?*

Ralph came waddling by. He was real cheerful too.

"Ralph, how—"

"Hey, watch it there, Princess. You left a little space in the line of dirt there. Remember, I told ya, no gaps."

"Oh." In my distracted state, I'd move the bag of dirt too fast and missed a spot. I poured more dirt there, saying, "This is some kind of protection too, isn't it?"

"You got it. You're picking up this thaumaturgy stuff fast."

"But what am I—" Angela walked into the room and I shut my mouth.

"Talking to yourself, T.J.?" She walked up to the stage, until she stood right beside Ralph.

"Just, uh, practicing lines." I glanced from Ralph to Angela and back. *Nope. She doesn't see him.*

"What do you keep looking at?"

"Sorry, Ange. I'm just real distracted. I keep staring into space."

She ran her fingers through her hair. "Yeah, I know what you mean. Um, T.J., you did arrange to have lots of people show up, didn't you?"

Ralph imitated her gesture with a wide, stupid grin. I had to cough to cover my laugh. *Bastard.*

"Sure, Ange. I put posters up all over. Didn't you see them?"

"Posters? No, I guess I didn't."

How could she have missed them? "Well, I did. And people seemed really excited about it."

"Glad to hear it. You thought about all I said the

other night, didn't you? About what a good act takes?" she persisted, worry all over her face.

I felt that strange, warm sensation in my chest again. *Oh, God, here it comes again. What am I going to say this time?* I looked Angela straight in the eye. "It'll be a good show, Ange. There will be lots of people. Take it easy. It's gonna be okay." *Phew. That wasn't so bad. Hope she doesn't get suspicious. I've never been able to talk to her like that before.*

Angela blinked. "Sorry. I'm bothering you, aren't I? I should probably just let you work."

"Well, um . . ."

Ralph whispered loudly up at her, "You're hungry. You want an early dinner."

"Listen, T.J., I'm gonna go grab some dinner. And a beer to drown the butterflies in my stomach. Can I bring you anything?"

"No, thanks."

"Okay. Warren will be here at six to let the crowd in. So keep that in mind, if you want to have the stage set by then. Or not. Up to you."

"Amscray," said Ralph.

"I gotta get out of here." Angela turned and walked quickly out of the club.

I turned to Ralph. "Did you hear that? That side effect popped up again."

"Stop fretting, T.J. Keep your mind on your work. It's important. Focus, that's what thaumaturges need."

"And how could Angela not see the posters?"

"We didn't make 'em for the likes of her," said Ralph. "She's not your audience."

Before I could ask him what he meant, he went bouncing away too.

"Am I ever gonna know what's going on?" I muttered to myself. I sighed and continued the setting up. I finished the cross and checked it for holes. Nada. I put the rock, with Dad's fixed hammer bound loosely on top of it, inside the hollow cross at the end of the arm pointing toward the audience. The other three arms each got a pedestal, which I had rented from a wedding supply place, at the end.

On the pedestal at stage right, I put the loaf of bread I'd baked. It smelled nice. Too bad I couldn't eat it. On the pedestal to the back, I put the doll under a green cloth. The pedestal at stage left got the book and a plastic cup holder.

And I was done. Simple set up. I hoped the final effect would be anything but simple.

I went back to the dressing room to start assembling my costume. First I smeared lumpy terra-cotta clay slip all over my skin. I wrapped aluminum foil over strategic places. Then I blended the clay into the foil so that it wasn't clear where the metal ended and the clay began. Once the clay dried, which didn't take long, I dabbed charcoal dust in splotches here and there to break up my apparent shape. I wanted to look as though I was made of rusted steel. I also rubbed clay slip into my hair and spiked it. Looked way cool.

The dressing room door opened and the sound of voices spilled in. Angela slipped through and closed the door behind her. She looked a lot happier than when she had left. In fact, she was grinning from ear to ear.

"Hey, T.J. Twenty minutes until showtime. Wow! That's some costume."

"Thanks. You have a good dinner?"

"Yeah. Got a nice surprise when I came back too. Don't know how you did it, kid, but when you keep a promise, you really keep a promise."

I blinked. "I do?"

"Haven't you seen the crowd out there?"

"No, I've been busy with the costume. I haven't even peeked."

"Well, take a peek now." She beckoned me to the door and opened it a crack. The crowd noise spilled in again.

The room was full; every table was crammed with people. Beautiful people. Tall, slim, well-dressed people, from the blouse-and-Birkenstock types to the Halston, Armani, Gucci types. All the people I'd seen checking out my posters. They were starting to line the walls, standing room only. They were talking excitedly to each other and eyeing the stage.

"They're all here for you," said Angela in my ear. "None of them had come for the main act. No one had to be sent away disappointed. And they're all ordering the expensive wine. Warren is doing jigs behind the cash register. I don't know how to thank you, but thank you."

"All for me?" My stage fright returned in full force.

"Yep." She checked her watch. "Fifteen minutes until showtime. Knock 'em dead." Angela made a motion as if she were about to hug me. But she stopped, seeing what I was covered with, and gave me a thumbs-up instead. She left, humming.

I walked back to the middle of the dressing room and just stood there a moment in shock. "Ralph!" I said in a loud whisper. "Norton!"

"Shhh!" came from behind the shower curtain.

I pulled back the plastic. "Norton, what are you doing in there?"

He glanced nervously at the door. "You shouldn't call us now. We're really busy backstage, okay? You need something?"

"Um. Only an extra dose of courage, if you got it. I'm having a bad attack of the shys."

"We can't make you no special tea right now. Look, don't worry. You'll do fine." Just do like we said and you won't get—You'll be okay. It'll all come together like we said. Trust us."

"Okay."

Norton did a rapid fade.

"Boy, that was encouraging," I muttered. I needed to do something with my hands before they shook

themselves off my arms, so I started to get the last
prop ready. I took a flashlight out of my backpack.
Over the lens I had Scotch-taped a small globe bowl,
the bottom of the bowl against the lens, so that the
whole thing looked like a cup with a long, thick stem.
I went to one of the sinks and put some water into
the bowl. From the dressing room fridge, I got a
small chunk of dry ice and quickly plopped it into
the bowl. It began to froth and steam nicely.

The door opened again. "Lights are down," Angela
said. "Anytime you're ready."

"Thanks. Tell Warren to give me two, then start
the music."

"Will do." Angela winked and closed the door behind her.

I turned on the flashlight. The prop became a torch
of glowing, bubbling smoke. I waited at the door
until the music began. Then, to the strains of Enya's
Ebudae, the torch held before me, I walked with mea-
sured step onto the stage. Soft, awed whispers drifted
up from the audience. I fought down my stage fright
by telling myself the people were just an illusion, not
really there.

Very carefully, I stepped over the line of dirt into
the hollow cross. I walked up the forward-pointing
arm and dipped the torch toward the rock with the
hammer on it. Next, I walked to stage right and
dipped the torch toward the loaf of bread. Turning
my back on the audience, I dipped the torch toward
the green cloth and what lay underneath. Finally, as
the music came to a close, I walked to the end of the
stage left cross arm and placed the flashlight in the
holder beside the book.

I returned to the center of the cross and raised my
arms. To the audience, I said, "Welcome. You may
believe you are here to witness death. Or a funeral.
But do not fear. Do not fear the unknown. Do not
fear death. For every death is a rebirth." I raised my
arms toward the ceiling and said one of the special

phrases Ralph and Norton had given me. The murmuring from the audience became louder, and my
skin began to tingle and hum as though I were wearing a bodysuit of live bees.

The next part was tough. I had only written it the
day before. Ralph and Norton had told me, "These
Yuppie types never think about death. They believe
it has nothing to do with them. So write something
about death. Stick it to them."

There was only one way I could do that. And it
was very, very hard.

I began a little dance toward the rock, singing,
"Once I built a railroad, made it run, made it run on
time—"

I stopped suddenly, as if seeing the hammer on
the rock for the first time. I crouched down and crept
closer to it, my arm outstretched as if to touch it. In
a monotone I recited: "Oh, Dad, poor Dad. They
called me at school. It was the landlady, telling me
she'd found you. She wouldn't tell me what had happened, only that she'd found you. And you were
dead. They wouldn't let me see you, so I imagined
a thousand horrible deaths." My voice began to
crack, but I pushed on.

"Your deaths filled my dreams. It was your heart,
they told me. But I still couldn't see you. Not until
the funeral, but there—it wasn't you. Just some plastic-
looking thing that wore your clothes and your face."
Tears ran down my cheeks, but I let them.

"You'd been laid off the week before. Was that the
wheel on which your heart had been broken? You'd
worked so hard. You'd worked so hard. And they
had even cleaned the dirt from beneath your
fingernails."

A shout welled up from inside me: "DID YOU
CARE THAT I WAS LEFT BEHIND, ALONE?" That
hadn't been in my script—it surprised even me. *Is it
that weird side effect again? Shit, I don't need it messing
up my act.* To cover for it, I slowly stood and turned

my back on the rock, trying to pull myself together. As gracefully as I could, I walked to the far arm of the cross, to the green cloth and what lay beneath it.

"But why mourn?" I said, trying to keep my voice light. I walked around the pedestal, barely touching the cloth with my fingertips. "All things die, don't they? What's this? Another grave? Who lies here, under the hill? What power draws me to this place?"

I reached under the cloth and whipped out the Barbie doll, wrapped in the glimmering material Ralph had brought me. I held the doll over my head and her gown sparkled under the stage lights. She wore a crown of violets that I had gathered myself. I cried, "Hail to thee, Shining Majesty, Queen of the Fair." I said another one of those special phrases and heard what sounded like gasps from the audience. "Pale, distant beauty; so wise, so high. Would you grant a boon to one so low as I?"

I felt the gathering warmth in my chest and saw the face of the doll subtly shift until it resembled the face of my mother. *No! Stop it! I don't need this, not now. Focus. Gotta focus. Keep the show going.*

I carried the doll forward to the rock. "Here is a throne for thee." I sat the doll, legs spread wide, on top of the hammer. Deep mutterings came out of the crowd. *Don't care for the symbolism, do you? Good.* To the doll, I said, "Do your magic, work your spell. Do that voodoo that you do so well."

On cue, Ralph and Norton did their first special effect. The hammer wriggled obscenely in its bonds, between the doll's legs. I watched a moment, then lifted the doll off. "Ah, you've done it, Majesty. He rises again." I set the doll beside the rock, raising its arm as if in surprise or summoning.

The hammer slowly slipped out of the binding cords. It rose, head up, cruciform, to hover two feet above the stage. I sat back, as if amazed.

"Is this a hammer I see before me, handle toward my hand?" The hammer obediently tilted its handle my way and I grasped it. I jumped up, laughing, and spun around, holding the hammer close to my chest. Then I stopped and looked back at the doll.

"Oh, but forgive me, Majesty, I am being rude. You must have your reward for this great gift." I went to the pillar, staying within the hollow cross, and picked up the loaf of bread. I brought it back to the rock and put it on top of the loose twine, then placed the doll, lying on her back, on the loaf.

"There, now. Comfy? You require an offering of food, Majesty. Here is food for thought. Rest a while, and I will read poetry to soothe you."

I went to the pedestal at stage left and picked up the book. It was actually blank inside, except for my lines, which I had written in the night before. "Listen, Majesty, and dream. 'The square of the hypotenuse of the right triangle is equal to the sum of the square of the two adjacent sides.' " Behind me, on a sheet hung on the wall, was projected a page from my old high school geometry textbook. Nervous laughter came from the crowd.

"Did you enjoy that, my Queen? Here's another." I proceeded to read Newton's First Law of Thermodynamics, with a slide of Magritte's painting of a man with an apple replacing the head.

"And here's another: $E = Mc^2$!" Behind me appeared the well-known photograph of Einstein with his tongue sticking out.

The doll rolled from side to side on her bed of bread. "Oh, do these dreams disturb you? They are troublesome, aren't they? For the Beast has discovered fire and has burned your forests. What will you do, Majesty, when the power of the Beast surpasses yours? What will you do when the Beast no longer hearkens to your call?" The image of a red-orange mushroom cloud appeared behind me.

The doll shuddered and rolled over, facedown, on the loaf. "Peace, my Queen, Peace! You must have peace. And I must have freedom. I can grant both our wishes. For now I have my hammer, and I'll hammer in the morning and hammer in the evening, all over this land." I approached the doll menacingly. "You know what they say, don't you? To someone who has a hammer, everything looks like a nail." I crouched down and thunked the stage with the hammer.

Continuing to creep forward, I intoned, "To one who has a hammer, everything looks like a nail. To one who has a hammer, everything looks like a nail." I got up to the rock and pulled out from beneath it an iron horseshoe nail. Staring intently at the doll, I placed the point of the spike between her breasts. "And her Majesty must have peace."

I raised the hammer, hearing gasps and cries from the audience. I began to sing an old slave work song, pounding on the nail after each line:

> "Take this hammer—" *Whack!*
> "Carry it to my captain—" *Whack!*
> "Tell him I'm gone—" *Whack!*
> "Tell him I'm gone—" *Whack!*
> "If he ask you—" *Whack!*
> "Was I crying—" *Whack!*
> "Tell him I'm laughing—" *Whack!*
> "Tell him I'm gone!" *Whack!*

With the final blow, red-dyed Karo syrup flowed out from the "wound" in the doll's chest, seeping into the glittering cloth, dripping down the loaf of bread. Muffled, amazed exclamations came from the crowd, and I thought I heard a woman sobbing.

Grinning in triumph, I stepped back, raising the hammer high over my head. When I stood again in the center of the cross, I folded my arms on my chest. "Your spell is broken. Your will has no power. I am free!"

The dirt of the hollow cross erupted into flame.

Lightning seemed to come down from the roof and flash around me. Behind me would be the image of a phoenix rising from ashes superimposed on a monster of Frankenstein. I began to rise into the air until I hovered three feet above the stage.

I couldn't understand the angry shouts from the audience, and now that the act was ending, my stage fright was again overtaking me. I closed my eyes and tried to soothe my nerves with the usual thought: *They're just an illusion.* Again I felt the gathering warmth in my chest. *Uh-oh.* I clenched my mouth shut and opened my eyes.

It was not the same audience. They were taller than before, and their skin was pale as moonlight. The women wore gowns of the same starshine gossamer material as I'd put on the doll. The men wore tunics and hose, and silver circlets sat on their brows. Swords and daggers hung at their hips. Their eyes glowed silver and they stared at me with the intensity of wolves, hungering to tear me to pieces.

Chapter 9

I stared out at the transformed audience. *My God, did I do that? Who—or what—are these people? Why do I see them this way?* As Ralph and Norton had instructed me, I did not move. Instead, I wrapped my arms tighter around myself and waited until the stage bumped reassuringly against my feet.

The pale, angry mob glared and fidgeted, clearly wanting to rush the stage but not daring to. The house lights came up and I blinked at the sudden brightness.

And again I saw the audience of normal, well-dressed young men and women, wearing everyday designer clothes. Some of them still looked sullen, a few had tears on their faces. They cast wary glances at me as they rose from their seats and filed out, some supporting others on their arms.

I stood still, bewildered. *This is getting crazier and crazier. Was it just one of Ralph and Norton's special effects? An illusion cast by the thaumaturgy of the performance? Or am I going nuts?*

One audience member remained, staring at the stage. He was a tall, white-haired, handsome gentleman, dressed in a well-tailored, expensive-looking gray suit. After a moment, he approached the stage, regarding me with an amused half-smile. He pulled out from within his suit coat a pair of gray gloves and he put them on. Then he reached in again and pulled out a rose. A rose made of metal. The light bouncing off its petals hurt my eyes.

He held the rose out toward me. Then, seeing that I would not move from where I stood, he placed the rose on the stage. Just within the hollow cross.

"Praise for the performer," he said in an elegant voice. "Brava. We will be watching the progression of your career with great interest, I assure you." The way he said it, it almost sounded like a threat. He bowed slightly to me, then departed after the others.

I breathed out a huge sigh. When the room was empty, I hissed, "Is it safe yet?"

Ralph's voice seemed to float in my ear. "Wait a sec. Okay. You can move now."

I slumped over, as if a huge floor-rug had just fallen on me. Following gravity's lead, I flopped cross-legged on the stage. "Ralph? What happened?"

"We'll talk later. You did good, kid. We got 'em."

"Yeah," I muttered. "But who, or what, did we get?"

I didn't get an answer. I reached forward and picked up the silvery rose. It was heavy. But it was beautiful, and very real-looking, as if it had grown naturally that way. *It was a gift, and Ralph didn't say I shouldn't take it.*

After staring at the rose for long moments, I stood up and stepped out of the hollow cross and shuffled into the dressing room.

As usual, I had hoped to be alone for a little while to settle my nerves. As usual, no luck. Angela was there waiting for me.

This time, she did hug me. Flakes of dried clay cascaded around my feet, and clung to her sweatshirt. "That was amazing, T.J.! That was the most stunning act we've ever had! You've outdone yourself! Warren said you should have warned us about the fire gag, but even he was thrilled"

"Thanks," I mumbled, falling into the rickety, overstuffed armchair.

"And what a great crowd!"

"Yeah? Yeah, I guess I impressed them or something."

"Oh, stop being so modest. You want to know what they told Warren as they passed him on the way out? They said 'We want to know whenever she appears again. We must watch her.' You've got a core of fans now, T.J. After tonight, I don't think you'll have to worry anymore about getting stage time."

And you get to keep your boyfriend and your job. I thought. *I worked wonders for everyone tonight. So how come I don't feel so good?*

"Clearly inscribed space works for you," Angela babbled on. "Kind of a conservative approach, but if you can breathe this sort of new life into it, I won't argue."

I closed my eyes. I felt so tired.

"Hey, that's a pretty flower. Gift from an admirer?"

"I guess. Sort of."

"I'm sorry," said Angela. "I shouldn't be talking your ears off right now. If you're pooped, you can come back tomorrow to clean up. I'll take you home."

"Great. Sounds great." Something inside me wanted to cry—maybe from relief that it was over. Maybe from tiredness. Maybe because of the small voice inside that kept saying I should be really afraid now, though I didn't know what of. I pulled myself out of the chair and stuck the metal rose into the inner pocket of my jeans jacket. Then I put the jacket down and took a shower.

The warm water struck the clay on my skin and sent it swirling down the drain, a rust-colored whirlpool. The shower did its usual magic of soothing my frazzled nerves. But what little energy I had left seemed to drain away with the clay, and I had to stagger out of the shower before I fell over.

I dressed while Angela closed the place down. There was no sign of Ralph and Norton and I didn't want to summon them. In fact, I didn't want to talk, or think, or move much at all.

Finally Angela returned, announcing that she was finished, and we walked outside. The moon was nearly full and shining through high, thin clouds. I could smell the river on the air. As Angela unlocked her car, I happened to glance to my left, back toward the Per Forma. Someone was leaning against the wall, watching us. His eyes glinted silver.

I jumped into Angela's car, slamming the door behind me.

"Let's go."

"What's wrong?"

"Some guy's watching us."

"Where?"

"Just go, will you?"

"Okay, okay." Angela peeled out of the parking lot, and I sank back into the musty upholstery with a sigh.

"Sorry," I said when we reached Liberty Boulevard. "I'm just in a weird mood tonight."

"Hey, no problem. Can't be too careful in the big city."

"Yeah." Though whatever I was afraid of, I was pretty sure it wasn't the usual sort of big-city danger.

Angela tried to start a conversation once or twice. She might have even mentioned a party coming up. I just sat, barely listening, tying my fingers into knots. While my body was as droopy as a beanbag chair, my mind was running races. *Shit. This is bigger than friendly little gnomes who fix things; bigger than horny leprechauns in velvet knickers; bigger than adding magic to performance art. Ralph and Norton haven't been straight with me. What the hell have I gotten myself into?*

As we pulled up to my mom's place, Angela said, "We might have an opening next week. Warren says you can have it if you want. Do you?"

"Huh? Oh. I guess so. Sure."

"You okay, T.J.?"

"What? Yeah. Sorry, I'm just really fried."

" 'Course you are. Go get some rest and I'll talk to you tomorrow when you come pick up your stuff. Okay?"

"Okay. G'night. Thanks for the ride." I got out and staggered up the stairs into the apartment. I flung myself onto the couch and said to the empty air, "Ralph? Norton? Okay you guys. Give. What's going on?"

They popped into the living room, grinning and high-fiving each other. "Ha ha hee, we showed the Sidhe," said Ralph.

"Ho ho ho, Sidhe gonna go," sang Norton. They danced around the room, their gray bodies bobbing up and down.

"Who's she?" I said.

"C'mon, T.J., celebrate with us!" said Ralph.

"Yeah!" said Norton. "You did it! You showed 'em!"

"Wait, *wait*, *WAIT!* You guys just settle down here and tell me exactly what I did. And who the hell were those silver-eyed people I saw at the end?"

They stopped, blinked, looked at each other, looked back at me. "You saw them in their real form? See, Ralph, I told you she had the talent," said Norton. He punched Ralph on the shoulder and zipped away into the kitchen.

"Real form?" I asked.

"Yeah, you know. Not like morts usually see them."

"Silver-eyed, armed with swords and stuff, and wearing dresses like that one we made for the doll?"

"You got it. You saw 'em in all their hoity-toity Seelie glory. Pitiful sight, ain't it?"

Norton returned from the kitchen, a can of Iron City beer in his twiggy hand. He hopped onto the couch beside me and popped the beer open. "Hee

hee hee, you showed the Sidhe." He nudged me in the side with his elbow and winked.

"For the last time," I growled, "who are these . . . Shee . . . Seelie . . . THINGS?"

Ralph tilted his head. "They was the people you wanted to shake up. You know, the nose-in-the-air immortals. The ones who are beautiful forever and want to rule everybody. The Seelie Court, the Fair Folk, what you call Boomies and Yuppers."

"Boomers? Yuppies? Those things weren't Yuppies! Yuppies are people! Human beings! That audience wasn't human!"

"Uh-oh," said Norton.

Ralph scratched his beard. "You mean, when you first gave us the job, you weren't talking about the Seelie Folk?"

"No! I just meant greedy, ignorant, selfish *people.* What are these Seelie things? And who is this "she" you keep mentioning?"

"Oh. *S-I-D-H-E,* pronounced 'she'," said Ralph. "Those featherbrained, good-for-nuthin', fancy-dressin, lazy, overbearing elves. Got it?"

"Elves?" I said.

"The Esteemed Nobility of our kind," said Norton. He took a huge swig of his beer and followed it with a loud belch.

"You mean, they're like you guys, and Luigi?"

"Huh. Like they'd ever admit it," said Ralph. "They're too pretty for the likes of us. All they do is dance and play music day and night. We do the work, getting our hands dirty. The Sidhe won't even touch iron, just to show how above-it-all they are."

"And they call *us* Unseelie. Hah." Norton belched again.

"Are these . . . Sidhe as powerful as you?"

"Oh, much more powerful," said Ralph.

"What d'you think we had you in that hollow cross for?" said Norton. "If we hadn't been protecting you, you woulda been toast."

My stomach felt like I'd eaten rocks. "You guys could have warned me."

"We thought you knew," said Norton.

"Yeah," said Ralph. "We figured you was pretty brave to want to go taking on the Sidhe like that. So naturally we had to help you."

I covered my face with my hands. "I just wanted to get a message across to some people. Just *people*."

"Well, now," said Ralph, starting to pace the rug, "how d'you know these Yuppies you're talking about are really human? The Sidhe run around disguised like you morts, when they're Upside. Usually morts can't tell the difference, though tonight, for some reason, you did."

"I didn't want to piss off any . . . supernatural powers," I moaned. "God, this has all been a big mistake."

"Maybe, maybe not," said Ralph.

"Somebody had to do it," said Norton. "Maybe you were meant to and just didn't know it."

"To do what?" I said, my hands balling into fists. "What exactly did I do tonight? Besides make a whole bunch of really dangerous new enemies?"

"Just what you wanted," said Ralph. "You woke up a lot of lazy, effete snobs. Showed them they aren't the only power to contend with around here. That they ain't gonna get what they want so easy."

He came over to the couch and put his spindly hand on my arm. He went on gently, "You done a good thing, T.J. Those people ain't good people. They don't care about you an' me, the workin' joe. They wouldn't care if mortals got wiped off the face of the earth. They'd like this whole place to go back to bein' forest primeval. They're trying to take over this town, and we gotta stop 'em."

"What do you mean *we*, gray-face?" I grumbled at him.

"Hey, why'd you think all the factories shut down

in this town, putting guys like your dad outta work?"

"I thought it was economic forces and stuff."

Norton chortled. "Yeah. That's what they'd like you to think."

"See," Ralph said, "all we're tryin' to do is get our own back. Like we told ya before, Pittsburgh is a workin' town, always has been. It's home to folk like us. But these Sidhe are moving in on our turf. We gotta show them they can't do that. Not without a fight."

"So," I said, "you're telling me that the magic in my performance act was just a way of telling them to go away?"

"Yeah, sorta. In part," said Ralph.

I squirmed, uncomfortable, and felt something hard and sharp-edged under my jacket. I zipped it open and pulled out the metal rose. "What is this, anyway? One of those . . . Sidhe gave it to me."

Ralph peered at it without touching it. "A rose made out of steel. Clever bastards. It combines two symbols, y'see."

"It's a token," said Norton, with a little difficulty. He seemed to be getting drunk awfully fast.

"A token of what?"

"To show they accept our challenge," said Ralph. "You know, like the old knights in your history. Taking up the gantlet."

"Gauntlet," said Norton.

"Whatever. Anyways, it means they know what they're in for. And since you picked it up . . ." Ralph shrugged.

"The battle is joined!" said Norton, flinging out his arms and dousing me with beer.

"Battle?" I said. "It's a battle now? Against them? They're more powerful than you and they're gonna fight back? Shit, guys, what have you gotten me into? Doesn't it break the contract that I was tricked into not knowing what I was doing?"

"Simmer down, Princess," said Ralph, patting my arm. "Don't worry. We're lookin' after ya. And I wouldn't go talking about breaking the contract right now. You need our protection more than ever."

"Great. Just great. I don't know why I ever listened to you two." I was starting to shake from fear, rage, and exhaustion.

"Because we're on the side of righteousness," said Norton thickly. "And so are you."

"Can you at least tell me," I said, trying to fight off the shakes, "what they're going to do? How they're going to strike back? What I should be watching out for?"

Ralph shrugged. "Nope. Those guys are sneaky. They might try anything."

"Yeah," Norton chimed in, nodding over his beer. "Shhhneaky."

I threw up my hands. "Wonderful. How am I supposed to protect myself? Or do you guys plan to be my bodyguards forever?"

"Oh, it won't be forever," said Ralph. "This thing will sort itself out pretty quick. By the end of the month, I'd expect."

"The end of May? That gives them a lot of time to jump me."

"Hey, we saved you the last time you got jumped, didn't we? Give us a little credit, will ya? You can trust us."

Norton started snoring beside me. Slowly he teetered over until his blobby, pointed head rested on my shoulder. Beer drooled out of his gaping mouth. I elbowed him in the side. He bolted upright. "Huh, hunh wha?"

"Ralph, I think you better take your buddy home. Wherever that is."

"Yeah, he never could handle mort brew. C'mon, pal." Ralph put an arm around Norton's back and guided him to the middle of the living room rug.

"I . . . I . . . think I'm gonna be siiiiiick," groaned Norton.

"Get him out of here!" I yelled. The last thing I needed was knocker-spew all over Mom's carpet, on top of all my other problems.

"We're goin'. Don't worry, T.J., you'll be protec— oops!"

Norton had covered his mouth with his hand, and his cheeks were bulging bigger and bigger.

"Gotta run!" said Ralph. And they were gone.

"And I'm trusting my life to these guys," I said, shaking my head. I picked up the steel rose again. It looked amazingly alive—veins on the leaves, tiny thorns on the stem. As if a real rose had been transformed into metal. *Maybe it was. And if these Seelie folk could do this to a rose, what might they do to me?*

Chapter 10

I woke up stretched out on the couch, the steel rose cradled in my hands. There were scratches in my palms from the metal thorns. I dropped the rose and sat up, licking my wounds. Vague images from my dreams flitted through my thoughts and faded—images of monsters lurking in the shadows.

The living room was filled with bright sunlight. I looked at the kitchen clock. It was 12:13. "Oh, God, afternoon already." I rubbed my eyes and checked the clock once more. Same result.

I got up and staggered to the bedroom closet and pulled out my favorite pair of old jeans, the ones with holes in the knees. But the holes weren't there anymore. They'd been sewn up with tiny stitches neater than a sewing machine would have made. *Luigi. He fixed things I didn't want fixed. Seems to be a pattern with these guys.* I pulled the jeans on anyway and a black T-shirt.

Breakfast was comfort food—black coffee and a banana dipped in Hershey's fudge syrup. I needed the caffeine/chocolate high to face the day. From the island counter, the apartment looked perfectly normal. Other than the steel rose on the couch, nothing special might have happened the night before. Out the kitchen window, Cypress Street seemed the same as always.

But I couldn't forget those silvery, shining eyes, those unworldly beautiful people armed with knives and long swords, and the hungering hate in their faces. Do elves walk around in broad daylight? I didn't know, and I didn't trust Ralph and Norton enough to want to ask them. I idly ran my finger along the scar on my cheek. I'd always wanted to do dangerous art. I just never expected the audience would be dangerous back. To think I had wanted to go rile up beautiful people. What's that they say? "Be careful what you wish for"?

What I wished for right at that moment was that I had paid attention to Mom's lectures about folktales and fairy stories. I gazed toward the bookshelves, thinking, *What I need to know might be somewhere in those.* Trouble was, it would take forever to find it, and probably the information I could use would be cluttered in academese.

I could call her. Claim I needed the info for a paper I was writing. No, she'd ask too many questions, and I'm not a good enough liar. And what if that strange side effect popped up again? God knows what I'd say to her.

I remembered how her face had appeared on the doll I had used to represent the Queen. Scary. I didn't know what it meant. The words I'd been speaking were about freedom.

Well, she has kinda controlled my life ever since Dad died. Where I live and go to school. I glanced around the apartment. *Why do I still live here? Yeah, sure, it's free, but I could always room with somebody for cheap. Have a place that's all mine, in a cooler neighborhood than this, maybe closer to campus or the Per Forma. It'd be better than staring at these old books and this ugly furniture.*

I put my head in my hands. *Because I'd need at least a part-time job, probably doing work I'd hate, taking time away from my art. I'm not ready to become a nine-to-five capitalist drone.*

So, I thought, changing the subject on myself, *do we stay at home like a sitting duck, or do we go out and brave the hazards beyond? Maybe I could call Grandma and ask her what she knows about elves.* Trouble was, she would believe me. And that could be worse. I didn't want to get her involved in this mess.

Damn. I can't stay cooped up in here forever, not even knowing what I'm watching out for. Maybe I'll go see what's happening on campus. At least it's familiar territory. Maybe there wouldn't be a line at the Administration Office and I could get my grades early. Not. Maybe I'd bump into people I knew. Maybe I'd just get out of this stifling place and stop thinking morbid thoughts.

I took a last swig of coffee, grabbed my backpack, and opened the front door. Something rattled on it. It was one of those rustic wreaths of branches and aromatic herbs. I never liked that style of decoration, but it smelled kinda nice. A white tag dangled from it:

Dear T.J.,
This should keep 'em out of your bedroom, anyway.

Your Pal, Ralph

Virtual rocks rattled in my stomach again. It hadn't all been a dream. I was still in deadly danger. Or something.

I scanned the stairwell, as if things might be lurking around the corners. Nada. I carefully locked the door. On the street, I looked both ways before stepping onto the sidewalk. As if silver-eyed warriors might run me down with a horse-drawn coach. Or maybe a silver-gray Cadillac. Who knows? But the street was clear. On the 54C bus, I tried to covertly watch the faces of other riders—in case I spotted one of Them. Didn't see any likely candidates.

It was a blustery day. The sun kept appearing and disappearing behind clouds, as if it couldn't decide whether to shine or not. The dogwood and plum trees beside the student union on campus were in full bloom, and the wind scattered their petals like pink rain.

Out of habit, I strolled toward the C-of-L. The Cathedral was also undecided, sometimes gray, sometimes golden. The grassy quad in front of it was deserted, except for some guys and a dog playing Frisbee. It was going to be kind of lonely here until summer session started.

I flung myself onto the Cathedral's heavy revolving door. It was cool inside, and quiet as a tomb. I went up to the second floor, where there's a gallery from which you look out over most of the Commons, as well as some large classrooms and a few of the Nationality Rooms. I leaned on the railing and stared out at the vaulted ceiling and ribbed pillars. With no students at the tables below, it was like gazing into the past. I half expected to see a knight in shining armor go clanking through or to hear a chorus of monks chanting.

Instead, I heard "Hey, T.J.!" and nearly jumped out of my skin. It was Crystal, coming down the hall. Her arms were loaded with books and papers.

"Hey, Crystal," I said. I fought down the nerves and tried to act cool. "What are you doing here? School's out, remember?"

"Not for everybody. My last final was today, and I had to turn in an art project. Also I have to take some books back to the library. By the way, I heard about your performance thing. Sounded way cool— way to go, kid!"

So knock me over a with a noodle. "What? You heard about it?"

"Well, actually, I read about it. Did you see your review?"

"Already? No. Where? Rawson in the *Post Gazette*?"

"In your dreams. No, it was in the *Art Paper*. Hang on, I've got a copy right here. Somewhere." She shuffled the books and papers in her arms, finally extracting a tabloid on slick paper. "Here. I think the review's on page six."

It was. The by-line was somebody named Ariel. The column was called "Performance Pieces," and I was mentioned in the last paragraph:

> The biggest surprise of the week was a new and shocking performance by young artist T. J. Kaminski at the Per Forma. Her multimedia piece "Death to the Queen" made ingenious use of music, props, and special effects, although her overall themes—revolution, vengeance and liberation—may have overwhelmed her talents. Nonetheless, this is a surprisingly powerful performer, and clearly an artist to watch out for.

"Wow," I said.

"Something, huh? Sorry I wasn't there. I wish I could have seen it."

"Oh, that's okay. You might have had trouble getting in. It was standing room only not long after the doors opened."

"Really? Are you doing another show soon?"

"Um . . . yeah. The Per Forma's manager said there's an opening next week she can give me."

"Cool. Let me know, 'cause I want to see the next one."

Huh. Wouldn't you know. A thing becomes important once it's been in the paper or on TV.

"Hey, Crys—T.J.! Is that you?" It was her pseudo-twin, Cyndi, coming down the corridor. Figured.

"No, it's just someone who looks like me, wearing my clothes."

"Stop that. Did you see your review?"

"Yeah, I showed it to her," said Crystal.

"How does it feel to be famous?" said Cyndi. "You've got cute guys asking after you and everything."

"Cute guys?"

"Yeah. There was one outside just as I was coming in who asked if I knew you, and if you were around. And here you are."

"Here I am. Who's the guy?" *Sam? No, Cindy knows Sam. She'd say if it were him.*

Cyndi shrugged. "I dunno. But he's tall, blond, and gorgeous. Maybe he's still out there. Wanna look?"

"Yeah, let's," said Crystal.

I shrugged as if I didn't care. I followed the Barbie twins over to a window in an empty classroom on the east side of the building. I was reminded of a TV Diet Coke commercial I once saw as a kid, in which a bunch of office chicks go stare out a window at some guy taking his shirt off. I hoped Cyndi and Crystal wouldn't start drooling and moaning.

"There he is!" Cyndi pointed at the tree nearest to the door. Beneath it sat a guy who was, indeed, tall, blond, and from what I could see, gorgeous. His long hair was pulled back into a ponytail. He wore a loose white poet's shirt and leather jeans with knee-high black boots.

"Yum," said Crystal.

"Clothes are kinda retro," I said. And I was getting a sinking feeling that he might be One of Them.

"All right, T.J. Is this some boyfriend of yours we don't know about?"

"Never seen him before."

"In that case, can I have him?"

"Maybe." I grinned at her. "Better let me check him out first. Wouldn't want you getting involved with the wrong sort of guy." I sauntered out the door and down the stairs to meet my mysterious stranger.

He seemed to be asleep. As quietly as possible, I walked up to get a closer look. He had a movie-star face, all right, though a bit too pretty-boy for my taste. A straight, long nose; nice lips. His hands had long fingers—I bet he could use them to play a girl's heart like harp strings. I hated him already.

He wasn't wearing a knife, that I could see. There might have been one in his boot, and that loose shirt could have hidden anything, but I wondered. *If he is one of the Sidhe, if I could just talk to him . . . maybe I could tell him it's all been a mistake. Maybe if I have a chance to explain, they'll leave me alone after that. It's worth a try.* And if he turned out to be dangerous, I could always call Ralph and Norton. I coughed to let him know I was there.

His eyes opened. I had never seen such an amazing shade of blue. "Are you the one called T.J.?" he said. His voice was light and musical, and I wanted to hear it forever.

"Um. Yeah. That's me."

He smiled and the sun rose for the second time that day. *STOP THAT*, I told my leaping heart.

In one fluid movement, he stood and held out his hand. "Truly, I am honored to have acquaintance of you."

I took his hand as if we were going to shake. Instead, he bowed and lightly kissed my knuckles. My skin tingled. *STOP THAT RIGHT NOW!* I told myself. "Um. And you are—?"

"I cry you mercy. You may call me . . . Chris." He smiled again as if at some private joke.

"Pleeztameetcha, Chris. You're not from around here, are you?"

"I'faith, no. I am from . . . Ireland. Forgive my poor use of your country's speech. I have not spoken it in some time."

Irish. Sure. "Really?" I said with fake enthusiasm. "My mom's family is from Ireland. Which county are you from? Donegal? Claire?"

His smile twisted downward. "None of those. But I craved your company as I have heard of your wondrous performance of yester-eve."

"Oh. You weren't there?"

"Alas, no. But some of my kin were and spoke most amazedly of it."

"Ah."

"Might there be someplace to which we might retire and refresh ourselves whilst you tell me of your art?"

It took me a moment to translate that. "Are you interested in performance art?"

"I am interested in yours."

Beneath his gaze, I felt deeply flattered. And disgusted at myself. Was this the Sidhe's best shot—a charmer who talked like Shakespeare? Perhaps I'd have the chance to tell my side of the story after all. This "Chris" guy didn't scare me. Or even impress me, much. As long as I stayed in familiar territory, around other people, I'd be fine. If I got scared, maybe I could run to the O and get some homeboys to beat him up. They might be more reliable than Ralph and Norton.

"Okay. I know a place we can go."

"Lead on."

MacDuff, and cursed be he who—I couldn't remember the line from *Macbeth*, but I did remember it was the beginning of a duel.

Chapter 11

I walked with Chris down Forbes Avenue. At every panhandler we passed, coins would appear in Chris's hand and he'd drop some into each cup. The beggars were all oh-so-grateful, but I wondered if the next time they looked in their cups, the coins would still be there.

I took Chris to Paul's Pub, on Bouquet Street, which is a bar with a small restaurant attached. They have good basic diner food, and I knew it wouldn't be too crowded at that time of day. If Chris had a problem with the place, he didn't say so.

I forget what I ordered. Chris asked for a glass of white wine. Our waitress, Tracy, had been in a couple of my classes, and as she left, she gave me a big grin and a thumbs-up. If nothing else, Chris was going to do wonders for my social rep.

I stared at him. *Now how do I tell him what I need to? Assuming he's One of Them. If he isn't, I might be about to make a real ass of myself. But if he isn't, he's not exactly sane and normal either.* "So," I started, putting my arms on the table, "you wanted to know about my performance last night."

"You are direct."

That put me off track a moment. "Yeah, well, um, you said you wanted to know about performance art. It's a big subject. Why waste time with small talk? I mean, how much can you say about weather and shit?"

He winced a little at my language. Guess the High

Seelie don't like swearing either. "It might amaze you," he purred, "what can be said of either. But as you will. My question will be one that you have doubtless oft heard: From what source did spring these fancies from which your rituals upon the stage were wrought?"

It took me a couple moments to translate that one too. "You mean, where do I get my ideas?"

"Brevity is e'er the soul of wit. Just so."

"Well—" My hands moved in circles in the air. "Everywhere. My life. The world. The garbage I see around me. Where else?"

"But your work displayed such skill—you have had . . . teachers, have you not?"

"Of course." I rattled off the names of three theater professors I'd had.

"Ah. Those are not names I know."

"I wouldn't expect you to."

"My friends who beheld your play told me—the matter of your father's death was clear, and most touching to the heart. But what led you to bring into it a queen, and to even name your work 'Death to the Queen'? In this nation, you have neither queen nor king, and royalty hath little import."

My hands went under the table, and my fingers began tying themselves in knots. *This might be my chance, if I can just handle it right.* "Well, you know, I was working off of the ideas of others, in a way. In fact, I have the feeling that the audience I was trying to reach wasn't the audience I got last night. Queens and kings are fairy-tale-type characters, and important symbols in our culture, but I wasn't expecting to get a fairy-tale-type audience, if you know what I mean."

Chris raised a pale eyebrow in restrained bewilderment. "Indeed?"

I had a moment of panic. *What if I am wrong, and he isn't a Sidhe? Maybe he's just some strange British actor who likes to charm American girls with his romantic way of talking.*

"Who is't," Chris continued with pointed interest, "who has steeped you thus in fairy lore? I am told th'effect t'was though you had stolen secrets from the Seelie Court itself."

Aha. One of Them, all right. I opened my mouth to explain, then stopped. I couldn't tell him about Ralph and Norton. I didn't know what he or the other Sidhe would do to them. But it hurt not to be able to say what I wanted. It made me mad, and I began to babble. "Look, a lot of performance art is just symbols, okay? Stuff pulled from childhood, from myths, from anywhere. You throw it at the audience, and they get to put it all together in whatever way makes sense to them. You do strange, shocking stuff to jar them out of their mental ruts, and then you hit them with ideas, images, actions, anything that might get them thinking in a new way. That's what art is about, you know?"

"So 'twas your intention to offend?"

"Yes, but not *that* audience! I only wanted to reach ordinary people—greedy, selfish people of a certain age and a certain lifestyle. I was hoping to wake them up to the reality around them, to show them they aren't the most important people in the world! That they aren't—"

Chris held up his hands. "I cry you mercy. 'Twas truly not my wish to thus distress you." He tilted his head as if looking at me in a new light. "If 'twould please you, we may speak on other themes."

I didn't know if he had understood me, but I felt immensely relieved. I let him take the conversation for a while, though I don't recall what he talked about. Something about rainbows. And fewmets, whatever they are.

Next thing I knew, the bill was paid—I think he paid it—and we were standing outside. It was much later than I expected, already late afternoon.

"There is a festival this eve," said Chris, "where three rivers meet and are cojoined."

"You mean Point Park?"

"The very place. I should like to see this fest, but alas, if truth be told, I do not know the way."

"I can tell you where it is and what bus to catch."

He gazed down at me. " 'Tis much to ask, I know. But would you kindly guide me there? I do confess, I am loath to leave your comp'ny. You are a most intriguing fair companion."

I would have been sad the date was ending too, strange though it had been. Perhaps this particular High Sidhe was really interested in performance art. Maybe pigs fly. Maybe I had gotten my message across after all and he was giving me a chance to make amends. He certainly wasn't threatening. Anyway, I didn't want to go back to a lonely apartment. And he was awfully cute. "Um, sure. I've got nothing else to do right now."

He smiled that million-watt smile again, and I felt glad all over.

As we turned to walk toward the bus stop, I asked, "Which festival is it?" Point State Park is the site of lots of events through the year. Pittsburgh throws festivals every chance it gets; anything to boost sagging civic pride. It's the only city that's had three centennials in a seven-year period. But late April was too soon for the Three Rivers Arts Festival, and way too soon for the Regatta.

"I know not by what name they call it. Somewhat in the stewardship of nature."

I puzzled this over as we walked up to Fifth and waited for the 71 bus. *Is it Earth Day?* I didn't think so, but I couldn't remember. The bus came in a few minutes and we got aboard. I think Chris paid our fares. Or maybe he just smiled real nice at the lady bus driver, and she forgot we ought to pay.

We didn't talk much as the bus trundled downtown. Chris seemed to be working hard at not looking uncomfortable. There are places along Fifth where the view of the South Side, across the Monongahela, is kinda neat. Narrow houses perch on the steep hillsides, and there's an enormous black clock face that never seems to show the right time. Up the river, eastward, you can see an industrial plant that adds to the scenery rather than ruining it, especially in the evening when its lights glitter against the hillside. Down the river is Station Square and the wharf where the paddle-wheel riverboats dock. Chris spared only a glance or two out the window, his eyes narrowed as if he vaguely disapproved.

We got off at Market Square, kind of a Disney version of a small-town square, though some of the shop buildings around it are actually pretty old. It must have been rush hour; men in suits and women in skirts and athletic shoes were striding past, trying not to see the homeless and the old black men on the park benches.

Chris and I walked the three blocks from the square to Point Park. There were no booths or anything on the first large grassy area we came to, but on the tunnel/bridge there was a banner. SAVE THE EARTH FEST it said, in big red letters. I hadn't heard of that one before. We seemed to be the only people going into the tunnel to the fair.

I've always thought the tunnel at Point Park was a cool place. It's actually the underside of a highway overpass. You walk through the tunnel over a concrete bridge that spans a pool of water. The floor of the pool is made of rocks arranged in a wave pattern. In a way, it's a bridge under a bridge. The acoustics are kinda interesting too. Someday I wanted to do a performance piece there.

As soon as we came out of the tunnel, it was like entering another world. Usually there's just another grassy open space where the foundations of old Fort Pitt show through. Paths lined with trees and benches run on either side. But for this fair, it looked like they'd transported a whole forest there. Every booth was surrounded by trees. I couldn't tell if they were real or fake.

The booths sold the usual stuff: T-shirts, mugs, posters, calendars, cookies and chocolate bars. All proclaimed proceeds went to this or that cause; saving rain forests, whales, pandas, baby seals, condors, spotted owls, black-footed ferrets, tropical tree frogs, Texas prairie chickens, you name it.

It all seemed harmless and pleasant enough. Until I began to notice the people—those manning the booths as well as those walking around them. They were tall, slim, long-haired, attractive, well dressed— just like Chris. Just like the audience last night. Now and then, I'd catch a glimpse of one staring at me. I started to feel distinctly uncomfortable.

"Art well?" asked Chris. "You have turned a lighter shade of pale."

"Um. Are you sure I should be here?"

"Fear not. We would not have come, were you unwelcome."

"If you say so." I relaxed a little. Was this their way of showing I was forgiven? I wished things were more clear and out in the open. I'd make a terrible spy. At least no one was acting like they were angry at me. And it wasn't like I didn't support the causes the booths advertised. After all, my first performance pieces were about ecology. *Hell with it. Why not stick it out?*

I went right up to one booth. "I'll take a Guava Crunch Bar, please."

The young woman behind the booth glanced up, quite startled. "Will you?"

"Yeah. If that's not a problem."

The woman flashed an embarrassed smile. "Not at all. Please do take one." She seemed flustered, as if at some pleasant surprise. She handed me the candy bar, took my two dollars, and said, "Will you wear one of our buttons? They are free to contributors."

She held out a round metal button pin with a colorful bird on it.

"Sure," I said with a shrug, and I put it on. The woman and Chris glanced at each other with expressions I couldn't read.

"What?" I said to Chris.

He shrugged too. "We are pleased you look upon us kindly. Come, let us walk further. There is much here worthy of our note."

We followed the path between booths that led to the center of the artificial forest. There was a gazebo in a clearing made to look like a wildflower meadow. On the gazebo platform, chairs were set at varying heights. In the middle, higher than the rest, was a couch or divan with a woman reclining on it. She wore a peach-colored dress suit and a matching round, wide-brimmed hat. Her dark hair was gathered in a knot at the back. She looked as though she had just stepped out of an Italian fashion magazine.

She looked my way as we got closer. I couldn't believe what a beautiful face she had. She wasn't young, but she wasn't old either. And she was tall and perfectly slim, like everyone else in the park. She smiled at Chris and me and beckoned to us with a peach-gloved hand.

"Ah, Fortune smiles upon us. Someone else desires your acquaintance."

"Who is she? She looks like a movie star."

"To say she is a celebrity would, indeed, hit close to the mark. Come." He led me up the steps of the gazebo, right up to the lady's couch.

"May I present you to Madame Reia Perry. Madame, may I present Mistress T. J. Kaminski."

My name sounded clunky in comparison to hers. She extended her gloved hand, and I felt like I should curtsy to it or something. Instead, I shook it briefly and said, "Hi."

"Welcome," she said in a voice even more musical than Chris's, but low like Kathleen Turner's. "So you are the brilliant young artiste. What a pleasant surprise this is. I have been hearing so much about you. Please do me the honor of joining me." Her eyes were an amazing dark brown. All her features were large, like Sophia Loren's, but they only made her seem larger than life. She gracefully scootched over and patted the empty space behind her. I squeezed in next to her on the fine upholstered couch, feeling awkward and out of place. I wondered if I had remembered to brush my teeth, and I was pretty sure I'd forgotten to comb my hair or put on deodorant.

Chris sat cross-legged at our feet and gave me an encouraging nod.

The lady pulled out a lace-trimmed handkerchief and coughed delicately behind it.

"Have you got a cold?" I said, trying to make conversation. I hate small talk. I'm bad at it.

She regarded me sharply. "A mere nothing," she said, an odd edge to her words. "I am recovering well. Though it is kind of you to ask."

"Good. I mean, I'm glad you're getting better." I felt so lame.

"What I have been told about your performance of last night is so extraordinary, I scarcely know what to believe. You must be a very talented young lady indeed."

"Um. Thanks."

"I confess, I had never heard of your particular form of . . . art. It had not come to my attention. I had no idea it had such potential. I assure you, I shall not make that mistake again."

I stared at my feet. "Any art can be powerful. Depends on how it's done."

"Or who does it? Of course. But this throwing together of random music, noise, movements . . ." She made a formless gesture with her gloved hand and shook her head slightly, as if to say it was all a bafflement to her.

I hoped I wasn't going to have to explain performance art again. I was getting tired of repeating myself.

"I crave your pardon, Lady," said Chris, "but our guest has said mayhap th'effect given was not the one she sought, nor the beholders those whom she had first intended."

"Truly?" Madame Perry raised a brow just as Chris had. "How can this be?"

Now was my chance. If only I could explain it right. "Well, it involves a big misunderstanding. See, I'd intended to shake up and offend a certain group of people—"

"You intended to offend?"

"Well, yeah, that's part of what I use performance art for. See—"

"Then does it matter who it is that you offend?"

"Yes! I had a particular message for a particular group I was trying to reach."

"But if you successfully offended the audience you had, then your aim must have been true, whether you knew it or not."

I sighed. This wasn't going well. "I'm sorry. Let me try again. See, last night's performance wasn't entirely just my ideas. I'd gotten some advice and help from . . . other sources, and that's where the misunderstandings came in."

Madame Perry tilted her head and raised her fine brows, gazing at me down her nose. "Ah, I see."

"I'm not being very clear, am I?"

"Clear as yon river in spring," said Chris with a wry smile.

"Forgive me," said Madame Perry, "but did I hear correctly, that this performance of yours was from the ideas of others?"

I nodded. "Some parts, anyway."

Madame Perry and Chris exchanged unreadable glances. This was getting annoying. The lady returned her gaze to me and said, "What, then, might we credit to your collaborators and what to you?

Who might these unnamed assistants be? It is not unfair to use their work without giving them their due acclaim?''

I felt pinned to the couch like a bug in a collection. My fingers began their snakes-mating routine again. *I should just tell them and be done with it,* I thought. *But what if it wouldn't make any difference and they'd still be my enemies? What if I need to hold something back, some insurance to make sure they don't hurt me?* And I didn't really want them hurting Ralph and Norton either. It wasn't the guys' fault, really, and they had rescued me from a rapist and helped me do the best performance of my life. The fact that they made me aim it at the wrong audience was just an honest mistake. I opened my mouth to say something. But nothing came out.

''The cats have your tongue, I see,'' said Madame Perry softly. ''Well, I've no wish to discomfit you. I will not trouble you further about it. Perhaps we might chat again later, when you are feeling less . . . shy.''

I swallowed. ''I'm sorry.''

''Think nothing of it. Please, enjoy our fair.'' She turned away, already dismissing me. To Chris she said, ''Treat her with such kindness as shall make her more free with us.''

He gazed at her a moment, then nodded solemnly. He stood and extended his hand to me. I let him help me up off the couch. My legs felt a little wobbly. He bowed toward the lady and guided me down the steps of the gazebo. Looking down, I noted my sloppy T-shirt and mended jeans. After sitting next to Madame Perry, I felt grubby and unclean.

''I guess I disappointed her, huh?''

''Let it not distress you. One's tongue oft cleaves to one's mouth in her presence.''

''Yeah. She's really something.''

''That is saying much in little words.''

We continued walking toward the point, past the

other booths. At last we reached the steps down to the fountain. Point State Park Fountain is right at the apex of the Golden Triangle, where the Allegheny and the Monongahela flow together to make the Ohio. The view from the point is actually pretty nice. To the left, on the far bank of the Mon, is the Duquesne Incline, its little red car chugging up the cliffside of Mount Washington. To the right, across the Allegheny, is Three Rivers Stadium, and beside that the silvery cylinder of the Science Center. There was a World War II submarine docked in the river beside the museum—I always thought that strange; I had fun imagining it sailing up the Mississippi to the Ohio, its periscope spying on the tourist-filled paddle wheelers it passed.

It was sunset, which added to the view, giving the world that copper-gold color you see in new car ads in magazines. The fountain glimmered and sparkled. It's a huge fountain, with a big plume in the center that spurts about 150 feet high and three fan-shaped sprays surrounding it. They say the water for it comes from a "fourth river" that flows far beneath the city. The round basin is big enough for lots of people to wade in, and they often do in the summer. But this evening Chris and I had the fountain to ourselves.

He put his hands around my waist and boosted me up to sit on the basin's rim. I kinda liked it. I was disappointed when he took his hands away.

"You seem ill at ease."

"Well, who wouldn't be?" I said. "After talking to her ladyship there, I feel, I dunno, like a toad or something." I also felt about six years old. I scuffed my heels against the stone basin, not looking at Chris.

"Naught is there amiss in this." Chris hopped up onto the rim beside me. He began to rub my shoulders with his long fingers. It felt exquisite. "Your

flesh is hard as steel," he said with a gentle laugh.
"I wonder that you can scarce move withal."

"I don't know. I hadn't noticed."

He moved his massage slowly down my back, his
thumbs pressing firmly into my muscles, but not so
hard as to hurt. I just wanted to melt into his hands
and flow into the fountain pool beside us.

" 'T. J.'—'tis a passing strange name. Is it the one
your sire chose for you? Or is it but in place of
other names?"

"Just initials," I said between sighs. "They stand
for Tiffany Jeannine, but don't call me that because
I hate it."

I could almost hear him smile, though he was behind me. "Wherefore hate it so? 'Tis a pretty name.
It speaks of things most precious, dear, and frangi-
ble." He leaned closer to me and I felt his warm
breath in my ear. "Tiffany Jeannine," he whispered.
"Tiffanny Jeannine."

His voice seemed to resonate within me. I suddenly felt as though I were completely naked, trans-
parent to him, vulnerable. Emotions welled up
within me—fear, wretchedness, an immense sorrow.
Everything I hadn't ever wanted to feel seemed to
be ganging up on me all at once. Tears began to run
down my cheeks. My sighs became sobs that I could
not control.

"Shhh," Chris whispered. "Dwell not upon past
sorrow. Turn your thoughts instead to beauty and
gaze upon soothing waters."

I turned, wiping my nose on my arm, and looked
into the fountain pool. With all the spray, the surface
is usually rough. But where Chris stroked the water
with his hand, it became smooth as glass. "Behold,
sweet Tiffany Jeannine. Give thyself that due regard
which thou hast earned."

I saw my reflection against a starry sky. What
stared back at me was a muss-haired imp, a child in
too-big clothing, eyes full of sorrow and fear. The

face was red and puffy and pouting. I looked just the way I felt—small, insignificant, ugly. *No wonder my performances were flops before Ralph and Norton showed up. Who would listen to a little brat like me? Why should anybody take what I say seriously? I'm just a spoiled kid with a huge chip on my shoulder. Nobody understands me. Nobody likes me. And why should they? I'm not worth it.*

I jumped off the fountain rim. "I gotta go."

"Wherefore now? What is't?"

"Nothing." I walked away quickly, taking the path that ran along the bank of the Allegheny. I didn't want anyone to see my tear-lined, snot-smeared face. I heard Chris following behind me. I didn't let him catch up to me, but I didn't try to lose him either. The water of the river was dark, and I wondered if it was cold and how deep it was. Lots of bridges nearby to throw myself off of if I wanted. But Chris or Ralph or Norton would probably try to stop me. Such desperate measures could wait. For now, I just wanted to get away.

The few other fairgoers I passed paid little attention to me. I made it to the other side of the tunnel/bridge without bumping into anyone. At Liberty Avenue, I stopped and gazed up at the night-lit towers of downtown Pittsburgh, wondering what to do.

Chris answered the question for me, flagging down a cab. He opened the taxi door for me, but just before I got into the backseat, he gave me a quick hug. "Forgive me," he said. I couldn't speak to answer him.

I clambered into the cab, but Chris didn't follow. He shut the door behind me and spoke to the driver through the window, handing him something. I curled up on the dark, soft backseat and let the taxi take me home.

Chapter 12

I don't know how long I sat on Mom's living room sofa, rocking and sniveling in the dark. My thoughts of throwing myself off a bridge had passed, but I still wanted to find a nice, deep, dark hole and hide from the world for a while.

"T.J.?"

I jumped at the sound of the gravelly voice. "Ralph? Norton?" There came faint popping sounds, and I saw their squat shapes appear before me.

"Where ya been, Princess? We had the feelin' something was wrong. We been worried about ya. Norton, get a light on here."

The floor lamp clicked on and I blinked in the light. "I don't know," I whispered.

Ralph gasped. "Cripes, you look awful! What happened to ya?"

Norton pointed to the button pinned to my T-shirt. "Ralph, lookit."

Ralph's eyes narrowed. "Those *bastards*. They got to her after all. Take that thing off, T.J. Right now."

My fingers fumbled at the button pin. After a few moments struggle, it came off and I threw it against the wall. Immediately some of my dark mood began to lift.

Ralph gently grasped my hand in his twiglike fingers. "You shoulda called us if you was in trouble, T.J."

"Yeah," said Norton. "We woulda protected you."

"I didn't think I *was* in trouble. I thought I could handle it. It all seemed okay until . . . until the end. And I thought about calling you guys. But they were all over the place and I couldn't get alone and I didn't know if it would be safe for you and I thought it was just me feeling bad and—"

"Hey, hey, slow down, slow down," said Ralph. "Just tell us everything that happened."

I wiped my nose. "Well, this guy showed up on campus this afternoon, asking for me."

"One of them Sidhe?"

"Yeah. But I didn't know it at first, and he didn't look dangerous or anything."

"So what did he do?"

"Well, at first he just wanted to talk to me. And I thought it might be a good idea, in case, well, in case they'd gotten the wrong impression."

Ralph and Norton gaped. "You didn't try to tell them it was a mistake, didja?"

"Well . . . sort of."

They both shook their blobby, pointed gray heads. "You shouldn't have done that, T.J.," said Norton. "They'll think you're a coward. They got no respect for cowards."

"Later, Norton," said Ralph. "What was this Seelie guy like, Princess?"

"Like any of them. He was tall, blond, really attractive. He talked like some character out of a Shakespeare play."

"Did he flirt with ya?"

"Um, yeah, sort of."

"Did he have a name?"

"He called himself Chris."

"Hmm. He could've been a Ganconer."

"What's a Ganconer?"

"You morts also call 'em love-talkers. Kind of a cross between Don Juan and Lee Harvey Oswald."

"Huh? What do you mean?"

" 'Kris' in their language means 'to cut like a

knife.' He might have been a hit man, T.J. Only, Gan-
coners kill with kisses, so to speak."

"Kinda like a vampire," said Norton, "Only, they
don't drink blood."

I went cold all over. "A vampire? An assassin? But
Chris didn't hurt me, at least not physically."

"Naw, 'course not. That wouldn't be elegant. These
guys are sicker puppies than that. They'd rather
break your spirit and let you live to remember it. So,
anyway, what did he do?"

"Well, he said he wanted to know about how I did
performance art. So we went to lunch and talked—I
didn't tell him about you guys."

"We know you didn't, T.J. It's okay."

"So, then, after lunch, he asked me to go with him
to some festival at Point State Park."

"The Point! T.J., that's their turf!"

"Well, I didn't know that! There was just this fair
with lots of save-the-earth type booths, and a fake
forest and stuff. It was kinda pretty."

Norton asked, "Did you eat anything there? Drink
anything?"

"No. Wait, I bought a chocolate bar, but I didn't
eat it." I pulled the Guava Crunch Bar out of my
jeans pocket. Ralph snatched it out of my hand and
tossed it to Norton, who stomped it underfoot.

"Sorry, T.J.," said Ralph. "Eating their food, 'specially on their turf, is bad news. So. What else did
you do?"

"Um, Chris introduced me to this really pretty
woman. He said her name was . . . Reia Perry."

Ralph and Norton stared at me wide-eyed for a
moment. Norton gave a low whistle. "Wow, you really are brave. How did she look? Was she healthy
and everything?"

"Healthy?" The question gave me the willies. "She
had a slight cough, but she said she was recovering."

Ralph and Norton grinned and elbowed each other
in the ribs.

"What's going on?" I said.

"Nuttin'," said Ralph. "But you had a close call there. How did she treat you?"

"Close call?"

"What did you say to her?"

"I tried to tell her that my performance might have been misunderstood. But she didn't seem to get it. And when I tried to explain, it was like I couldn't talk around her. She asked the same sort of things Chris did and I couldn't tell her."

"'Course you couldn't, T.J. But at least our protections are working."

"Will you guys quit being secretive and just tell me who the fuck she is?"

"Ow, oooh," Ralph covered his nonexistent ears. "Okay, T.J., just don't go talking like that, all right? This Reia Perry you met, she's one of the most powerful of Them. 'Reia' means 'queen,' you know. She's got lots of other names."

"Like Queen Mab?"

"On the nose, Princess."

"And Queen of Air and Darkness," added Norton.

I felt cold all over, as if I'd been turned to stone. "This is the queen my act was aimed at, isn't it? The one I wished death on?"

"You catch on quick, T.J. But you got by her all right."

"*Got by her?* I don't understand. She made me feel like shit. I'm not all right!"

"T.J., you walk right into a nest of vipers and you're surprised you got bit a little? We're just glad you ain't dead!"

"Or worse," said Norton. "So she's the one who got you, huh?"

I shrugged. "Nobody *got* me. Chris took me to the Point Fountain."

"Figures," growled Ralph. "That's bedrock water they got in that thing. Lotta juju for elves in that. Bet they planned that from the beginning, whoever they talked into building it. Did you know that, before the fountain idea, the city fathers were gonna put up a big statue to Joe Magarac, the steelworker. Now *that* woulda been a suitable monument for Pittsburgh. But nooo—''

"Ralph," said Norton, "let her get on with the story."

"Oh, sorry, Princess. So this Chris guy takes you to the fountain."

"Yeah," I said, wincing at the memory. "We talked some more. He rubbed my back and it felt real nice. He asked me what 'T.J.' stood for."

Norton's eyes went wide. "You didn't tell him, didja?"

"Well, yeah. It didn't seem like any big deal."

Ralph smacked his forehead with his hand. "Princess! You don't go telling those guys your real name! It gives 'em an edge."

"Wait a minute, I thought that rule only worked for you guys. Besides, I've told *you* my real name."

"Yeah," said Ralph, "but you can trust us. We won't misuse it. Now that we're workin' together, we got to follow some of the same rules."

"Then why didn't you tell me not to tell them?"

"Because we thought you wouldn't 'cause you said you hated it! Look, it probably wouldn't have mattered so much if you weren't bothered by your real name, but there it is. So this Chris guy started using your real name."

"Yeah. And he told me to look at my reflection in the water. The basin water was really smooth when he touched it. I saw my reflection, only . . . somehow . . . I just looked so childish and ugly and stupid—'' I had to stop talking to keep tears from spilling out of my eyes again.

"Aha!" Ralph growled. "The old 'soul-in-the-mirror trick.' They make you think you're seeing your real self, but you only see the worst, or whatever they want you to see."

"Chris wanted me to hate myself? Jeez, I nearly felt like jumping off a bridge! And I'd been trying to be friendly to him and the others."

"See? Didn't we tell ya these were not good people?" said Ralph. "Do you believe us now? Do you understand why we don't want 'em taking over this town?"

"I see that now," I mumbled. Learning that Chris had deliberately tried to hurt me tore at my heart in a way I couldn't understand. And I couldn't stop thinking that the magic water in the fountain had shown me as I really was, and it wasn't anybody worth being. "But I think you guys picked the wrong person to be your hero. I can't do this. I'm not that brave. I'm not strong enough. Just go away and leave me alone, okay?"

"We better do something for her, Ralph," said Norton. "She's still in a bad way."

"Yeah. We gotta break this spell. Hey, I got it. Maybe a little trip downstairs can help her."

"You sure that's a good idea?" said Norton.

"It'll be okay, long as we don't stay long. C'mon, Princess." Ralph tugged at my arm.

"What? I said leave me alone," I whined.

"Relax. We're just goin' to a party."

"I don't wanna go to a party. I don't know if I should go anywhere with you guys. You don't tell me everything, and you get me in trouble, and I feel tired and I look awful and I just want to go to bed and forget you Seelies and Unseelies ever existed."

Ralph said, "You want those Sidhe to get the better of you?"

"I don't care. They already did. I'm not going anywhere." I folded my arms across my chest and shut my eyes.

I felt their arms slide around my back and under my thighs.

"Hey! What are you doing?"

"We're not gonna let those guys make a wimp out

of you. One way or another, you're coming with us."
They lifted me and carried me a few steps.

"Stop it! Stop or I'll swear! I'll swear . . . and I'll
whistle!" I puckered up my lips—

"TIFFANY JEANNINE KAMINSKI!" Ralph boomed
in my ear.

My whole body snapped to attention. It was the
tone that Mom had used when she discovered I had
colored in her academic books. It was the "listen-to-
me-right-now-and-no-back-talk-young-lady-or-you're-
going-to-your-room-for-the-rest-of-the-day" voice. It
was the Voice That Must Be Obeyed. "Ye-yeah?" I
said timidly.

"Sorry I had to do it, Princess, but you was getting
carried away there. Now you gonna be nice and come
along quietly?"

"It's for your own good," said Norton.

"Okay, okay. Put me down."

"Good. But keep your eyes closed."

"Why?"

" 'Cause seeing is disbelieving." They stood me up
somewhere in the middle of the living room carpet.
"Now just step down like there was stairs here."

"Stairs?" I slid my right foot forward and, sure
enough, the floor dropped away. I carefully lowered
my foot until it found a hard surface.

"There ya go. Just one foot after the other. That's
right."

I took another step down, and then another. And
then many more, with Ralph and Norton squeezed
in tight beside me. Wherever we were going, it was
a long way down. The air began to smell earthy, and
I could hear echoes of our breathing. Finally the guys
jerked me to a stop.

"You can open your eyes now."

I did. There was a big metal door in front of us,
studded with rivets. Ralph let go of me and pushed
with both hands against the door. Slowly it opened
a crack. A deep, throbbing bass sound spilled

through the opening, something like the music I'd heard at industrial metal clubs. If there were instruments playing on top of it, though, the mix was way unbalanced and not in their favor. Ralph and Norton pushed the door open wider, and warm air swirled in around us. They pulled me through the opening and . . . I wasn't in Pittsburgh anymore, Toto.

Ahead of us was an enormous cavern, complete with stalagmites, stalactites, rocky ledges, pillars, and pedestals. Furry, raggedy, spindly creatures of all shapes and sizes danced on the rocks, in the niches, on the ledges, in the shadows. They hung from the ceiling and scuttled on the cave floor. It was like entering a demented episode of *Fraggle Rock*. "Wow!" I said and started to step forward.

"Watch out!" Ralph grabbed my arm and held me back. Right in front of me was a narrow-gauge railroad track. From a tunnel to my left came a loud roar, rattle, and clatter. A rust-brown iron mine car, filled with chunks of shiny black coal, came rocketing out of the tunnel. A strange-looking critter with long, furry arms, big eyes, and big teeth sat atop the pile of coal.

"Wwaaahhhh-ha-ha-HA-HA-HAH-HOOOOO-eeeeee!" cried the creature as the mine car plummeted past us and down another tunnel on our right.

"Uh, thanks," I said, rocking back on my heels. "Where on earth are we?"

Still holding my hands, Ralph and Norton jumped over the rails, pulling me along with them. "Under the Hill!" said Ralph.

"But on the Wrong Side of the Tracks," added Norton.

"Right. Very funny." The deep, throbbing music was getting to me. As we walked into the midst of the bobbing, weaving throng of . . . things, my feet kept trying to dance. The critters around me weren't fighting the feeling at all; they were boogying everywhere. Even Ralph and Norton were bouncing along beside me in rhythm, big grins on their faces.

"Is this place great or what?" shouted Ralph.

"If there's a mosh pit down here," I said, "I don't want to know."

"Hey!" Something in the crowd shouted at us. "Who's the mort?"

The music stopped, and all of them turned and stared at me.

"Leave this to me," said Ralph. He bounded on top of the nearest stone pedestal, bumping off the gnome that had been dancing there. "Listen up, everybody. This here's T. J. Kaminski. She's the thaumaturge who gave it to the Sidhe last night. They tried to get back at her today; she'd been whammied bad and ain't feeling so good. I want you all to help cheer her up. She scored one for our side, so we all owe her a big welcome. Let's hear it!"

"HURRRRRAAAAHHHH!" Their cheering was louder than the music, so much louder that I had to cover my ears. "T.J.! T.J.! T.J.!" they chanted. It was strange, but their voices helped to lift the clouds from my mind even more.

Ralph hopped down and pounded me on the back. All sorts of other elf-things—some naked and hairy, some well dressed, some fat, some thin, some ancient, some childlike—came up to meet me. Ralph told me each species of critter, though it went in one ear and out the other. Folletti, Erdluitle, Wichtlin, Korred, Fees, Martes, Domoviye, Fir Bolg—it was impossible to keep up with the list. They all shook my hand, patted my arm, kissed my cheeks, smiled at me. After a while I did feel welcomed, even appreciated. I even began to smile myself.

The music started up again, and I let the crowd push-pull me around, dancing with it. The pounding beat drove the last bits of sadness from my thoughts. The world became all movement and sound, and I was just a mote of dust on a speaker cone, bouncing with it.

Chapter 13

I paid no attention to where in that enormous cavern I was, and after a while I found myself dancing at the edge of the critter crowd. An entrance to another tunnel loomed nearby. I was happy but getting tired, and my feet were showing no signs of stopping. I slipped away from the mass of movement and boogied down the tunnel, hoping I could find a place to rest.

As I shuffled further down the side passage, the throbbing music quieted and my feet began to behave themselves. I could almost walk normally. Golden-red light glimmered on the crystals on the walls and ceiling of the cave tunnel. I continued down the passage out of sheer curiosity, wondering where it led.

The air became warm and there was a faint smell of smoke. I heard new sounds: metallic clanking, hissing, and the grinding of machinery, punctuated by the occasional distant roar.

I went around a bend and the tunnel split into three. Now where to? The tunnel to my left seemed to slope upward. The tunnel ahead of me was totally dark. The tunnel to my right was where the orange-yellow light was coming from, as well as the mechanical sounds, so I went down that way.

The walls were veined with mineral stains, some of which had a faint fluorescent glow. I wondered if gold or silver or gems might be found down here. Would they be magical?

I was so distracted, I didn't notice the pounding sounds approaching. They were different from the music I had just escaped. Pretty soon I realized it was the footsteps of Something Big coming down the tunnel behind me. I pressed myself up against the wall, not sure whether I should run.

"Dum-di-dah-dee-doo-di—" someone was singing in a booming voice. The someone came more into the light as he walked, his footsteps nearly shaking the ground. He was big, all right; he filled the tunnel. He wore drawstring pants and work boots but was naked from the waist up, except for a cap on his brown-haired head. My God, what muscles!—they rippled and shone in the fiery light. Handsome mustachioed face too. I began to think I knew who he was.

The big man stopped when he saw me and tipped his cap. "Evening, Miss," he said with a smile.

"Hi. Uh, are you, by some chance, Joe Magarac?"

His grin got even wider. "That's me, Miss. Magarac the mule, 'cause I work like one." He rapped his knuckles on his chest, and—so help me—there was a clank like metal against metal.

"My dad used to tell me stories about you." Sheesh, I was gushing and blushing like a fluff-chick.

"Your dad a steel man?"

"Yeah. Used to be. He's dead now."

Joe lowered his cap to his chest. "Mighty sorry, Miss."

" 'Sokay. But I thought . . . I mean, Dad told me the story where, in 1944, you threw yourself into the furnace so you could improve the steel to be made into weapons and that's why we won World War II.

Joe laughed a big, booming laugh. "Ho, ho, lots o'tales been told about Joe. Some of 'em true, some of 'em not."

"I heard they were going to put up a statue of you at Point Park."

He shrugged. "Don't need a statue. Just humble Joe. I'm going my house now. Want to come visit wi'me?"

"Well, sure!" It's not every day you get to talk to an American Legend. Besides, he outdid Fabio in the hunk department by a mile.

I let him squeeze past me in the tunnel and I followed him. We came to a bend, and as I came around it, I had to stop.

If I had thought the first cavern, where all the dancing was going on, was big, I had to change my mind. This chamber ahead of me was *enormous*. The tunnel ended at a ledge halfway up the chamber wall. In the center of the chamber was a full-size old-fashioned blast furnace steel mill. It was built of brick, with large rectangular windows lining the walls. The tall chimneys had been fashioned in the shape of dragon's heads, and they spouted fire and cinders. Beside the building, the nose cone–shaped Bessemers shot out flames like roman candle fireworks. You couldn't see the roof of the chamber because of the black clouds billowing there.

Off to one side of the furnace was an incline rail track leading to the building's roof. A mine car was climbing up it—maybe the same one I had seen before. It still seemed to have a furry critter riding it.

"Ain't it beyootiful?" said Joe.

"Um," I said, nodding to be polite. It was impressive, sure, but "beautiful" wasn't the word I'd use.

"Just like the 'Burgh in the good old days. Come and see." Steps led down from either side of the ledge to the floor, and I followed him down. When we got up to the mill, I felt as if I'd shrunk to dwarf size. The mill had been built to Joe's proportions, not mine. He pushed open the big steel door and bowed me in.

Wow. Memories from when I was a kid flooded

back. Dad had once taken me to a mill, shortly after
it had shut down. I had only seen pictures of mills
in operation. And the pictures were nothing like this.

It was awesome. A crane the height of a two-story
house reached down from the mill's ceiling and
hooked onto a metal ladle the size of a Volkswagen.
With lots of clinks and whirrs, the crane rolled sideways, pulling the ladle over to where we stood. A
shunt opened in a round container above us, and a
river of glowing, molten metal flowed like a waterfall
into the ladle. The flow stopped, the shunt closed,
and the crane rolled sideways again to another part
of the mill, where the ingot molds would be, if I
remembered right.

"Pardon me, Miss. Gonna freshen up a little." Joe
strode over to the ladle and opened the tap at its
bottom. The liquid iron flowed into a fire-brick trench
below. Joe reached into the glowing stream and
splashed some of the molten metal onto his face and
arms as if it were tap water.

I turned to gaze out one of the big windows. Liquid metal might be harmless to Joe, but it made my
skin hurt just to watch. Out the window, instead of
seeing the cavern, I saw what Pittsburgh must have
looked like long ago. It was dark as midnight, and
street lamps were lit all along the banks of the Monongahela. Other mills across the river belched fire and
smoke. It was a scene from some inner circle of
hell.

"Whatta view, yes?" said Joe behind me. He
smelled of hot metal. Well, it was better than some
colognes I've known.

"Um, yeah, it's really something."

"How 'bout you stay and have a late supper
wi'me?"

"Okay. Sure."

Joe set up a folding table and spread a red-and-
white-checkered tablecloth over it. From somewhere
he brought out steel plates, mugs, forks and knives,

and laid them out neat as you please. He went over to the trench, below the huge ladle, and pulled a drawer out from under it with his bare hands. A scent of hot meat pies reached my nose, and my stomach growled as I remembered I hadn't eaten in a while.

Joe put the sheet of hot pastries on the table and held my chair for me as I sat. "Help yourself, Miss . . . um, I not catch your name, please?"

"T.J. T. J. Kaminski."

"Miss Kaminski." He did a cute little bow, doffing his cap. "I go bring us drink. Enjoy!"

I carefully pried a couple of the pastries off the sheet and onto my plate. They were ground sausage and rice and cabbage and spices wrapped in a flaky crust. The first bite nearly burned the roof of my mouth, but, man, they were good. *Boy, if only I could tell Mamu about this*, I thought.

Joe returned with an earthenware jug and poured a thick, dark liquid into my mug. I admired the way the orange-gold light reflected off his muscles as he bent toward me. I didn't pay much attention to what was in my mug until I took my first sip of the thick, sweet stuff . . . the alcohol burned all the way down to my belly, leaving my mouth feeling like the aftermath of an explosion.

"PHEW! Whoa, what *is* this stuff?"

Joe laughed. "That prune jack, Miss. Best drink ever. Strong as me, nearly." He downed his mugful in one gulp.

"Uh, yeah, I think you're right." I continued to only sip at it while nibbling the meat pie. Even so, my head started swimming pretty quickly, and I was getting awfully warm. I wished I could take off my T-shirt.

"You sad, Miss Kaminski?"

"Huh? What?"

"Your eyes. You look sad."

"Oh. I dunno. I've just been knocked for a loop

lately. I don't know what to believe anymore—about
the world or even myself. What do you believe in,
Joe?"

He leaned back in his chair and scratched his head.
"Hmmm. Work. Hard work. Laughing a lot. Being
good sport. Being good friend and neighbor." He
looked at me. "Pretty ladies."

I blushed, staring at the floor. "Sounds like good
stuff to believe in," I murmured.

" 'Nother thing. Not being too serious. Music!" Joe
called out to the room. "Need music here someone!"

From behind the machinery appeared the long-
armed furry creature that had been riding the mine
car. He was carrying an accordion.

A muppet with a squeeze box. Why not? I thought.
Nothing else has been normal down here.

Mr. Long Arms began a polka, and Joe leapt to
his feet. He bowed again, saying, "Will you dancit
wi'me, Miss?"

"I'd be delighted," I said. Well.

My feet hardly touched the ground. Literally. Once
Joe picked me up in his massive, strong arms, I
danced mostly on air. He whirled me around the
floor of the steel mill, and I got dizzy watching the
light from the glowing ingot molds flash by. Somehow, Mr. Long Arms got the polka to match the
rhythmic thumping and clanking of the mill machinery. Thoughts of Chris fled far from my mind.

Joe's skin was smooth as steel and warm, the muscles beneath were firm. I was beginning to wonder
if other parts of him would be just as firm and strong
and warm. The song ended and he gently set me
down.

For a long moment, I didn't move. I just stared up
into his big, brown eyes. I wondered if he was thinking what I was thinking. There had been stories
about Joe that Dad had told when he thought I
wasn't in the room. Like how Joe had a way of pleas-
ing steelmen's wives on the sly.

There came a banging on the mill door, and we both jumped. The door creaked open, revealing the tiny silhouette of Ralph in the doorway. "Hi, Joe. You seen a girl named T.J.?"

I came out from around the big guy. Reluctantly I said, "I'm here, Ralph."

"Aha! There you are, Princess. C'mon. We oughta be getting you home."

"Do I have to go *now*?"

"Hey, time works a little different down here. You don't wanna get back and find it's a century later, do ya?"

"I dunno," I grumbled. "Might not be so bad."

Joe thunked me on the back. "Best you go now, Miss Kaminski. But you come back soon, yes? We talk and dance more, okay?"

"Okay. Thanks for dinner. 'Bye." I smiled at him and wobbled off toward Ralph, who scurried on ahead. Despite some difficulty keeping my balance, I got to the ledge at the top of the stairs, then turned for a last look at the mill. Joe was standing outside the door. He raised his cap and waved at me, wearing his adorable grin.

I smiled and waved too before I ducked into the tunnel, where Ralph was waiting for me. The prune jack was starting to hit hard, and I just stood there wavering, not knowing which way to go.

"What's the matter, T.J.?"

"Nothin', Ralph," I said thickly. "Just . . . feeling too good."

"You drink something with Joe?"

I grinned at him. "Yeah. Prune jack. It was awesome. Wish I could bring some back with me."

"Eat anything?"

"Yeah. He made these meat pies that were really good."

Ralph shook his head. "You morts. You never listen. Oh, well."

"Oh, well what? What's the problem now?"

"Never mind. I'll tell you when we get you home. C'mon."

I let Ralph take my arm and guide me back. The pounding music was still going in the dance cave, and my feet did the fandango while we hooked up with Norton. It took both of them to pull me out of the dance cave, back across the tracks, to the stairs.

I turned for one last look at the cavern and had a desperate desire to stay. "Aw, guys, can't I dance for just a little longer?"

Norton looked at me funny. "What's with her? We have to drag her down here, now we gotta drag her back."

"Prune jack," Ralph said. "Meat pies."

"Oh." Norton took a firmer grip on my arm. "She don't like to make things easy, do she?"

"What are you guys talking about? Why can't I stay?"

"Later, T.J. C'mon."

"Later, later, everything's later with you guys. You're just like my stupid parents."

"Yeah, yeah, close your eyes. That's a girl." They tugged me up the stairs, and I felt like a four-year-old being dragged to the dentist.

Norton said, "So I guess the Sidhe spell got worn off you pretty good, huh?"

"What spell?"

" 'Nuff said."

"Well, that's good, anyways," said Ralph. "Don't worry, T.J. We won't let them getcha down again."

"Are we there yet?" The steps seemed to go on forever, but at last the earthy smell was gone and there were no more stairs to climb.

"You can open your eyes now," said Ralph.

We were back in the apartment, but it wasn't as depressing as I'd expected. In fact, thanks to the prune jack, I still felt pretty good. I didn't mind at all that the room was spinning and going in and out of focus. "Great party, guys. Thanks."

"No problem, Princess, but we better get you to bed."

"Yes, daddy." It helped to have them to lean on as I made my way toward the bedroom. "Know what I think? Those Shhhheeelie were really mean to me. Here I was trying to be nice to 'em, and Chris and that lady made me feel lousy. I think you guys were right, and those guys aren't good at all. Not like Joe. He's nice."

"Yeah, T.J., we know."

"Know what else?" I asked as they sat me on the bed and pulled off my shoes and socks. "I'm not so afraid of them anymore. They're not so tough. They're just Yuppies who talk funny, you know? I think I wanna do another performance piece, just for them. Just to show 'em. Hit 'em again, harder, harder." I flailed my arms, pretending to be a cheerleader.

Ralph and Norton looked at each other and shrugged. "Sure, kid," said Ralph. "Whatever you say. You wanna do another stage thing, we'll help you all the way. We're in it together now. Almost like family. We'll take good care of you."

"I know," I said as I fell back on the mattress, already drifting off to sleep. "Pals forever."

"Pals forever," Ralph agreed sadly.

Chapter 14

It wasn't a normal hangover. My head didn't hurt. My stomach wasn't upset. But I'd waked up kneeling in the middle of the living room floor, my fingertips raw and red and the carpet in front of me all scuffed, with some threads pulled up. There were tears on my face. I had dreamed I was trying to find the stairs leading down to Under the Hill. I guess it hadn't been a dream. *Now what the hell is wrong with me?*

My hands were trembling uncontrollably. *Coffee. I need coffee.* I ran to the kitchen and flung open the cupboard doors. The shelves were almost bare— Ralph and Norton had been cleaning me out. But I found at the back of one lower shelf a jar of instant coffee. *At least they left me that—maybe Ralph and Norton don't like the taste of it.* I nuked some water and put in two tablespoons of the brown powder. It smelled wonderful. The jangle of warmth, bitterness, and caffeine drove the crazies back into the darker corners of my brain, and I could begin to think a little more clearly.

I sat at the counter, hunched over my coffee mug, and tried to access my misfiring memory chips. I remembered I'd been really depressed after going to the fair with Chris. Ralph and Norton said the Sidhe made me feel that way. The guys took me to a party Under the Hill, where the Unseelie fairy types live. I'd danced with a lot of weird creatures and met Joe Magarac and had some prune jack and pastries and . . .

uh-oh. That's what Ralph was talking about. I'd eaten on their turf. Ralph and Norton had said it was bad news in Sidhe territory, but what did it mean in theirs?

As I turned to get more coffee, I noticed the answering machine light blinking. *Three calls. I gotta learn to turn up the volume on the phone.* I punched the retrieve button.

"Hi, T.J., this is Angela. Listen, um, since you didn't come back for your stuff, I've just put it in a corner of the dressing room. Warren says you can have next Tuesday at seven, so if you're going to do the same act, you can just leave the stuff here if you want. Whatever. Give me a call and let us know what you decide, okay? It's too late for the *In Pittsburgh* ad, but we might be able to get you listed in the *Post Gazette.* Just let us know. 'Bye." *Beeeep.*

Shit. I forgot about my props. I really am losing it.

"Hello, Tiffany? This is your mother, dear—"

Mom! What does she want?

"I know you're not the sort to write, but you've left me in the dark about your plans for the summer. Now that classes are over for me, I may be taking a couple of months off from the academic grind and coming back to Pittsburgh. This means, of course, that I'll be needing the apartment. So we'll need to talk about arrangements and so forth. Oh, and your grandmother called to say she was worried about you. I know Sadie is prone to odd notions, but I'd be reassured to hear from you that everything is all right. So please give me a call as soon as you can. Bye-bye." *Beeeeep.*

I jammed my fingers into my hair. *She's coming back. She'll need the apartment? How will I keep her from learning about this fairy shit? Maybe I could live somewhere else for a while. But where?*

The next message started, but there was only a background hiss, maybe faint music in the background. *A wrong number.* I was about to hit the delete button when the eerie voices began:

> "O goblin's thrall and regent's bane;
> Think twice before you err again.
> Powers of air and stream and wood
> Hunger for your bones and blood.
> Keep your bestial talons sheathed,
> Lest, unleashed, those wights aggrieved,
> Come creeping to your slumber bed,
> And cut your throat and take your head.
> By Rowan, Ash, and barleybreak,
> Do not our sleeping ire awake.
> For you are but a mortal small,
> O regent's bane and goblin's thrall."

The voices faded, and the final *beeeep* startled me off the stool. I fell back against the kitchen cabinet and landed clumsily on the floor. I pulled my knees to my chin and swallowed hard. *They're just trying to frighten me*, I told myself. *But, dammit, it's working.* The bravado given me by the prune jack seemed to have fled with the morning sun.

Are the Sidhe serious? If I do another performance act aimed at them, will they try to kill me? I better ask Ralph and Norton, and this time they'd better be straight with me or I'm breaking the contract. Wonder if the Unseelies have their own lawyers.

It took a couple of tries to get my voice to work. "Ralph! Norton!"

A faint ball of light appeared in the air before me. Ralph's voice said, "Hiya. Sorry we are unable to answer your summons right now. Please leave a message after the chime and we will show up just as soon as we can. If this is an emergency, say so and an alternate will be sent to assist you."

"This is an emergency, goddamn it!"

"Please hold on. Your local alternate will be sent to you shortly." The chimes sounded.

"Great, just great," I muttered. "Of all the times they pick to not be available. Well. I'll call Angela and tell her I don't want the gig Tuesday. That'll help." I pulled myself back onto the kitchen stool and dialed her number with a shaky finger.

It was busy. Angela hated call waiting, so she'd never had it installed, and she could be on the phone for hours. I hung up.

I turned, and who should be standing there on the counter but little Luigi, in his black velvet suit. He bowed to me, smiling hopefully.

"You're the alternate?"

He nodded. *"Si, bella mia."*

"Figures. And I'm not your beauty." I buried my face in my hands.

"Che posso fare per lei, Signorina?"

Slowly I said, "You can tell me where Ralph and Norton are."

Luigi shrugged and shook his head.

"Wonderful." I wandered out into the living room. I opened the front door. The herb wreath was still hanging there. I wondered if it would do more good hanging around my neck. I needed protection of some sort, that was clear. And I needed to find Ralph and Norton.

I turned back to the little Italian folletti. "Luigi?" I said as sweetly as I could.

"Signorina?"

I stood in the middle of the rug and pointed down. "Show me where the stairs are. Stairs down. You know?" I closed my eyes and mimed walking down stairs—not easy to do standing in one place. I opened my eyes. Luigi was looking up at me, his head tilted in bafflement like a cat.

I sighed. Again, slowly, I said, "Where are the stairs?" With my fingers, I pantomimed walking downstairs.

"Aha!" He flew to the apartment door and opened

it. He pointed toward the stairs that led down to the street. *"Là!"*

I smacked my forehead. "No!"

Luigi shut the door with a disappointed pout.

"Underhill," I said. "I need to go under the hill. Down. Where you live. Take me under the hill, please?"

Luigi's eyes widened. He shook his head, clicked his tongue and waggled his finger. *"No, no, Signorina. E proibito. Pericoloso."*

"I'll give you a kiss if you do."

He blushed and looked down at his feet. *"Posso avere il bacio primo?"*

"All right, I'll give you the kiss first."

He wasn't bad, if you like kissing children. I pushed him off after ten seconds. He spun around joyously, faster and faster, until he was a blur. The little whirlwind passed close to me and caught me up with it, spinning so fast the room was a blur. Then the floor dropped out from under me and I fell, still spinning, straight down through darkness. When I had something solid again under my feet, I stumbled to my knees, still dizzy. I was in utter blackness, cold stone beneath my hands, a cold, damp breeze in my face. "Where is everybody? Luigi?"

There was a soft hiss and a flame appeared, Luigi's cherubic face behind it. He was carrying a candle in an old-fashioned brass holder. The flame did not illuminate much. The chamber we were in was empty and silent. I could dimly see a narrow-gauge rail to my right and beyond that a set of iron doors. So at least we were in the same place. Maybe.

"E felice ora La Signorina?"

Something inside me had relaxed, like the slowing down of a windup toy. I stood unsteadily. "Yeah, happy now, thanks, but now I've got to find Ralph and Norton. Or Joe."

I heard scuttling in the darkness, and two wrinkled gnomes came into our dim sphere of light. They carried between them a large, heavy basket that was covered with a blanket.

"Soft now," said one. "There's a mort—oh, 'tis you, T.J. Hail and well met."

"Um, hello," I said. "Has either of you seen Ralph or Norton?"

"Who?"

"The guys who brought me down here last night and introduced me to all of you."

"Oh, them. Nay, we've not seen a hair of their beards."

The other gnome nodded and then shook its head. Something under the blanket wriggled.

"Your pardon," said the first gnome. "We must be about our duties. May fortune follow you, T.J. For your courage, our thanks."

"Um, yeah. Sure."

They shuffled off into the darkness, and I heard a muffled gurgle and cry.

"Luigi . . . was that a baby in that basket?"

Luigi shrugged and sighed, as if to say, "What can one do?"

I'd heard of stories of fairy-types snatching babies, but even after meeting Ralph and Norton I never expected them to be true. Mom always said such tales were a cover for infanticide. *I could chase after the gnomes and grab the baby myself . . . but then what? What if they wouldn't tell me where they got it? What would I do with it? Besides, I've got enough problems right now.*

With a pang or two of guilt and helplessness, I peered around in the dim light. "I should be able to find Joe's place at least. He might be able to help." I walked forward, bumping my shins on stalagmites and tripping over rocks. I could now and then see passageways leading out of the chamber, but none of them were lit and they didn't seem to be where I remembered them.

A yellow light came bobbing around a corner and

out of one of the tunnels. It was a lantern, held up
by a short fellow with a long white beard. Behind
him were two others just like him, carrying picks and
shovels. I almost laughed aloud—they looked like
they'd just stepped out of *Snow White*.

"Hey, there!" I said, waving at them.

The three dwarves turned, and the one holding the
lantern lifted it higher. "Who calls?"

"It's me, T.J. I was here last night. Can you guys
tell me how to get to Joe Magarac's place?"

The one holding the lantern spit off to the side.
"Can't get there from here."

"Oh, c'mon. That's impossible. I got there from
here last night." I stepped closer to them. I couldn't
help myself—I asked, "Say, which one of you is
Grumpy and which one of you is Doc?"

The one with the lantern smiled a cold, foul smile
of yellowed teeth. "I'm Grungy, he's Sleazy, and he's
Creepy. Wanna come dig coal with us, little girl?"

I staggered back. "Um, no, thanks. I've already got
a guide."

"Suit yourself." Chuckling darkly, the three dwarves
marched off down another tunnel.

"Jeez, Luigi, this isn't at all like yesterday. What
rabbit hole have you taken me into?"

He didn't seem to understand the question.

I sat on the cold stone with my knees pulled up
to my chin, trying to think what to do. After a few
moments of silence, I seemed to hear faint music;
something like a guitar and flute were playing a
sweet melody.

"Luigi, can you tell me where that music is coming from?"

"*Eh.*" He looked around a moment. "*Lassù!*" he
said, pointing at another tunnel entrance.

"Okay. Let's go there. At least we might find somebody civilized." I scrambled into the tunnel, Luigi's
candlelight bobbing behind me. He was babbling
something in Italian that I didn't catch.

The tunnel sloped up and became more narrow. The floor was soft dirt instead of rock, and pale roots stuck out from the walls like finger bones.

The music was louder now, but the tunnel stopped at a round wooden door. It was fastened with a beam across it. I could put my ear against the door and hear the music clearly. Frustrated, I lifted and pulled on the beam.

"No, Signorina—"

"Shut up." After some heaving and shoving, I got the bar dislodged, releasing a cloud of dust. I dropped the beam and sneezed.

"Yi!" I heard Luigi cry, and his feet pattered away down the tunnel behind me, leaving me in darkness.

"Some help you are," I muttered. I pulled on the edge of the round door and it slowly creaked open.

Fresh, cool air hit my face. When the space was wide enough, I squeezed out past the door. I was no longer in a cave, but wherever I was, it was night. Impossibly bright stars glimmered in a velvet-black sky. By their light, I could see the silhouettes of trees and a wide meadow in front of me. The music was coming from a grove at the far end of the meadow. I was struck by a surge of déjà vu. This was the place I had seen in my dream at the Beehive.

There was a large bush with pale flowers to my left. Something tiny and glimmering came around the bush and hovered over one of the flowers. At first I thought it might be a very small hummingbird, until it paused to look at me. It was a tiny person, with dragonfly wings and pearlescent skin. And very large eyes and an extremely long tongue. It hovered for a moment, then took off at high speed for the trees across the meadow.

"Wow," I whispered, and I stepped out to follow the creature.

Something grabbed my right arm and yanked me back inside the round door.

"What in Mab's name do you think you're doing?" cried Ralph in my ear.

"Ralph! There you are! I've been looking for you guys."

"Well, this is a helluva place to look. Norton, shut that door."

"You bet, Ralph."

I was pulled back further into the dark tunnel, and I heard the wooden beam slam home.

"Now, what's the meaning of you comin' down here uninvited?" asked Ralph. "You tryin' to give us trouble or something?"

"No! I needed to talk to you guys and you didn't answer the summons."

"Oh, really? Is that why you was gon' over to the other side?"

"Other side?"

"Who do you think lives out there? That's High Sidhe country. Once you got out there, you wouldn't be comin' back."

"I think I hear something comin' on the other side of that door," said Norton.

"Let's get outta here!" said Ralph.

I was hustled down the tunnel back to the main chamber. Luigi waited there with his candle.

"Take us up, Luigi."

The folletti did the whirlwind act again. This time it was like riding a very fast elevator to the penthouse suite. My stomach was in my shoes by the time I was standing on the living room rug. I fell over onto the couch, gripping the cushions until the room stopped spinning. It was strange being suddenly back in daylight.

But it looked a lot later than it should have been.

"As for you, pipsqueak," Ralph growled at Luigi, "you got a lot of nerve, putting her in danger like that. We'll deal with you later. Beat it!"

Luigi disappeared with an "Eep!" and a pop.

"It's not his fault, Ralph. I talked him into taking

me down there. I just needed to find you guys, and you wouldn't answer when I called."

"Hey, we got busy lives too, you know. Especially now. So what is it you want?"

I sat up slowly. "I wanted to say . . . I'm not sure I want to do another performance for you guys."

Ralph and Norton looked at each other, then back at me. "Why not? You were rarin' to tear at them last night."

"I think you'd better listen to this." I staggered to the answering machine, rewound the tape, and played it. Angela's message played, then Mom's. Then there was a long, hissing stretch with nothing on it. "It's gone!"

"What's gone?"

"The Sidhe left a message, a poem, a threat. It really scared me. They kinda said that if I bother them again, they'd kill me."

"The Sidhe left a message on your answering machine?"

"Yeah. It's not here now, but you've got to believe me, I heard it."

"We believe you, Princess. What we don't believe is that just because they made nasty noises at you, now you wanna quit."

"Yeah, doncha get it?" said Norton. "Because of the way you acted at the park, they probably think they got you on the run now. They think they can keep you from causing trouble just by leaving scary messages. You ain't gonna prove 'em right, are ya?"

"I dunno." I sat heavily on the kitchen stool. "This is all so much bigger than I expected," I said. "So much riskier. I didn't want to start a war. I didn't want to hurt anyone. Physically. I just wanted some people to think differently."

Ralph narrowed his eyes at me. "So. Yeah, it's bigger than that. This is bigger than any mort dream you ever had. It's got more risks than you been used to. That's life. That's part of growing up, kid. Facing risks. Taking chances. You think them politicians in their big offices or those lawyers in their fancy cars let every little death threat scare 'em outta their job? You said you wanted to do dangerous art. Well it's gotten dangerous, kiddo. You got what you wished for. Now what I wanna know is, have you got the guts to handle it? Or are you gonna go back to being little miss nobody loudmouth, squirting ketchup on people?"

I winced and stared down at the floor. "Well . . ."

"You always dreamed of making a difference, didnja?" Ralph went on. "Now here you've got the chance to change the whole future of this town. Maybe to save the lives of thousands of people for miles around. And because of some little scary poem, you wanna run away?"

God, I hated to admit it, but he was right. It stung to think I didn't really have the guts for "dangerous art." Could I ever respect myself if I just walked away?

"Besides," said Norton, "even if you didn't do another thing for us, what makes you think the Sidhe will leave you alone? They've noticed you now, and that ain't a good thing. You still need us, T.J. And we still need you."

"Especially since," Ralph added, "you had to go and eat and drink Under the Hill."

"Oh. Is that why I keep wanting to go back there so badly?"

"You got it. See, you ain't so dumb after all. It's like you left a piece of yourself there, and it'll never leave. You ain't become one of us, exactly. But you're not what you used to be, either. And it's permanent. You'll never be the old T.J. again. That's a thing you gotta know about Seelie and Unseelie folk. What we do, we do for keeps."

"Why did Joe give it to me, then?" I said softly. "Didn't he know what the food would do?"

"Joe, heh, he's such a sweetheart. A real hospitable

guy. Didn't even occur to him what it would do, I'll bet. Good man, but he's not the brightest bulb on the Christmas tree, if you know what I'm sayin'."

"Oh."

Ralph scratched his beard. "But no need for you to mope like that. So long as you stick with us, we'll make sure you can get back Under the Hill whenever you want. Maybe, someday, live there for good."

"And when you do that," said Norton, "you won't nevermore grow old or die."

Wow, I thought. *What a carrot to hold out.* "You guys are as bad as drug dealers."

"Hey, we didn't tell you to go drinkin' no prune jack."

"Okay, okay," I sighed. "You guys are right. Guess I'm still on the team. Whether I like it or not."

"Don't look at it that way, Princess. You still got a glorious adventure ahead of you. Norton and I, we got plans. We'll get this town workin' again. And you're gonna make it all happen."

"Yeah. Great. Go team go." I felt brave. *Not.* I stared out the window and it was sundown already. Where did the time go? So many changes so quickly. If Ralph and Norton were right, I wasn't even myself anymore.

Chapter 15

"Okay, here's the plan," Ralph said Friday afternoon, as we sat around the living room in a nest of pizza boxes. "We've shown 'em we've got the power. Now we gotta hit 'em where they live."

"Turf wars!" enthused Norton.

I began to get a bad feeling about this. "But you guys get mad at me every time I go into their territory."

"That's 'cause you ain't been prepared," said Ralph. "Now we've got a specific plan of attack. Did you nail down the gig for this coming Tuesday?"

"Yeah, I finally reached Angela and told her I'd do it and that it was going to be a whole new act."

"Good, good. It's gonna be a big day, Tuesday, T.J."

"Right, Ralph."

"No, really. It's Beltane Eve. April thirtieth. Night before May Day. Big Fairies' Night Out, know what I mean?"

"Oh. Does this mean there'll be even more of them than last time?"

"Naw, maybe fewer. But we'll be interfering with their fun, ya see. Because they can't ignore you—they'll have to check out what you're doing. And that means they can't go party. At least, not until we're done with 'em."

"And they may not wanna party once we're done with 'em," said Norton.

"Great," I said. "That'll really piss them off."

"You got it."

"Which means they'll strike back even harder next time."

"We'll be ready for 'em. Don't you worry, T.J. We got it all under control now."

"Yeah. Right."

"Now don't start getting cold feet again, Princess. We're in this thing to win, remember."

"Yeah, Ralph. I remember."

"Now here's what you're gonna call this act: 'Salt of the Earth.' Like it?"

"Not as grabby as the first one."

"Hey, just think about it a minute. It's got a double meaning, see? 'Salt of the earth' means workin' types like us, right? But 'salting the earth' means—"

"Means nothing can grow there," I said. It conjured up images of deserts and wastelands.

"Exactly!" said Ralph, beaming.

"And another thing," Norton said. "Elf-types don't like salt. In fact, I'll bet they're behind this antisodium kick you morts are on. I learned about that on the TV."

"Sure," I said. "Next you'll be claiming that the Sidhe killed JFK and Marilyn Monroe."

"Wouldn't put it past 'em," said Norton with a knowing nod.

"Getting back to the subject," growled Ralph, " 'assaulting the earth' means attacking it. Which is what the Seelie are afraid of you morts doing. So the title has three meanings, none of which they'll like. Got it?"

Norton clapped his twiggy hands. "Brilliant, Ralph, simply brilliant!"

"Maybe you guys oughta do this on your own. Sounds like you don't need any ideas from me."

"Aw, now, don't put yourself down like that, T.J. You got the power that's gonna make this all work. Ain't that right, Norton?"

"You said it, Ralph. We couldn't do it without you, T.J."

"What a relief. I guess."

"So what you gotta do is an act based around natural stuff—chopping down trees, that sorta thing."

"I gotcha."

"Knew you'd catch on fast. Now we gotta do some preliminary groundwork—"

"Yeah," said Norton with an evil grin. "Groundwork."

So Saturday morning found me walking into Frick Park with a backpack full of greasy machine parts and a trowel.

Frick Park is a huge patch of forested land on the East Side of Pittsburgh. It's pretty obviously Sidhe territory. It used to be the estate of Henry Clay Frick, the guy who ran Carnegie's steel mill in Homestead back in the Bad Old Days at the beginning of the century. His name is a dirty word around steelworkers. Even though Frick was long dead, my dad never had a nice thing to say about him. But old HCF gave his land to the city, so he gets a big park named after him.

Most of the park is natural woodland, but here and there you can find wild apple and orange trees that used to be part of the orchards on the estate. If you look closely underfoot, you can sometimes find broken horse troughs and the foundations of gazebos and other garden buildings, now grown over.

I avoided the groomed lawns of the exercise trail and the kiddie park. Instead, I went through the woods, the smaller and less-traveled the path, the better. Now and then, I'd step off the path and dig a hole. Then I'd reach into my backpack, with gloves on, and pull out a greasy, grimy gear cog or piece of pipe, or a hunk of metal that I couldn't even identify. I'd plop the thing into the hole and cover it up, then move on. Just call me Johnny Wingnut-seed.

I didn't like what I was doing. It seemed ugly and

stupidly destructive. More like junior high school vandalism than striking a blow for the "working joes" of Pittsburgh. But Ralph and Norton said it would keep the park from being a comfortable place for the Sidhe to gather. It would fit into the theme of the performance act. It would keep the Sidhe nervous, unsettled, not knowing what to expect next.

Well, the Sidhe weren't the only ones it made nervous. Behind one stand of oak trees, as I buried a greasy gear, I thought I heard whispering overhead. I looked up and saw only sunlight filtering through the rustling leaves, but I couldn't help feeling like I was being watched. Out of the corner of my eye, the bark of a nearby tree seemed to wrinkle into a frowning face. But when I looked straight at it, the face was gone.

I told Ralph about this when I got back.

"Sure, you was bein' watched. I'll bet they got tree sprites, nixies, and pixies all over that place. That's why you had to go midday. Nighttime, you woulda been in hot water."

My stomach went cold again. "Ralph, if you're trying to scare me some more, I really don't need it."

"I'm not trying to scare ya! Just clueing you in on what's going on. You said you wanted to be better informed about this stuff, right?"

"Yeah, Right. Thanks. So any nature spirits are all on the side of the Sidhe?"

"Your so-called nature spirits ain't on nobody's side but their own. Most selfish critters around. But they can be bribed, and let's face it, the Sidhe got more to bribe 'em with. So I'd keep an eye out for 'em from now on if I was you."

I put my head in my hands. "How come the longer I'm around you guys, the more of these . . . things keep popping up?"

"They always been there, Princess. You're just able to see them now, now that you're learning about your powers. And you've eaten our food. Better get used to it."

I sighed and closed my eyes. Back before meeting Ralph and Norton, I hadn't even gotten used to being human yet. Now I had to get used to a whole new world of strangeness on top of that. *In my next life*, I thought, *I want to come back as a slug. Something simple that doesn't have to think.*

Sunday and Monday I made and bought props. I spent a lot of time in hobby shops, at Goodwill, and in gardening stores. On posts and bulletin boards, the new poster appeared. In white letters along the top, it read SALT OF THE EARTH. The 3-D picture showed me rising out of a cracked, barren landscape like a weed, holding a scythe in one hand and a hammer in the other. I was in one of those Socialist-realist poses you used to see in communist paintings. Even I had to admit the poster was well done. It would probably get lots of attention. Unfortunately.

Monday evening I stopped by the Per Forma to pick up the props from my previous act.

"So it's going to be a whole new show?" asked Angela.

"Yep. We . . . I like to keep my audience guessing."

"Okay. Fine with us. We've had people coming by already asking about your show tomorrow."

"Yeah? Guess I can promise you a crowd this time, too."

"Great! Hey, Warren wanted me to let you know he's having his May Saturday bash next week. You're welcome to come, if you want."

So. I'd finally arrived. I guess I should have been thrilled, but I wasn't. Especially since it wasn't ex-actly my natural charm and talent that had got me there. "Thanks, Ange. I expect I can make it."

"Good." the phone rang, and she bounced off to answer it, saying, "Well, see you onstage tomorrow. I'm looking forward to seeing what you'll do next."

I wished I'd felt as happy about it as she did.

Tomorrow. Tuesday. May Eve. I went early, so it would be daylight when I got to the Per Forma. There were several tall, attractive people strolling down Penn Avenue as I got off the bus. They watched me as I passed.

Ralph and Norton had rigged up a different kind of protection for me this time. The front of the stage was lined by a small, rustic-style "fence" of wood— the same kind of branches they had used in the wreath on my door. The strangest part was, they'd added salt-encrusted pretzels as part of the fencing. Ralph and Norton seemed to think it was some wonderful joke. I thought it was okay just because it was absurd—you always ought to have something absurd in a performance act, in my opinion.

But from the edge of the stage, the fence continued up the wall and across the track lighting on the ceiling and down the other side, forming a frame. Artistically, I didn't like it. Anything that separates the audience like that allows them to keep a mental wall between themselves and what the artist does. On the other hand, the frame was reassuring—I wasn't ready to die for my art. I guess that makes me a phony. So sue me.

It took me a couple of hours to set up the stage. I had glued lots of those miniature trees that toy railroad buffs use to a set of green army tarps. Around the trees, I put the moss that the hobbyists use to represent bushes and so on. When spread out, with pillows beneath to make them lumpy, the tarps looked like forested hills. At the back of the stage, I lined up some more pillows in dark green cases, folded and positioned to look like distant mountains. I set some blue ribbon, sprinkled with glitter, between some of the "hills" to make streams.

I checked out the effect from the back of the room. Looked pretty nice. Almost a shame, given what I was going to do to it. My costume was very simple this time. A leotard and tights beneath a T-shirt,

denim overalls, and a red bandanna on my head.
Since I didn't need much changing time, I could
watch the audience come in.

I got some surprises. Crystal and Cindy were there.
And Sam! His dark face was easy to spot among the
pale, unsmiling Sidhe. My nerves began to jangle. I
know it sounds strange, being more nervous about
performing in front of someone I liked than performing for a bunch of powerful nonhumans, but
that's shyness for you. One of God's little sick jokes:
the people who need friends the most are given the
most problems in making them.

Then I saw Chris, and my heart seemed to stand
still. He looked relaxed, sprawled out in a chair, staring blandly at the stage. And despite what he had
done, despite what Ralph had told me about him, I
wanted to be near Chris again. I wanted to hear him
whispering my name in my ear, to feel his long,
strong fingers kneading my back. So strong was the
hunger that it took effort to turn my eyes away.
Damn. What has he done to me?

I wondered if he carried a weapon. I wondered if
the pretzel fence/frame would be enough protection
if he did. A sick part of me wondered what it would
be like to die by his hands.

I bet the Sidhe brought him here just to psyche me
out. A small voice in the back of my mind whimpered. *But what if he's really interested in what I do,
what if he wanted to see me again?* I tried to summon
the courage to shut the dressing room door.

Luckily, Angela came by then and noticed me peeking out at the audience. She grinned and gave me a
thumbs-up. "Five minutes!"

I nodded, swallowed hard, and shut the door.
Then I went to stand by the shower. "Ralph! Norton!" I whispered loud.

A gray shadow appeared in the shower stall. "T.J.,
haven't we told you not to call us so close to show
time?"

"Sorry, but Chris is out there! I thought you should know."

"Who?"

"You know, the Ganconwhatever. The Sidhe who whammied me at Point Park."

"Oh. Him. He ain't the biggest of your worries. Forget about him. Now let us get back to work, okay?"

"He's not? But who—"

The gray shadow was gone before I could finish asking just what my biggest worry should be.

The door opened and I jumped around. It was just Angela again. "Warren says any time, T.J."

"Um. Thanks. I'll be right out." I took five deep breaths, grabbed my first prop, and stepped out and onto the stage.

There was no background music this time, just sound effects of birds chirping. As I walked across the stage, I whistled, "Hi ho, hi ho, it's off to work we go." I saw some faces wincing in the audience. I guess the Seelie don't like whistling any more than the Unseelie do.

The prop I was holding was an ordinary weed whacker bought at the local Kmart. I started it up and casually strolled around the stage, happily cutting down all the little trees. I heard nervous laughter in the audience but worked on ignoring it.

After I'd turned all the trees into plastic confetti, I set the cutter aside and, chin in hand, gazed over the newly chopped landscape. A folksy recording of "Old Macdonald Had a Farm" began playing in the background. I took some plastic toy cows and sheep out of a box at far stage left and tossed them, willy-nilly, all over the stage. Then I stopped and looked at the scene again, chin in hand.

I shook my head and went to the box again. I pulled out squares of brown cloth with green and yellow stripes painted on them. I dropped these here and there on the tarp, not caring where they fell.

Again, I stood back to survey my handiwork. Then I bent down and moved the blue ribbons so that each connected to one of the striped patches. I sat and rocked from side to side, grinning, as "This Land Is Your Land" played for a while.

My hands scrabbled around the stage in front of me, until I pretended I had suddenly found something. I brought up from under the tarp a black rock, a gray rock, and reddish-brown rock. I examined these closely, my mouth open in wonder. I began to juggle them, giggling like a child. They fell to the stage (I don't juggle very well), and I reached under the tarps for more.

"Working in a Coal Mine" was the music on as I piled up black rocks in one place, gray rocks in another, and the reddish ones in still another spot. The tarps were starting to get pretty messed up.

Then a gold painted rock came tumbling down from the pillow mountains behind me to land at my feet. I held it up, again pantomiming joy and wonder. Turning around, I acted surprised, as if seeing the mountains for the first time. Pulling a knife out of my pocket, I ran back to them, tearing open the first one I came to. I reached into the pillow and pulled out another gold nugget. I laughed and tossed it in the air, then tore into the next pillow. I pulled out silver-painted rock this time and tossed that away too. The next pillow held a copper-painted rock. I tore into every pillow, pulling out rocks and stuffing and strewing them all over the stage.

"This Land Is Your Land" began playing again, only at double speed. Like a maniacal child, I pulled back the tarps and dug out all sorts of things—hubcaps, knives and forks, toy radios and TVs, clocks, a toaster, old vinyl records, whatever had been cheap at Goodwill. I tossed these everywhere too. I picked up an ugly plastic red rose and tossed it out into the audience.

I lay down on the tarps and rolled around on

them. With a loud "Wheeee!" I made an utter mess of the stage. It was no longer recognizable as any sort of landscape at all. I got up and ran to stage right, where there was a large broom. With this, I swept everything into a pile in the center of the stage.

Now came the pièce de résistance. Kinda literally. A toy wagon rolled onstage carrying a big silver box. Tubes stuck out from the top of the box, and there was a crank on the right-hand side. I took the box out of the wagon and plopped it on top of the pile. I sat right behind the silver box and put my hand on the crank.

Suddenly "Fanfare for the Common Man" swelled in the club, and I began to turn the crank. I rocked and laughed mechanically as I did so, like a windup toy monkey. Steam and smoke began to pour from the chimneys on top of the box.

It was no ordinary steam. There was nothing in it that would hurt people—mortals, that is—unless they had allergies. But there were certain herbal oils mixed in that were bad for the Sidhe; Saint-John's-wort and red verbena, clover and holly juice. Through the mist, I saw the Sidhe rub their eyes and faces. Some of them sneezed and coughed.

Images appeared in the steam, projected from off-stage—human faces, money, cars, televisions, computers, telephones, skyscrapers, freeways, airplanes, the space shuttle. One by one, the Sidhe got up and headed for the door, rubbing their faces. None of them shrieked in anger, like the last time. Tears ran from their eyes, but probably not from sorrow. Their only expressions, when they bothered to look my way, were hard scowls and glares.

At last the steam ran out. I got up and stood back. Solemn organ music began, over which I intoned, "The Earth is the repository of sin. It drags all who worship it into lives of idleness, materialism, and sensuality. The Earth is a false whore, whose only purpose is to serve mankind. When it can no longer serve us . . ." I kicked the silver box over. A ladder descended from the rafters above. I climbed up it, as the music swelled into "There's a Place for Us."

From the catwalks, I called down, "Look what I found! Another planet!" I threw down a watermelon that made a loud thunk as it splattered on the stage. I clambered down the ladder again and squatted beside the watermelon. As the house lights came up, I munched on pieces of the watermelon, spitting out the seeds, smiling and waving bye-bye to the crowd.

There weren't many people left. I didn't see Chris anywhere. Crystal, Cyndi, and Sam all sat at one table. The girls looked baffled. Sam started to applaud, then noticed he was the only one clapping. He stopped and shrugged at me. I shrugged back.

Only after all the Sidhe types were gone did I get Ralph's "All clear" in my ear.

"What about the worst of my worries?" I muttered under my breath.

"What? Oh, the suit. We're keeping him occupied. Be careful when you leave the club, though, just in case. Gotta run. We'll talk again later."

The suit? I'd noticed the guy who had given me the steel rose in the audience, but he hadn't looked threatening. He'd even seemed . . . amused.

Chapter 16

I used the large broom to sweep the debris on the stage into a bin at the side. I felt different than I had at the end of the last performance. I wasn't nearly as drained or shook up. Maybe I was getting used to this thaumaturgy stuff. It helped that there weren't any surprises. And then I realized, the "side effect" that had caused such problems in the first act had never showed up this time. In fact, I hadn't felt that funny energy in the chest in a while. I wondered if it had just faded, or if maybe something had cured me of it. Maybe the prune jack, which I could easily believe could drive off anything, from the side effect to the common cold.

Crystal and Cyndi walked up as I swept. "Hi, T.J.," said Crystal. "That was, um, really interesting. I mean, I don't know if I exactly get it, but the special effects were really neat."

I didn't do it for you. I smiled at her. "Thanks. Thanks to both of you for coming."

"Oh, no problem. We were really curious, you know. After the article."

Cyndi said, "The air in here really smells nice. What was in that smoke, anyway? Maybe you could sell it as air freshener."

"Or perfume," added Crystal.

"Uh, yeah. I'll think about that." I could see the ads now: Ralph and Norton posing naked, gray and wrinkled skin glistening between the pages of *Allure* magazine, holding bottles of Elfbane Parfum.

"Why did everybody else leave so early?" said Crystal.

"I think they had a party to go to," I said, starting to sweep again.

"Party? Where? Think we could crash it? Some of those guys were really cute."

"I dunno. Some park somewhere. You'll have to ask one of them." The idea of one of them dancing with Chris was laughable . . . and I didn't like it.

"Schenley Park," said Angela, walking up to us. "Apparently it was supposed to be at Frick, but something made them change venue at the last minute. One of those willowy blondes sweet-talked Warren into going, so I don't see why you couldn't." I'm not usually good at people vibes, but I got the distinct impression I wasn't the only one feeling jealous.

"Well," said Cyndi, "guess we'll go check it out. Nice seeing you, and your act. Maybe we'll catch the next one too."

Won't hold my breath. "Okay," I said. "See you."

"By the way," said Angela, holding out an envelope to me, "here's your percentage of the house. You should've gotten paid last time, but Warren was being a bear about the bookkeeping. So this is for both performances."

I took the envelope. It held a thick wad of bills. "How much is it?"

"About a hundred. Most of it's from tonight. There's a slip in there stating the exact amount."

"Wow!"

"Congratulations," said Sam, patiently standing nearby.

"Thanks," I said to both of them and put the envelope in my overalls pocket.

"You deserve it, kid," said Angela. "I owe you one. I'll check to see when our next open slot is and let you know, okay?"

"Okay."

Angela winked and strolled off. Sam said, "Hey, got any plans for after you're done here?"

"Not really. Why?"

He shrugged. "Thought you might like to go out for coffee or something. Do some catching up. Been a while since we talked."

I almost dropped the broom. *Sam's asking me out. Sorta. Wow. Is my luck fairy making up for lost time or what?* "Uh, sure! Love to."

"Great." His smile was a lot warmer than Chris's.

"Cool," I said. "Just let me finish up and I'll be right with you."

As we left the Per Forma, I was really glad to have Sam beside me. I kept glancing at dark shadows, looking for people with silvery eyes. Especially one in a gray suit.

"You okay, T.J?"

"Huh? Yeah, why?"

"You just seem a little nervous, that's all."

"Just post-performance jitters. You know, adrenaline and stuff."

"Yeah, I know the feeling. Lasts about half an hour and then you crash."

"Just remember to catch me before I hit the ground, okay?"

"For a chance to hold you in my arms, anything."

I blushed and wondered if he was kidding.

We ended up at a tiny Chinese cafe about a block from the club. I hadn't gotten around to eating dinner before the show, and I was starving. We ordered hot and sour soup, pot stickers, spring rolls, and tea.

"I gotta say, T.J., either you've gotten more subtle in your work or you changed your tune while I wasn't looking."

"What?" My brain wasn't exactly firing on all cylinders.

"I mean, you used to be really an out-front, in-your-face tree-hugger. With what you seemed to be saying up there on the stage tonight, you almost seem to be leaning the other way. Or maybe you were being sarcastic. I couldn't tell. Then again, maybe that's what you wanted."

I opened my mouth, shut it. Then said, "I'm aiming at a different audience these days."

"Yeah, I noticed. That was quite a crowd you had there. They didn't seem to be happy when they left, though."

"Performance art isn't about making people happy."

"Yeah, yeah, I know. But is it making T.J. happy?"

I stared down at the table. "It's what I've always wanted to do."

"Sounds like you aren't so sure anymore."

I gazed up at the plastic Chinese dragon on the wall. "I dunno. Sometimes success has a big price tag."

"Huh. Hope I get to see that tag someday." He frowned at me a moment. "Where'd you get that scar on your cheek?"

My hand jumped up to my face. "What? This? Stage makeup," I lied quickly. "Really tricky to get off, you know?"

"Uh-huh," Sam grunted. I don't think he believed me. "Did you, uh, ever make it to the health service, or shouldn't I ask?"

"Been too busy."

"Yeah. Well, you seem more, I dunno, connected. Maybe working more pulled you out of whatever condition you were in."

"Yeah, maybe." I needed to change the subject. "So how did *Midsummer* go?"

Sam shrugged. "It went okay, I guess. I don't think people really know how to react to Shakespeare anymore. They just watch it because it makes them feel cultured. Laura, the director, was saying I should think about doing some tech work this summer. Lighting and shit like that. She says I got the knack.

Says a black tech man can just about write his own ticket these days."

"Huh." I'd thought it was just the warmth of the tea, but suddenly I recognized a certain feeling in the chest. Out of nowhere, I said, "I think Warren was looking for a tech guy for the Per Forma. You want me to give him your name?" *Ulp. So the side effect hasn't gone away after all. I don't even know if Warren really needs a tech guy.*

Sam's eyes widened. "Would you? Hey, thanks. I'd appreciate it. Do they pay okay?"

My turn to shrug. "I guess that's up to Warren. Show him you're worth it and he'll pay accordingly." The weird thing was that I wasn't sure if I was disappointed that I still had the side effect or glad.

The bill arrived with the usual pair of fortune cookies. Sam cracked his open fist.

"What's yours say, Sam?"

" 'Reach for your dreams and success will follow.' "

"Between the sheets," I added in the usual game.

"There's a thought," said Sam with a wink. "What's yours?"

I cracked it open and fished out the slip of paper. " 'Your life is full of surprises.' Man, ain't that the truth."

"Not sure if you'd want surprises between the sheets."

"Depends on the surprise."

Sam looked up with a slight frown. A slim, pale arm descended in front of me, putting another piece of paper on my plate. I turned my head—it was Chris. My heart filled with warm ice as he rested his long fingers on my shoulder.

"Another act, sweet Tif, to pierce our souls," he said in his smooth, resonant voice. "As e're, bold and unforgettable. We must meet again and speak of it." Chris turned to Sam, gave him a slight, gentlemanly bow, and departed. My hand went to my shoulder, too late to keep his fingers there.

"Boyfriend of yours?" Sam said, one eyebrow arched.

"No." I stared with dread at the paper on my plate. "Just someone I met a few days ago."

"He seems awfully interested in you. He was sitting at the table behind us this whole time."

"He was?" It surprised me that I could feel joy and terror at the same time.

"Yep. You aren't in some kind of trouble, are you? This guy stalking you?"

"No. Not exactly." I picked up the paper, my hand shaking. I unfolded it. In elegant calligraphy, it read:

Those who heed not warnings doom themselves.
My kin have shown you patience and forbearance.
Such kindness hath its limit. 'Twill not last.
Yet, on your behalf, I have begged mercy.
And you are granted one last, precious chance.
Meet me this night, past midnight, in the court
yard of Black Crystal Tower, nigh the Point.
Hold you this missive close and speak my name.
No harm will befall you thus, I swear.
Do not fail, sweet Tiffany, I pray you.
You have not earned the blows they mean to give.

Chris

Sam snatched the note out of my trembling fingers and read it. "What kind of deep shit are you in, girl?"

I shook my head. "It's hard to explain. Some people don't like what I'm doing."

"You mean your performances?"

I nodded.

"Who? Religious Right nuts?"

"No. I guess you could say they're eco-freaks."

"Like Greenpeace?"

"More like Earth Firsters. You know, plants before people?"

"Oh. The real fringe. So somehow you pissed them off."

"I was *trying* to piss them off. Well, not *them*, exactly. But they ended up getting mad anyway. Worked too well, I guess."

Sam threw the note back on the table in disgust. "You know, there's something I don't get about all this ecology shit. It's like, both sides—the tree-huggers and the big corporations and labor—all of them are really reaching for the past. The eco-freaks want a world before people, and the corporate honchos want the world of the mega-moguls, like Pittsburgh used to be. Nobody's dealing with reality, the way the world really is and is gonna have to be. Now, some of us know there's no point in looking to the past—it was not a good place to live for some folks, if you know what I'm sayin'. My family's got stories that would make your skin crawl. We gotta hope for changes ahead. Look to the future. Not this wishful-thinking shit."

I wrapped my hands around the warm teacup. "You got a point, Sam. But some people are doing some powerful wishing." I drained the last of my tea. The leaves on the bottom of the cup made an interesting pattern, but I couldn't read it.

That was something that had bothered me about the act. Sure, it was in the face of the Sidhe, but it wasn't saying anything nice about humanity either. I wondered if the Unseelie, like Ralph and Norton, were really on the mortals' side, or if they were just acting like they were.

Sam got up to pay the bill. "You want a ride home?"

"Yeah, I'd like that. Thanks."

In his car, on the way to my place, he said, "So, you gonna meet this Chris fucker?"

"Not unless I can figure out what he means by 'the courtyard of Black Crystal Tower'."

"Sounds like something out of *Hercules* or *Xena:*

Warrior Princess." After a moment Sam began to laugh.

"What? What's so funny?"

"C'mon, think about it. What in downtown Pittsburgh looks like a black glass castle tower?"

I thought. "Oh. PPG Place."

"You got it. I bet that's what he means."

"Yeah, I bet you're right."

"But you're not gonna meet him, are you?"

"I dunno."

"He sounds like a real nut case. I'd blow it off, if I were you. Or take some friends with you. Friends with guns."

"Yeah. Maybe."

"I'll come along, if you want me to."

God, no. I don't want to get him involved in this. "No, I think I'll just blow it off, like you said. You're right, he's probably a nut, just trying to scare me."

"Yeah, well, if he starts giving you trouble, you let me know, okay?"

"Okay, Sam. I will."

We drove the rest of the way to Cypress Street in silence. Sam managed to find a parking space right in front of the building. Without my asking, he got out of the car with me and walked me up the stairs. At the apartment door, as I turned to ask him if he wanted to come in, we heard someone moving inside. And it sounded like the TV was on.

"Shit," I said softly. *Probably Ralph and Norton come to do a victory dance again.*

"You got a roommate?" said Sam.

"No."

"Think we oughta leave and call the cops?"

"No! I mean, it could be a couple of friends of mine dropped by. They have a key." I got mine out and quickly, if clumsily, unlocked the door. Sam stood to the side, back to the wall, like a guy on a cop show.

I opened the door a crack and peeked in. The couch

had been moved and someone was sitting on it, silhou-
etted in the television glare. It wasn't Ralph or Norton. I swallowed hard and stepped in.

The person turned and stood. "Oh, there you are,
Tiffany. I was wondering when you'd be getting in."

"Mom?!"

Chapter 17

"You look surprised, dear. Didn't you get my phone message? I told you I'd be coming back."

"Um, yeah. I mean, I just didn't expect you so soon." I glanced around the apartment for signs of Ralph and Norton, but the place was clean. *Luigi must have been here.*

Sam stepped in behind me. "Everything okay?"

"Sam, this is my mom. Mom, this is my friend Sam Waters."

"Evening, Mrs. Kaminski."

"Very pleased to meet you, Sam." She said it with a warm smile. She wasn't freaked at all. After a moment of awkward silence, she said to me, "Well, don't I get a hug hello?"

"Um, sure." I let her come over and hug me while I tried to recover from the shock.

Sam said, "I, uh, guess I oughta leave and let you two do some catching up."

"Yeah, guess so," I said. I walked him out the door.

"You gonna be okay?" Sam said softly. "You look like you been hit by a brick."

"I feel like it. I didn't need this. Not on top of everything else."

"Hey, families exist to be inconvenient. Well, take care, girl. You need anything, just let me know."

"I will, thanks."

His hug was a lot nicer than Mom's, but I didn't

get a kiss good night. Oh, well. I watched him go down the stairs, took a deep breath, and went back inside.

"When did you get in?" I said, just to say something.

"Early this evening. I called from Carnegie to give you warning, but I see you haven't been home for a while."

"I was doing a performance this evening. Why is the couch scootched back?"

"So I can pull out the hide-a-bed. That's better than having you sleep on the floor, isn't it?"

"Oh. Yeah. Of course." *Shit.* I suddenly felt like an alien in my own home. I mean, I never felt it was really my place, but now that *she* was here, it was like she left territorial markings all over. The place was totally *hers* again. I didn't know where to sit or stand, or be. I was emotionally homeless.

"Well. Take off your coat and stay a while."

"Yeah." I slipped off my jacket and draped it over the back of the sofa. Then, after another awkward moment, I sat on the stool at the kitchen island counter, just to keep a safe spread of Formica between me and her.

She sat on the arm of the couch. "Listen, Tiffany—"

"I keep telling you not to call me that, Mom!"

"I'm sorry. I'd forgotten. T.J. Look, I know this won't be the most comfortable arrangement for a while, but it's not like I can afford another apartment, or three months of hotel bills."

"I know. I understand."

"Besides, now don't be alarmed, dear, but I had some minor chest pain about a week ago, and while I hope it will prove to be nothing, you never know. I'm going to have some tests done at the medical center, and you know my insurance won't cover those."

I think my jaw must have dropped onto the counter.

Oh, God. Did I hurt her too, the same time I was voo-dooing the elf queen? I thought about asking her what night it happened but decided I didn't want to know.

"Oh, dear. I'm sorry. This is a lot to drop on you all at once, isn't it?"

I ran my hands through my hair. "No. Well, yeah. But I've been really wrapped up in stuff, Mom. I haven't been paying a lot of attention to real-world things lately."

"Oh. Of course. You must have had finals by now. How did your classes go, dear?"

I hated the way she could make me feel twelve years old with just a few words. Hated it. I wanted to yell at her, *All the time I was living with Dad, you wanted as little to do with being a mom as possible. But now that I'm here, you put on the mommy act. It's a little late, isn't it?* Good thing the side effect wasn't happening right now or God knows what I would have spewed out. "Fine. I dunno. I haven't gotten my grades yet. Okay, I guess."

"My, you are distracted these days."

"I've been doing art, Mom. Art requires mind-space, you know." *And, boy, have I got a lot to think about now.*

"Of course," she murmured. A slight frown appeared between her fine, graying brows. "You're still doing your performance art, then?"

She made it sound like it was a little hobby of mine. "Yep. I'm getting steady gigs now. Good audiences, too." I was about to tell her a little bit about the Per Forma when she crossed her arms and glanced down at the floor, scuffing one foot on the rug. I knew those gestures. *Uh-oh. Lecture coming.*

"T.J., now that classes are over at Pitt, have you given any thought to getting a summer job? Even regular actors, you know, find fill-in work as waiters or typists or something."

I glared at her. "I have a job. I've been onstage at

the Per Forma twice this month and they want me back again next week."

"Oh. Does that pay at all well?"

"I got around a hundred dollars tonight, for the last two weeks."

"Hmmm. I see. But even if you work every week, two hundred dollars a month would be hard to live on, don't you think?"

"What? I don't understand."

She sighed and sat down on the edge of the couch. "I was thinking a lot about you on the drive up from Georgia. I know you've gone through a rough year since your father passed away. And I've been happy to let you stay here without paying rent while you pulled yourself together. I thought I was doing the right thing. But it has been a year . . . and, well, you haven't made quite the recovery I'd hoped."

"What do you mean?" I also hated the way she made me feel like one of her anthropology subjects, an object of study.

"Well, perhaps it's time you started taking a little responsibility for your life. You know, learn how to get and keep a job, how to get an apartment, and so on. These things are an important part of being grown up. I'm afraid your father may have spoiled you by not teaching you—"

"He did not spoil me!"

"All right, I was out of line. I'm sorry. I know he's still a hero to you. Sometimes I've wished I could have inspired that kind of worship in you."

There was that bitterness in her voice again; it showed up anytime she talked about Dad. *Maybe if you'd been around more, visited more after the divorce,* I thought.

"Thank you, by the way, for keeping the place so tidy. I confess, I was worried about what I'd find when I got back."

"I had help," I said with a tight smile.

She picked up an empty wineglass from the coffee

table and frowned at it. "You know, it's funny, I could swear this was full a minute ago."

Yep. Luigi was here, all right.

She shook her head. "I'm getting forgetful in my old age. Well. We can talk more about future plans in the morning. I've put out sheets and a pillow for the hide-a-bed. I get up at six these days, so I can't guarantee not to wake you."

"Uh-huh." *Shit. This is gonna be impossible!* I stomped to the bedroom and opened the closet. Already my clothes had been pushed far to the side to make room for Mom's stuff. I took down my black leather jacket and put it on.

"T.J., what are you doing?"

"I gotta go, Mom. I forgot, there's somebody I gotta meet."

"You're going out again tonight? But it's already after eleven."

And suddenly I felt it . . . the growing heat in the chest, the gathering of radiant energy in my heart that told me the side effect was about to manifest itself. Part of me felt elated, ready for the release of all that ugly emotional shit I had building up inside, ready to fling it right at her. "Mom?"

"Yes?"

What came out was, "I forgive you."

"What?"

I was so confused, so surprised, that I didn't answer her. I just ran out the front door and slammed it behind me. I ran down and stepped out onto Cypress, not having a plan of what exactly I was doing. I felt disappointed, hurt, and more than a little scared. *How could I say that when there was so much important stuff to say?* There was a loud *BLAAAAAT!* behind me. I shrieked and spun around.

Ralph and Norton stood there, wearing party hats, noisemakers in their hands.

"Hey, I didn't call for you guys!"

"You don't hafta," said Ralph. "It's May Eve. We

can go wherever we wanna tonight. Just like the Seelie folk."

"Yeah, party time!" said Norton. "We woulda
joined ya sooner to celebrate, but you haven't been
alone."

"So's that your mother up there?" said Ralph, with
a jerk of his head back toward the apartment.

"Yeah. That's her all right."

"Looked like she was moving in."

"She is, for the summer," I said. "But it's her place,
not mine, so I don't have much say-so about it."

"Want us to drive her out?" said Norton.

"What? No! I mean, I don't like it, but it is her
place. She pays for it. That wouldn't be fair."

"So what are you gonna do? It's gonna be kinda
hard for you and us to do our work with her
around," said Ralph.

"I know. I don't know. Um, is there some chance
that I could maybe go Under the Hill with you guys?
Just now and then, like to sleep?"

Ralph shook his head. "Nice try, kid, but not a
good idea. Like we told ya, time works different
there. You think you sleep eight hours—you come
back up and it's been ten years. Or maybe a hundred.
Or maybe you won't feel like coming back at all. I
mean, we're flattered you like our place, an'at, but
you oughta know what you'd be choosing."

"Can't you guys use clocks or something? You
know, like they have at some TV news stations that
show the time in different places, so you could
keep track?"

"Clocks!" said Norton, laughing and holding his
sides. "She thinks we can use clocks!"

"Here's what a clock does Under the Hill," said
Ralph. He waved his twiggy hands and an illusion
appeared of a clock face. The hour and minute hands
were spinning forward and backward, out of control.
With a pop, the illusion disappeared.

"Okay, I get the idea," I grumbled. "Listen, guys,

I gotta tell you. That side effect from the tea you
gave me a while back—it's still happening. And it's
making me say really weird things. Not what I think
I'm gonna say, but something else entirely."

"Like what, T.J.?"

"All sorts of things. Sometimes good things. Good
for other people, that is. Sometimes just weird. Like
just now, I told my mother I forgave her."

"Forgave her for what?" asked Norton.

"That's just it. I don't know," I said, frowning. Or
rather I suspect part of me did know and I didn't
like it. I didn't want to give up my hate, give up my
anger. *That's a part of who I am, isn't it? I've got legiti-
mate reasons for it. Don't I have a right to it?*

"Sorry, but like I said, we can't help you there,"
said Ralph. "We ain't no pharmacologists. But we
could rig up a silencing spell for ya or something if
it gets real bad."

"No, thanks. Guess I'll just live with it." *Along with
the hunger to go underground and this scar on my cheek.*
I shivered. The night felt cold and dark and closing
in on me. "Um, so, guys, if all you people can be
wherever you want tonight, what's to protect me
from the Sidhe sending someone to do me in for
getting in their face again?"

"Because it's party time! They wouldn't wanna
spoil their fun making trouble on their big night
out."

"Yeah, they might. I saw Chris again. He gave me
this." I pulled his note out of my jeans pocket and
showed it to them.

Ralph made a low whistle. "Looks like they
mean business."

"Smells like a trap to me," said Norton.

"Is PPG Place their turf?" I asked.

"Naw, that's neutral territory," said Ralph.

"What will they do to me if I don't go?"

"Nothin' if we can help it," said Ralph.

"What if you *can't* help it?"

Ralph puffed air out of his nonexistent lips. "All sorts of things. But you don't need to think about that, T.J. We got 'em running scared, that's all. They're getting desperate."

I sighed. "Well, I'm scared too. Listen, if Chris has some sort of deal to offer, I think I oughta talk to him. Are you guys willing to go along as protection or not?"

Ralph and Norton looked at each other. "The trap isn't for you, T. J.," said Norton. "The trap is for us. They're hoping we'll come along with you so's they can nab us."

"So what you're saying is, you can't protect me?"

Ralph grimaced. "Look, T.J., we don't know what this Chris guy's game is. The Sidhe do stand by their word, one of the few good things about 'em, and if he says he won't hurt you, he won't. But they're slippery, and you gotta pay careful attention to what they say and don't say. Even if he offers to cut you a deal, it might not be what you think it is."

"Yeah," said Norton, "he might make you turn us in or something."

"I wouldn't do that."

"We know you wouldn't plan to, T.J., but these guys got a lotta tricks up their sleeve. Now maybe . . ." Ralph put his hand to his chin and paced up and down the sidewalk a little. "Just maybe we can use what he tells you to our advantage. Maybe we can find out where the factions are now among the Sidhe. Anything they love more than tormenting morts, it's politics. Sounds like this Chris guy may know what's going on. We might be able to use what he knows to double-cross 'em."

"You want me to spy for you?"

"Yeah," said Ralph, his eyes lighting up. "There's a thought. If you can get 'em to think you're leaning toward their side."

I didn't like the way this talk was going. "I told

you, I'd make a terrible spy. Remember what happened at Point Park?''

"That's 'cause you were unprepared, that's all.''

"I don't even know what you want me to find out.''

"Their weaknesses, Princess—you know.''

"Then we can really stick it to 'em,'' said Norton.

"I thought we already did that,'' I grumbled. "Through the performances.''

"Naw, that was just a love pat, compared to what we'd like to do. Just a wake-up call. Now we gotta drive 'em back Under the Hill and slam the door.''

"Why does this agenda of yours keep changing every time I turn around?''

"Hey, hey, hey! We ain't changed our agenda. You ain't been paying attention, that's all. Didn't we tell ya this was gonna be a war? The little guys against the hoity-toits?''

"Well, it's not a very organized one.''

"Hey, we just been going through a—whatdaya-callit, Norton?''

"A learning process,'' Norton said carefully.

"Yeah. A learning process. It's not like we do this sorta thing every year, ya know. But now we've found out what we can get away with. So now we push harder. And we keep pushing while the Sidhe are off balance. And we drive them out of Pittsburgh so's they can't come back.''

"And just how are we going to do that?'' I asked.

"We're working on it. So, okay, you go meet with this Chris fella and find out what his line is. Pay real careful attention to what he says. But whatever you do, don't go anywhere with him. Stay on neutral ground. You got that?''

"I got it.''

"Good.'' Ralph handed the note back to me. "You're a brave kid, T.J. I knew we had the best. Worst comes to worst, you can try to call us. We'll rescue you if we can.''

I didn't like the sound of that either. I pocketed the note and saluted. "Purple Power Ranger is on the case."

"Huh?"

"Never mind. See you guys later."

"Call us soon as it's over. Anything we can do for you, meantime?"

"Yeah. Find me a new place to live."

"You got it." Ralph and Norton did a final blast on their noisemakers and disappeared.

Chapter 18

The bus was nearly empty as I rode it downtown. In the darkness beyond the windows, a few buildings were selected by the moonlight to glow, bone-white, amid the shadows.

I stared straight ahead at the seat in front of me. I felt adrift. It was like Mom's returning shook me up more than anything the Sidhe might do, and I resented her for it. *What's wrong with me?* I wondered. *I've thought of leaving Mom's place before. Getting a place of my own. Why don't I want to now? What would I be giving up? What don't I want to let go of?"*

The still voice inside answered me all too clearly. With my dad dead and gone, all I had left of my past was Mom, her place, her stuff. The past? Is that it? Am I like all those people Sam talked about, wanting to go back to some rosy time, not wanting to look ahead? Thinking about where I would live now was like thinking about stepping off a twenty-story building.

I hunkered down in my oversized jacket and wished I had a teddy bear. *So that's it. I don't want to grow up. If that's true, Ralph and Norton are wrong. I'm not brave. I'm too chicken to even face my own future.*

We entered the Golden Triangle, the western point of downtown Pittsburgh. Strange stone faces and stone lion heads stared down from building cornices at me. Lots of lion heads on Pittsburgh buildings. I wondered why. The Allegheny County Jail, with its massive stone wall and towers, seemed an ancient fortress transported here from another time. I felt small and truly on my own. I knew it wouldn't be good to face Chris while I was feeling insecure, but I didn't seem to have any choice.

The driver gave me a dubious look as I got off at Market Square. Downtown, so far as I knew, was neutral territory for the local gangs. Which didn't mean fights didn't happen. I pulled my black leather jacket tight across my shoulders and tried to look bad. I needn't have bothered. The few knots of kids standing here and there were too involved with each other, joking and laughing. They didn't even notice me.

I strolled the half-block south into PPG Place. Sam had it right—the huge central plaza did look like the courtyard of some strange, fantastic palace. On three sides of the plaza were modest-size buildings, all faced with dark, silvery plates of glass, topped with pointy towerlike projections. Their entrances were framed by tall, angular archways. To the east was the main tower itself, rising forty stories high into the night sky. The moon was reflected hundreds of times on its surface.

I pulled the note out of my pocket and walked toward the center of the plaza. A squat stone obelisk, supported by four stone balls on a square stone pedestal, stood there. "Chris?" I said softly.

He stepped out from behind the obelisk as though he had been waiting for me. He also was dressed in a black leather jacket and leather pants and boots. Had to admit, he looked way cool. "Well met again, sweet Tiffany."

"I'm not your 'sweet' and don't call me Tiffany."

He held out his arms. "I cry you mercy. If such terms mislike you, I forgo them. Let this be a happy meeting. A perfect place for our trysting, is this not?"

I stuffed my hands in my jacket pockets to hide my trembling. "I was told this is neutral territory to you guys."

"It is. Consecrate only to Mammon and his ilk."

"Who's Mammon?"

"The soul of Avarice, in mortal ken."

"Whatever. So, okay, I'm here. What did you want to talk about?"

"Why, you are what I truly wished to speak on. And your future, sith you shall have one."

I shuddered. As New Agers would say, the karmic forces were all too much in agreement tonight. "I was just thinking about my future myself. But why should you care?"

"You have been told, perhaps, we do not value mortal qualities and human skill. But we have oft admired great gifts or virtue among your kind who dwell above the Hill. You have evinced yourself a soul of courage, if unwisely used and poorly led. In thaumaturgy, you have shown a talent, yet 'tis poorly taught in you," Chris said. "You are due more honorable care."

"Was it honorable to weasel my real name out of me and try to ruin my self-esteem?"

Chris turned away from me and sighed. " 'Twas not my wish to prick you so. I was compelled to't."

"You were just following orders."

"You state the matter neatly. 'Twas hoped you would forsake your foolish acts and turn to other things that better suit."

"So, it's true. I do scare you people."

He looked at me sidelong, over his shoulder. "Do not mistake disquietude for fear. What you have done, thus far, has taxed us not; no more than the mere buzzing of a fly. And we have waved our hands to keep you distant. Do not compel us now to slap you down."

"Us? Sounds like you're speaking for everybody. Do all of you hate me now?"

Chris shrugged. "There is variance among us, as with mortal hearts. Hate? That is a word that I am loath to use."

"You answer by not answering. For all I know, you're bluffing. You and your Sidhe-folk might have already hit me with your best shot and it didn't work."

He turned to face me, wearing an incredulous smile. "The courageous puppy barks. Then I shall bare my teeth also." He walked slowly toward me. "There are those among us, sweet, more cold than I. There is one, whom you have met, who at a touch would wither you or make you deadly ill. 'Twould please him to do thus. There are others who would hold you fast in ice, or stone, or undersea, for their disport. Some, with songs so fair 'twould drive you mad, and some would fain enslave you for their lust. I am all that stands 'tween you and these."

"No, you're not. I have other . . . protection."

"Ah, now we come to't. We know 'twas not your fancy to arise nipping at our heels to raise our ire. Those of my kin may yet become convinced to think you blameless. To do so, we must know who set you on. Tell me the names of those who have misled you, and you shall be absolved of all offense."

My jaws froze shut. I now knew that Ralph and Norton had whammied me not to be able to betray them. And that was my out. "I can't tell you," I said. "I don't know their names."

Chris stared at me for a moment. Then he began to laugh. "Certes, your keepers are not common fools. Their true names they would leave unknown to you. It matters not. Say but those words by which you summon them. The rest we will uncover for ourselves."

Damn. I looked down at the pavement stones and said nothing.

I felt his hand under my chin, lifting my face until my eyes met his. His fair brows rose. "You have been . . . altered."

"You mean the scar?"

"I speak of things beneath, not on, the surface."

Maybe he'll know. What can I lose? "I . . . there was this herbal tea I was given. It was supposed to heal me, but it has a strange side effect. Do you know what it is?"

"What manner of effect is't you speak of?"

"I get all warm in my chest and then I say strange things."

His gaze bore into me, and I felt my arms and legs go stiff with fear. *This was a mistake. I should never have mentioned it.*

Chris closed his eyes at last, with laughter sad and dark. "Alas, sweet Tif, your healing is a curse."

"A curse!"

"Your counselors are either fools or more cruel than I."

"What? What kind of curse?"

"You speak such truths as you are meant to hear. You do such good as your soul is meant to bear."

I couldn't tell if he was quoting something or what. "I don't understand."

"You will, sweet Tif, one day, and will rue it. But I am remiss. I have spoke of poison but no cake. The Sidhe are not unkind to those who aid us. I see, as well, that you have tasted of fey foodstuff."

"How do you know?"

" 'Tis marked clear upon you. Forever you will hunger for our world." He stepped back, toward the obelisk. Reaching to one edge of the pedestal, Chris pulled something aside as if it were a door. And the obelisk, indeed, became a doorway. Through it I could see the night land I had entered Under the Hill—where the trees glimmered in starlight and distant music tugged at my heart.

I took a step toward it.

"See, it calls you." Chris flung his arm out to grasp my shoulder, barring me from entering. "Tell us your advisers' names, and you shall have a home forever with the Sidhe beneath the Hill. You may taste of all our pleasures, sing and dance to elvensong. Every dream and wish be answered"—he leaned low and said softly in my ear—"and all desires fulfilled."

And I felt all those desires at once. I desperately longed to enter that world, drink their wine, hear their songs, dance to their music, lie under the stars with Chris in my arms—*Bastard! It's like teasing a junkie by holding out a fix.* I shook myself out of his grasp and turned away.

I heard him sigh behind me. "What more may we yet offer?"

"Respect."

"You shall have it."

"I don't believe you."

"By Oak and Thorn, what oaths must I bespeak you?"

I turned back to face him. "Look, it doesn't matter. I shook hands on a contract with . . . with those who are helping me. I can't break it."

Chris tilted his head. "Hold they you fast with threats upon your life?"

"No. They just said it would make them mad. Besides, they saved my life once. And they've helped my career."

Chris laughed, but when he looked back at me, his eyes were again sad. "Know you for certain that their timely rescue was not intended long before the time?"

"What? You mean a setup? They couldn't have . . . wouldn't do that!"

"Would they not? And it is our attendance on your plays that have brought you now the fame you sought. Had you not brought your act to our attention, who perchance would your admirers be?"

I had no argument for that. So I changed the subject. "Anyway, how can you ask me, a mortal, to join with you when your plan is to wipe mortals off the face of the earth?"

Chris's eyes opened wide. "Who is't speaks this vile calumny? Have I not said we value mortalkind?"

"Sure you do. As playthings."

"A hit. 'Tis partly true, we do. And 'tis true we love the forest wild. But there is much we give one to the other. Is not your world more rich because of us?"

"If you like mortals so much, how come your kind hide behind fairy tales? Why not come right out in the open and show yourselves?"

Chris sat on the stone pedestal, chin resting on his hand. "That would do more harm than good, for we have seen what mortals do e'en to their own kind. As your friend of dusky hue can well relate. We prefer to keep our friendships few."

Point to their side. "Well," I said with a shrug, "I guess we'd better call it a draw. You haven't convinced me. And I don't think I could betray my friends, even if I wanted to."

"Once within our fold, no one may harm you."

"Like I said, I'm not convinced. Look, I'm dealing with a lot of things right now, okay? Your threats and bribes aren't helping. So I'll just go and think about what you've said and I'll get back to you." I turned my back and started to walk away.

"Tif—T.J.!"

I stopped. "What?"

Chris leapt off the stone pedestal. He shook his head, laughing without humor. "My kin do chide me right for my kind heart." He stopped and tilted his head as if listening to something. When he looked at me again, his face was colder and more distant. He raised one pale hand and pointed at me. "My Queen hath gi'en the order. Hear me, then, and tremble. 'Tis no game. Throughout this month, my kinfolk wander freely. But at May's end, we once more quit the world. And at that hour, you will be coming with us. Pray, let it be as friend and not as foe."

"What order? What is this, more threats? Just how are you gonna take me with you if I don't want to go?"

Chris didn't answer. He just turned, walked into the obelisk, and disappeared.

"Oh, I'm soooo scared," I said. Because I was.

Chapter 19

Mist hovered near the street lamps in Market Square. I crossed the cobbled square, heading for the bus stop on Fifth, feeling like I'd accomplished nothing. I hadn't lost, but I hadn't won. I'd just gotten riddles about my side effect. And there was that new threat to worry about.

I heard a pop behind me. "Hiya, kid."

I whirled around. "Ralph! You shouldn't be here. Chris might be watching."

"Naw. We'd know it if he was. So how'd it go?"

I stuffed my hands into my jacket pockets. "I'm a lousy double agent."

"Aw, don't be so negative, T.J. Tell us what happened. You didn't give in to 'em, didja?"

"Still here, aren't I?"

"We knew we could count on you. What'd ya learn?"

"Not much. He was pretty cagey. He said there were different opinions among them, but he didn't name any factions. He implied he was the only Sidhe on my side and wanted to help me. But I guess he was lying, huh?"

Ralph shrugged. "Who knows? Maybe he is sweet on you. These high 'n mighties take some weird fancies sometimes. Like I told you, they're sick puppies. But what did they say?"

Something inside went *hop* when Ralph said Chris might like me. *Just who is the sick puppy here?* "The usual carrot-and-stick stuff," I said. "If I'd tell them how I call you, they'd give me anything I wanted, blah, blah, blah."

"That's typical," said Ralph.

"I asked him about the side effect, and he said something about it being a curse."

Ralph rolled his eyes. "Natch he's gonna put the worst spin on things. Any spell can be looked at as a curse. What else? No ulty-matums or nothing?"

"Well, he got real strange before he left and said that at the end of this month, one way or another, I'd be going under the Hill with the Sidhe. That the Queen had ordered it."

"Heh. Don't she wish."

"Why would they do that?"

"Like I said, the Sidhe like unusual things. They collect mortals with special talents the way you morts collect butterflies. You've shown you've got special talent, so they wanna study you. Close up and personal."

"Oh. Can you stop them from snatching me?"

"Sure. Lotsa ways. Meanwhile, we got some places you can stay the night."

"Oh, good. Where?"

"There's some space under the Sixth Street Bridge. And an abandoned mill down by Coraopolis—"

"Hey! Do you want me to live like a homeless bum?"

Ralph looked offended. "Norton and me live in places like that, when we ain't Under the Hill. Besides, I thought you liked bridges."

"Not to sleep under, thank you." I sighed and rubbed my face. "Well, thanks anyway, but I guess I'll just stay at Mom's for now. I'm too used to soft beds."

"Suit yourself. You sure you don't want us to make your mom vamoose? We'd only have to scare her a little."

"You don't know my mom. She's stubborn, and

she doesn't scare easy. She doesn't believe in ghosts or . . . you guys."

"Hey, it's the ones who don't believe that scare the easiest. Could be fun."

"I said forget it!"

"Okay, okay, I was just joshing ya."

"None of you people take us morts seriously, do you? Seelie or Unseelie, we humans are all just toys to you."

Ralph raised his twiggy hands in protest. "You got us all wrong, T.J. You're important to us! Really! Don't be so touchy, Princess."

"And another thing. Chris hinted that maybe that attack on me back when I first met you might have been arranged. Maybe you planned it to get me to trust you."

Ralph gaped in exaggerated shock. "He didn't! That mud-worm, that bum-sore, that nose-in-the-air wood shark! How dare he say such a thing!"

"But is it true?"

"I can understand why you're upset, hearing such tripe. Lemme do you a favor. I'll take you home. Save you a bus ride. Close your eyes."

I closed them. "But—"

A gust of wind blew me off balance and I just barely kept my feet. I opened my eyes and I was standing in my—mom's living room. The lights were off. The bedroom door was closed, and I could hear my mom snoring.

"There ya go," Ralph whispered. "I'll let you get to sleep now. Thanks for sticking with us, T.J. You're a real trouper."

And he was gone. Without answering my question.

I awoke the next morning to the sound of the coffee grinder. From the couch-bed, it was hard to ignore. I propped myself up on one elbow, squinting in the light from the kitchenette. Mom was standing there in a peach-colored bathrobe.

"Oh, did I wake you, dear? I'm sorry. I should

have set up the coffee last night, but I was so tired I forgot."

"Mffmrmf," I muttered through the blanket.

"How was that?"

"What *time* is it?"

"It's, um, six thirty-five."

I moaned and flopped back to horizontal.

"You got in pretty late last night, didn't you?"

"I dunno. Did I?"

"Well, I didn't hear you come in." She opened the fridge. "Tsk, this cupboard is pretty bare. Guess I'd better make a run to Giant Eagle today. Tell you what, if you feel like you're going to stay awake, I'll just have some coffee while you shower and dress, and then we can go to breakfast together. How does that sound?"

I had to think about it. But tired as I was, my stomach was complaining too loud to ignore. "Okay," I groaned.

We ended up at Ritters, because Mom had missed eating real diner. food. She said it was a relief to be someplace that didn't have grits on the menu. I played with the turn-knob on the booth jukebox selector, trying to find song titles that sounded silly together, while Mom babbled at me. Wouldn't you know, she's a morning person. I sure didn't inherit *those* genes.

"—and you think Pittsburgh is bad in summer, you haven't suffered until you've experienced Southern humidity. T.J.? Are you listening?"

"Hmm? Oh. Sorry. I'm just not awake yet."

"How many cups of coffee does it take to make you conscious these days?"

I shrugged and yawned. "I don't keep count."

"Hmm. You know, I want to apologize for last night. It wasn't fair of me to come right out and carp at you about your getting a job or finding a new place. It wasn't a nice way to say hello, was it?"

I stared at the steam rising from my coffee cup.

"No, you were right." God, how I hated to admit that. "I should have been thinking about it. I've been letting myself drift too much. I oughta start believing I have a future. I need to get a life." I tried to smile, but I'll bet it came out more of a wince.

"I'm glad to hear you say that." Mom reached over and squeezed my hand. A good thing our breakfasts came just then, or some embarrassing water might have run out of my eyes.

"When did you get that scar on your face?" Mom asked after several bites of scrambled eggs and home fries. "Looks like it's been there a while."

I shrugged. "Cut myself while setting up props for my act." Well, I couldn't exactly tell her the truth, could I? She'd freak and demand I call the cops.

"Hmmm. Well, it's not too noticeable. A little makeup will cover it up nicely. I have some foundation that might be your shade, if you want to try it."

"Mmm. Thanks." I hate makeup. *What's Mom going to do next, tell me to inflate my hair and put a big bow in it?*

"By the way," she said, "before I forget, mark your calendar for Friday evening. We're going over to your grandmother's for dinner."

"We are?"

"I talked to Sadie a couple of days ago, and she said she hadn't seen much of you since you came back to Pittsburgh."

"You talked to her?" One shock after another— Mom and Grandma Kaminski didn't especially get along, even when my parents were married.

"She was worried about you, and she called me. Apparently you stood her up the last time she invited you over."

"I had finals that week, Mom!"

"I know, but finals are over now, and we ought to let her see you so she knows you're all right. And then she'll stop the subtle guilt trips about how I shouldn't have left you alone. I tried to tell her how you're a big girl now, but, well, you know how she is."

"Yeah. Okay," I grumbled. *I hope Grandma doesn't ask me about the scarf.*

She stared at me pensively. "And maybe before we go, we could do something about your hair."

After we got home, I stared at the newspaper ads for a while, pretending to be looking for jobs. When it got late enough that I figured Angela would be at the Per Forma, I called her.

"Hey, you must be psychic," Angela said. "I've just been talking about you."

"To who?"

"Well, for one, to Warren. Seems the chicky-poo who dragged him to the party last night didn't like your act. She tried to seduce him into not letting you perform again. Warren usually thinks with his dick more than his brains, but fortunately his wallet speaks louder than both."

"So he'll still give me gigs?"

"Hell, yeah. He hopes we can fit you in again next week. Oh, and the other thing. Could you come down to the club about six this evening? I've got a surprise for you."

"What kind of surprise?"

"The good kind. Can you be here?"

"Um, sure. Listen, Angela, my mom's come back from Georgia for the summer, and I'm gonna be needing a place to stay. If you hear of anybody who needs a roommate, could you let me know?"

"Sure, I'll ask around. But if your ship comes in, you can buy your own place, right?"

Ship comes in? "Yeah, right. In my dreams."

"Dreams can come true, kiddo. See you later."

"Later."

I spent the afternoon in a tizzy, trying to think what Angela meant. *Did Warren let go more cash to pay me?* I got the feeling it was bigger than that.

Maybe they want to offer a steady weekly gig. Hey, I'd have a real job, doing what I wanted. That would be cool. No question I'd be at the Per Forma at six.

Besides, it gave me a good excuse not to have dinner with Mom.

When I strolled into the club, right on time, the place was nearly empty. The tables were set up and candles lit on them. One couple had a table by the far wall, reading each other's faces like road maps. At a table on the opposite wall sat a tall, silver-haired gentleman in a very well-tailored gray suit. I'd seen him before. He was the one who had given me the steel rose.

"There's your surprise," Angela said in my ear. "His name's Brian Amadan. He talks like a big producer. He's very interested in you. This could be your chance for the bright lights, kiddo."

"There aren't any big producers of performance art."

"Hey, Spaulding Gray got into the movies, didn't he? Besides, this Amadan guy dropped names. He mentioned . . . um, shit—I can't remember them now. But isn't he the dashing type? If he's working a casting couch, I'd consider auditioning."

"I remember him," I said. "He was at my last two performances."

"There you go. He must have been impressed."

"Look, Angela, I'm not sure this is a good idea."

"Come on, you aren't afraid of success, are you?"

"I'm not dressed to meet any high Hollywood type." Which I knew bloody well this Amadan wasn't.

"T.J., you're an *artist.* You're expected to look funky. What kind of swank drink should I send to your table?"

"Perrier. Look, Angela—"

"I won't hear another word." She grabbed my shoulders and hustled me over to the gentleman's table. "Mr. Amadan? Allow me to present T. J. Kaminski."

He stood, the picture of grace, and nodded to me. He didn't offer a hand to shake, so neither did I. "A pleasure," he said, like a purring tiger.

"Hi," I cleverly said back. I was now sure this was the "suit" I'd been warned about. And I wasn't in the mood to be brave. I tried to call for Ralph and Norton, but their names never got to my tongue. Because he was watching. The whammy was still in effect.

"Good luck," Angela whispered in my ear, and she quickly made herself scarce.

The Sidhe types always made me feel like I was in the wrong clothes. I wished I was wearing a black leather miniskirt and a sheer black silk halter rather than my usual T-shirt and jeans. And I should wear dark purple lipstick, have my hair slicked back, and carry a long, gem-studded cigarette holder. Life just isn't fair.

When in doubt, be cool. I took one of the chairs at the table, turned it backward, and straddled it, my arms draped over the back. "So. How was the party last night?"

He smiled. There were no lines on his face, but his eyes seemed old. And cold. "You do like to make an entrance, don't you?" he said.

He didn't talk like Chris. Neither had Reia Perry, come to think of it. I guess the Seelies all picked their own affectations. This guy was trying to be James Bond. I shrugged. "I'm a performer. Life is performance. Everything is an act. Who knows where the stage ends and reality begins?"

"An excellent point. As one of your great artists has written, 'All the world's a stage.' My card." He held out a business card in a gray-gloved hand.

I took it. It read: Brian N. Amadan. There was no phone or address, or occupation. The card was white, but it shimmered and glistened as if made of frozen starlight. I stuffed the card in my jeans pocket. "What can I do for you, Mr. Amadan?"

He rubbed his upper lip with a gloved forefinger. "I understand an offer was made to you recently that you rejected."

Oh. "I said I would think about the offer."

"The one who made it suspects you do not take us seriously."

"Sure I do. I just haven't made up my mind yet."

"I see. What further information do you require in order to make your decision?"

I shrugged again. "Don't know yet." *Sheesh. This really is like a bad spy movie.*

Mr. Amadan sighed, shook his head and clicked his tongue. "You are being a difficult child."

That pissed me off. "If I'm just a child to you, what are you so worried about? Can't you just leave me alone?"

"To allow you to continue would set a dangerous precedent. Some of our distant kin seem to have forgotten their place. It is important that we remind them of it."

"My kind of people would call that racist."

He laughed, but no humor reached his eyes. "Equality may be appropriate for your kind of people. The differences between mortals are minuscule, imperceptible, compared to the gulf between the Seelie and the Unseelie."

"I'd bet that gulf is smaller than you think."

His eyes narrowed. "You are being rude."

I grinned snidely. "Part of my calling in life."

"Unfortunate. Even Puck has some semblance of courtesy." He began to tug gently on the fingers of the glove on his left hand.

"Look, the folks you should be talking to, if you want a deal, are . . ."

He gazed at me intently.

". . . are the Unseelie guys. Your so-called distant kin. If they're unhappy, maybe there's a reason. Maybe you ought to find out what it is and meet them halfway, or something. I'm just their microphone and speakers, amplifying their message to your ears. You might consider listening."

Mr. Amadan sighed. "Either you are a disingenuous fool or you think me one. Not all the Unseelie Court is in revolt. It is arrogance, not unhappiness, that drives the rebellious ones. As I believe has been made clear to you, it would be of great help to us if you could be specific as to whom we should . . . listen to."

I felt my jaw begin to freeze up again. "You know I can't, even if I wanted to. I wish you people would stop asking me that."

"Very well." He pulled the gray glove entirely off his left hand. It was pale, with long, tapered fingers. The effect was as though a sword had been unsheathed.

"Look, I'm sure your folk have other places all your own. Why not let the Unseelies have Pittsburgh? What does it matter?"

"You understand nothing. The verdancy of these hills has been hard-won. Or perhaps you would like to live on a belching smoke-wreathed, fiery slag heap."

"Where people, mortals, could live and work."

"And die, of various cancers. And send their poison downriver for others to enjoy."

I paused. "It doesn't have to be that way."

"That is how the Unseelie would like it. Or haven't they told you that?"

"They haven't, and I don't believe it's true."

"And do you believe they would stop at one city? Or even at the mortal world? I have heard they intend to depose our sovereign queen and set you in her place."

"What? That's stupid!"

"I agree. And we shall see that it does not happen."

I slapped my forehead, exasperated and scared. "Why are you being such pickles-up-the-butt about this? Look at mortal history. We manage to resolve territorial disputes, why can't you?"

"Indeed? What example should we emulate? Bosnia? Ruanda? Israel? I really should learn not to waste time arguing with fools. You will come to respect our way of things, one way or another. In time." He reached over with his bare, pale left hand and gently grasped my right shoulder.

Pain. Cold—icy—pain flowed slowly down my arm. The muscles contracted tighter and tighter until my arm was bent, fingers curled into rigid claws. He let go and the pain and paralysis remained. I couldn't scream, couldn't speak. Tears ran down my face, but he ignored them. I looked around desperately, but the club was empty.

He put a five-dollar bill on the table and stood up. Gazing down at me, he smiled and said, "A pleasure meeting you, Miss Kaminski. Perhaps we shall have the chance to speak again soon. Please think over what I have said. I hope we can come to some agreement. Good evening." He made a little bow and casually strolled away.

Gasping, I managed to stand, knocking the chair over. No one came into the room. I couldn't cry out for anyone, not even Angela. I staggered to the club door and fell against it. It opened, and I stumbled into the evening air. I leaned on Angela's car and breathed, "Ralph, Norton, help me. Oh, God, help me!"

They popped up right beside the car. "Where's the fire T—'Sdugs! What happened to ya?"

"My arm . . . Amadan . . ."

Norton tapped Ralph on the shoulder. "Oh-oh. Looky there."

At the corner of the building, stood Chris and Mr. Amadan, watching us. I didn't know why Chris's eyes were wide or why the older Sidhe was restraining him.

"A trap!" said Ralph. "Let's get below, fast! Close your eyes, Princess."

I did, and I screamed as the ground dropped out from under me. I fell feet-first straight down, as though I'd stepped into an empty elevator shaft.

We hit bottom, and I rolled on a cold, rocky floor. Ralph and Norton picked me up and carried me some distance, through dark tunnels. All I could do was keep holding my useless right arm, trying not to whimper in pain and panic.

At last we stopped. Ralph and Norton were breathing hard from exertion or fear, or both.

"Do you think they heard her?" said Norton.

"Dunno," said Ralph. "But if they did, we're in deep doo-doo."

They paused, waiting for something.

"Please, guys," I moaned. "Please fix my arm. It hurts so much. Please!"

"I think we got lucky," Ralph said softly. "Hang on, Princess. We'll do what we can." To Norton, he said, "Go get a bandage."

"I'm on it." Norton disappeared.

Ralph sighed. "S'balls, T.J., why didn't you tell us you was goin' to see the Amadan? We woulda warned ya not to go. He's just about the worst of 'em!"

"I didn't *know* I was going to meet him. Angela wanted to surprise me. And once I was in front of him, I couldn't call you guys because of your spell!" The pain in my arm was settling down to a dull throb, though I still couldn't move it.

"Some friend you got there if that's how she surprises you."

"I think he tricked her into believing he was some big Hollywood producer."

"Sounds like their sort of trick. Just take it easy now."

Norton reappeared. "Here's a bandage. Hope it helps."

"A bandage?" I said, as their twiggy hands tore away the sleeve of my T-shirt. "That's all?"

They didn't answer, but wrapped a warm, soft cloth along the length of my right arm. It smelled faintly of sulfur, and other minerals, and herbs. My arm began to relax and the pain slowly began to flow away. I could, at last, start to breathe normally.

"Thank you," I said. "I was really scared."

"You're not out of the woods yet," said Ralph.

"Hunh?"

"We can't fix everything," said Ralph. " 'Specially the Amadan's work. 'Fraid you're gonna have some permanent damage there."

"Permanent . . . damage? Oh, God, no."

"Shhh, will you stop swearing like that?" said Norton. "Remember the Rules."

"I'm sorry. I'm just worried. About what you mean by permanent damage."

"Good thing you was never a doctor," Norton said to Ralph. "Your, uh, bedside manner leaves a little somethin' to be desired. Lookit her, she's white as a ghost."

"Oh, like you've seen a lot of ghosts," said Ralph. *"WILL YOU PLEASE TELL ME WHAT YOU MEAN BY PERMANENT DAMAGE?"*

"No need to yell, Princess. Besides, it's kinda hard to know yet how bad it's gonna be. But that arm ain't gonna work the same again, I can tell ya that."

I tried to move my hand. Sharp twinges of pain shot up through the arm again. "But I'm right-handed!"

"Guess you'll have to learn to be amby-dextris, or whatever."

I slid down the cavern wall until I was sitting on the cold stone floor. I cradled my aching arm on my lap as though it were a sick baby. It had all seemed a kind of bad dream, kind of unreal. Even what Chris had done. But this . . .

Ralph and Norton talked in their own language,

sounding like two distant avalanches rumbling at once. Ralph turned back to me. "Did the Amadan give you anything?"

"Yeah. A card. In my pocket." I fished it out with my left hand and gave it to Ralph.

"All right! A calling card. This may give us something here."

"But if you call him, he'll know who you are. Maybe that's what he wants you to do."

"Well it's not what we're gonna do. Not exactly. This is all happening sooner than we thought, but if that's the way they want it, then so be it."

"Whaddaya thinking, Ralph?" said Norton.

"I think we're through playing games, Norton. It's time for the big showdown. No more poking 'em in the ribs."

"I can't do performance art like this," I said.

"That's just it," said Ralph. "We've gone beyond that now. As a Mister Bugs Bunny once said, this means war."

Chapter 20

"We better be getting back," said Norton. He draped some broadcloth over my shoulder, improvising a sling. He and Ralph each grasped an armpit and hauled me up to standing. The cave blurred around us and we rocketed upward. I think I left my stomach on the floor.

When I opened my eyes, I was standing in Mom's living room again. Mom was putting down the phone receiver, staring at me wide-eyed. Then she saw Ralph and Norton and she screamed.

"Listen!" Ralph said to her. "You don't see us. Your daughter hurt her arm in a fall. You were with her at the hospital last night. But everything's jake now. Got that?"

"Yes. I understand," Mom said in an eerie monotone.

Ralph turned to me. "We got some planning to do. You just hold tight, Princess. Don't go meeting any more Sidhe, okay?"

"Okay. But—"

"No buts. 'Bye." Ralph and Norton dropped through the floor again as if it wasn't there.

Still dazed and in pain, I just stood there. Sunlight was coming through the window. I wondered what time it was.

"How is your arm feeling now, dear?" said Mom. She was wiping the counter in the kitchen as if nothing had happened.

"Oh, still hurts." It did, especially when I flexed my fingers.

"Well, the doctor told us we had to expect that, didn't he?"

"Um, yeah."

"Just a good thing no bones were broken. Guess you'll have to eat left-handed at your grandmother's tonight."

"Tonight? It's Friday already?" *Shit, time does work weird Under the Hill.*

Mom looked at me curiously. "You feeling all right?"

"Sorry, must be the painkillers they gave me. Really disorienting, you know? I just forgot what day it was."

"I told the doctor not to give you too heavy a dosage, but you were pretty insistent you needed something strong."

"Uh, yeah." *Where was all this coming from? Did Ralph put all that in her head or is she making it up?*

"I was thinking it'd be nice to go to Phipps Conservatory today. Their spring flower show is almost over, and I'd like to catch it before it ends. Want to come along?"

I had pleasant childhood memories of Phipps. I remember going there every year for their Christmas shows, looking at all the decorated trees, plants in the shapes of animals, bright red poinsettias and deep green holly. Even though it was spring, not winter, I felt I could use a comforting trip down memory lane.

"Sure. Sounds good."

We drove up through Oakland, past Pitt, the Cathedral, the Carnegie Museum, over the Schenley bridge and parked along Flagstaff Hill. Water was running in the Columbus fountain and children were splashing beneath the stern gaze of the Italian explorer. The dogwoods and cherry trees were in glorious bloom in the outdoor garden beside the conservatory, white and pink froth against the white-painted steel-frame building. It was one of those rare clear and beautiful days in Pittsburgh, and I was filled with the intense appreciation of someone who has narrowly avoided death. Everything was precious, and I wanted to cling to it forever.

The thought did cross my mind, as we strolled up the path lined with wrought-iron park benches and tall, old-fashioned street lamps, as to whose turf this was—Seelie or Unseelie? Sure, there were trees and flowers here, but they were controlled, surrounded by iron and steel. Would the Sidhe think this an awful place or would they like it? Well, it was broad daylight, and there appeared to be the usual heavy crowd, so I put worries aside. Phipps was my childhood friend. It wouldn't betray me.

Even though the conservatory had been recently renovated, it hadn't changed much from what I'd remembered. There was the bottleneck of people at the gift shop at the entrance. There were the grand palm trees in the Palm Court. Pathways led between red-brick flower beds, filled with pink and white blossoms. In each room there were topiary bushes shaped like bunnies or ducks or mice and cats, or Easter eggs.

Mom always goes through Phipps slowwwly, because she wants to look at *everything.* I told her I'd catch up with her later, and I quickly headed for my favorite place, the Orchid Room. I liked it because it had always seemed more "jungly," a little wilder than the other rooms. There was a pool of water in the center, overhung by a gnarled old tree, whose limbs were covered with orchids of all different shapes, sizes, colors. The walls of the room were also covered with orchids in moss-lined hanging baskets, orchids on driftwood, orchids in rock-lined beds. Some orchids were tiny and looked like colorful spiders, others were large, with petals that were runway landing strips for bees.

I looked at each kind, shuffling along the narrow, winding path that circled the pond. Traffic flow is always a problem in the Orchid Room, since everyone views the flowers at a different speed. At the far end of the room, as I examined one pot of bright purple blossoms, someone bumped into me hard from behind.

"Hey!" My foot went into the pond, and my right shoulder crashed into the gnarled tree. I glanced back to see who might have pushed me, but nobody in the nearby clumps of little old ladies was even looking my way. I heard a dry chuckle to my right— there was a face in the trunk of the tree, and it was leering at me. Twigs like clawed fingers dug into my sling and pulled me toward the trunk. A long slit in the bark split open, and a hole gaped wide.

"Help," I whimpered, unable to scream. I tried to pull away but only succeeded in stumbling closer to the hollow trunk. "Help."

"Oh, dear." There was a tap on my left shoulder. I twisted my head and saw a group of four elderly nuns in short habits peering at me through their bifocals and looking concerned.

"Help?"

"You seem to have got your sling caught on a branch, dear. Here, hold still a moment and I'll try to dislodge you." With deft fingers, the closest nun plucked at my sling, and it came free. I looked at the tree again: the hole in the trunk had closed and there was no face.

"Um, thank you," I said to the sister as she helped me step up out of the pond.

"Not at all. Happy to assist," she said with a smile. She patted me on the shoulder. "God bless you, dear."

The group of nuns toddled away into the crowd. No one else was reacting as if anything odd had happened.

Shaking all over, I tried to find Mom and get out

of the conservatory. But Phipps is something like a maze, and on a busy day there are no quick paths to the exit. I stumbled through the Desert Room, where my sleeves and pant legs kept getting caught on cactus spines. In the Seasonal Display Room, my shoelaces got caught between the teeth of a straw rabbit. In the Fountain Room, the pillar of water that spouted up from the pond took the shape of a thin, beautiful woman. She smiled at me, showing glistening fangs.

That did it. I shoved people aside and jumped over partitions to get to the path that led to the door, ignoring the shouting behind me. I hadn't found Mom.

I stumbled out through the exit and sat heavily on one of the iron park benches. "Ralph? Norton?"

Pop, pop. "What's up now, Princess?"

"I'm so stupid," I gasped. "In there . . . A tree tried to grab me. There's vampires in the water, and the plants all tried to stick me—"

"Whoa, whoa, slow down."

"They're alive. They tried to get me and it's still daylight and there's whole crowds of people and some nuns had to save me."

"There's Sidhe in there?" Ralph jerked a thumb toward the conservatory.

"Not Sidhe. Things in the plants and the water. They kept trying to pull me in."

"Sounds like nymphs and sprites, all right," said Norton, rubbing his chin. "Remember, we warned you about them, T.J. But they don't normally show up in such a crowded place."

Ralph made a rumbling noise in his throat.

I was calming down some. "You said nymphs and sprites are mostly on their own side. Do you think the Sidhe could have sent them after me?"

"Naw," said Ralph. "The Seelie Court don't control nymphs and sprites much. Those things are kinda wild, and they got the smarts of your average housecat. They probably wanted to snatch you for themselves."

"Snatch me? Why?"

"You been marked," Norton pointed at my right arm. "You got the glamour on you now. If you're worth the Sidhes' notice, you get noticed by any of 'em."

"But what would they want me for?"

"I dunno," Norton said with a shrug. "Probably wanted to mate with you or something. Everything's sex with them. And it's May, you know. That thing in the water was probably a glaistig. A bit of mortal blood would taste real good to them about now."

"This ain't good," said Ralph. "I bet the Sidhe are making it easier for the nature spirits to be out and about. See, this is what's scary about them takin' over, T.J. Today it's just you in this park, but before long, every mortal's gonna have these problems everywhere."

"Yeah. I see what you mean." I looked back at the conservatory entrance, and panic shot through me. "My mom's still in there."

Norton put his ear to the ground. "She's on her way out. Hang on."

The group of four nuns appeared at the entrance and pointed at me. My mother was in the midst of them, and she nodded enthusiastic thanks to them before heading my way.

I sighed my relief. "Guess you guys oughta go now."

"Yeah, there's big plans in the works. But we'll have to give you more constant protection if stuff like this is gonna keep happening."

"Protection like how?"

"Whatever we can manage. Later." They popped out of sight just as my mom came up to the beach.

"There you are! What happened, T.J.? I was told you went running through the conservatory like demons were after you."

I rubbed my forehead and covered my eyes. "I'm sorry, Mom. It must be this medication I'm on. I just had a panic attack and I had to get out. Sorry. Didn't mean to ruin your day."

She sighed. "I think we'd better talk to your doctor about changing your prescription. C'mon, let's go home and I'll make the call."

Uh-oh. How long is this fable gonna hold up? I tried to think of some way to turn her thoughts to other things as we got in her car.

"Mom, you know a lot about folklore, right?"

She laughed. "That's a huge subject, T.J. I know a few things from here and there. What culture or what part of the world did you have in mind?"

"Huh. I dunno, let's say Europe. What I'm wondering about are all those stories about fairies stealing babies or snatching people to take Under the Hill with them. Why are there so many stories like that, do you think? I mean, what would fairies want with mortal people, anyway, if they're all magical and powerful and stuff?"

"Well, that narrows it down a few notches, but that's still a lot of questions in one. Why do you ask?"

"Oh, I've been looking through some of your books for inspiration for my performance acts and just got curious, that's all."

"I'm glad to see you taking a broader interest in things. Anyway, let's start with the legends of snatching. There's all sorts of possible origins for those stories. A deformed child might have been explained away by calling it a changeling—and that way the parents could avoid shame. And doubtless there were occasional disappearances when someone wandered away from the village and got lost. Easy to say the fairies had taken them. You know, I find there's an interesting similarity between the tales of fairy snatching and the modern-day alien abduction stories you see in the tabloids—"

"Yeah, okay, I can figure all that. But do they ever try to justify why the fairies would want a healthy baby or a grown-up human?"

"Oh, I see what you're getting at. Well, the usual things people would steal people for: slaves or wives—which were much the same thing in past days. It might be a reflection of the tradition among some ethnic groups of exogamy—marrying outside your group."

"Yeah, to get variety in the gene pool; I heard that in a history class once. But how much did medieval people know about genetics?"

"Well, they passed along the observations of generations, but, you're right, that's only one possible explanation for exogamy. After all, some groups encouraged inbreeding in order to strictly control lineage, such as ancient Egyptian royalty. But another explanation for exogamy is to make ties with enemies or allies, so there is always some line of communication between their countries. That might be reflected in the tales where a half-human can live both in our world and the supernatural world. And yet another reason might be to bring cultural knowledge or talents into the family, so that no kinship group becomes too isolated or set in their ways. If I recall rightly, the fairies like to snatch particularly beautiful or talented children. Some cultures had a taboo against boasting for just that reason. Is this at all what you wanted to find out? I know I tend to ramble when I'm talking shop."

"Yeah, kinda," I said, mulling it over. "There might be something to all that. Maybe I'll take an anthro course in the fall." *If I'm still around.*

"I'm pleased to hear you say that. I was afraid I'd scared you off by too much childhood exposure. I'll be interested to hear what you think of it when you do."

The distraction seemed to work; Mom didn't mention the doctor again.

So maybe that's it, I thought. *The Sidhe want to snatch me for my talent, and maybe because having me around would make it easier to get into the mortal world somehow. I know I've made it easier for Ralph and Norton. Do the Seelie want me at the end of May so that they can keep coming back after their free-pass month is over? If I go Under the Hill to Ralph and Norton's side of the tracks, will the Unseelie be able to appear in our world more often? And is this a good thing or a bad thing?* Ideas were flying like arrows through my head, and I didn't like the way they were pointing.

Chapter 21

We wasted a couple of hours wandering through import shops on Craig Street. I was glad none of the Thai god masks made faces at me, and the bronze sphinx didn't lash its tail.

When we got back to Mom's apartment, I flopped down on the couch, ready for some mind-numbing TV.

There was someone beside me. I turned, and Luigi smiled up at me. "Lemme guess," I said softly. "You're the protection."

He nodded. "A tuo servizio."

"Great. You against the Amadan. I can see it now."

"How's that, T.J.?" said Mom, coming out of the bathroom.

"Nothing, just muttering to myself."

"Well, we'd better get you changed for dinner."

I looked at my kinda grimy jeans and T-shirt, then at my right arm. "Do I have to, Mom? It'll hurt my arm."

She crossed her arms on her chest. "You've been wearing those clothes for two days now. *You* may not care, but as a courtesy to your grandmother and me, you might do what you can."

"Okay, okay, maybe I can pull on a skirt or something."

"I'd be happy to help."

"I can manage, Mom," I said, stomping into the bedroom. But after long minutes of fumbling my jeans off, and getting the T-shirt off my left side, I was pretty discouraged.

È da servire?" said Luigi, standing beside me.

I glared at him. "Can you do it nicely? No funny stuff?"

He took off his cap and bowed, solemnly. "Naturalmente, Signorina."

I sighed. "Okay, do what you can. But make it quick."

Me and my big mouth. I was instantly caught in a buffeting whirlwhind—as if the Tasmanian Devil was doing my wardrobe. Cloth swirled around me; my hair stood on end. I was turned and tugged at and tipped this way and that until I forgot which end was up. But I gotta admit Luigi was quick.

By the time Mom stuck her head in the bedroom door to check up on me, I was wearing a flounced denim skirt. My T-shirt was clean and had a new, lower neckline and was embellished with red sequins. Not what you'd call fashionable, but, then, what would a centuries-old folletti like Luigi know about fashion? Just look at the way *he* dressed.

"Well, hey there, Cinderella," said Mom. "You look very nice. How did you do that with your hair?"

I reached my hand up. My hair was now curly. "Um, a blow-drying trick. I learned it from a friend."

"Cute trick. You'll have to teach it to me sometime. Okay, if you're ready, let's go."

"We got in Mom's car, and Luigi hopped onto my lap. "Oh, this is going to be fun," I muttered sarcastically.

"What, dear?"

"I said this is going to be fun. I haven't seen Mamu in a long time."

"Well, some of that is your fault."

"I guess so." I said to Luigi, "Try anything and you're toast."

"How's that?" said Mom.

"Um, I said I'm so hungry I could eat toast."

"What *was* in those painkillers they gave you?"

"I dunno, but I could sure use more of it right now."

We drove down Fifth through Oakland and took the Smithfield Bridge to the South Side. Luigi behaved himself the whole way. Finding parking north of Carson Street was a challenge, until Mom complained out loud. Luigi waved his hand, and a car pulled out just a few feet from Grandma's place.

"Thank you," I muttered.

"Niente," he said with a smile.

Grandma Kaminski met us at the door and made her usual fuss over me. She's shorter than I am, with short gray hair and an apple-shaped body. She was wearing a pink beaded sweatshirt and polyester stretch pants. She looked like such a typical grandmother—that's part of what I like about her.

"How nice to see you, Tiffany. I've been so worried about you. Oh, you're so dressed up—how pretty you look! What happened to your arm?"

"Fell down the stairs," Mom and I said simultaneously.

Grandma glanced back and forth between us. "How awful! When did this happen?"

"Last night," we chorused again.

Grandma blinked. "But, Sarah, I have a call from you on my machine from last night. You said you had not seen Tiffany and were wondering where she might be."

I jumped in, "Oh, uh, that was before she found me. At the bottom of the stairs."

"That's right," said Mom. "I'm sorry, Sadie. I should have called you again, but we went right to the hospital and things have been terribly busy since then."

Grandma stared at my mother. "Of course they have. Of course."

Something rubbed against my leg. I glared down,

but it was only Grandma's white Persian cat, Cassandra.

"You remember Cassandra, don't you Tiffany, dear?"

I've been pretty indifferent to cats since I got over my childhood fears about seeing ghosts between their ears, and they usually feel the same about me. But I squatted down and scratched her head to be sociable. "Hi, Cassy."

She sniffed my right arm and sling with great interest, then drew back her head and hissed.

"Well, same to you."

The cat then saw Luigi, who was cautiously peeking out from behind my skirt, and her eyes went huge. She took off for the dining room and disappeared.

"I wonder what got into her," Grandma murmured. "Well, but come in, both of you. Sit down. Be comfortable. I will pour wine. Would you like wine, too, Tiffany? I suppose you are old enough now."

"Sure." I sniffed the air as Mom and I sat down at the dining room table. Fish. Of course it would be fish, it was Friday. And something else . . . cinnamon. "Grandma? Did you make struchla?"

She popped out of the kitchen bearing wineglasses and an embarrassed blush. "Well, yes, dear, I did."

"You made my favorite pastry, and it isn't even Christmas! Thank you, Mamu!" I leaned over and kissed her cheek.

"Well, I know how much you like it, dear, and I thought this was sort of a special occasion. I haven't seen you in so long." She set down the wineglasses and poured them half full with a white wine, then went back to the kitchen.

Four chairs were placed around the table, though only three places were set. Guess who sat in the fourth chair.

"I don't think she's redecorated in decades," Mom murmured, glancing around at the faded still-life

paintings and portraits of angels, the carefully pol-
ished silver candlesticks, the bright woven tapestry
runners, the simple wooden crucifixes, the straw animal knickknacks, and so on. On one sideboard was
an old photo of my dad, and as I looked at it something caught in my throat.

Luigi reached out a long arm and snatched Grandma's wineglass. He downed the wine in one gulp
and set the glass back exactly where it had been. I
glared at him. He shrugged with a rueful smile.

Grandma came out holding a tureen full of fish
fillets in a bland cream sauce. Mom helped her set it
on the trivet on the table. Grandma saw her wineglass. "Goodness, I could have sworn I had poured
for myself."

Mom laughed. "You know, I did that just the other
day. Thought I'd filled a wineglass only to find it
empty. Our minds are going, Sadie."

Grandma said nothing but went to the kitchen and
returned with the wine bottle. She sat down and
poured herself another glass. We paused a moment
while she closed her eyes and murmured grace in
Polish. Luigi shuddered but stayed in his seat.

Grandma noticed that I was watching the fourth
chair when she opened her eyes, so she looked at it
too, then back at me.

"I was just wondering why there are four chairs
at the table," I said with a shrug.

"Because there were four in the dining room set."

"You'll have to forgive her, Sadie," said Mom. "the
painkillers have made her a bit out of it."

I nodded. "Strong stuff."

"So what is the matter with your arm?" asked
Grandma, as she ladled out fish onto each of our
plates. "Did you break a bone?"

"No, I just badly bruised some muscles. It's
kinda paralyzed."

"Hmm. Elf-shot."

I jumped in my seat, knocking my wineglass over, spilling wine onto the table and into Mom's lap.

"T.J.!" Mom said, urgently dabbing at the spots on her skirt.

Grandma was staring at me.

"Sorry. I . . . I'm just real clumsy with my left hand."

"It is just a folk expression," Grandma said. "It is said when one is hit by a fairy arrow, or is struck by the hand of a fairy, that one will be paralyzed or ill."

Mom said, "That was just the way agrarian cultures tried to explain heart attacks and strokes. Excuse me, I'm going to have to try and wash these spots out." She got up and headed for the bathroom.

For once, I desperately wanted her to stick around. Instead, I had to face Grandma Kaminski across the table.

Too casually, she asked, "Do you still have the blue scarf?"

Shit. "Um, sure, Mamu."

She tilted her head with gentle accusation. "You lost it."

"No, really, I didn't. I, um, loaned it to someone." Luigi flashed me a quizzical look, but I tried to ignore him.

"Hmmm. Well, then, no matter. That scarf has a way of returning to its rightful owner."

Cassandra chose that moment to leap onto the table, sniffing at Luigi. Her tail fluffed out and she growled low in her throat.

Luigi shrank back in the chair and made shooing motions at the cat.

"Cassandra!" said Grandma. "Where are your manners, girl?" She got up from her seat and came around the table behind me. "What is it you see?" As she put her hands around the cat's middle, Grandma peered between Cassandra's ears.

I held my breath. *Will she see him?*

"Ah," was all Grandma said. She picked the cat

up off the table and set her on the floor. Grandma came around the table and sat again, smiling. "Do you think your little friend would like some fish?"

"What? Who?" *She saw him! She saw him!*

Grandma took a salad plate and scooped a little bit of the fish on it. She placed the plate in front of the fourth chair.

Luigi gobbled it down instantly.

I was almost too stunned to speak. "Mamu! You . . . you can . . ."

"I assume your mother does not know," Grandma said with a conspiratorial wink.

"Um, what? Oh, no. She doesn't."

"He is not the one who touched you, is he?" She nodded toward my arm.

"No. In fact, he's supposed to be protecting me from the one who did."

"Ah. A guardian spirit, then?"

"Yeah. Sort of."

"Ah. Cute little fellow. Does he have a name?"

I lost my chance to tell her because the toilet loudly flushed and Mom came striding back to the table.

"I would have to have on a linen skirt tonight," Mom grumbled.

"I'm sorry!"

"Oh, that's all right, Tif. You couldn't help it. Now, Sadie, you know belief in witchcraft and so on was just an attempt to understand things that primitive cultures had no way of knowing the true cause of—"

And she was off. I'd heard this lecture before. Grandma just nodded pleasantly, without argument. I tuned Mom out and watched Luigi, who was busy snatching crumbs off Grandma's plate. She seemed to be helping him.

Now I wanted desperately to talk to Grandma, but Mom was in High Babble mode, talking about her year in Georgia. I concentrated on trying to get some dinner to my mouth with my left hand. I was mostly successful.

But even through the struchla and coffee and washing the dishes, I wasn't given a private moment with Grandma again.

When we were standing at the door to say goodbye, Grandma Kaminski said to me, "You know I'm always here, dear. Anytime you need me for anything, just give me a call. Please."

I hugged her tightly, even though it hurt my arm. "I will, Mamu. I will. Thanks for dinner."

"It was nothing, dear. Please don't be a stranger for so long this time." In my ear, she whispered, "You can bring your little friend again, if you like."

"Um, sure."

On the drive home, Mom said, "I'm always amazed when modern people retain such primitive notions. I know people are entitled to their beliefs, but it's nonsense to imply that your arm was hurt in some supernatural way."

"It's okay, Mom. Grandma didn't mean anything by it." But the fingers on my left hand were writhing as hope and fear fought inside me. Hope because now I might have a new ally. Fear because I desperately didn't want Mamu getting hurt in all this.

"Luigi," I whispered to him as he sat on my lap, "is there some way we can protect her too?"

He spoke a long string of Italian, the gist of which seemed to be that Grandma could probably protect herself pretty well.

"I hope you're right."

Mom frowned over at me. "We'd better get you to bed."

Chapter 22

Once on the couch-bed, I couldn't sleep. I tossed and turned, my brain too crowded with thoughts. Though Mom would never know it, a lot of what she had told me made sense. Either because I was too dangerous or too valuable, or both, the fairy world had tagged me to be their next inductee. I didn't want to be a breeding cow, or a Princess of the Goblins, or an ambassador between worlds. But I did like feeling important and that I had special powers. The High Sidhe were beautiful but nasty, and the Unseelie seemed friendly but the world they wanted would be ugly and grim. Both had tried to manipulate me without being straight with me. I guess, on close examination, I didn't like either side all that much. The city of Pittsburgh wasn't going to be any better off with either the Seelie or the Unseelie in charge.

And yet—especially when I closed my eyes—I could envision the starlit meadow and the enchanting music, or the wild parties in caverns far below, or dancing with Joe Magarac. I would almost whimper with the longing to be there. Then I'd open my eyes and sit up, disgusted with myself.

I wanted my own life, dammit, with me in control. I was just beginning to get a taste for what life would be like as a successful performance artist, and I wanted more. I wanted to be with Sam more, and see more of the world.

I was beginning to get a picture of what I needed
to do. But it was going to take guts—something I've
had short supply of in my life. I would have to learn
what I could from Grandma Kaminski and keep my
eyes open for chances. And I'd have to do it all behind Ralph's and Norton's back, and out of sight of
Luigi. If I didn't succeed, by the end of May I'd be
dragged Under the Hill anyway. Nope, this wasn't
going to be easy.

The next morning I was on the phone to Angela.

"I hope you haven't already scheduled me for next
week," I said. "Because I hurt my arm the other night
and I won't be able to perform."

"Oh, no! What happened?"

"Fell down the stairs." I was saying it so often,
even I was starting to believe it.

"That's awful. I know Warren was hoping to
squeeze you in again as soon as possible."

"Yeah, sorry to disappoint you guys."

"Oh, hey, you just take the time to heal, okay?"

"Listen, there is one date that I'd really like to
have, if you've got the room."

"When's that?"

"May thirty-first."

"Lemme check the schedule. May thirty-first is
a . . . Thursday. Sorry, T.J., we already have a couple
of people signed up. I'd feel really bad about bumping anybody."

"Maybe you don't have to. I want a late show—
eleven o'clock to midnight."

"We don't stay open that late on weeknights."

"Please, Angela. It's really important. It's vital to
the performance."

"Hmmm. Well, seeing that it's you, I'll talk to Warren about it. Or you could—you coming to his party
tonight?"

"Is that tonight? Wow, I've really been losing track
of time. Yeah, I'll try to be there."

"Good—then we can both work on him."

I got Warren's address from her and said good-bye. One piece of the puzzle almost in place. Now if I could just call Mamu. But there was this problem. He was small and Italian and sitting on the couch, watching a replay of "Three Tenors" on PBS. Sublime tears rolled down his cherubic face whenever Pavarotti sang.

"I didn't know you enjoyed opera," said Mom as she walked in from the bedroom.

"Well, performance is performance, you know. Besides, Placido Domingo is kinda cute."

"I suppose. Who were you just talking to?"

"Angela. I was setting up another gig for the end of May."

"Hmmm. Do you think your arm will be healed enough by then?"

"If it isn't, I'll just work it into the performance somehow."

"I hope the performances will be steady enough work for you. I expect your arm injury would get in the way of job hunting."

I nodded. "Kinda hard to fill out forms and take typing tests."

"Not to mention making employers nervous about giving you health insurance. I guess we'd better just plan on your staying here for the time being."

"Yeah." To my surprise, I felt disappointed. I was strangely looking forward to being driven from the nest, to finding my own corner of the world.

Mom sat on the couch, almost on top of Luigi, but he scooted aside. "Do you mind if I change the channel? *Days of Our Lives* is on and I want to catch up."

"Fine by me."

She picked up the remote and clicked it. Luigi stared up at her, devastated. I had to laugh.

"What's so funny?"

"Nothing. I just hadn't thought you were the soap opera type." *Now what's Luigi going to do?*

"Don't knock it. They're seriously addictive."

Luigi snapped his fingers. The TV suddenly switched back to Pavarotti.

Mom stared at the remote. "Now how did that happen?" She clicked it again and the opening theme from *Days of Our Lives* swelled from the speaker.

Luigi glared up at her and snapped his fingers again. The TV switched back to the tenors.

"Well, now, how—" Mom shook her head, exasperated. "I think this TV's on the blink, T.J."

I didn't answer as I silently got off the couch and snuck out the front door.

No luck. Luigi stood on the landing, frowning and shaking his finger at me.

I squatted down and put my hand on his shoulder. "Luigi, if I told you that it was very important that you stay here and protect my mother, would you do it?"

He shook his head and said firmly, "No, Signorina."

"Not even for a big kiss?"

He paused a moment, then shook his head again with sad regret.

"Let me guess. You're going to stay right beside me until Ralph and Norton tell you otherwise, right?"

He nodded.

"How the heck do they expect a little elf like you to protect me?"

Luigi drew himself up, arms crossed on his chest. "La forza di coraggio!"

"Wonderful," I muttered. Looking up, I noticed that the herb wreath that had been hanging on the front door was gone.

I went back inside. "Hey, Mom," I said, "what happened to the wreath that was on the door?"

"Oh, I threw it out. Some of it was wilting, and it didn't smell very good. I'm sorry—did you still want it?"

"I was going to use some of it in my next performance."

"Well, it's probably still down in the barrel."

I ran down and around the back of the building. I pried open the top of the plastic garbage container—not easy to do one-handed. Yep, there was the wreath jammed in among the garbage sacks. It didn't smell any better for it. I pulled it out anyway.

Luigi, hovering in midair beside me, backed up a little.

Hmmmm. "Luigi, would you be a dear and carry this for me?" Luigi shook his head rapidly.

Keeps his kind at bay too. Worth knowing. I ran back upstairs and stuffed the wreath into a plastic bag for future use.

"Did you find it, T.J.?"

"Yeah, thanks, Mom."

"Sorry, I should have asked. The TV seems to be working now. But I wanted to mention; I tried using the Apple last night and I couldn't get it to bring up a file."

"Yeah, it's been kinda buggy lately."

"I swear, it must have a gremlin in it."

"Mom! You don't believe in gremlins."

"Hah! Gremlins are about the only supernatural creatures I would believe in. Given my experience with computers, something's got to be the enforcer for Murphy's Law."

"Okay, I'll check on it." I slid the bag with the wreath under the couch and went into the bedroom. Luigi drifted along right behind me.

I shut the door to keep out the sound of the TV and sat down at the computer desk.

Pop. Pop. "Hiya, T.J."

"Wha?" After unjangling my nerves, I turned around. "Don't you guys ever knock anymore?"

"Naw, don't have to." Ralph's leather apron and skin were grimy, and Norton was beaded with sweat.

Just like I thought. I make it easy for them to get here. "So. What have you guys been up to?"

"Workin' in Joe's mill, making weapons and stuff for the battle."

That made my stomach turn cold. "So this war stuff is for real, huh?"

"Yeah," said Norton, with a big grin. "But we figured we'd take a break and come talk to you for a bit."

"I'm flattered. Well, as long as you're here, do you guys know anything about gremlins?"

Ralph blinked. "Enough to know they're trouble."

"They ain't our kind," said Norton.

"They're not?"

"Nope," said Ralph. "Gremlins are more like the wild sprites you saw in Phipps there. Or maybe some sorta mutated Lutin or kobold. I wouldn't mess with them if I was you."

"Didn't say I was gonna mess with one. My mom thinks there's one living in this computer. If there is, could you get it out?"

"If there is, you wouldn't want to. Listen, if there's a gremlin in that box, better to leave him where he's happy. Let him loose and who knows what he'd do."

"Well, like what?"

"Like wreck somebody's day, that's for sure. Might blow up your water heater for the fun of it. Might shut down a whole factory down the street. Anywhere there's machinery, the more complicated the better, gremlins will wanna go. They love throwing orderly things into chaos. Gremlins are bad news. Forget about it."

"Do the Sidhe hate them too?"

Ralph and Norton burst into laughter. "Everybody hates gremlins!"

Hmmm. Something else to keep in mind. "So, how's this big battle of yours shaping up?"

"It's looking good. We think we got enough Unseelie signed up. Now we're just thinking about what would be a good place to do it. It has to be our turf or neutral, though. We're thinkin' over several spots. You got any ideas?"

A thought came to mind. "How about Homestead? My dad told me stories about the fight there back in 1896 between the steelworkers and the Pinkertons. Since you're worker guys battling snooty wealthy types that are trying to throw you out, it'd be kinda like history repeating itself."

Ralph and Norton stared at me wide-eyed. "Homestead! That's brilliant, Princess! We weren't thinkin' about so far out of town, but you're right, it's perfect. See, Norton, I told you she'd have the answer."

"Yeah, but where do we put the line?" said Norton. "By the monument or something?"

"My dad told me the main fight was down on the riverbank by the mill. The Pinkertons came up the river in the middle of the night. Most of the mill-works are torn down now, but I think there's a couple of buildings left. So, anyway, if you want to be really historical, the riverbank east of the High Bridge would be the best place."

Ralph nodded. "You're right. That's the place."

"But tell me something, guys," I said. "If you are all immortal and powerful, what's this battle going to prove? It's all a game if nobody's really going to get hurt."

Ralph and Norton looked at each other. "She doesn't get it," said Norton.

"T.J.," Ralph said, "immortal don't mean nothing can hurt us. It just means we don't die of disease or old age and stuff. But the sword of a Sidhe can cut me up just as well as it'd cut you."

My stomach began to sink. "But even if you're cut down, you just go back to living Under the Hill, like Joe Magarac, right?"

"She still doesn't get it," said Norton.

Patiently, Ralph explained, "Look, we don't know where you morts go after you bite the Big One. But us, we don't go nowhere. If we get dead, we're gone. Kaput. Outta the picture. The Big Zero. Got it?"

"Ain't you ever heard?" said Norton. "We don't have souls."

I just stared at them. "You mean, you're willing to die a real death . . . for Pittsburgh?"

Ralph stood up straight. "You got it. 'Course, we hope we don't."

"And the Seelie Court . . . Chris, Amadan, they can die too?"

Norton chuckled darkly. "We ain't building weapons for nothing. We're gonna give as good as we get."

"This is the stupidest thing I've ever heard! You guys are gonna risk your immortal lives over a stupid city. Why?"

Ralph tilted his head and scratched his scraggly beard. "Why not? You young morts today kill each other over shoes, jackets, or wearin' the wrong color. What's so strange about fighting over having a place of your own to live in?"

"But you have a place—Under the Hill."

"Can you imagine living there forever? Norton and me, we're born to work. We love workin' side by side with you morts. That's what we live for. That's why we need Pittsburgh to stay a workin' town."

"Couldn't you guys just move somewhere else, like Detroit?"

They shuddered like jelly. "Uh-uh. You don't wanna know who's taking over there. Besides, our kind sticks to one place, pretty much. This is where we belong. We wouldn't feel comfortable noplace else."

"Isn't being uncomfortable better than being dead?"

"Not for us, it ain't."

"Oh." I rubbed my paralyzed, aching arm. I didn't know what to say. Ralph and Norton had been strange companions, and I couldn't always trust

them, but they were still almost buddies to me. I
might want them to go away, but I didn't want them
to die.

"You guys will let me know if you're all right after
it's over, won't you?"

"Heh. Won't have to. You'll be there to see it all
yourself, Princess. You'll get a ringside seat."

"*I'll* be there?"

"Don't worry! You won't have to fight or nothin'.
You just have to be there."

"Why?"

"It's . . . a ceremonial position. It's important."

"Why?"

"You'll just think it's metaphysical mumbo jumbo."

"WHY?"

"Okay, okay, quit bursting your Bessemer there.
Listen, you've walked in our world, Under the Hill,
and you're a part of your world, the mortal universe.
So you might say you represent both. And with your
thaumaturgy skills, you can summon our forces into
your world, onto the battlefield, and help them stay
there for the fight. Understand that?"

"I thought during the month of May you guys could
go anywhere you want."

"It's complicated," said Ralph. "Some of us Unseelie can, and some of us can't, 'cause of the work we
do. The Sidhe got that advantage over us, since they
ain't beholding to no one. But us workin' types, some
of us are stuck in one place, one house or one farm
or one mine, depending on what we do. For those
guys, May just lets them be out in their working turf
more often. But what you can do is bring them out
of their turf to where we need them."

"A go-between," I murmured. *So I was right.* "So
that's what this has all been about, isn't it? You
picked me so that you could bring an army of your
people into Pittsburgh. You needed a mortal, and I
was the chump who got the job."

"Hey, hey, don't look at it like that. We didn't plan

it that way. We didn't know it was gonna get this far. We were hoping the Sidhe would give up easy. But they didn't. You gotta admit we been fair to ya, T.J. We gave you what you wanted."

"Yeah. Maybe. I didn't count on losing the use of my arm when this started."

"We'll try and make it up to you, T.J. Honest."

"Assuming we win," said Norton.

"Uh-hunh. Just what are you guys gonna do if you win?"

"Oh, it'll be great, Princess! Think of it! All them smokestacks lighting up again. All that black, shiny coal will come out of these hills. The rivers will be filled with barges, bringin' iron from Minnesota, limestone from Michigan. People will flock here from all over the world, our kind too, to work the biggest mills the world has ever seen!"

"Oh." I found I was beginning to hope they'd lose. "When's this battle supposed to happen, anyway?"

"Don't know yet. According to the Rules, if we choose the place, the other side gets to choose the day."

"Seems like a dumb way to run a war. Why don't you just sneak-attack the Sidhe somewhere when they aren't expecting it?"

Ralph and Norton stared at me, aghast. "We'll forget you said that, T.J. We may just be workin' joes, but we still got our pride, and sense of honor, no matter what the Seelie say. You morts may not care about that sorta thing anymore, but we do. Now, we gotta continue our preparations. We'll be getting back to you when we got more for you to do." With backs straight and heads held high, Ralph and Norton sank slowly and majestically into the floor.

I noticed Luigi sitting over on the bed. "Are you going to be in this battle too?"

He nodded proudly. "Per la gloria e patria!"

"Lucky you." I stared at the static on the Apple monitor. *Can't win for losing, as my dad used to say.*

Chapter 23

That evening, Mom drove me to Warren's place in Shadyside. Luigi came along, of course, this time in the backseat.

"I can come get you if you don't stay too late," Mom said as I got out of the car.

"That's okay. I'm sure I can get a ride."

The door to Warren's town house was open, so I wandered in. Luigi floated along right behind me. "Hello?"

"T.J.!" Angela waved to me from the stairs.

"T.J.?" said someone from a dark corner. "T.J.'s here?"

Suddenly the room began to fill with people. Ankoya, Barb, Daniel, Marissa, they all spoke to me, hugged me, wanted to know what happened to my arm. People I'd never met before came up and introduced themselves. People who looked nothing like the Sidhe. They wanted to know when I'd be performing next and what issues I'd be working on.

I knew it was all just because of my newfound celebrity. These people would have treated me like shit before I hooked up with Ralph and Norton.

And you know what? I loved it. It didn't matter why people were now paying attention to me—I had their attention. I guess that makes me a bad person. So what? Success is the best revenge, they say, and I believe it.

"Hey, where's Warren?" I asked nobody in particular.

"Out back," said someone whose name I'd already forgotten. "Slaving over a hot grill."

I went out into the backyard. I recognized Warren by his shoulder-length brown hair and glasses. Sure enough, he was flipping burgers on a barbecue grill. Sheesh, for an art maven, he was acting downright bourgeois.

"Hiya, Warren. You been moonlighting at McDonald's? I know the art world don't pay much, but that's kinda extreme."

He grimaced. "Glad you could make it, T.J. Wanna burger?"

"No, thanks."

"Sorry about your arm. Angela told me you fell or something?"

"Yeah. Badly bruised some muscles."

"Ooooh. You gonna be able to do another performance for us sometime soon?"

"I told Angela I wanted May thirty-first."

"Did she say it was open?"

"No, she said it was booked, but I want to do a late show. Eleven to midnight."

"We don't stay open that late. Can't get a crowd at that hour on weeknights."

Sheesh. That side effect never shows up when I need it. I thought. *It's so good for suggesting things to people. Wonder what would happen if I pretended it was there?* It was a strange idea, but when you want something bad enough, even strange ideas sound good. I planted my feet on the ground and looked Warren right in the eye and tried to speak from my belly. "I need to do it then, Warren," I said. "The timing is important. It's part of the act. I'll bring in lots of people. You won't lose money by it. And I'll only ask for it this once; never again."

Warren peered down at me and raised his eyebrows. "You'll bring in lots of people? Promise?"

"Definitely."

He gave a casual shrug. "Then, sure, you can have it. Since you put it that way, T.J. Yeah, we can open up a special late slot. Sell it as a special event. The other acts that night will probably appreciate it—you'll bring in extra audience for them. Good idea. Tell Angela you got it."

"Thanks." And while I was on a roll— "By the way, if you need more tech crew, I know somebody looking for a job. His name is Sam Waters and he's very good."

"Sam Waters," said Warren. "Okay, bring him by and introduce him sometime. I'd be glad to talk to him."

"Great. You'll like him, I'm sure." And then I noticed it. The energy in my chest wasn't as strong as when the effect showed up on its own, but it was there. *So I can summon it! I can use it. Sort of. Wow!* That was enough luck-pushing for now.

"Something else on your mind, T.J.?"

"Uh, yeah. Where's the beer?"

"In the kitchen. Dave is playing bartender tonight. Ask him."

"Okay." I saw Luigi pilfer a burger patty off the grill and toss it down. He didn't even get burned. "Can't take you anywhere," I growled at him as I wended my way back inside the duplex.

In the kitchen there was a large crystal bowl of pink liquid sitting on the counter.

"What's that?" I asked the guy standing behind it.

"Some sort of wine cooler punch Warren mixed up," he said cheerfully. "I'd watch out for that stuff—they say it packs a wallop."

"Really?" Wheels began to turn in my fiendish mind. I found a quiet corner beside the refrigerator and told Luigi, "Find out if there are any Sidhe in this house."

Luigi saluted and disappeared in a streak of light.

In a moment, he was back, his black velvet cap just slightly askew.

"Well?"

"No, Signorina, nessuno."

"Good." That meant that Luigi's services were not needed at the moment. That meant I had a chance to phone Grandma Kaminski and pick her brain. If I could just get Luigi distracted.

I went back to Dave the bartender. "I'll take two big glasses of the punch, please."

"Two?"

"One's for a friend."

"Yeah, right." But he filled two large plastic cups for me. "Um, how do you wanna carry these?" He said, nodding at my slinged arm.

"One at a time." I carried the first cup outside and found a secluded corner of Warren's garden. I set the cup down on a low brick wall. "Here, Luigi. This is for you, for being such a good protector."

Luigi hopped up onto the wall and took the cup in both hands. "I'll go get the other one and I'll be right back."

I did, and when I returned, Luigi's cup was empty and he was sitting, just a little tilted, on the wall. I sat beside him and sipped at the wine cooler. *Bleah.*

"Luigi, this is really too sweet for my taste, but I don't want to waste it. Would you like my wine punch too?"

"Hmmmm?" He grinned and blinked at me.

I gently took his cup out of his hands and replaced it with mine. His eyes opened wide and he gulped all the punch down in a single swallow.

His eyes began to turn red at the edges and he was definitely having trouble sitting up. "È multo buono," he said, his voice slurry.

"I'm glad you like it. Let's see what else is going on at the party." I took his hand and headed for the town house basement. Luigi seemed unable to decide whether he wanted to walk or fly. He was unsteady either way.

From the giggles and the muggy, chlorine smell drifting up from the basement, I was pretty sure the rumors I'd heard were true. Warren has a hot tub down there, and they say at parties he keeps it filled with naked chicky-poos.

I wasn't disappointed.

"Hey, T.J.!" said one of the two men in the tub, "gonna join us?"

"Not right now, thanks. I forgot my swimsuit."

"Who needs a swimsuit?" a couple of them said in unison. Yes, indeed, the ladies were unclad. I glanced at Luigi. He was boggling—a classic cartoon take, body stretched horizontal, eyes bulging, tongue hanging out.

"Maybe I'll think about it," I said and ducked into a dark corner of the basement, pulling Luigi with me. "Listen," I whispered in his ear, "I have *got* to go to the bathroom for a while. And we know the house is safe. That water looks mighty nice. With all the bubbles, the girls probably won't even know you're there. If you want to join them, why don't you go ahead? I'll come back in a few minutes. Go on! It'll be fun."

That was all it took. Luigi zipped out of my grasp and soon there was a splash and more giggles in the hot tub.

"Yes!" I said to myself and dashed up the stairs.

I bumped into Warren in the kitchen. "Warren, where's your phone? Can I use it?"

"Sure—there's one in the living room, one in the bedroom."

"Thanks!" I ran off, leaving laughing speculation behind me. I decided on the bedroom, for more privacy. Fortunately, no drunken couples had decided they needed to use it yet. I picked up the receiver— and realized I didn't know Grandma's number. I'd always used speed-dial before. *Shit.* I looked around the bed table for a phone book—found one. I flipped madly through the pages, hoping she was listed. Yes, there she was, S. Kaminski.

The phone seemed to ring forever, then "Hello?"

"Hello, Mamu, this is T.J.!"

"Tee . . . Tiffany, dear, is that you?"

"Yes, Mamu, it's me. You said I should call if I needed any help and I need help!"

"Goodness, this is rather unexpected, dear. But what can I do for you?"

"I'm sorry to call out of the blue, Mamu, but I need to know a few things—about elves and fairies and stuff."

"Oh. Does this concern your new little friend?"

"Not exactly. I've made some other acquaintances less friendly than him."

"Oh?"

"Yeah. For one thing, you were right about my arm. The first thing you said. Elf-shot."

"I was? Dear me, I—you aren't joking, are you, Tiffany? I never know when you're joking, you know."

"I'm not joking!" I nearly screamed into the phone. "I'm in trouble! I need to know how to keep fairy folk away from me, and there isn't much time to talk to you, so I need to know it quick!"

"Well, well, I can answer your second question more quickly off the top of my head. To keep the fairies away, of course, prayer and making the holy sign are the most efficacious. Are you a believer, dear?"

"Not really, Mamu. I haven't been to church in a long, long time."

"Hmmm, well, you'd probably better not rely on that, then. Dear me, what were the other things? They don't like to touch iron. Bells are supposed to drive them off, though I can't imagine why. I've heard stories that turning your clothes inside out makes it hard for them to recognize you."

"I can't believe these guys are that dumb. What else?"

"Um, all sorts of herbs that I can't remember right at the moment. I'd have to go check some of my books."

"Okay, forget about that right now. How about if I wanted to break a contract I'd made with them? What would I have to do?"

"Contracts? Oh, that's a much more serious thing, dear. Sometimes, if you learn their real names, or steal their clothes from them, you can gain power over them."

"Steal their clothes?" I heard something behind me and I turned.

Luigi was standing there, dripping wet, a sad and angry pout on his face.

"I gotta go, Mamu. Nice talking to you." I hung up.

"Giocasti un tiro a me," Luigi said sadly.

"I wasn't playing a trick on you, I was just talking to my grandmother. She worries about me, that's all. You like my grandmother, don't you?" But it was no good. I knew that he knew that I was lying. And he knew that I knew that he knew, and so on.

Without another word, Luigi turned into a tiny tornado. He spun over to where I sat on the bed and swept me up in the whirling wind. When the world stopped spinning, I was in Mom's apartment, just inside the front door. And I was sopping wet.

Mom was reading on the couch, her back to me. I looked around but didn't see Luigi anywhere. I turned and reached for the doorknob. Loudly, I opened and shut the front door.

Mom turned around. "T.J., you're home early."

I shrugged. "Wasn't my kind of party."

"And you're wet. Is it raining outside?"

"No, um, I got thrown in the hot tub. That's why I left."

"Sounds like more fun than I've been having."

"Why don't you get out more, Mom?"

"At my age?"

Ralph and Norton popped out of the floor right in front of her, but she looked right through them. Ralph said to Mom, "You feel sleepy. Why don't you turn in for the night?"

Mom yawned and stretched. "I think I'm going to turn in for the night. If you're going to stay up, try not to make too much noise, okay?"

"Uh, okay." I wasn't happy about the way Ralph ordered her around. "Good night."

" 'Night." She wobbled off to the bedroom and shut the door.

Ralph walked right up to me and planted his fists on his nonexistent hips. "Luigi tells us you tried to lose him."

No point in lying. "Look, I had him check to make sure the house was safe. We were in no danger, and I just wanted some time to myself for a while, that's all."

"He wasn't, you know, bothering you or nothin', was he?" said Norton. "He promised us he was gonna behave himself."

I could have said yeah, but Luigi didn't deserve that. "No, he behaved himself, he was just *around*, you know? Always there. I couldn't ignore him, and I couldn't have a normal good time at the party with him right beside me all the time."

Ralph grimaced and spun around. I could almost see steam spewing out of where his ears should be. "Whadda you got, a death wish? You want Mr. High and Mighty Amadan to come do your other arm?"

"I told you, Luigi said the house was safe!"

"Maybe at that moment, but you never know when those sneaky Sidhe might show up."

"So what would Luigi have done if one did?"

"Luigi's got a lot of skills you don't know about," said Ralph. "Anyways, he says you was talking to your grandmother about how to keep us away."

"How to keep *any* elf type away. I figured you guys weren't doing such a good job of protecting me, so I'd better learn some stuff for myself."

Ralph and Norton looked at each other. "Don't you trust us, T.J.?" asked Norton.

"I don't know anymore." I sat down on the couch and tried to fold my arms across my chest. That only hurt my right arm, though, so I settled for scowling at the wall. So much for trying to do anything behind Ralph's and Norton's backs. They'd find out no matter what I did.

Ralph and Norton looked at each other, then back at me. Ralph stepped forward, almost humble. "Look, Princess, I know we've had our misunderstandings. But Norton and me, we've never lied to ya. We never wanted you to get hurt. We thought we could all help each other. And you been a great help to us. Haven't we helped you?"

"I'm not sure what you've done for me," I said. "You gave me big audiences, but they were all Sidhe. The performance acts I did weren't all my own creation, either."

"Listen, we understand that you're scared," said Ralph. "And some not too good things have happened to ya. But some good things have happened to you too, you just don't know it yet. Don't worry. It's all gonna be over soon."

"Okay, but . . ." I sighed, trying to get my courage up. "Could we maybe put an end date on our contract? I mean, it sounds like this battle you're planning is going to decide things, anyway. If you lose, I'll just have to do what I can to keep the Sidhe from snatching me at the end of the month." I decided not to mention that I'd set up a gig for another performance on the thirty-first. I needed that to be my backup. "But if you guys win," I went on, "you won't need me anymore. And I'd really like to get my life back. So, what do you say we call it quits on June first?"

After a dubious scratching of beards, Ralph and Norton walked a few paces away to confer. When they came back, Ralph said, "It's true we'll know by the end of the battle who'll be running this town. So your offer for an end of this contract sounds fair, T.J. But we'd like the chance to make you another deal afterward. It's not true that we won't need you if we win."

"One of the Sidhe types said you guys wanted to set me up in place of their queen. Is that true?"

Ralph twitched uncomfortably. "Well, we're gonna need a figurehead, sorta. And you're already a hero to our folk Under the Hill. So why not you? If we win, that is."

This was really making me nervous. "I don't want to be any kind of queen! Is that what I'm gonna do at the battle itself? Be a figurehead for you?"

"Naw," said Norton. "You're gonna formally summon the Sidhe to battle, using that steel rose you got. Sorta like a herald-tribune."

"Herald!" said Ralph. "*Herald-Tribune* is a newspaper, dummy. But, yeah, T.J., you'll just start things off. Once everybody's there, you retire from the field, as it were, and we all go at it."

"You're sure I won't be in any danger?"

Norton snorted. "That would be stupid. If you got killed, we'd all have to go back to where we came from. End of battle."

"Wait a minute. If killing me stops the battle, what's to stop the Sidhe from attacking me first?"

Ralph threw up his hands. "Leave it to a mort to think of something like that."

"You mean you haven't?" I asked.

"We haven't 'cause it ain't gonna happen."

"Why not?"

"You just don't think like we do. Listen, one thing about the Sidhe, they always follow the Rules. Tradition and Order is everything to them. Especially in war. They're powerful but predictable. Even if you were on the battlefield, they wouldn't harm you."

"It would be unsporting, donchaknow," said Norton in a fake British accent.

"Was it sporting of that Mr. Amadan to freeze my arm?"

"Entirely within the Rules, I'm afraid," said Ralph.

"That reminds me," said Norton "Shouldn't we tell her the other thing?"

"What other thing?" I said. "Why is there always one other thing?"

"We been asking around Downstairs," said Norton, "about trying to fix your arm. Turns out, if you decide to come live with us Under the Hill, your arm will eventually heal and you can use it again. But as long as you're here in the mortal world, it'll stay like it is. Useless. The Seelie probably rigged it that way so you'd have more reason to let them take you to fairyland."

"Oh, fucking great." This just gave that part of me that *wanted* to live there one more excuse. "Look, if I decide I want to live Under the Hill, I'll let you guys know before June. Okay?"

"That's what we mean," said Ralph. "We'll cut off the current contract midnight, May thirty-first, if you wanna. But just give us the chance to make a new offer. See, win or lose, if we take you to our side of the tracks before the Sidhe get to you, then you'll be safe with our kind of folks. The Sidhe won't be able to snatch you. So you might wanna let us know what you decide before the battle. That way, if we get axed, we can have picked someone else to make sure you get Under the Hill."

Talk about a high-pressure sales pitch. "I'll *think* about it, okay? You guys aren't making this any easier for me."

"We're trying to make it easier for you, T.J., but it's up to you. Whatever you wanna do."

"Yeah. So when's this battle gonna happen, anyway?"

"Like we said, the Seelie Court gets to choose that. Oh, that reminds me, we need you to deliver the invitation."

"Invitation?"

"You know, declaration of battle or whatever. The Sidhe like things formal, so we have to give them formal notice. You got that note from Chris, so you can call him up anytime you want. Unless you'd rather talk to the Amadan, since we have his card."

"No, thanks," I said quickly. "I'd rather talk to Chris." Although the thought of seeing Chris again scared me for entirely different reasons.

"That's what we figured. So you call him and give him this . . ." Ralph pulled out from within the folds of his gray skin a huge square envelope made of heavy light-brown paper. It even had a wax seal on it.

I took the envelope. "Okay. When do I give it to him?"

"Soon as possible. But be sure to call him on someplace that's our turf. Or neutral. Just so long as it's not in a park or by a river. Just to keep him from trying any funny stuff."

I tapped the envelope against my right hand. "Not near a park or a river? That's pretty tough in Pittsburgh. We're surrounded by rivers. And there are parks everywhere."

"You're a bright kid, T.J. We're sure you'll figure something out."

"Look," I said, getting exasperated, "I keep getting burned whenever I deal with the Sidhe—"

"It's a formal job you're doin' here," said Ralph. "This Chris guy won't do anything to you once he knows that. It would look really bad. Image is a big thing among the Sidhe."

"Right," I growled. I hoped the battle would be real soon. It was gonna be so good to get my own life back. *Ever since I put that sandwich on Mamu's scarf—* Inspiration struck! "There's something you haven't mentioned about my role in this—it's a small thing, but to you guys, symbols and formal stuff is important, right?"

"Yeah, some of it. Whatcha got in mind?"

"I remember from the old movies that at a tournament a lady wears a token of the side she supports. Since I'm gonna be a figurehead for your side, I oughta have a token, right?"

"Sure, okay," said Norton. "What should we give her, Ralph?"

"No, I want something specific," I said. "I want the blue scarf I gave you two when I first met you."

Ralph paused in thought a moment. "Yeah . . . yeah, that's a good idea, Princess. In fact, that's perfect. That scarf is meant to bring luck to a mort, so if you wear it on the field, that might bring luck to us too. Okay, you got it. We'll give it to you just before the battle."

Figures. He probably knows I'll help willingly in order to get the scarf back. But at least he's confirming that the scarf has some magic, and that magic may give me some protection if I use it later, on the thirty-first. "Thanks."

"No problem. Now we gotta go. You just hand over the invite and we'll take it from there."

"Yeah, okay. Fine. See ya."

Ralph and Norton waved and waddled down the invisible stairs, disappearing into the middle of the living room rug.

I flopped over on the couch. "I hate it when life gets complicated," I groaned, to no one in particular.

Chapter 24

So later that same night, I'm standing hunkered down in my leather jacket on Baum Boulevard, which runs between the neighborhoods of Bloomfield and Shadyside. *I must be nuts,* I told myself. *Certifiable.* But if I'd waited until morning, Mom might have bollixed up the schedule or Chris might not have wanted to show. Better to get it over with.

My right arm ached in its sling, and I tried to keep the jacket pulled over it. Car headlights went by, but thankfully none of them slowed. There were a couple of strip joints along Baum Boulevard, and men sometimes get the funny notion that any female near such a place must be a whore.

It had taken careful searching on a Pittsburgh street map to find a place not near the rivers or a park. A real challenge, but this area was the best I could do—a street of used-car lots, fast-food joints and diners, square warehouses, apartment buildings that might as well be warehouses, gas stations, and a couple of posh restaurants I'd never seen the inside of. It's about as empty of nature as any place in Pittsburgh—there's not even much graffiti on Baum, except for the club with that name, which is where local bands go when they're dead. Certainly nothing here to interest the Sidhe.

Chris's note was curled up in my left hand. Finally, when there was no traffic on the street, I called softly,

"Chris? Come here, Chris. Earth to Chris, do you read me? Here Chrissy, Chrissy, Chrissy."

"I am not a cur," I heard behind me, "to be called as if you had a bone."

I whipped around. "There you are!"

"Here am I." He was wearing a long black leather coat and an ironic smile. He seemed paler, however, and glanced over his shoulder often, as if uncomfortable in his surroundings. His long blond hair was loose and disheveled.

"You should be careful going out like that in the big city," I said. "Homeboys would kill you for that coat."

"I think not," he replied with a smirk. "How fares my merry mischievous maid?"

"Could be better. One of your people zapped my arm pretty good." I pointed at the sling.

He gazed at me sadly. "I did warn you. If you had given thought to all I said, this would not have befallen you."

"Okay, okay, I know. You told me so. Anyway, look, I called you because I have something to give you."

"Ah, a gift! How kind of you to think of me so."

"You won't say that when you see what it is." I pulled the parchment envelope out of my sling. "They told me to give you this." I handed it to him.

Chris took the envelope and gazed at the wax seal. His expression turned grave. "Ah. We have been awaiting such a missive." He turned the envelope over and over in his hands but did not open it.

Awkwardly, I said, "I was told you guys get to choose the day."

He nodded. "That is the form of it."

"And . . . they say I'm to be the herald or something. That I'm supposed to stand where you're going to fight and summon all of you to the field."

"A more sweet voice to call us could not be chosen from all the nightingales i'the world."

I jammed my fingers into my hair and shuffled from foot to foot until at last I blurted out, "You aren't really as stupid as the rest of them, are you? Are you going to go to battle, and maybe die, for . . . for Pittsburgh?"

"Wherefore not? We are summoned to the field, and we must answer."

"But you're immortal!" Something came over me, and I walked right up to him and grabbed his leather lapels in my left hand and shook him. "How can you give up all that life for a stupid lump of real estate? That's crazy!"

He smiled, sadly amused. "You do not know the very land you live on. These wooded hills lie nestled 'twixt two rivers that cup it close as if 'twere lover's hands. The richness of the earth serves all who dwell here. E'en the cloud-choked skies of decades past could not stop its surging fount of life. This place has beauty dear to those who see it. It must not be wrecked by thoughtless fools."

Gotta admit, I'd never heard Pittsburgh described that way before. I realized I was losing, but I kept on. "So it's kind of a pretty place. So what? Aren't there lots of places like this around the world? Why lose your life over it? Can't you find some other place to go, or some way other than war to solve your problems?"

Chris gazed down at me. "Beshrew my heart. I think thou dost love me."

"I do not!" I let go of his coat and backed away. "I just think war is stupid, that's all! There's no point to it!"

He caressed my cheek with the edge of the parchment envelope. "War is a drug, sweet. It blends the rush of poppy syrup with the fellowship brought of good ale, with the pricks to the intellect of strong, hot tea. It is the Great Hunt, the festival dance, and a game of chess all rolled in one."

"No, it's not. It's ugly, it's messy and destructive, and people get hurt and die."

"Aye, that as well."

"I thought you people were supposed to be superior to us mortals. But you've got all the same blockheadedness and you do the same stupid things. You Seelie just do it with better style."

Chris made a mocking bow. "Thy praise I will accept on behalf of those who claim that style is all."

I balled up my fist and growled, "You're hopeless!"

"Hope is a sentiment that you mortals bear more often than my kind. In truth, it does bemuse us to behold how such a silk-fine thread sustains you so. Dost thou truly wish to stop this war?"

"What? Of course I do."

"Then know that the method for it has always been within thy grasp."

"It . . . it has?"

"Thou hast known the answer all along."

If he was going to tell me to click my heels together and say, "There's no place like home," I was going to scream. "Well? What?"

"Give us the names of those who sent thee hither." He placed a finger on my lips. "We know thou has been ensorcelled not to speak. But come with me 'neath the Hill before our Queen, and she will have the means to free thy speech. The one who withered thee might yet be grateful and there restore thy use of thy right arm."

I paused. "But you'd kill the ones I name, wouldn't you?"

"I? Nay, 'tis for our Queen to judge and pass the sentence."

"But she'd have them killed, wouldn't she?"

"I cannot say. She might consider death too kind a fate."

"Thought so. Look, I wouldn't betray them, even

if I could speak their names. I couldn't do such a ratty thing."

Chris nodded. "Thy loyal silence is a sign of valor."

I stared at the sidewalk, not feeling particularly valorous. "So. Nothing can stop you? What if I just don't show? You know, what if I just throw that metal flower away and go hide in a church all day and don't come out until June? What would you do then?"

Chris stood taller, almost seeming to grow in height, towering over me. The wind tousled his hair and he seemed a wild thing, grown like a weed in the crack of a sidewalk, splitting the illusion of the tame modern world. Though his face was young, he looked ancient, as if I could see the centuries that had passed before his eyes. "If not now, then soon. If not thee, another. But wherefore wouldst thou shirk so grand a fate? Destiny hath lain its hand upon thy head, and thou art chosen midwife to our future. Thy race's fate as well sits in thy hands. Wherefore give this up to ones who may not quit themselves so well as thee?"

He's saying it could be worse. It's true that there are people who are more power-hungry than I am, who might use the power the Seelies or Unseelies give them for awful things. Maybe if I back out now, the Seelies will have too much of an advantage the next time and Ralph and his guys will just be wiped out. Too many possibilities. If I go to the battle, maybe there will still be something I can do to stop it. I swallowed hard and said, "I see. I guess I'd better be there."

He inclined his head to me, a salute. "Again thy courage shines, a glowing beacon brighter than the stars amid the night. I honor thee." Chris came up to me and placed a cool hand beneath my chin. Gently he lifted my face toward his. And then he kissed me. Just a bare brushing of the lips that sent delicious shivers down to my toes. I didn't die. But I wouldn't have minded if I had.

Chris stepped back and said, "I must away to render thy missive unto my sovereign Queen. Therefore, farewell, my sweet. 'Tis next on the field of battle we will meet." He turned and walked away. In a few steps, his coat became a shadow on a wall, his hair a spill of light from a nearby window.

I could not tell when one became the other.

Chapter 25

When I woke up late the next morning, Mom was out. She had left a note on the refrigerator:

T.J.—
I didn't want to wake you, so I went off to breakfast on my own. I'd appreciate it if you could do some of the dishes in the sink. With two of us here, they pile up quickly. I know it's difficult with your arm injury, but do what you can. By the way, the Apple has become impossible to work on. I know you're more comfortable with that computer than I am. Could you check it over or call a tech help line to get it fixed?

And could you please call your grandmother again? Sadie called last night all concerned about you, but she wouldn't say why. You know how she is. Thanks.

Mom

I sighed. *Why does she always have to be so . . . mom-like? Aren't I grown up enough that she can treat me like a human being?* I scarfed down some coffee and a couple of blueberry Pop Tarts. And then I did the dishes. Man, was it awkward with only one useful arm. My right hand could sort of hold the scrubber while I moved the plate or cup around with my left hand. Once I got the hang of it, though the process went okay. The hot water was soothing, and the mindless work gave me time to think.

One way or another, unless the fey guys wiped each other out or I managed a miracle in my next performance, I was doomed to go Under the Hill at the end of the month. Only question was which side of the tracks I'd be on, Seelie or Unseelie. Forever. The Sidhe were better dressers, but I couldn't help thinking Ralph and Norton's bunch would be more fun to party with. And the hunger to go was still there, gnawing at my hindbrain like a cross between homesickness and a bad craving for chocolate. All I had to do was accept their deal.

So what would Mom and Grandma think when I suddenly disappeared? That I'd run away? What would Sam and others I knew think? Sam had his suspicions already. Would they get the FBI to try to track me down? Heh. Calling Agents Mulder and Scully . . .

What if, after I was gone, nobody really missed me at all?

I stopped washing a moment and rubbed my cheek with the back of my hand. It wasn't soapsuds on my face but tears.

See, it was like thinking about death. That's what leaving the world forever is, isn't it?

Some people, I'll bet, would argue that I was nuts. Why stay in a world full of crime, poverty, war, stupidity, and pain? Why not live forever in a magical world full of wonders?

Yeah, well, if their world is so wonderful, why were the Seelie and Unseelie always trying to come onto mortal turf? Even Ralph and Norton said they didn't like living Under the Hill all the time. I was beginning to learn that I shouldn't trust everything fairy critters tell me. Or even everything I see.

The truth was, I wasn't ready to go. To "die," even though I knew what that particular afterlife looked like. There was so much left to do up here in the mortal world that I hadn't done yet. I'd never had a real boyfriend; not for long, anyway. Other than Pittsburgh and L.A., I'd never traveled much—I wanted to see Paris and London and Rome. I wanted to see all the beautiful art in the world. I wanted to know what it was like to have my own apartment, to have more friends, more money, to know more stuff, maybe even learn how to understand people. Or at least myself.

It wasn't fair—to have to choose. It wasn't right. I was only nineteen.

The phone rang and I jumped back, dripping soapy water all over. I quickly dried my hands on a paper towel and grabbed the receiver on the third ring.

"Hello?"

"T.J., this is Sam."

I swallowed and wiped the tears from my face. "Hey, Sam, howzit going?"

"Going great. I talked to that guy you told me about. You know, Warren at the Per Forma?"

"Yeah? How'd it work out?"

"Well, I'm starting there next week. Almost seemed like he was ready to hire me even before I showed him what I know. Guess I owe you a lot of thanks."

"Hey, no problem. I didn't tell Warren much about you, just your name and that you were looking for a job. You must have impressed him right off."

"That, or he's way into affirmative action. Anyway, I think I owe you a dinner or something. Whaddaya say?"

Wow. Another date with Sam. Yep, this is worth hanging around for. "Uh, sure!"

"Cool. Warren wanted me to talk with you, anyway, 'bout what you wanted in the way of lighting and so on for your next performance. He seemed real concerned that I oughta keep you happy."

I grinned. "Oh, I think you'll manage that."

Wheels began turning in my brain again. "I am going to be wanting some special help in my next act. It's going to be the most important performance in my career, I think. I might even need you helping out onstage."

"Me? Shit, I've never done performance art."

"Doesn't matter."

"You're not gonna need me to throw up or spread garbage all over, are you?"

"No, Sam. I don't know what it's gonna be yet, but you won't be doing anything like that."

"Okay, I'll trust you. I got a reputation to uphold, you know. So, how about dinner next week? Say, maybe early on Wednesday? We can discuss in intimate detail this career-making performance thing."

"Sounds great."

"Think about where you'd like to go and I'll give you a call Tuesday or something."

"Cool."

"Take care, now. 'Bye."

I hung up and breathed a long sigh. *It's gotta be possible. There's got to be some way I can stay. There are so many Rules that fairy critters live under . . . and it's always some Rule that trips them up in fairy tales, isn't it? Something that lets the mortal win?* It was like doing a jigsaw puzzle with some of the pieces missing.

I stared at the phone. *I could call Mamu again. What had she said before Luigi found me at the party? Something about bells and putting your clothes on backward.* I reached for the receiver and hesitated. *What if they're watching? What would they do to her if they suspect she's helping me?* I couldn't get Mamu in trouble, even if Luigi thinks she can protect herself.

I got up and walked into the living room. *Somewhere in all these books, there's probably an answer. But I don't have all month to read them. Maybe when Mom gets back, I can ask her.*

That reminded me of her note, so I went into the bedroom and fired up the Apple. Just as Mom said, it wasn't working right at all. Clicking with the mouse gave random results. *Definitely we've got gremlin infestation.*

Hmmm. *What if it is more than a joke, and something lives in here that no fairy critter likes? I wonder if it can be talked to. I wonder if I can summon it out? I'm supposed to have all this thaumaturgy power, aren't I?* I rubbed my left hand on my jeans and prepared to do some major mojo. Placing my hand on the monitor screen, I took a few deep breaths. Static crackled lightly up the skin of my arm, making my hair stand on end. "Gremlin in the machine," I intoned, "come forth! I summon you. Show yourself!"

The itching on my left arm became intense and I had to pull my hand away. But something came with it, emerging from the screen. It fell away from my hand and darted around me, sparkling like bright television static "snow." When I could get a glimpse of it, it looked about five inches high, with vague arms and legs and head.

So it is real! "Hold still!" I commanded.

The gremlin stopped on the edge of the desk. But it spun in place so fast that although I could tell where it was, I could no longer see its shape.

"Why were you in my computer? Speak!"

In a high-pitched voice, it replied, "Random interface optimal energy nexus local environs."

I scratched my head. "Can you talk more coherently?"

"No."

Well, at least it was capable of a direct answer. *Maybe if I ask only yes/no questions.*

"You create chaos where there is order, right?"

"Yes."

"Any kind of order?"

"Yes."

"If I asked you to disrupt something for me, could you?"

"Probabilities divergent infinite sample unavailable—"

"Okay, okay, I asked that wrong. Um, can you disrupt things outside of the computer or other machinery?"

"Yes."

"Things that are not machines?"

"Probability variable dependent."

"Heh, I almost understood that. If I asked you to do such a thing, and you did it, is there something you would want in return?"

The gremlin spun this way and that but did not reply.

"Too complicated a question. Okay, is there anything that would make you happier?"

After a pause, "Yes."

"What would it be?"

"Modem access."

"Aha. You'd like to be able to move into bigger systems."

"Yes."

"An on-ramp to the information superhighway, right?"

"Yes."

I'll bet. Now what? There were moral dilemmas all over this business. If I set the gremlin free, like Ralph said, who knew where it would go? If I agreed to give it modem access to other systems, I'd be the cause of foul-ups someplace else—maybe some poor nerd's web site, or the Internet itself. But the facts that gremlins made chaos out of order and that the Sidhe loved order had to be useful somehow. At least as a distraction during my performance, provided I could control it. More to think about. For the moment, the safest place to store the gremlin was back in the Apple.

"If I release you, will you let the computer work normally for my mom and me?"

"Yesno."

"I could bind you into the toaster."

"Nonononononono!"

"Promise to behave?"

"Yes."

"Okay." I put my left hand under the spinning creature and held it up to the monitor. "I hereby release you. Return whence you came."

The gremlin hopped onto the screen and melted into it. And I got a big static shock. I pulled my hand back and sucked on my fingertips. "Nasty critter." But the screen suddenly changed to the standard front page, and the mouse was able to work normally. Files appeared when they were clicked on, and they contained the right stuff.

"Thank you," I said to the screen. "I'll think about that modem thing."

A smile of static briefly flickered on the monitor.

The front door opened and banged shut. "I'm back. Are you home, T.J.?"

"I'm in the bedroom, Mom."

In a minute she came to the door. "Thank you for doing the dishes, dear. That's a big help. How's the computer doing?"

"Fine. You were right. There's a gremlin in it."

Mom raised her brows. "Well, so should we call Apple or the Orkin man?"

I grinned at her. "I fixed it for now. If it gives you more trouble, just let me know."

"I'm impressed. Glad they teach you something worthwhile at school."

"Um, Mom? Remember how we were talking about fairy abductions the other day? After Phipps? You know, I've been wondering how, in those stories, mortals ever won against the fairies. I mean, if they've got all this magic and power and stuff, what chance would any mortal have against them?"

"My, you have been dwelling on this, haven't you?"

"Well, um, I was talking to Sam and he was in

Midsummer Night's Dream this term and we were discussing that."

"Ah, yes, Oberon and Titania." She frowned. "But I don't remember any fairy abduction in that play."

"Well, the subject came up anyway and, so, aren't there stories about how mortals fight fairies?"

"You mean like Queen Maeve?"

"Who?"

"Queen Maeve, or sometimes it's Medb, of Connaught. She was a warrior queen, a mortal—though some call her a goddess—who fought the great Cuchulainn in order to steal the Brown Bull of the Sidhe."

Hearing her say the name of the Seelie made me sit up straight. "Did she win? What did she do?"

"I believe she won. She used up the lives of a lot of warriors, as I recall. And she was said to be treacherous and sneaky."

"But do you remember anything *specific*?"

"No, dear. It's all in the great cycle *The Tain*. I'm sure the library must have a copy."

As if I'm going to get a chance to do library research, I thought sourly.

"But that isn't abduction anyway," Mom went on, "Unless you mean the bull. Now Tam Lin is a story about preventing abduction, and there, I recall, his lover has to keep hold tight of him, no matter what happens, in order to keep him bound to this world."

"Really?" Now we were getting somewhere!

"Yes, I remember several stories like that. The lover or spouse has to hold the potential abductee, no matter what they see or hear or what shape the victim takes. Is this what you were looking for?"

"Yeah! That's it! Anything else like that?"

"Well, not that I can remember off the top of my head. Let me think about it a little. You are enthusiastic for this topic, aren't you?"

I shrugged, not knowing how to explain it to her. "But I had another question, Mom. I mean, don't the families of the abductees notice they've been snatched? Would the families go after the fairies in revenge, wipe 'em out or something?"

Mom laughed nervously. "T.J., you sound as though you believe these stories were real. Folklore is never that logical. In some stories, the abductee's absence is noted, but sometimes the fairies make a stand-in, a fake golem of the person they're stealing, made out of moss or heather or I suppose whatever's handy."

"Oh. I see . . . so they might never know the real person's gone."

"Unless they notice a certain earthy smell or that their loved one has a more wooden personality, I guess not. Now, if you'll excuse me, since the computer's running I'd like to get on it and get some work done."

"Oh. Sure." I stood up and let her have the chair. As she sat, I kissed her cheek and said, "Thanks, Mom."

She looked startled. "You're welcome. What for?"

"For being you. I'm going to the library. See you later."

Chapter 26

Naturally, they wouldn't let me go to the library. In fact, they wouldn't let me go anywhere.

I stepped out the apartment door, ran down the steps, and hit a wall of molasses. Or so it felt. It looked just like ordinary air, but with a strange yellow tint to it. I didn't see any other people, but cars went by at their usual speed.

Using my arm as well as my legs, I tried to press on further, almost swimming through the invisible density around me. But every step was an enormous effort. I got about two buildings down, when I had to give up and sit down on a low brick wall.

A long-haired black cat jumped agilely onto the wall and sat down beside me.

"Hi, there," I grumbled at it. "You don't seem slowed down any. Aren't you lucky."

"Under the right circumstances," the cat replied. "Top o' the day to ye, Miss."

I jumped and immediately felt stupid. "A talking cat. I should have expected it."

"I do apologize for appearing in this form," the cat said. "Ordinarily, I'd be in a more noble shape, a proud stallion or a great black dog. But no, 'be a cat,' they told me. 'Horses are rare in this place and large dogs must wear leashes. Cats are more common, more accepted and less noted.' I ask ye, what debased times are these, when cats are more welcome than a right noble dog?"

I grinned. "People live in smaller places and cats fit better. But if you aren't really a cat, what are you?"

The cat's eyes widened in surprise. "So, 'tis true what the boggies were sayin', that we are no longer known among the mortal folk. I, my dear, am a pooka."

I snorted. "Why do you critters always have such stupid names?"

The cat growled, "Here, don't you go makin' a mockery now, or I'll bite ye and scratch ye, princess or no."

"If I'm a princess, why aren't you calling me 'Your Highness'?"

The cat drew itself up proudly. "For I am a cat, and we don't go highnessin' nobody."

"Oh, you'll be a cat if it suits you?"

"Precisely."

"Uh-huh. So are you here to protect me, watch me, or harass me?"

"Oh, I can do all three. Right talented we pookas are."

I rolled my eyes. "What did they *send* you to do? And are you a Seelie or an Unseelie critter?"

"We long ago cast our lot with the workaday world, for it grieves us how you mortals grind yourselves down with labor. Makes you no fun at all, it does. Though, truth be told, there's many a mort who's enjoyed a wild ride on my back o'nights to find themself dumped in the drink at dawn." The cat winked at me.

"So I guess that makes you Unseelie. Why are you here instead of Luigi or Ralph and Norton?"

"All, all, gone to train for the wars, don't ye know. Seelie and Unseelie alike. The world is quite bereft of them these days."

"But if the Sidhe aren't around, why worry about me? Why not just let me go about my business?"

The cat shook its head. "The sprites and spriggins have no chain upon 'em now. You'd have to beware the very grass beneath your feet. And the mortal world has dangers enough to protect you from. You've an important part to play, and we'll not have ye breakin' a leg before your time to strut the stage."

"I see. So I'm a prisoner until the battle."

" 'Twill not be long."

"When is it going to happen?"

"Soon."

"Can't you be more specific?"

"No."

"You're as stubborn as a cat, too."

"When it suits me." The cat bared its teeth in what might have been a grin.

"So why aren't you off training for the wars?"

"No need. We pookas don't use weapons, oh my me, no. Only tooth and claw, hoof and horn. We need only be ourselves, in all our dazzling variety."

"Oh. Well, I guess I might as well go back home, then, if you won't let me go anywhere else. Can you at least make it easier for me to get there?"

The cat jumped down from the wall and fluffed its black furry tail. "Follow me, and I shall clear the way."

"Thanks." It was a normal walk back up the stairs. The cat sat on the landing as I opened the door. "Want to come in for a saucer of milk?" I said. When I turned around to look, the cat was gone.

"That was fast," Mom called out from the bedroom as I walked in. "Forget something?"

"No." I slumped down on the couch.

"What happened?"

"A black cat crossed my path."

"Poor dear," she said sardonically. "Bad luck is just piling up on you lately, isn't it?"

I closed my eyes. "Tell me about it."

Late that night, I was shaken awake.

"Hmmm? Mom?"

"Not exactly, Princess."

"Ralph! What time is it?"

"It's *that* time."

I rubbed my eyes and sat up. It was still very dark. I could barely see Ralph's and Norton's silhouettes in the street light filtering through the curtains. "What time?"

"We got an appointment in Homestead. Remember?"

"Oh." I threw back the covers and sat up on the couch bed. "The pooka said it would be soon, but I didn't think it would be *this* soon."

"The Sidhe want it over with. So do we. Norton, let's have some light."

I expected the lamp to go on, but instead a dim blue flame appeared in Norton's hand. I stood, half awake, feeling as though I were still in a dream. I was wearing only a T-shirt and underpants. "Listen, my clothes are in the bedroom, and I don't know how I can dress without waking up my mother."

"No need," said Norton. He held out his arm, which had a heavy cloth draped over it. It turned out to be a long hooded wool robe with wide sleeves. Ralph helped me put it on, especially over my uncooperative right arm. The robe was lined with soft fur and was very warm.

Next, Norton handed me another length of cloth. "This is a tabard. You wear it over the robe so's people know who you are." It was just a long length of fabric with a hole in the middle for my head. Ralph draped it over the robe so the tabard hung down front and back. It was made of a dark-red satin and had a rose embroidered on it in silver thread.

Then Ralph took the actual steel rose the Amadan had given me and placed it in the crook of my right arm so that its blossom was cupped in my curled, useless hand.

"Okay, is that everything?" said Ralph.

"Shoes," I said.

"Oh, yeah. Luigi?"

I heard a pop in the room but didn't see him. Suddenly my feet were warmer, and I looked down. I was now wearing fur-lined black leather boots that came up to my calves. I would have thought they were way cool, had I not known the occasion for which I was wearing them.

"Ready?"

"Can I have something to eat first?"

"No."

"Not even coffee?"

"No. Believe me, you'll thank us later, Princess. Let's go."

"What about the scarf?"

"You'll get it when we get there."

So that was that. I was awake enough now to be scared shitless, but I couldn't think of any more ways to stall them. Ralph had been smart not to warn me about when the time would come. I was so frozen with fear and uncertainty, it was easy for them to take my arms and lead me into the living room wall.

It was like walking down the moving sidewalk they have at the airport, only the "sidewalk" was sliding so fast, the surrounding landscape was just a dark blur. I let Ralph and Norton hold me up and guide me along, as if I were going to my own execution.

The blur receded and we were standing on a riverbank. The air was chill and a damp fog was rising off the river. The water flowed like black ink just a couple of yards from my feet. To my left, I could see the Homestead High Bridge, whose street lamps shone a harsh, glaring light. Behind me loomed dark, squat buildings, the remnants of U.S. Steel's mills, the ruins of the place that workers had called "Fort Frick."

My eyes were adjusting to the dimness. and I could now see that Ralph and Norton were dressed in heavy leather robes, studded with metal circles. They had each a bow and a quiver of arrows slung over their backs.

Norton was tying something to my upper left sleeve.

It was the blue scarf. "This was a good choice, T.J. This cloth was woven to bring luck. With you wearin' it, maybe it'll help us win."

"Aren't you guys afraid?"

Ralph shrugged, his face grim. "We can't afford to be. Now, we figured there might be a problem with you holding the scroll that lists our names, what with your arm like that. Also, you might not be able to pronounce some of them. So we're gonna do something else instead."

While I was looking at Ralph, Norton took my hand and I felt a sudden pain on the tip of my index finger.

"Ow!"

"Sorry, Princess. But what we need you to do is to put a drop of your blood on everybody's forehead as we call them here. That will fix them to the mortal world so's the Sidhe can't just send us away. So put a smudge right here." He tapped his face above his eyes. I thought about poking one of his eyes out, but didn't. I wiped my finger on what passed for his forehead.

"Thanks. Norton, too."

Norton bent his head forward and I did the same for him. He stepped back and pulled out from under his armor an enormous scroll. Standing to my left, Norton unrolled the scroll and began to read aloud a list of names. "Tom Cockle, Billy Blind, Botuchan Sowill, Gentle Annie, Cutty Soams, Lob-Lie-Bythefire, Gull, Patch, Hinky Punk—"

As each name was called, they came out of the dirt on the riverbank and bowed before me; big, hairy goblins with long arms; neatly dressed little men with red, blue, or green caps; withered little women with pendulous breasts and hooked noses; long-bearded dwarves in chain mail armor. On each one's forehead I placed a drop of my blood. I felt like some strange sort of priestess, giving bloody benediction to these would-be warriors from the otherworld. Perhaps, in some way, I was.

This went on for a very long time. I was surprised I didn't faint from blood loss. But at last Norton rolled up his scroll, and the motley mob collected themselves in a line some yards from the river.

I tried to remember what I could about the original battle between the steelworkers of Homestead and the Pinkertons sent by Frick to break their strike. The millworkers had been ready for that sort of move on Frick's part, and so when the boats carrying the Pinkertons were sighted, the workers and their families lined up along the river. The Pinkertons tried to land, and a volley of bullets was exchanged, each side claiming the other had fired first. But, after several men on each side died, the Pinkertons surrendered and were forced out of town.

I hoped history would repeat itself.

Ralph spit on the little wound on my finger and rubbed it. In a moment, it was healed.

"Thanks," I said. "Now what?"

"Now you summon the Sidhe," said Ralph.

"How?"

"Throw the steel rose into the water and say, 'You are summoned to the field,' or something like that."

"Okay." I turned and took one last look at the ragged line of rebellious Unseelies. "You sure you wanna go through with this?"

Ralph sighed and rolled his eyes. "Just do it, will ya?"

I walked to the river's edge. The fog was thick now and I couldn't see the opposite bank. I took the steel rose out of the cradle of my crippled hand. Holding it high over my head, I said, "Warriors of the Seelie Court, Knights of the Sidhe, we summon thee onto the field of battle." I threw the rose over the dark water and heard its distant splash.

For long moments nothing happened. I heard a low wail, far to my right. A factory whistle.

The streetlights on the High Bridge dimmed. The clouds overhead parted, revealing the full moon. Out of the mist ahead of me, strange white shapes—boats in the form of giant swans—emerged. The Sidhe had arrived.

Moonlight glinted off their plated armor, their feathered helmets, their painted shields, their long, unsheathed swords. They rode enormous pale horses whose eyes glowed red like hot coals and whose nostrils steamed with hot breath.

Oh, shit. My legs seemed to freeze in place and my stomach went cold. I glanced back over my shoulder at the motley mob behind me. The weapons they carried were farm tools, rough spears, some bows and arrows. Many wore no armor at all. *To hell with history,* I thought. *They're going to lose.*

The boats kept coming slowly toward the shore. There were three of them, immense swans carved to look fiercer than eagles. In the lead boat I recognized Brian Amadan, and I rubbed my right shoulder protectively. He now was wearing full plate armor instead of a gray suit and riding a huge gray horse.

But beside him, even more fierce and terrifying in appearance, was the lady Reia Perry, on an armored white steed. Her long hair stood out in wild disarray from beneath a helmet topped by two raven's wings. A gold bird sat on each shoulder of her silver breastplate. A purple cloak billowed out behind her. In her left hand she carried a long, light lance, and a sword was strapped to her side.

A warrior queen, like Queen Maeve or Medb. Mab. Wait. Wasn't Queen Mab the name of the fairy queen in one of those monologues in Acting class? Could it be . . . that she was real, and once a mortal, and the fairies snatched her because she was such a good fighter? Interesting as this line of thought was, it didn't reassure me at all. I could only stand and watch the Sidhe approach, frozen in awe.

The swan boats stopped just a few yards from the

shore. Reia Perry called out, "We thank you, herald, for your service. For your safekeeping, I pray you quit the field."

I suddenly woke up to the fact that I was not in a good spot. I bowed to the boats and trotted a few yards to my left.

A loud "Cawwk!" broke the eerie silence. A huge black raven had settled onto one of the ruined foundations near the riverbank. I shivered and dared not go near it.

From the line of Unseelie warriors, someone called out, "Do not try to land here, gentleman, for we have come to look to our land and families."

"Now, my less than fair folk," called the Amadan, "we are coming ashore to guard this land, and we would have no bloodshed. Three hundred are behind me and you cannot stop us."

A high-pitched voice from the multitude on the riverbank replied, "Come on, then. But if you come, it shall be over our carcasses."

Events then moved quickly. The Amadan threw a spear that landed at the feet of the Unseelie line. From the Unseelie came a rolling roar like an avalanche, screams like the tortured metal in a train wreck; a volcano of sound that, I realized after a moment, was their war cry. A volley of silver arrows flew from the ragged line, most falling in the water, some too near me for my comfort.

Then, from the Sidhe, came a high-pitched wail, the scream of metal guitar, mixed with the moan of bleak winter wind through bare trees, the howl of a thousand enraged cats, an atonal chorus of damned souls. My hair stood on end and I stood frozen, unwilling to even breathe.

The swan boats lowered their heads until they touched the water, forming ramps toward the shore. The Amadan raised his sword and lowered it. And then the Sidhe charged, their horses plunging into the shallow river's edge and thundering up the bank.

The two armies rushed at each other like two floods undammed. The sound of their collision was horrible—screams of horses, men, and inhuman creatures, metal striking against metal and flesh. I tried to run further along the riverbank, but the fighters flowed around me and my way was blocked. No one harmed me—I was ignored, but I was not able to make headway against them.

I was splashed by hot, dark liquid, and I smelled blood. I looked down and saw a hairy severed hand twitching, saw a severed head spouting black ichor. Its eyes still rolled, and a long tongue whipped about its foaming lips.

I knelt at the river's edge and retched. Nothing came out but bile and saliva as the waves of nausea rolled over me. *This was why Ralph wouldn't let me eat. How kind of the bastard.*

The incredible noise continued behind me, and after I had heaved enough I tried again to run further downriver, not looking at the ground. I tried to ignore the sounds and movement around me, letting it become a blur of color and noise, indistinct and meaningless.

Something caught my left ankle. I glanced down and saw Luigi hanging on to my leg with both hands. "Scusi, Signorina. Perdona, ma—"

I bent down and tried to stand him up. His arms and legs flopped like a rag doll's. And little rag-doll guts came spilling out of a gaping wound in his belly.

Oh, God. I swallowed down nausea and awkwardly picked him up with my left arm, pinning him against me as best I could with my right. A space opened up in the clashing bodies ahead of me, and I ran. As soon as I found myself away from the battle, I lay Luigi on the cool dirt of the riverbank.

"Acqua, per favore," he said softly. His eyes were no longer focusing. "Sono tanto assetato."

I ran to the river's edge and cupped the dark water

in my hands. Trying not to spill any, I hurried back to Luigi's side. I clumsily poured water into his tiny mouth, and it spilled out again. His eyes stared at nothing.

"Luigi?" I shook him. I pressed my thumb against his neck. Dead. The true death.

I turned and looked back at the battling throng, hoping I could see Ralph or Norton. They were good at fixing things, weren't they? They would help him. I stood and staggered toward the fighters ahead of me. "Ralph? Norton?" I didn't see them, and I doubted they could hear me over the noise.

Suddenly the scene in front of me came into focus—one Sidhe rider was surrounded by Unseelie. His helmet was off and his pale hair writhed in the wind. It was Chris! He slashed about with his sword, but the Unseelie were pulling his horse down. His head snapped back as a scythe cut across his neck and three arrows pierced his chest.

"No!" Like a madwoman, I rushed into the throng of Unseelie fighters and pushed them away. They moved aside for me, and I fell to my knees at Chris's side. He, too, was dead, eyes wide and unseeing. I bent over him and pounded on his chest. "Was it worth it, you stupid idiot! Is it worth it now?"

Naturally, he didn't answer. But as I stood over him, seeing the blood on his body and Luigi's blood on my hands, a molten-hot anger welled within me. Sorrow and rage and fierce disgust all built within like I was a volcano ready to explode. I raised my left fist into the air and with everything that was in me, I screamed, "STOP!"

Instantly, the shouts and sounds of war died down to a soft, astonished murmur. The Unseelie shuffled into a line in front of me, confusion and wonder in their eyes. I turned around. Brian Amadan and Reia Perry were riding up to me on their great steeds, but they stopped a couple of yards away. The Amadan stared at me with . . . what? Amazement? Admiration? Rage? I couldn't tell.

"The herald has called for a cessation of arms," he shouted into the silence. "By what Right or Rule does the herald compel us?"

It was the side effect, I realized. The good old helpful side effect had given me the power to stop the fight. But now it was gone. Spent. And as the silence stretched longer and longer and I felt the stares of all of them upon me, I thought, *Shit. What do I do now?*

Chapter 27

The whispering among the Unseelie behind me became louder, although I could not understand what they were saying. Reia Perry tilted her head and regarded me curiously. "Does the herald," she said at last, "bid us hold in the name of mercy?"

"Mercy!" I said, latching on to that word as though it were a life raft. "Yes! In the name of mercy, I bid you hold!"

She and Brian Amadan looked at one another, darkly amused.

"You did have some once, didn't you?" I said to her. "When you were mortal? When you were the warrior queen of Connaught?"

There came a soft, astonished gasp from the Sidhe line and their stares became more intense. *Yes!* I thought. *That's it. I know her true identity, her true name, if Mom told me the right one. True names have power. That's one of the Rules!*

The Sidhe warrior queen smiled at me, and that smile was more terrifying than her armor and lance. "No," she said. "I never did. That is why some of your kind call me La Belle Dame Sans Merci." She nudged her horse and rode very close to me. She drew her sword and placed the bloody blade on my shoulder, its edge against my neck. "Have you any requests, herald?"

Any final requests, does she mean? So this is it. I'm about to die. Unless I say the right thing. I began to shake so bad I could hardly stand. Tears leaked out of my eyes and I had to grit my teeth to keep from sobbing. I finally whipped my left arm across my chest and grabbed the scarf armband to try to hold myself together. I didn't have any moxie or mojo left. All I had was me. "By . . . your name," I said, "Queen Maeve of Connaught, who won . . . the Brown Bull . . . I . . . demand that . . . you call . . . a truce."

A very long second passed. And then she flicked the sword blade away. Loudly, she proclaimed, "In my name, the herald has asked for a truce. Therefore, let it be done. We will depart the field. Let us arrange to have representatives meet for more amicable settlement of our dispute."

Cheers and shouts arose from Seelie and Unseelie alike. Me, I collapsed beside Chris's body, bent over double, feeling like I was going to be sick. My whole insides ached, but I didn't throw up. I just knelt there, moaning, as the Sidhe took Chris away.

One by one, the rest of the Seelie Court turned and walked or rode into the river, disappearing into the thickening mist. All around me, the pools of blood and bits of bodies evaporated into nothing.

The raven I'd seen before the battle flew down from its ruined wall and landed right in front of me. It tilted its head this way and that, regarding me with dark eyes. I had the feeling it did not approve of me or what I'd done. It spat out a "Caw!" and took off into the night.

I stood up slowly, still shaking. The Unseelie were gathered in clumps on the riverbank, some tending to each other's wounds.

"Hey! T.J.! T.J.! Over here!"

To my right I saw Ralph lying on the ground. I hadn't thought my heart could sink any lower.

I hobbled over. Ralph lay on the dirt. He was alive, but his twiglike legs had been snapped off. He smiled up at me, his eyes leaking tears and blood.

"All right! We knew you could do it! You stared her down, just like we knew you would."

"You *knew* I could do that?"

"Well, we hoped it, anyways. They always say it's important to have a mort on the battlefield. Heh. Now I see why. Anyhoo, I'm glad I lived to see that. But now . . ." He looked down at his twiggy stumps, then back at me. "Ya might as well gimme the koo-dee-grass, Princess. A knocker ain't much good without his legs." Ralph held out a jagged-edged dagger toward me.

I pushed his arm aside. "No! There's been enough dying today! Can't you be fixed or something? Can't you heal yourself? You aren't dying. You aren't even bleeding. You guys are good at fixing things. Where's Norton?"

"Over there," Ralph said morosely. "No, don't look. You don't wanna see, believe me."

But I did look and saw a couple of dwarfs bearing away a shapeless gray mass.

"God, I'm sorry, Ralph."

"Hey, didn't we tell you not to swear? Anyway, it's not your fault. My best buddy, more'n three hundred years." Ralph sighed. "Like they say, we knew the job was dangerous when we took it." He held the dagger out to me again.

"No."

"Look, T.J., I can't be fixed. Once my legs were cut by those elven swords, nothin' can put them back on again."

I clenched my fist. "That doesn't mean you have to die!"

"Whaddaya want me to do? They don't make wheel-chairs for knockers."

I wracked my brain, trying to think of something, anything. "That's not the only answer. When morts lose arms or legs nowadays, they just get artificial ones. So . . . so why not have Joe Magarac make you a pair of legs? A magic metal pair of legs. He'd be good at that." It sounded stupid, but at least I could keep Ralph arguing.

"Hey," Ralph blinked and looked up at the lightening sky, "that's a thought. Metal legs. Sure, Joe could do that. They'd probably be even stronger than the originals. Could do more with 'em. See, that's what we love about you morts. You guys can come up with stuff like that. I coulda never thought of that."

"Are you sure you weren't just being overly dramatic?" I suggested.

"Who, me? You morts are strange, ya know," said Ralph. "Sometimes you treat us knockers like we're nothing, and sometimes you act like we're better'n real people."

"Don't be so surprised," I said. "We morts treat each other the same way." I called out to a couple of hairy, long-armed Unseelie types nearby. "You! Come here. Take this guy Under the Hill, to Joe Magarac's mill."

They looked at each other uncertainly a moment, then rushed up and grabbed Ralph's arms.

"You sure you don't wanna be queen?" asked Ralph. "You're a natural, ya know. Hey, careful, there," he grumbled at the Unseelie. "Got a bruise or two, ya know what I mean?" As they hustled him down into the earth, Ralph waved. " 'Bye, T.J. Offer's still open, ya know. Hope to see ya later."

"I'll think about it," I said softly.

The Unseelie, what was left of them, were milling around, occasionally glancing at me. I heard a horse approaching behind me and felt a tap on my shoulder. I looked up.

Reia Perry, or Queen Maeve, smiled down at me. "You must tell them to depart. They await your order."

"My order?"

"It is your blood that holds them here."

"Oh." I stood and yelled at the mob. "Go! It's over! Go home, all of you!"

They scurried down into the earth as fast as they could. I was alone on the riverbank, except for the Fairy Queen. Warily, I waited to see what she would do.

She held out her hand to me. "As we are the last upon the field, it would be my honor to let you ride before me on my horse and thereby escort you home."

She's treacherous, Mom said, I remembered. "No, thanks. I can catch a bus."

The warrior queen chuckled. "You are cautious. It shows you are wise as well as brave. But I am more honor-bound now as a Sidhe than I was in mortal life. We have promised you these last days on earth and will not take you until the last hour tolls upon the last day of this month."

"Good. I'm counting on that," I said. Then I quickly added, "I'm doing a last performance on the thirty-first. Kind of a way of saying good-bye."

"We will be most pleased to attend and bear witness to your leave-taking. Now, if it pleases you, will you ride with me?"

I looked around. It would probably be a long walk to the nearest bus stop. And I didn't know which ones went from Homestead to Pittsburgh. And I didn't have any money with me. And I couldn't call Mom to have her pick me up. What would I tell her? Guess I had to trust La Belle Dame Sans Merci. "Okay. But I've never ridden a horse before."

"It will not matter." She tapped her horse's shoulder and the animal went down on one knee, as if bowing. This lowered the saddle enough that I could climb on behind her. The horse stood up again and began to canter across the bridge. But the bridge disappeared before we reached the other side. I could swear we were riding through the clouds. It was perfectly smooth . . . I had no trouble staying on.

"Can I ask you something?" I said over her shoulder.

"Ask what you will, though I may not answer."

"So, they snatched you from the mortal world, just like you're going to snatch me, right?"

"I was not snatched, as you put it. They offered and I accepted."

"Why?"

"To live forever, immortal, among those who admire one's skill? Whyever not?"

"Okay, in your case I guess it makes sense. But why me? I'm not beautiful, or powerful, or brave—"

"But, surely, the events on the field this day show you are powerful and brave enough."

"But I was just mad, that's all. I mean, I'm usually really a coward. I'm afraid of *people*, for Christ's sake—"

The horse stumbled. "*If* you please," said Reia Perry, as the animal caught itself and continued its run.

"Sorry, didn't mean to swear. Anyway, I'm afraid of growing up, afraid of getting a real job, all that stuff."

"And yet you live and persevere and even dare to hope."

"Well? So? What else is there to do?"

"The quality of courage does not belong to the fearless. It belongs to those who feel the fear, yet overcome it. This very morn I watched as your soul melted in terror, yet you said those things that needed to be said."

I had no answer to that. A few moments later, the clouds parted and we were standing in the apartment living room. Here I was, sitting on a horse, behind the Queen of Elfland, in my mom's living room. If I'd had the energy, I would have laughed.

Instead, I slid down off the saddle. "Thanks for the ride."

"You are most welcome. Sleep now and let rest ease your troubled thoughts."

"Chris is really dead, isn't he?"

"He will not rise again."

"Was it worth it? This battle, I mean."

She smiled. "In ways you cannot imagine. It was glorious."

Yep. Ralph was right. Sick puppies, the lot of 'em.

"We shall see you again in a fortnight, I expect," she went on.

"Yeah," I said with a feeble wave. "Later."

The warrior queen looked at the couch-bed and wrinkled her pretty nose. "Dear me, what is that dreadful smell?" She backed her horse around, and it leaped into the window curtains.

I expected to hear breaking glass, but I didn't. I sniffed the air. She was right—there was a faint sickly herb scent coming from somewhere. I knelt beside the couch and pulled out the wreath in the plastic bag. The smell was clear even with it wrapped. I lay down on the couch, still dressed, and hugged the wreath to my chest with my good arm. In moments I fell asleep.

Chapter 28

Some hours later, I was shaken awake.

"Mmmm. Ralph?"

"Who's Ralph? No, dear, it's me."

"Mom?" I opened one eyelid, then the other. Yep, it was her. There was too much light in the room, and I shut them again.

"What time is it?"

"It's nearly eight."

"Eight?" I moaned. "Why did you wake me?"

"You were tossing and making all kinds of noise, dear. I thought you might be having bad dreams."

Heh. I'll bet they were. A wild hope seized me and I sat up. *Might it all have been—?* But beside the couch were the black fur-lined boots, the soles caked with mud. The blue scarf was stuffed in one boot. The robe and the tabard with the embroidered rose were draped over the back of the couch.

Mom had gone off to the kitchen. "So, who's this Ralph? Some boyfriend you haven't told me about?"

"No. Just a . . . just a friend." I rubbed my face with my left hand. I noticed I no longer had feeling in my right arm at all—no pain but nothing else either. There was a thought knocking on the back of my forebrain, wanting in. "Mom? Where's the wreath I was holding? I had it on the couch here and now it's gone."

"It's out by the front door, dear. I knew you wanted to keep it, but it was reeking so much, I had to put it in another bag and put it outside. If you're going to use it, at least please throw out the wilted part or store it better. It smells like parts of it have rotted past redemption."

"Okay. Sorry, Mom."

"I'm going out for breakfast. Want to come along?"

"No. I'm not feeling hungry right now."

"Suit yourself. I'm planning to call your doctor today to get your prescription changed and have him examine your arm again. I don't like the way it's looking. Do you happen to remember the name of the doctor we saw? Or which clinic it was? I've been hunting for the number, but I can't remember where I put it."

Wonderful. All Ralph's spells are unraveling. What am I going to tell her? "I'll look for it while you're gone, Mom."

"Thank you, dear. I appreciate it. I swear, while we're at the clinic, I should have myself tested for Alzheimer's. Well, see you later. Try not to sleep all morning."

"I won't."

I sighed a big sigh after the front door closed behind her. I was about to lie down again when Ralph appeared on the bed near my feet. Bandages covered his short leg stumps, and his gray face and body sagged more than before the battle. He now more resembled a partly melted Hershey's kiss than a fireplug.

"Ralph? What are you doing here?"

"You called for me."

"I did? Oh, I just said your name because I thought Mom was you when she woke me, that's all. How are you doing?"

He shrugged. "Not bad, considering. Joe's workin' on a new set of legs for me and they're pretty swell-lookin'."

"Good. I'm glad that'll work out. But, if you can

just disappear and appear where you want, and I've even seen you fly, why do you need legs at all?"

Ralph grimaced. "Let's just say there's been places where I needed 'em and without 'em I'd be real stuck."

"Okay, I'll take your word for it. I . . . I'm real sorry about Norton."

"Yeah, me too."

"And Luigi. He's dead too, you know."

"Yeah," he said, more softly.

I asked him the same thing I asked Reia Perry. "Was it worth it?"

Ralph looked up at the ceiling and scratched his beard. "I dunno. Maybe. Maybe the Sidhe will respect us a little more. Be a little more careful before they mess with our turf again. They'll probably respect morts a little more now, too, after what you done."

"But I didn't do hardly anything! I mean, what pisses me is, why couldn't I have used my thaumaturgy, whatever you call it, to bring Luigi back? Or even Chris? Instead all I did was manage a truce for you guys. And from the way Queen Maeve was talking, it's all going to happen all over again someday."

"I can't answer that for you, Princess. Wild talent like you got sometimes seems to have a life of its own. Wizards study for years to learn how to control it, sometimes they never do. So don't beat yourself up over it. You stopped the battle before more folk were killed, and now we'll have some peace for a while. It's a good deal for everybody."

"Yeah. Okay. I'll try to live with that. Listen, as long as you're here, Ralph, I noticed your spells are unraveling. Mom's starting to wonder who my doctor is, and she's going to start asking questions about my arm soon."

"Sorry. I been a bit distracted lately. At the moment, I don't have the strength I used to. But I can keep that delusion with your mom going a little longer. Lucky for you I survived."

"Yeah, thanks," I said with a worried frown. What would have happened if Ralph had died too? I didn't really want to know. "And could you look at my arm, here? It seems to be feeling worse. That is, it isn't feeling anything at all."

"Sure, bring it here."

I leaned closer to him and let him poke at the arm. Even though he pinched and prodded and sniffed at it, I didn't feel a thing."

"Strange," he said. "Like there's something missing."

"I'll say. Like all my nerve endings."

"No, that ain't it. Worse than that. Nobody hit ya during the fight, did they?"

"Not that I can remember."

"Hmmm." He narrowed his eyes at me. "None of them Sidhe touched you recently?"

"No . . . except . . ."

"Except?"

"Well, when I delivered the parchment envelope you gave me for Chris, he—well, he kissed me."

Ralph smacked his forehead with the palm of his hand. "That's it! You nincompoop! Didn't we warn ya? You're missing a little bit of your soul!"

"But it was just a little kiss, hardly anything. And anyway Chris is dead now."

"Yeah, that's probably why you're arm is dead too. You're lucky he took just that shred of yourself, or more of you would be reporting in missing, know what I'm saying?"

"Oh, Jeez."

"Hey, hey, hey!"

"Sorry."

"Well, look, Princess, there's nothin' I can do for your arm here. We can hope that once you come Under the Hill we can rig something up so's you can at least use that arm."

"Uh, yeah."

"Hey, maybe we could chop it off and have Joe make you a nice shiny new one."

"Ralph!"

"Sorry, T.J., that was a joke. Guess I'm not too good at jokin' right now. So, anyway, since the battle's over, you can come Under the Hill anytime now."

"Um . . . I wanted to stick around a while longer, Ralph."

"Sooner's better than later, kiddo. Those Sidhe are itchin' to snatch you, since you faced 'em down."

"The queen told me they promised to leave me be until the thirty-first. I've set up a performance for that night, and I want the chance to do it, since it might be my last, you know?"

"I understand, T.J., but that's cuttin' it a little close, ain't it? Some of them Sidhe will probably come watch your act, and it'll be hard to take you to our side of the tracks right out from under their noses."

"Let me worry about that, Ralph. It's my life, after all."

"Yeah, guess so. Well, I better be gettin' back. You change your mind about comin' Downstairs sooner, just let me know."

"I will, Ralph."

He slowly began to fade.

"Wait! What do I tell my mom about my arm?"

"Uhh, tell her you called the doctor and he'll see you in a little over two weeks." And with that he disappeared.

"Thanks." *Why didn't I just tell him I wouldn't be going underground, if I could help it?* Maybe I didn't want to disappoint him so soon after he'd lost his friends. Maybe because it'd be good to have his help in my last performance—though that might mean tricking him into it, and that didn't feel good either. *Sheesh. Get involved with these critters and it's just one sticky mess after another.*

A healthy case of paranoia can do wonders for keeping you focused. I cleaned up the herb wreath and threw away the rotted part. I whittled shavings off the wood and lined my jeans pockets and my shoes with them. I made crude little daggers from the longer, sharper chips. I made Grandma's scarf into a sling and used that for my right arm. I started wearing a silver crucifix (Madonna may be out of style, but so what?). I stayed away from parks and rivers. In fact, I mostly stayed home for the next couple of weeks, plotting my great escape.

That is, except for the night I went to dinner with Sam. We went to the Eat n' Park in Squirrel Hill. Not very romantic, given that it's a family-friendly chain restaurant, but it was comfy. I had a hamburger, with grilled stickies for dessert. Sam had soup and salad and a couple of Eat n' Park's trademark smiley-face cookies.

After we'd stuffed our faces and gone through the usual small talk, it was time to talk shop.

"So," said Sam, "what's this new performance gonna be called?"

"I thought I'd call it 'Declaration of Independence.' "

"Oh, so it's gonna be about American history?"

"No, not at all. It's about *my* independence."

"That's all right, then. I might have felt uncomfortable about my role in this thing if it was historical."

"No, what I have in mind isn't really a dramatic-type role for you. You'd just be there helping out, like one of those Japanese puppeteers, what do they call it?"

"Bunraku?"

"Yeah, that. I just need help with props and moving around because of this arm."

Sam nodded. "I could do that. I'm surprised to see you're still wearing a sling. Must have been some fall you took there."

"It was a surprise to me, that's for sure."

"Do the doctors say when you'll be able to use that arm again?"

"Maybe never."

Sam winced. "Ouch. No shit? That'd be a damn shame."

I shrugged. "Well, you know doctors. They like to tell you the worst. They aren't always right. And, anyway, I figure if Bob Dole can run for president with a withered arm, I can still do performance art."

"Guess so. So what kind of special effects you planning? Warren says you're a real wizard at stagecraft."

"Yeah, well, kinda," I said with a secretive smile. "But this time there won't be that much in the way of special effects. Just a couple of tricks up my sleeve, that's all."

"If I'm onstage with you, any lighting changes are gonna have to be pre-set. No chance for flexibility, and that light board Warren's got isn't exactly state-of-the-art."

"That's okay. Most of the performance can be under one setting—maybe a change at the end, if possible. But the end is the most important part, where I'll need you onstage the most."

"Okay. No gels, gobos, or other fancy stuff?"

"Nope. Those would just get in the way, I think."

"Well, heck, you're easier to please than I expected." He picked up the check. "Cheap date, too."

"Cheap and easy, that's me."

Sam raised a brow. "We'll see about that."

We spent the next couple of hours strolling down Murray Avenue. Squirrel Hill started as a Jewish community, but it's become pretty multicultural now. There are neat bookstores, two movie theaters, delis, a coffeehouse or two, and a few great restaurants. Just off Murray are oak-lined streets with old red-brick houses and apartment buildings.

"You seem kinda wistful," Sam said, his arm around my shoulder.

"Just thinking about the future," I said. "Mom's trying to kick me out of the nest, and I was thinking this would be a cool area to live in."

"It is. I live not too far from here."

"Really?"

So Sam took me to his place. What happened there is nobody's business, but the rumors are true. He's a real gentleman. 'Nuff said.

Mom didn't say anything when I came in the next morning, though I knew she was dying to. We had an awkwardly silent breakfast and then she went off to do some shopping.

After she left, I checked the calendar. Nine days until May 31. I had a concept, some props, and Sam's help lined up. Now for the hard part, which I wasn't looking forward to.

I fished out the battered manila time card from the bottom of my bookpack. "Ralph?"

"Hey, hey!" He appeared wearing a grin and a shiny new pair of metal legs. "How do you like 'em, T.J.?" Ralph kicked and danced around the room. "Pretty spiff, huh? I could kick some serious Sidhe butt with these, lemme tell ya."

"Wow! Joe did a good job."

"Yeah! This worked so well, some of the other guys who lost parts in the battle are gettin' metal replacements too. Them that ain't allergic to iron, that is. You're a real hero Downstairs."

"Thanks. Um, listen, I wanted to ask a couple of last things of you."

"Last things?"

"Well, we've still got a deal, right? Until the end of the month? I'd like to ask you for some help with my next performance. On the thirty-first."

Ralph stopped prancing around and scratched his beard. He sucked his breath through his sharp, triangular teeth. "I dunno, Princess. Without Norton around, I can't do as much as I used to. And with this new treaty we got with the Sidhe, we have to be real careful about annoying them again. That's not what you were thinkin' of doing, was it?"

"No, not really. This is more a personal thing, about me. I just wanted to let the Sidhe know they can't have me."

"Well, I'll go along with that, but you sure like to play things the hard way. On the thirty-first, huh? What time?"

"Eleven to midnight."

" 'Sdugs! T.J., you can't—" Then he stopped and stared at me, real serious. "You aren't coming Under the Hill with me either, are you?"

Damn. No point in lying. "Ralph . . . I can't. I'm only nineteen. I've barely lived up here yet. I'm not ready to go anywhere else. Look, I don't want to fight you over this. I mean, I'm real flattered that you folks want me to live with you. But I can't. Not now."

Ralph's face slumped sadly. "You won't have to fight me, T.J. It was just an offer, that's all. We're not like the Seelie—we won't force you to accept."

I breathed a sight of relief. "Thanks. I'm glad."

" 'Course, Joe is gonna be mighty sad that you won't be coming Downstairs. He was really looking forward to dancing with you some more."

And I suddenly remembered the taste of the prune jack and the pastries and sound of the music and whirling in Joe's arms, and all the hunger to return below hit me full force. "Ralph!"

"Okay, okay, I'm sorry. That's the kind of dirty trick the other side would do. I shouldn't have done that to you. But you oughta know that you're always gonna feel that way."

"Yeah, all right, I know that."

"And you oughta know something else. After the thirty-first, I can't invite you Downstairs again. The Rule among us is, you only get one chance to choose. Only one."

I rubbed my senseless arm, knowing what the choice I was making meant. "Okay. I understand."

"Just so's you know that. You still got nine days. Don't rush your decision. So, anyways, what were you wanting me to do for your act?"

"Oh. I don't need your help in the act itself. But I need you to do the publicity. You know, the posters and stuff."

"Well, maybe, if we can keep it simple."

"Doesn't have to be elaborate."

"Got a title for it?"

"I'm going to call it 'Declaration of Independence.'"

Ralph tilted his head and narrowed his eyes at me. "Heh. You are sticking it to the Sidhe again, aren't ya?"

"Well, maybe but only for my sake. This performance is just about me. I've still got the right to stick up for myself, don't I? Your treaty doesn't cover that, does it?"

"You're right, T.J. It doesn't."

"Yeah. It's just that, because of this stupid useless arm, I need help with some things. Will you do the posters and put them up for me?"

Ralph paused, turning this way and that. "Oh, all right. A deal's a deal. Don't know what I'll tell the gang Downstairs, though, about your not coming down."

"Tell them whatever you want. It's not because I hate them. I just like being a mortal too much."

"Dunno if they'll understand that."

"Not sure I understand it either, but it's true."

"Well, I guess since this is the last job I'll be doing for ya, I better get started. Wanna do it right, an'at. Guess we probably won't be seeing too much more of each other."

"Guess not."

Ralph looked embarrassed and even a little shy. "Well, lemme just say, while I got the chance, it's been great workin' for ya. Whatever else happens, I wouldn't have missed it for the world."

"Yeah, thanks. It's been really . . . something."

"Yeah, not every mort can claim they had a knack for knockers."

"Yeah, that's true."

"Somethin' to tell your grandchildren."

"If I have any."

"Well, guess I'll be movin' along then."

Is this a Midwestern good-bye or what? "See ya."

"Yeah. 'Bye." With a face full of regret, he finally dropped into the living room carpet and disappeared. All except his two metal legs. A moment later Ralph's upper half resurfaced out of the rug, and he snatched up the legs. "Heh heh. Still not used to these." With an embarrassed grin, he sank under the carpet again.

"Thanks for everything," I said to the empty spot where he had been.

Chapter 29

The stage was a mess. *Stupid, stupid, stupid!* I mentally kicked myself for not realizing what a pain it was to be the last act of the night. I'd been spoiled; being first opener had always given me lots of time for setup. Now, from the dressing room door, I watched Sam and Angela hastily trying to put out my props while Marissa was still cleaning up hers.

On top of that, my mother had insisted on coming to the club. She said she wanted to "get a look at what was so important" in my life. And she brought Grandma with her! I couldn't talk her out of it, so there they sat at a side table, looking a little lost and confused.

It was if everything that could possibly make me more nervous was piling up, almost as if the Sidhe were conspiring to discombobulate me. If Ralph had put posters up, I hadn't seen any, but the Per Forma was full anyway.

I missed Ralph and Norton. I realized as I watched Sam and Angela struggle to put up the seven-foot-tall iron cross at the back of the stage that I had underestimated all the help the knockers had given me. Sam had gotten the metal from a cousin's junkyard, and we'd draped chains over the arms of the cross, but he and Angela couldn't seem to stand it straight. I hoped that wouldn't matter.

They'd managed to find a long enough extension cord to plug in the Apple computer, which sat on a low table in the middle of the stage. Now Angela was shaking wood chips out of a plastic bag. The chips had been shaved from the wreath Ralph had given me. There hadn't been quite enough wood in the wreath, so I'd added oak and redwood chips bought at a garden store and hoped they wouldn't dilute the effect. *Don't leave any gaps in the circle!* I mentally commanded Angela as she poured the chips in a line around the computer and the cross. I'd told Sam to especially watch out for this, but he was busy bringing the bell stands onto the stage.

I'd blown my budget on cowbells, sleigh bells, imported bells from India, in hopes that Grandma Kaminski was right about their deterrent factor. I'd wanted to hang the bells in strings from the rafters, but Warren had nixed it.

I looked back at the audience. I recognized people I'd met at Warren's party, and others I'd seen on previous nights for other acts. The club was full, although very few in the audience seemed to be Sidhe. But they'd sent the big guns—Brian Amadan and Reia Perry had taken the front-row-center table. She was wearing a silvery evening gown that reminded me a lot of the armor she had worn. There was someone else sitting between her and Amadan. Reia Perry noticed me peeking out at them and moved slightly back so I could see who it was sitting beside her. I gasped. It was Chris.

But he was more pale than I had ever seen him, and a white scar ran across his neck. He slowly turned his head and looked at me. His eyes were gray, and dead.

I slammed the dressing room door shut and pressed my back against it, my heart pounding. *He's alive, but he isn't! Can fairy zombies exist? She's sneaky, all right, that Queen Maeve. She must have brought him back somehow just to shake me up. Damn it, it's working.*

There came a knock on the door, and I jumped away from it. "Who is it?"

"Fan mail for you." The door opened a little, and the hand of Barb the waitress popped in, holding an envelope.

I snatched it from her. "Thanks."

"Break a leg." The arm disappeared again and the door shut.

I stared down at what I was holding. It was a peach-colored envelope, and I knew immediately who it was from. *It wouldn't be an elvish letter bomb, would it? Or some spell? They'd promised they wouldn't interfere.* I was putting a lot of faith in the fairy sense of honor. Of course, I was also wearing my clothes inside out, as Grandma had suggested, and a crown of daisies on my head, and four-leaf clovers in every pocket, along with iron horseshoe nails for good measure. I took a deep breath, opened the envelope, and pulled out the note inside. It read:

Our Dear Miss Kaminski:

Rejoice! I bring you good news. As you have seen, one whom you thought had fallen is still with us. It appears that you had shared with him a trace of your life spirit, and with that thread we have been able to save him from final oblivion. But the thread is slender and will not hold long. Therefore we hope you will not dally or toy with us, and will accompany us without delay at the time appointed. With your help, Under the Hill, the one you know as Chris can be fully restored to life. Without you, he is doomed.

We look forward to enjoying your final performance. We expect it will be every bit as entertaining as the others we have seen.

HRM Maeve

I crumpled the note and threw it on the floor. *What more can they do to me?* I banged my head against the wall, lightly, three times. *If I don't go, Chris dies. For sure. But if I do go, how do they expect me to help him?* The answer hit, dark and terrifying. *A shred of my soul sustains him, a Ganconer. A love-sucker. The only way I can restore him is if he gets the rest of it. I'll bet the process feels wonderful, but what would be left of me when he's done? Would I wither away and die myself? Might I become a soul-sucking vampiric elf, sent to seduce unwitting mortals to their doom? Worse yet, would I enjoy being one?* Mythology isn't my strong subject, but I was pretty sure whatever happened, it wouldn't be good.

Fuck them. I didn't ask him to get killed in some stupid war. I didn't ask him to kiss me. It wasn't fair of him to take what he did. And it isn't fair to them to ask me to sacrifice my life for him. This is just another sneaky trick on the queen's part to get me underground. Well, we'll see about that. I began to understand how the Unseelie had felt when they decided to battle the Sidhe. They probably knew they would lose, but they had to try . . . and so did I.

The door opened again and I jumped again. But it was just Angela bustling in. "Sorry, T.J., you're going to be starting late. I didn't know it would take this long to set you up."

"Huh? Oh. That's okay, so long as the stuff I've timed goes off at midnight."

"Well, that's up to Sam, I guess. At least the crowd is sticking around, despite the delay."

"Yeah."

Sam hustled in behind Angela. He was dressed all in black, including a loose hood with a slit cut for the eyes. *Like an executioner*, I thought morosely. "Hey, T.J., did you want that folding chair that's over on stage right to stay?"

"No, that's left from Marissa's act."

"I'll take care of it," Angela said, rushing out the door.

"Other than that," Sam said to me, "I guess everything's set and ready to go."

"Okay. Just remember, Sam, in the very last part, whatever happens, whatever I say, or do, or whatever you see or hear, don't let go of me, all right?"

"Yeah, yeah, I remember."

"I'm dead serious, Sam."

"All *right*. No need to be naggin', girl. I got it. But if you've got surprises planned, you should have told me."

"This is live theater, Sam. There are always surprises."

"Heh. Tell me about it."

Angela stuck her head back in. "All set. Warren says come out whenever you're ready."

"Okay. Go," I said to Sam, and he hurried off to take his position backstage.

Courage, I told myself. And to the strains of Aretha Franklin singing, "Think, think about what you're tryin' to do to me . . ." I walked to the stage as if going to the headsman's block.

Sam waited, crouched beside the iron cross. I stepped over the circle of wood chips and stood beside him. He put my left arm out against the arm of the cross and wrapped the chain around it. He took another length of chain from the upright and wrapped it, loosely, around my neck. Then Sam again sat down on the stage. The music cut out abruptly the third time Aretha sang "freedom."

"The Past wants to make me its prisoner," I began. I tugged on the chain with my left hand. "The Past is my father and mother. It brought me forth and supports me, yet now it hangs, a weight, upon my soul." I thought I saw my mom wince in the audience, but I had to push that sight away.

"The Past is dead!" I kicked a plastic skull out of the circle, into the audience. "And yet, its rotting fingers clutch me still . . ."

Sam slipped behind the cross and took up two

plastic skeletal arms with hands. One he reached around one side of the cross to cover my breast, the other came around the other side reaching for my crotch.

". . . With half-forgotten fairy tales of ghouls and goblins infesting my brain." A tape cart ran with sound effects of eerie moans and gibbering, with some low voice saying "T.J." now and then.

"Enough!" I cried and the voice stopped. "Enough of this eternal Halloween. The Land of Night shall not claim my soul."

I heard hisses in the audience but ignored them. I slipped my left arm out of its chains and knocked the skeletal hands away from my body. The hands moved to my throat as if to choke me.

I reached into my left pocket and pulled out a handful of salt. "Begone!" I tossed the salt up on the skeletal hands and they shook and slid away. Sam pulled the chain's coils from around my neck, making it slither as if it were a snake. I stepped forward from the cross.

"Who among you are ghosts of the past, your hour come 'round and gone?" I stared straight at the table with Amadan, Reia Perry. And Chris. It was strange how the words I had written happened to apply so well to him. "You're up way past your bedtime. This waking, living world is not for you. It's time to rest. Here, I've brought some flowers for your grave." In a deconstruction of Ophelia's speech in *Hamlet*, I tossed some flowers and herbs at their table. They let them fall and did not touch them. "There's a daisy. I would give you some violets, but they withered all when my father died. There's rue for you, and some for me." At this last, I rubbed some of the herb on the sling on my right arm.

To Chris, I tossed a wilted rose with herbs tied to it. "There's rosemary, that's for remembrance." He stared at the flower as it landed on the table, but his face showed no reaction that I could read.

I danced back to the center of the circle as Aretha sang a couple more bars, then cut out again. Sam flipped a switch and all the lights went out except for one spot that shone down from directly above me. I looked like I was trapped in a column of white light.

"I am a prisoner of the Now." A large copper bell from India was on a stand within reach. I pushed its clapper so it rang once, a clear, full tone. The Sidhe in the audience winced. I placed my left hand here and there at the edge of the light circle, mimelike, as if it were a wall. "I am without depth or form, one-dimensional." A tape ran of Tibetan monks chanting. Sam swirled a bit of colorful cloth, a road sign, an advertisement poster, and other things through the light column ahead and behind me, so that they would be only briefly glimpsed by the audience. "I drift blindly, without power, without thought. Beside me and ahead lies only darkness. I am afraid of the dark."

As the sound effect of a chain saw started up, I pulled a flashlight from my pocket and mimed cutting a doorway in the column of light. Then I staggered through the "doorway" as if blind, my left arm out in front of me.

"I will seize my future, I will welcome it." As if I had grabbed a rope, I pretended I was being pulled toward center-front stage. "The future . . . the future . . ."

I stood in front of the Apple computer. "The Future Is Now!" The main lights suddenly snapped on.

"The future cannot hold me prisoner. Here are no walls, and chaos reigns. All is possible. The future is freedom." I knelt down in front of the computer as if it were an altar.

Suddenly Tchaikovsky's *1812 Overture*, the last section with the bells and cannon, blared out through the club's speakers.

"Three minutes to midnight," Sam said in my ear.

"Shit, I'm behind! Start ringing the bells, any of them." I had to jump ahead to my last surprise. I put my left hand on the Apple monitor screen. "Spirit of the Future!" I intoned, "Come forth! Be free!" I got a static shock again, and as I jerked my hand away, the sparkling, spinning gremlin popped out of the machine.

"What the hell is that?" said Sam.

Amadan and Reia Perry stood up, aghast.

Sam began ringing the cowbells, the little brass bells, whatever his hands fell upon. The Sidhe put their hands over their ears and grimaced.

The gremlin danced around the stage, squeaking "Free! Free! Free!" Then it found the extension cord and zipped along it to the wall socket and disappeared.

"So much for that trick," I muttered.

The lights flickered. Blue. White. Purple. Red. Off. On.

"What the fuck?" said Sam.

"The gremlin's gone into the light board!"

The stage lights strobed as if run by a demented roadie at a rock concert. In one blue-tinted flash, I saw the Amadan pull off his glove.

BONG. The recorded chimes of Big Ben began to sound.

"One minute to midnight!" said Sam.

"Quick! Tie me up to the cross again!"

In a yellow flash, Chris had stood and was holding out his right hand to me. My right elbow rose up, pointing to the Amadan. With a jerk, I was pulled forward, toward him.

BONG.

"Sam!"

"I gotcha." Sam wrapped his arms around me and pulled me back toward the iron cross. He looped the chains around my body, then stood behind the cross, holding me against it, his arms around my waist. The iron felt like it was both burning and freezing my back, but I withstood it.

BONG.

In a flash of blue light, I saw that the Amadan had left his table and was now reaching his hand toward . . . my mother.

"NO!" I cried. I kicked and writhed, but Sam held me fast. Then Grandma stood between them, her mouth moving. I don't know if she was saying a prayer or a curse, but the Amadan stepped back, surprised. Luigi had been right—she could protect herself, and others.

BONG.

A voice came from the far left of the stage. My voice. "Sam, I'm over here! Let her go, she's a fake!" I turned my head and saw . . . myself. In nicer clothes and looking better than I ever did. She was grinning and waving.

"What the—" Sam murmured. His grip loosened.

"Don't let go!" I yelled. "It's an illusion!"

He held on.

BONG.

Reia Perry, alias Queen Maeve, stood in front of the stage and waved her arms as if doing ballet. The audience behind her vanished, replaced by a beautiful, starlit meadow. I could smell the trees and the perfume of the flowers. A harpist played a haunting melody. Chris stood beside the queen, looking as he had in life, impossibly attractive and desirable. The incredible homesickness welled up in me and I struggled against the chains, moaning.

"You all right, girl?"

"Hold . . . on . . ." I wailed.

BONG.

Brian Amadan reappeared beside the queen. Scowling, he held out a glimmering object . . . I couldn't tell if it was a wand or a dagger. His lips moved, and suddenly I felt something moving inside my sling. I looked down and saw that my right arm had turned into a python, which was slithering up my chest to wrap around my neck.

BONG.

"Holy shit!" Sam cried.

The python tightened around my neck, until I couldn't breathe. Sam let go of me to struggle with the snake, trying to pull it off my neck. I tried to shout, "No!" but I could only move my lips. No air came out. I felt myself yanked away from the cross—

BONG.

Chris stood beside the Amadan and grabbed his wrist. Slowly and with apparent great effort, Chris pulled the Amadan's hand to the side and, turning his arm, ran himself onto the dagger in the Amadan's hand, plunging it into his chest.

BONG.

As Brian Amadan stared in disgust and disbelief at Chris, who had slumped to the floor, my arm turned back to its dead, paralyzed self and I was able to stagger back to the cross and Sam's arms.

"What the flying *fuck* is goin' on here?" Sam breathed in my ear.

"Tell you later. Just hold on."

BONG.

Queen Maeve again. This time she stood in full battle array, with an expression that said she was through playing nice. She drew her sword and with one sweep cleared away the line of wood chips at the front of the stage. So much for that protection. Lance in one hand, sword in the other, she stepped onto the stage and came toward me.

BONG.

The entire club went black. No light. There came a clang, a grunt, and a thud as a body fell on the stage in front of me.

"Hoo boy, am I in trouble now!" I heard Ralph say in the darkness.

"Ralph?"

"Yep, these legs kick serious Sidhe butt. Good luck, T.J.!"

BONG.

Silence. Darkness. Rustling and murmuring in the audience. Slowly, the house lights came up, and I saw Warren scowling at the board in the light booth. Brian Amadan, Reia Perry, and Chris were gone. I still stood against the iron cross. Sam stood beside me, shaking his head and rubbing his eyes.

Awkward laughter rippled through the club. Then applause and even a few whoops and cheers. I let the chains fall from my body and took a deep breath.

"What . . . the hell . . . was going on here?" said Sam.

"I won. I think." In front of me lay one of Ralph's metal legs. Beside it lay another peach-colored envelope.

People came up to the stage, their faces flushed and exhilarated, telling me what an amazing show I'd done. I saw my mother, her eyes and mouth wide in astonishment, being led gently away by Grandma. *Maybe she can explain better than I can*, I thought. I heard people asking me how I had done it, and when my next show would be. I shrugged and said, "I don't know."

To far stage left, where the illusion of myself had appeared, there now stood a human-shaped thing made of moss and twigs and leaves. I shuddered, wondering what Sam would have thought if he'd taken *that* home tonight.

After five minutes, when most of the crowd had left, I reached out and picked up the envelope. It was sealed with a blob of silvery wax, embossed with the symbol of a rose.

"Fan mail from some flounder?" said Sam.

I didn't answer. I tugged open the envelope and pulled out the peach-colored card inside.

My dear Miss Kaminski,

Oh, very well. Congratulations. Anyone who fights so mightily, with such stalwart allies, in order to stay in the mortal realm, deserves the granting of their wish. So stay, and may you have joy of it.

Nevertheless, it would please me to one day have at my side such a clever and courageous fighter. Therefore, be it known that my invitation stands. Should you ever choose at last to live among us, use this note and call my name. It would delight me to have nearby one who annoys Amadan so.

Warm regards,
HRM

"As if," I muttered. But I didn't tear up the note.

With a pop, Ralph appeared, standing one-legged beside me. "Heh, heh, I think I left something behind here. Can I have my leg back?"

"Sure," I said, handing it to him. "And thanks. We still friends?"

Ralph looked sheepish. "Hey, the guys Downstairs would never have forgiven me if I didn't help. And . . . and they wanted me to give you this." He pulled out from a fold in his skin a time card made of steel and handed it to me. "Joe made it for ya special. It's kinda bending the Rules, but after all you done for us, we couldn't see how we couldn't do it."

I wiggled the metal card in my hand until it made a *wubba-wubba* noise. "Cool. What is it?"

"An invitation. Joe says anytime you want, if you get tired of this mort world stuff, you can come down and stay with him."

"I thought I only got one chance."

"I wasn't allowed to invite you again, but Joe could. Good thing he likes ya, huh?"

"Thanks. This is really nice of you guys. I'll keep it in mind."

"Good. Well, so long. It's been fun. Maybe we'll do this again sometime, huh?"

"Yeah. Sometime."

Ralph turned to a goggling Sam. "And you, you take good care of our princess, you hear?" Before Sam could work out a reply, Ralph sank down into the stage, waving his leg good-bye.

When Sam finally found his voice, he said, "That . . . that gray thing. That was what you were talking about before, wasn't it? The thing you saw in the park."

"Yep." I walked over to him and leaned my head on his shoulder. "I guess there's a lot I ought to fill you in on."

" 'Sokay," he said, putting his arms around me. "I got all night to listen."

Epilogue

Two days after my showdown at the Per Forma, I stood on the overlook next to the Duquesne Incline on Mount Washington. From the clifftops there, you can get a great view of Pittsburgh. One of the better-kept secrets of this city, I think, is that from a few places, a few times a year, it is truly spectacular.

I could see from Brunot Island on my left to the Allegheny Observatory hill in front of me to the distant top of the Cathedral of Learning on my right. Just below me was the Golden Triangle of downtown Pittsburgh, buildings glittering like giant glass jewelry boxes in the summer sunlight. The Monongahela River flowed past, its banks loosely stitched together with bridges as far down as the eye could see.

I had to admit Ralph and Chris had been right—this was a special place. But I was glad it wasn't just trees and hills, or the smoke-choked forest of factories it used to be. Pittsburgh was a pretty good place for people, mere mortals like me, and I hoped it would stay that way.

As for me, well, my right arm still won't work, but I don't have to let that get in my way. Warren and Angela are willing to give me stage time at the Per Forma anytime I ask for it. Cindy and Crystal are working in a little New Age shop in the South Side, and they want me to help develop some products for them. I think I got some ideas. Won't hurt to have a little more elfbane spread around, just in case. I could always call up Grandma if I need a recipe or two.

Sam's let me know about a couple of neat studio apartments opening up in Squirrel Hill, and Mom says she'll help me out with rent for the first couple of months to get me started. And though I might keep on with a theatre major at Pitt in the fall, I think I'll slip in a Mythology course now and then.

It's all looking up. 'Course, if it doesn't work out, there's always those invitations to go Under the Hill. I can take that way out any time. But those are strictly one-way tickets—no coming back to the mort world. Someday I may get tired enough, bored enough, old enough. But not yet. Not yet . . .

THE ROC FREQUENT READERS BOOK CLUB

BUY TWO ROC BOOKS AND GET ONE SF/FANTASY NOVEL FREE!

Check the free title you wish to receive (subject to availability):

☐ **BLACK MADONNA**
Shadowrun®
Carl Sargent & Marc Gascoigne
0-451-45373-5/$5.50 ($6.50 in Canada)

☐ **DARK LOVE**
Edited by Nancy A. Collins, Edward E. Kramer, and Martin H. Greenberg
0-451-45550-9/$5.99 ($7.99 in Canada)

☐ **EGGHEADS**
Emily Devenport
0-451-45517-7/$5.99 ($7.50 in Canada)

☐ **ICE CROWN**
Andre Norton
0-451-45248-8/$4.99 ($5.99 in Canada)

☐ **STARGATE™: REBELLION**
Bill McCay
0-451-45502-9/$4.99 ($5.99 in Canada)

☐ **THE WHITE MISTS OF POWER**
Kristine Kathryn Rusch
0-451-45120-1/$3.99 ($5.50 in Canada)

To get your FREE Roc book, send in this coupon (original or photocopy), proof of purchase (original sales receipt(s) for two Roc books and a copy of the books' UPC numbers) plus $2.00 for postage and handling to:

ROC FREQUENT READERS CLUB
Penguin USA • Mass Market
375 Hudson Street, New York, NY 10014

Name: _____

Address: _____

City: _____ State: _____ Zip: _____

E-mail Address: _____

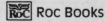 Roc Books